Unmasked II:
More Erotic Tales of Gay Superheroes

Edited By
Eric Summers

Herndon, VA

Copyright © 2009 by STARbooks Press

ISBN-10: 1-934187-56-9
ISBN-13: 978-1-934187-56-2

This book is a work of fiction. Names, characters, places, situations and incidents are the product of the authors' imaginations or are used fictitiously. Any resemblance to actual events, locales, or persons, living or dead, is purely coincidental. All rights reserved, including the right of reproduction in whole or in part in any form.

Published in the United States by
STARbooks Press, PO Box, 711612 Herndon VA 20171.

Printed in the United States

Herndon, VA

About the Cover

Kosher Man first appeared in *Unmasked: Erotic Tales of Gay Superheroes* (STARbooks Press, 2007) in the story, "Kosher Man and the Shegatz" by Milton Stern.

Jose A. Dennis created the image of Kosher Man based on Mr. Stern's narrative.

Acknowledgments

Many thanks to graphic artist John Nail for the cover design. Mr. Nail may be reached at: tojonail@bellsouth.net.

Many thanks to Jose A. Dennis for the cover image of Kosher Man, a character created by Milton Stern. Mr. Dennis can be reached at gryphta@gmail.com. His Website is http://www.josedennis.com.

STARbooks Press Titles by Eric Summers

Muscle Worshipers

Love in a Lock-Up

Unmasked – Erotic Tales of Gay Superheroes

Don't Ask, Don't Tie Me Up

Ride Me Cowboy

Service with a Smile

Never Enough – The Lost Writings of John Patrick

Unwrapped – Erotic Holiday Tales

Can't Get Enough – More Erotica Written by John Patrick

Unmasked II – More Erotic Tales of Gay Superheroes

Teammates

CONTENTS

- THE BAT'S DILEMMA By Stephen Osborne 1
- JUNIOR OHO ... SORT OF By Troy Storm 13
- TOOLMAN By Wayne Mansfield 27
- MASTER MIND'S DOWNFALL By Jay Starre 41
- SAVING TERRA By Armand 57
- THE OTTER By Rob Rosen 69
- UNDOING TANTRAMAN By Owen Keehnen 79
- THE ICE KING COMETH By Tom Cardamone 95
- SAVING CAPTAIN CUM By Gerrard Jones 109
- KOSHER MAN GETS PORKED By Milton Stern 121
- HUMMINGBIRD II (GETTING BEHIND ON THE JOB)
  By Sedonia Guillone 131
- ANTIMATTER MATT By Derrick Della Giorgia 145
- THE LEGACY OF CALIBAN By Kale Naylor 155
- RAZED By Evan Gilbert 165
- RIGHT HAND MAN By Erastes 177
- FORGET-ME-NOT By Logan Zachary 189
- CAPTAIN VELVET DOWN UNDER By Ryan Field 203
- LOVING CALVIN PANARO By Jamie Freeman 219
- THE CAPTURE OF CLOUD RUNNER By Jay Starre 235
- SUPER SLIDER AND THE WARDEN OF BATON ROUGE
  By Jay Starre 251
- LEATHER MAN By Wayne Mansfield 267
- HERO WORSHIP By Stephen Osborne 283
- ABOUT THE AUTHORS 293
- ABOUT THE EDITOR 297

THE BAT'S DILEMMA
By Stephen Osborne

Mark Marshall settled down in front of his television set, a cup of tea by his side and a smile on his face. It was early afternoon, and Mark was preparing for one of his guilty pleasures – the soap opera *As the Green Globe Turns*. Not even his partner in crime fighting (as well as partner in bed), Juan, knew about his addiction to the trials and tribulations of the fictional town of Carthage, Maine. For an hour every day, Mark lost himself in the lives of doctors, lawyers, hookers, and other sundry characters played by exceptionally pretty people. Mark thought he deserved a little escapist fun. Being the only superhero team defending Indianapolis against the forces of wrong and evil, Mark and Juan, in their guise as The Bat and The Raven, worked hard every night beating the snot out of the criminal element. Who would deny, Mark thought to himself, that he deserved a little silly diversion?

Still, Mark never told Juan that he watched the show. Mark even ensured that his housekeeper, Carla, was out doing the shopping while *As the Green Globe Turns* was on.

He sipped his tea as the program began, feeling his pulse quicken as it always did when the opening credits came on the screen. He hoped that today Jenny would tell Dr. Cary that the baby was indeed his. That would show the smarmy bastard.

The first scene did not, however, concern the busty Jenny and her offspring. This storyline concerned young Kenny, who it was rumored was to become one of the first gay characters on the soap. On screen, Kenny was gazing deep into the eyes of Will, the high school football captain.

"Have I ever told you," Kenny said, looking longingly into Will's big blue eyes, "that I've watched every game you've ever played?"

Unmasked II

Will in turn looked as if he was about to eat Kenny alive. "Have I ever told you," he said, leaning in close until his lips were nearly brushing Kenny's, "that I've made every touchdown thinking of you?"

Just as the two were getting ready for what looked like one hell of a lip-lock, static filled the screen. Mortified, Mark stared at the screen. "No! No! No!" he screamed, already thinking of the nasty letter he was going to write to his cable company. Nothing should interfere with *As the Green Globe Turns*.

The screen cleared, but instead of the two young men kissing, there were two outrageously outfitted men smiling into a camera. They were wearing what appeared to be baseball uniforms, but the costumes were tight-fitting and festooned with lots of sparkles. To anyone unfamiliar with them, the two might be mistaken for mere sports fanatics with bad fashion sense, but Mark knew them as the supervillains, The Pitcher and The Catcher.

"Sorry to interrupt the programming," The Pitcher said, smoothing out his large black mustache.

"Well," The Catcher said, shrugging, "actually we're not sorry. We're kind of proud that we managed to intercept the signal and are broadcasting into your homes."

"Think of this little break as the seventh inning stretch," The Pitcher went on to say. "Anyway, we're sending out this message to both the Indianapolis Police and that spoil sport known as The Bat."

"We're back, in case you haven't noticed," The Catcher said, chuckling.

"We've broken out of prison, and we're ready to take our revenge on this stupid city and more importantly that stupid clown, The Bat."

"We've got a plot that we're ready to hatch. One that can't fail." The Catcher crossed his arms, looking pleased with himself. "And just to ensure that The Bat won't interfere with our plans, we've kidnapped his little bird-brained buddy." The Catcher pointed off to the left and seemed surprised when the camera didn't pan to the side.

"There's no cameraman," The Pitcher pointed out. "One of us will have to actually turn the damn thing."

With a deep sigh The Catcher rose and walked off-screen. After a pause, the camera panned to the left and showed what seemed to be a disused locker room. By one of the lockers, tightly bound and gagged, was Mark's crime-fighting partner, Juan Martinez. Juan must have been in his Raven outfit when he'd been captured, but the villains had stripped the young man so that now he was nude save for his black mask and black boots. Juan seemed to be unconscious.

The camera went back to The Pitcher. "Nothing will happen to your young friend, Bat, as long as you leave us alone."

Now that the camera was again locked in place, The Catcher returned to his seat next to The Pitcher. "Yeah, we're tired of getting beat to a pulp every time we try to rob a bank or something. You broke my nose the last time, you caped bastard!"

The Pitcher gave his partner a glare. "We're getting a little off topic here, Catch. Anyway, our new plot, like I said, is fool-proof, but then that's what we thought of the last dozen or so plots we've had, and we've always had our asses whooped by the Caped Duo. This time, though, if The Bat tries to stop us, his little partner gets it. We're going to fuck him good."

"You mean fuck him up good."

The Pitcher smiled evilly. "Both."

Laughing, The Catcher looked directly at the camera. "So that's it. Try to stop us, and The Raven's going to lose a few feathers."

"We now bring you back to our regularly scheduled program," The Pitcher said, smoothing out his mustache again.

Mark stood up, cold fury running through him. The only thing worse than preempting his favorite soap, in his mind, was to capture Juan and threaten to fuck him. Mark looked over to the closet where his superhero costume was kept. The Bat would have something to say about this ...

Nearby, two old women were seated on a well-worn couch, their attention on the television set in front of them. "You know, Martha," one of them said as the image of The Pitcher and The Catcher faded from their screen, "I'm not sure I'm going to continue to watch *As the Green Globe Turns*. The plots are getting rather silly, and I don't like some of the characters they're introducing."

The Bat was nearly finished putting on his outfit when his housekeeper, Carla, returned with the groceries. The rather plump, middle-aged woman didn't even blink when she spotted the man in the midnight blue tights and cape standing in the living room. She set her bags down on the kitchen table and sighed. "You wouldn't believe the price of tomatoes," she said, shaking her head.

Mark, frozen in place with his hands adjusting the mask over his face, stammered a bit before managing to say, "I bet you're wondering what I'm doing dressing up like this."

The woman grunted as she took a can of corn out of one of the grocery sacks. "You're The Bat, and your boyfriend is The Raven, like it's a secret. Please. I've known for ages. You're always leaving gadgets and things all over the place for me to put away. It doesn't take too many times shoving Bat Smoke Bombs into drawers before one gets the idea, you know."

"Yes," The Bat slowly replied, hoping his uncertainty didn't show in his voice, "I knew you'd figure out our identities sooner or later."

Looking unconcerned, Carla opened the refrigerator to stow away some sausages. "So are you off to fight some crime? Maybe foil those two goons in the baseball outfits and rescue Juan?"

The Bat frowned. "How did you ..."

His housekeeper shrugged. "They interrupted the radio show I was listening to. One minute, Howard Stern, the next Twiddle Dee and Twiddle Dum."

The Bat pounded a fist onto the kitchen table, rattling the grocery bags. "If only I knew where to find them! They've got The Raven, and goodness knows what they'll do to him."

Carla opened a cupboard and put away a box of cereal. "Probably fuck him up the ass and then kill him. That's my guess. You'd best go rescue him and leave me alone, so I can mop your floor. You've got bloodstains on your linoleum, you know."

"If only I knew where they had him! They could be anywhere."

With a sigh, Carla said, "Well, since these two have baseball on the brain, I'd say the most likely place they'd be hiding out would be the old Victory Field stadium. The new stadium has been in use for several years now, and no one goes to the old Victory Field much anymore ..."

The Bat suddenly leaned down to kiss the woman on the cheek. "Brilliant! Remind me to give you a raise!"

His housekeeper frowned. "I'd be happy if you'd manage to piss into the toilet for once. I thought bats were supposed to have good radar. You couldn't hit the broad side of a barn."

The night was dark as The Bat pulled his car into the Victory Field parking lot. The place seemed deserted, but his Bat senses tingled as he bolted from his vehicle and headed toward the building. A bright autumn moon illuminated the way as The Bat raced to the front entrance. The doors were, of course, locked, but a swift kick splintered the aged wood. A second kick sent the doors flying open. It made more noise than The Bat would have liked, but he didn't feel like wasting time, not with The Raven at the mercy of those two goons.

Once inside, The Bat paused, trying to decide which direction the locker rooms would be. Finally, he found a corridor leading to the back of the building that looked likely. He was rewarded by a sign pointing to the locker rooms, telling him he was on the right path.

The Bat allowed the anger to build up inside him. He'd teach The Pitcher and The Catcher a lesson they wouldn't soon forget. They'd think twice in the future before kidnapping his Juan.

Bursting through the doors marked LOCKER ROOM, The Bat found himself confronted by the two villains, who were standing in front of a set of old, tarnished lockers. Behind them, trussed up like a Thanksgiving turkey, was the nearly naked Juan. The Pitcher and The Catcher were obviously waiting for The Bat, having been alerted to his presence by the noise of his entrance to the building. Each had in his hand what looked to be a plastic baseball.

"You're going to have to pay for that door you broke," The Catcher said. "It's certainly not coming out of our loot."

The Bat advanced on them menacingly. "Let The Raven go now," he said through gritted teeth, "or I'll break every bone in your bodies."

"Stay where you are, freak," The Pitcher said, holding up the plastic baseball. "You don't want me to drop this."

The Bat stopped, frowning. "What's in those baseballs? Poison gas?"

"Something much worse," The Catcher replied.

"These," The Pitcher went on, holding the baseball even higher, "are filled with a special formula we designed ourselves. All we have to do is break open the baseball by throwing one against any hard surface and our Eroto-gas will be unleashed."

"Eroto-gas?" The Bat asked.

"Anyone getting a sniff of this stuff will have an uncontrollable urge to have sex," The Catcher informed him. "See, we just toss one of these into, say, a jewelry shop. The patrons and the clerks working there will be too busy getting their rocks off to try to stop us from robbing them blind. Another one tossed outside will stop any police from entering and annoying us."

"It was the perfect plot," The Pitcher went on to say. "We knew you'd come up with some gadget, some Bat-Sex-Gas Mask or something, so we kidnapped your little friend to keep you from bothering us." He paused, seemingly lost in thought, before going on. "It didn't really work, did it?"

"You're about to find out just how much it didn't work," The Bat said, tightening his fist. He lunged forward so quickly that the two villains had no time to react. The Bat shot out a punch that connected with The Catcher's jaw at the same time as his left boot came up and slammed into The Pitcher's chest. The Catcher fell back, hitting a small wooden bench before he slumped to the floor, but still conscious. The plastic baseball he held rolled safely out of his hands, coming to rest right next to where The Raven was held. The baseball that had been in The Pitcher's hand, however, went flying as the criminal fell back. The Bat lunged, nearly catching it. He only managed to brush against it as it fell, however, before it smacked against the concrete floor and broke open.

"The Eroto-gas!" The Catcher screamed as the area instantly filled with a sweet-smelling, oily vapor. The villain scrambled to his feet frantically, trying to get out of the way of the quickly gathering cloud.

"Now we're fucked," The Pitcher said, rubbing his chest. "Literally."

The Bat cocked his fist, ready to pummel The Catcher with another shot to the head. He sniffed, breathing in some of the gas. "It doesn't seem to be working," he said, letting his fist fly.

The Catcher fell back onto his ass. The Bat couldn't help but notice the enormous bulge that suddenly appeared in the criminal's tight crotch area.

Staring at the villain's stiffy had been a mistake, giving The Pitcher time to get up and prepare for a counter-attack. The Bat turned, only to see The Pitcher poised to strike. Fists ready, the man came forward. "I'm going to fuck you up," he snarled, unleashing rights and lefts at the Superhero. The Bat was able to parry most of the blows, but he seemed unable to fight back. Suddenly punching The Pitcher didn't seem to be the thing to do. He wanted to see what the man looked like naked and wondered what it would feel like to have The Pitcher's cock up his ass ...

Oh, no! The Bat thought. The Eroto-gas was starting to affect his judgment.

The Pitcher ceased throwing punches. The effort had caused him to suck in huge amounts of the tainted air, and the man was now looking hungrily down at The Bat's crotch. "Whoa," he said, licking his lips. "Talk about batter's up!"

The Bat looked down. Sure enough, his tights were stretched to nearly the tearing point by his large, rock-hard cock. He felt as if he'd die if he didn't get off immediately, so when The Pitcher dropped his fists and began stroking The Bat's hard-on, he gave in to the waves of pleasure filling his body.

Smiling, The Pitcher squeezed The Bat's dick and balls through the slick material. "Hmm. He's got two balls and no strikes against him!" With a few awkward tugs the villain managed to yank The Bat's tights down until his stiff cock was free. "Turn around," he whispered in The Bat's ear. "I want to step up to the plate and show you what a real hitter can do."

The Bat did as the criminal suggested. The Pitcher pulled his own garments down quickly and stood close so that The Bat could feel the man's hard cock nuzzling his ass. The Catcher had managed to get back to his feet and was standing in front of them. His tights were down as well, and he was jacking his own cock furiously. To The Bat, the huge dick looked like a tempting treat he couldn't pass up. He leaned forward until he could engulf the man's pole in his mouth. The Catcher groaned as The Bat began to greedily suck his cock.

The Pitcher, still behind The Bat, nearly slobbered in anticipation as he watched his partner force The Bat's face further into his crotch. "Let's make a Bat Sandwich," he growled, eyeing The Bat's ass, which was hovering temptingly before him. "Now that's what I call a moon shot!" He clutched the Bat's hips and quickly shoved his hard cock into the masked man's waiting hole.

The sudden intrusion of The Pitcher's dick would normally have made The Bat yelp with pain, but the effects of the Eroto-gas, plus the fact that his mouth was full, resulted in him just emitting a low moan. It took a few moments for the threesome to get a rhythm going, but soon The Pitcher was slamming into The Bat's rear, forcing him further onto The Catcher's cock.

"This is a true double play!" The Catcher crowed.

The Pitcher grinned as he continued to slam his pole into The Bat's ass. "You could say the bases are loaded and I'm up at bat ... or up in Bat!" He smacked his palm hard against one of The Bat's ass-cheeks. "I must say, this one is high and tight!"

"A real backdoor slider!" The Catcher yowled, grinding his hips so that The Bat was forced to deep-throat his stiff rod.

The Bat let the two villains continue with their silly baseball banter. He concentrated on jacking off his own cock. Even under the influence of the Eroto-gas, he reasoned that the first person to come would be the first to shake off the mind-control. He thought of The Raven, tied up only a few feet away – unconscious, but oh so beautiful. He thought of Juan and himself in bed, fucking like mad. He thought of Juan's beautiful cock ...

The Bat grunted as he shot his load. The two criminals didn't seem to notice, being too focused on their own oncoming ejaculations.

"I think I'm going to come!" the Catcher groaned.

"Give me your Bronx Cheer!" the Pitcher said encouragingly.

"Oh, FUCK YEAH!" The Catcher took his cock out of The Bat's mouth just as he shot. The thick, gooey stream hit The Bat on the cheek and even covered part of his mask.

That better not stain, The Bat thought to himself.

Unmasked II

The Pitcher rammed his cock into The Bat like a madman. He began to let out a series of tiny grunts before he finally exploded. "Oh, yeah!" he screamed. "It's a home run!"

The Bat didn't even wait for The Pitcher to remove his cock. As The Bat had reasoned, coming had released his mind from the effects of the dastardly vapor. He knew he had to act just as the criminals shot their wads. He cocked his leg forward and then slammed his boot into the miscreant's midsection. At the same time, he shot his left fist into The Catcher's gut.

The villains fell back. The Bat found moving with his trunks down around his knees was difficult, but he managed to scoot forward and grab hold of The Catcher.

"Here's a Grand Slam!" he said, hitting the crook with a bone-jarring right fist. The Catcher slumped to the floor, totally out. The Bat turned his attention to The Pitcher, who was attempting to scramble to his feet.

"And you've just struck out!" The Bat hissed, giving the man a hard uppercut that connected right on the tip of the chin. The Bat saw The Pitcher's eyes roll back as he collapsed.

The Bat quickly yanked his tights back up before checking on The Raven. The lad was beginning to show signs of life. A light tap on the cheek brought him around.

"Where am I?" The Raven asked, his voice thick and heavy.

"You're safe now," The Bat assured him. "I've got you." He untied the young man and helped to rub life back into his aching limbs. It took a few moments before The Raven was able to stand on his own and even then he looked shaky.

"The last thing I remember," he said, still massaging his wrists, "was walking into an alley and seeing two goons in baseball outfits waiting for me."

The Bat nodded to the two unconscious figures. "The Pitcher and The Catcher. I've subdued them."

"Why are their trunks pulled down to show their willies? And just what," The Raven asked, picking up the baseball that had been dropped by The Catcher, "is in this plastic baseball?"

"It's a long story," The Bat replied, pressing a button on his belt that sent a special signal to the police department. "Let's get the men in blue here to take these two idiots away, and then I'll explain everything."

"Suits me," The Raven replied, tossing the baseball behind him.

The Bat lunged, but he was too late. The plastic ball hit the concrete floor and shattered. Immediately the thick gas wafted up and engulfed the two superheroes.

When the police arrived, The Raven, still wearing just his boots and mask, was slamming his huge cock into The Bat's ass.

The Bat was smiling giddily.

JUNIOR OHO ... SORT OF
By Troy Storm

"It's a great boner," Junior thought, driving his throat down the full length of his partner's throbbing morning mast. "Super meat for a super junior dude ... but ..."

He sighed, pushing his nose into Senior's still smooth pubes, feeling the older potential superhero's powerful shaft glide smoothly past his uvula and settle comfortably into his non-gagging gut.

Settle ... comfortably ...

His own dick – in the prime of its bonerhood and certainly not junior-sized but nonetheless nothing like the mass of mature manhood he was masticating – was also comfortably settled between his senior partner's quietly sucking jaws as they quietly sixty-nined another boring, waiting morning away.

Comfortably settled ... quietly ... boring ... waiting ...

Junior shook his head – mentally – trying to shake the errant thoughts away and applied himself diligently to efficiently vacuuming a gutful of premium protein from the massive meat pole stretching his lips.

Diligently ... efficiently ...

Groan. Holy Fucking Heroes-in-Waiting!

He had to stop thinking this way! It wasn't Senior's fault they were still ... still in line for the next Superhero opening. Criminently! How many years had it been, now?!? A few more fucking eons waiting for a current superhero to croak – fat chance! And, Junior would be anything but at the top of his powers. Senior was already beginning ...

Uh, oh. He'd better not go there, either. Even in his most private thoughts.

He loved the old guy. For real. And for a man Senior's age, the superdude was in fantastic shape. It wasn't his fault the League kept them both waiting ... waiting ...

Unmasked II

Oh, well, what the fuck. They were allowed super powers every now, and then and Junior had learned to take a massive amount of rock-hard manhood down his gut without upchucking and up his butt without ...

He chuckled – there were compensations. The League was proud. He and Senior had a fucking plaque ... on the wall ... kept dusted.

They also kept the neighborhood safe; they kept the local retired superheroes up to sexual snuff; they kept the up-and-comer superstuds coming.

He could wait. He would have to. And, if the senior partner could be patient and keep himself ready to leap into the breach – if it ever occurred – so could his junior partner.

His junior partner applied himself and promptly shot a couple of gutfuls of prime morning cream into Senior. The old guy, licking his satisfied chops, moved on to lap earnestly at Junior's butt hole, preparatory to blasting Junior's prime ass with his past-prime super salami.

Earnestly ... past prime ...

Junior gritted his teeth – not literally, since streams of senior cum had just been ejected down his throat and Sen's sensational protein shots always fired up the cockles of his cock. So he was a second banana to an overripe big banana, and neither of them would probably ever get promoted to SuperBananadom. Tough ... banana. He would be the best superhero-in-waiting there was, supporting his Top Banana all the way.

Probably into retirement ...

Junior flipped and presented his butt to his senior pal, knowing its shafting would put a deserved glow in old guy's eyes.

Inside his blasted anus, the young man clenched his sphincters and gave his partner the best butt-milking he had had in a month of fucks.

#####

Eric Summers

"Aaagh!" Junior banged his head onto the bar's countertop. "And that's when he dumped me! Kicked my fucked ass right out the door. Aaaagh!" His pounding fists echoed throughout the empty dive as the resigned bartender deftly swooped an empty beer glass out of harm's way.

"But you wanted to be on your own, right?" he reminded the soused young man. The barkeep's cool assessment set off another round of drunken wails from the ousted sidekick, only slightly mitigated by the older man's muted English accent.

"Yeah, but, I didn't want to hurt his feelings! He's a great dude! But, shit! He fucks me like never before, and I think I'm being cool letting him know I'll always be there for 'im, and then he kicks my beat-up butt right outta th' neighborhood sayin' it's for my own good."

The bartender tried not to roll his eyes yet again. "And, indeed, it sounds as if it might be; if you can prove to the ... Council?"

"The League! Fuckers!"

"Right. The League, that you can make it on your own, perhaps they might consider allowing a single sidekick to bypass his somewhat aging mentor – if such an opening were to occur – in addition to continuing to consider you both as a replacement duo."

Junior concentrated. Compound sentences were difficult at this stage of his alcoholic intake, but the gist sounded right.

"Six months, I've got. Jeez, I'm gonna miss 'im. He's the greatest fucker!"

As he methodically re-polished the counter, the older man's sudden interest tightened on the handsome, drunken sot "D' you mean that lit-trally?"

"Huge dick. Rock hard, even at his age. Shoots gallons of cum."

"I'd be more than happy to oblige," the bartender offered quietly. "I'm rather well-equipped for such an endeavor. And gallons *is* about right."

Junior sat up, eyes wide. "You could be my sidekick! Like one of those 'faithful servants'! I've always wanted one of thos'!"

The older man winced. "I rather lean toward 'faithful associate.' As it happens, I have been recently dumped from my accustomed position, myself. I'm rather good at oral as well as anal, if that's a further inducement."

"Oh, man, you'll love my dick. I'm hung like a fucking horse." Junior staggered off the barstool. Unsteady, but delighted at his turn of good fortune, he unzipped his pants and shoved them down. The unmistakable massive bulge in his straining Calvin's showed he didn't lie.

With astonishing dexterity, the middle-aged barkeep bolted over the bar. Junior's underwear joined his pants at his ankles. The suddenly released, half-hard trunk of meat leaped toward its young owner's firm pubes and climbed toward full bore as the man's eyes widened happily, his delighted mouth hanging open in hungry anticipation.

Easily lifting Junior, the Englishman seated him on the bar, spreading his legs wide and licking at the beautifully sculpted dickhead already exuding gut-greasing goo.

"Wow!" Junior blinked, grabbing the head of thinning hair. "I'm gonna get a blow job." He began to sniffle. "I haven't had any sex in a week." Shaking his head sadly, he noted, "I just might blow you right through the wall when I come."

"One can only hope." The barkeep happily swallowed the super dick whole.

#####

"Whoa ho! You are good, Edgar!" On his tummy spread-eagled, Junior munched an apple with one hand as his other hand firmly gripped the bedpost of the bouncing bed in the man's nearby flat. "Whoever the dude was that dumped you, must have a very lonely asshole now."

"One can only hope," the hard-working top muttered grimly, smashing his crotch into Junior's ripe melons. With a suppressed groan, he shot a final load up the young lad's ass and collapsed onto the broad, muscled back. He caught his breath, reached under to give Junior's tits affectionate tugs, and continued. "My former master was ... is a very angry young man. He needed some time alone to assess his situation, he informed me. I'm sorry I wasn't able to fulfill his needs ... not nearly as well as I seem to be filling yours." He licked Junior's neck affectionately.

The pleased young stud giggled, twisted to kiss the older man on the cheek – eliciting an embarrassed blush – and wiggled his ass, happily. "If your dick gets sore fucking my fab butt, you're welcome to start sucking again. Okay if I watch some TV? I oughta keep up with the news. Just in case." He snagged the remote.

Re-hardened, Edgar began to drill Junior's fab asshole again. "So you really have super powers ... just in case?"

"For about an hour, once a day." Junior flipped through the channels. "And we can't fly. I mean ... I can't fly. Neither of us ... Hey! Some action!" As Junior eagerly crouched on his hands and knees, the older man pistoned his dick in the well-oiled hole and reached under to simultaneously jack off the young super dude as they both watched the television screen.

"It's a hideous nightmare!" A frantic on-the-spot correspondent screamed as buildings toppled behind him. "Some crazed superhero is destroying midtown! Amazingly, no one has been hurt yet, but it can only be matter of time! Aaagh!"

"Wow," Junior marveled. "Look at that. He's really efficient at knocking stuff down. You think it's a super virus or something in his super brain? Like a Godzilla germ or something?"

"I think it's a psychological maladjustment puncturing his pinhead," Edgar hissed tightly, as his hips and hands increased their tempo. "Let's bring this home, gorgeous rump ... sir. You need to get downtown right away and prove your prowess."

"You're coming with me, right? Sen and I always ..."

"But, sir, I've no super powers." His face suddenly contorted. "Oh, yeah, buddy babe! We're almost there!"

"You could watch my back – my ass looks great in Spandex."

"I would be honored to serve as your lookout, sir – Yeah! Yeah! Blowing a big one!"

With a somewhat unseemly plaintive howl, Edgar power jetted a final series of pure English cream shots up the young stud's heroic American ass.

"How do we get there?" he sighed contentedly, stroking the broad, muscular back.

"I'll carry you and run really fast. We'll suit up as we go. Grab some duds and grab my backpack."

#####

Whoosh!

Junior raced through the city streets, his new "associate" hanging on for dear life, while at the same time attempting to get his new charge properly outfitted.

"Sir, Captain America? Isn't his attire copyrighted?" he shouted.

"It's a knock-off. The Captain doesn't have a cape. I had to use off-the-shelf stuff. Sen always said the League would take care of how we looked."

"Perhaps if I make a few alterations. I've a penknife. We want your first public outing to be effective."

"Uh, Edgar, you're not leaving a lot to cover me up."

"A mask, a cape, briefs and boots. I think it makes a statement."

"Wow! The Naked Avenger!"

"I'm afraid that's copyrighted also. Let's see what I can Magic Marker onto your cape. How about JO?"

"Jerk Off?"

"Oh, right. I was thinking Junior On-His-Own. We do want your Senior to be proud."

"J-OHO! I love it! Yo ho, JoHo!"

"HoHo! Splendid." Edgar chuckled, continuing to pare away as they dashed toward the area of collapsing buildings. "Just a bit more off the briefs."

"Oh, wow! There he is! What a mess!"

Screaming fleeing pedestrians. Circling helicopters. Flashing police cars. Howling fire trucks. The roar of raining bricks and twisting steel. "Not a very attractive scene," Edgar noted as Junior deposited him on a nearby building overlooking the chaos before racing into the midst of the mayhem to reconnoiter. He dashed back, gasping excitedly.

"He's really mad. But he's really good-looking. Young guy. Like me. Great outfit."

Edgar humphed. "Skin-tight, iridescent steel-gray unitard. Not very original, but I suppose it does display his assets. Did he see you?"

"He glanced my way, but I was running pretty fast. He keeps moving, too. He's totally determined to make a mess."

"Hmm. Perhaps that's how he maintains his powers."

"By making a mess?"

"By keeping moving."

"Wow. I never thought of that. Sort of like a self-generating dynamo, you mean? Maybe if we could immobilize him for a minute, he might run out of juice."

"What an excellent idea, sir."

"Gee, but how? I don't have any rope or stuff, and he's probably really strong."

"Well, there is that large crane. It might pin him down for a bit."

"Right!" Junior's excited look changed to a puzzled one. "But …?"

"You might start the crane to fall, then quickly lure the young man under it."

"How would I do that?"

"Take off your cape, and I'll take a bit more off your briefs … to allow more freedom of movement. And, turn down those boots. Show a bit more calf."

"Edgar ...?"

"Well, he's all dark and moody and very angry and you're all bright and muscular and eye-catching. Perhaps you might divert his attention long enough for the crane to flatten him."

Junior grinned. "You're a dirty old man. You and Senior would be great pals."

An explosion of bricks and the shriek of tangled steel signaled the path of the destructive young man. Junior quickly calculated the trajectory the falling crane might take and using his available super strength ripped a couple of strategic retaining bars loose. The giant latticework of metal began to tremble.

Racing through a rain of debris, Junior dashed into the path of destruction. "Nyah, nyah, messy man! Wanna come play in my junk yard?" He struck a fine superhero pose, muscular arms akimbo, expanding his bare chest. The dark clad destructive force stopped and stared. Out of the corner of his eye, Junior caught the crane beginning to sway in their direction.

"Or maybe you don't have enough to play with?" He dropped his briefs to give the guy a good look, then yanked them up and raced toward the pre-calculated spot.

With a roar of anger, the young man flew toward Junior, reaching out to catch the backside of his bright red, altered trunks and rip them off. "I'll show you who's got enough to play with, junior jerkman!" He grappled Junior to the ground.

The crane plummeted toward the tangled duo.

From the top of a nearby building, Edgar gasped in horror!

Junior fought dirty. Grabbing his furious opponent by the nuts, he planted his foot in the flat, hard groin and shoved. With a painful yell, the costumed dude slid backwards into the path of an encaging tangle of crashing steel.

Staggering backwards, slightly wincing at the thought of the deserved pain he had inflicted on his adversary, Junior peered through the billowing clouds of dust and debris, his hands protecting his exposed dick and balls.

Edgar dashed up, quickly wrapping the doffed knock-off cape around Junior's naked mid-section. "You did it, sir! Remarkable timing. I thought you both were goners."

Junior puffed his super breath to clear the air. "He might be, Edgar. Super powers are tricky stuff. You noticed he was only destroying old condemned brick buildings. He might not be immune to collapsing glass and steel."

The trapped young man seemed to be unharmed. At the sight of the unlikely couple emerging through the dust his face reddened with rage.

Junior leaped into the air, punching his fists victoriously. "We did it, Edgar! We flattened him right on his good-looking super ass! Oops." The protective cape came loose and fluttered to the ground. The pinned opponent's eyes widened as they flicked back and forth between Junior and his associate, then narrowed menacingly as his firm jaw clamped shut.

"We got you, buddy! No more, Me Bad!" Junior leaned into the tangle, taunting. "What do you say to that?!?"

"He appears to say nothing," Edgar noted dryly, as the young man snapped his head away, refusing to acknowledge defeat. "Perhaps we should move the operation along, sir," he suggested. "The authorities and crowds may be here soon. You might wrap a few girders around him to keep him immobile and run the lot of us back to our lair."

"Neat-o! We've got a lair?"

Edgar blushed. "It's rented. I was going to, um, surprise you later if our ... relationship seemed to be working out."

"Wow. You're really thorough, Edgar," Junior noted admiringly as he hoisted Edgar and the trapped super villain, who raged soundlessly, furiously rattling his entrapping girders.

Unmasked II

Later at the lair – "Actually, a rather amateurish attempt at a neighborhood S&M playroom," Edgar sniffed in apology – the ebullient, On-His-Own, part-time Superhero and his proper English associate stood assessing their prize, securely shackled to the wall, a la DaVinci's Detruvius man, though still clothed in his rather splendid Spandex.

"Funny he doesn't talk, now," Junior said. "He sure yelled the hell at me."

Edgar shrugged. "Perhaps he swore never to speak to someone again, and now that he's lost his superpowers that he used with such poor discretion, has remembered his ridiculous oath." He humphed and turned away.

"What's your problem?" Junior asked, stepping forward. "You made sure nobody got hurt, and you only destroyed buildings that were going to come down anyway. You coulda been a hero instead of a hot-headed bad guy."

The young man glared furiously at Junior and Edger for a moment, then imperiously turned his head.

"What do you think, Edgar?"

"I'd rather not say, sir. Perhaps it's hormones. A childish delight in knocking things down. An adolescent sense of inadequacy." He sighed. "I'll go prepare tea." And left the room.

Junior stroked the Spandex. "You're really hot, you know that? Senior – my old partner, I mean, he's my partner, except we're not together right now because, well, never mind – he'd cream in his jeans over you."

The young man looked surprised and puzzled. "Sure, we share," Junior explained. "Some of the guys in the neighborhood are really something. 'Specially the up-tight married ones. And the wives tell us what a great job we do, getting their tired ole dudes to loosen up and ... go with the flow." He shrugged, sadly. "Boy, do I miss that. Being able to pull community service."

He absently plucked at the young man's protruding nipples as the young stud gasped and writhed. "It would be a shame to turn you over to the cops – man, are they making a fuss on TV about your getting away. Gee, what great abs you've got." Stroking up the young malcontent's inner thighs, Junior's big hands cupped his crotch and massaged, causing the young dude to gulp and writhe even more luxuriantly.

"Maybe you need a good blow job," Junior suggested, digging his fingers into the stretched fabric and ripping it from the throbbing bulge he had created. "Hey, nice, really nice. I thought you might be from when I grabbed you before. Sorry about that. I'll make it up to you." He stroked his tongue slowly across the glowing head of hard meat. "But you gotta ask nicely." Pulling his mouth away, he left his tongue hanging, millimeters away from the throbbing flesh.

"Please ... sir ..."

Junior vacuumed in the dude's dick and grabbed at his balls, suckling furiously.

"Oh, God, yes!" The bad superguy bellowed happily as the young part-timer bounced his head up and down the bone-hard peninsula of self-lubricating meat.

The clatter of the plate of cucumber sandwiches hitting the floor as a stunned Edgar reentered the room failed to dislodge Junior from his community service task at hand.

"See, fucker, what a great blow-job a real pro can give! Even with inadequate goods, you cockney dork!"

Edgar stormed forward. "Master Reginald, I'm extremely competent in all my requirements. I would have been ..."

"Would have been doesn't cut it, Irish lout!" The young man forced himself to look pained, though he was obviously in the throes of utter delirium from Junior's concentrated efforts.

"He doesn't seem to have a problem with my being a dickless wonder!"

"Master Reg, I was angry! You were a very recalcitrant youth! I didn't realize you felt so ... inadequate."

"What the hell should I feel ... compared to my own servant! Ohmigod, ohmigod, Edgar, this guy is unbelievable!"

"You were my ward! Yes, I know how unbelievable he is. There was no way I could have properly laid hands on you ... You had better hang onto your balls, sir. He'll scarf them right down, too. Your father ..."

"Shithead Dad! Stud?! Me!? I've been wanting you to lay hands on me for years, and when I finally reached majority, when I finally looked like a manly, superhero, you were repulsed by my lack ..." He gritted his teeth, his lower half happily erupting. "OhgodI'mcoming! I'mcoming! I'mcoming!"

"Go with it, Reggie, babe!" Edgar pulled out his dick and began whanging away. "Let the good times fire away! I was not ... repulsed ... by the size of your ... cock. I was angry. You were brutal toward my trying to maintain ... a proper ..."

Reg slowly collapsed as Junior continued to nurse his deflated dick. "I didn't know how to get through your damn Scottish dourness," he gasped. "We English are so fucking reserved."

"Master Reg – ungh, ungh – you dismissed me."

Reg grinned. "I caught you pounding the pork ... like now."

"Trying ... to prevent myself ... from 'making a man of you,' as the Lord instructed, though I don't think that's quite what he had in mind ..."

"You're huge, Edgar. I was shocked. I thought you would never be satisfied with my mere ..."

"And then ... in a moment of peckishness ... I used an unfortunate phrase ... Excuse me, lad, I've got to pop off or my nuts will explode."

Junior pulled his mouth off Reg's rebuilt rebar. "Put it up my ass, Edgar. I love getting worked at both ends."

Edgar shook his head in wonder as he shafted Junior. "These Americans are delicious," he noted.

"I think it's the mixed blood," young Reginald sighed happily, readying himself for a rematch with Junior's amazing mouth, as did his older mentor, earnestly screwing into Junior's equally efficient engulfing anus.

Reg leaned over Junior's shoulder to kiss the startled Edgar on his thinning hair. He looked up, and Reg kissed him full on the mouth. "Come back home? Please ... sir?"

Edgar bit his stiff upper lip and forced back a sniff.

"Will do ... sir."

They all came ... home.

#####

"You know it was all arranged by the League? To test you. I thought that was pretty underhanded, but ..."

Junior happily bounced up and down on Senior's dick, scratching at the older man's chest hair, tweaking his nipples. Home again, home again.

"I figured something was fishy," Junior replied, between ecstatic grunts. "I've watched too many English movies to believe those accents."

"But I'm so proud you made a good showing. You're on the fast track, now, Junior." Senior's happiness was less than unbridled. "But I didn't think it was necessary to choose superhero actors who were so ... well endowed."

"They had to live up to the guy I was being taken away from." Junior leaned down and clamped his mouth to Senior's as the older guy thoroughly hammered his ass home.

Home again, home again.

At least for now.

TOOLMAN
By Wayne Mansfield

I noticed him immediately as I was coming down the hallway toward the photocopier.

"What's his name?" I asked Tracy, the seventeen-year-old office assistant who was fond of wearing too much make-up.

She looked at me, chewing as always, and shrugged. "I dunno. He's the new accountant. That's all I know. Why? Ya fancy him?"

Now it was my turn to shrug. "Dunno yet."

What was I talking about? He was a walking wet dream. At over six feet tall, solidly built – I could see the muscle definition beneath the fabric of his shirt – short, dark hair and a well manicured moustache, he was everything I could ever want in a man. I hovered by the photocopier, making myself look as busy as I possibly could while waiting for him to turn, so I could sneak a peek at his package.

Rachel, the receptionist, red hair piled up on top of her head and also wearing too much make-up, was keeping him occupied. Shameless bitch! If that chest of hers was thrust any further out, she'd dislocate a vertebra. And, that stupid little laugh she had sent shivers down my spine, but at least I got to see his perfect smile, dazzling white behind red, oh-so-kissable lips. And then, he turned. My eyes dropped to the massive bulge in his pants and stayed glued there. Could he be any more perfect? Impossible!

"Jake. Jake!"

Rachel's dulcet tones wrenched me from my examination of the juiciest crotch bulge I had laid eyes on in months. I looked up to see both Rachel and the hottie looking back at me. I must have turned beetroot red.

"This is Jake, and he'll be working with you in accounts," said Rachel, her smile evaporating as she glared at me. "Jake, this is Calvin, and he is your new boss." The smile reappeared as she looked at Calvin.

"Pleased to meet you," I said extending my hand.

Calvin shook it, a manly, powerful shake. I caught a whiff of his cologne, understated, earthy; the scent of a man. I felt something stirring in the front of my trousers as I looked into his sparkling green eyes.

"Pleased to meet you," he echoed.

"Well I guess I should show you where you'll be working," I said, casting a snide smile at Rachel.

The look on her face was like frozen thunder. But, it soon thawed. Her face literally beamed. "Now Jake, you know that is my responsibility. So if you don't mind ..."

I cut her short. "Oh it's no problem, Rach. I was going there anyway. I'm sure you have better things to do."

I could feel the daggers in my back the moment I turned it on her.

"I'm sorry about that," I said as I escorted Calvin to the small office we would be sharing. "She gets a bit possessive of any attractive man that arrives at the reception desk."

Calvin nodded thoughtfully. "So you think I'm attractive?"

I nearly choked. As I thought of something witty to reply with I heard him laugh.

"Just kidding," he said.

Later, the following day, as I was showing him the contents of the various computer files he'd be using, I became aware of him staring at me. At first, I ignored it and continued banging away at the keyboard, bringing up file after file, but then I began to wonder if he was taking any of what I was telling him in. I didn't want to have to go through it all again. I turned to face him. He smiled.

"You know I saw you checking out my package yesterday," he said with a half smile; the dark brown moustache accentuating the bright white of his teeth.

I didn't know where to look. Unfortunately, I looked down, my eyes landing squarely on that heavenly crotch.

One of his hands was resting on his thigh, his thumb gently brushing the base of his engorged cockhead, the outline of which was clearly visible through the tight fabric of his pants.

I looked back up at his face.

"You know you're a very handsome guy, too," he said, his voice taking on a serious tone. "I have a thing for guys with black hair and blue eyes."

I cleared my throat and swallowed.

"You're in luck then!" I said with a laugh, not knowing what else to say.

"Could you and I go out for a drink this evening, after work? I don't usually do this kind of thing, especially with colleagues, but I just moved here, and I don't really know anyone. Plus, I think we might have a few things in common."

I considered my answer for about five seconds. "Sure," I said, figuring I might as well.

We went out for a drink and ended up having half a dozen. Throughout the evening there were furtive glances and lots of "accidental" touching. We even ended up in the toilet together at one stage and caught a glimpse of each other's semi-hard cocks.

"Can I drive you home?" he asked me at the end of the night.

"You really shouldn't drive," I cautioned. "You've had just as many as me."

"Alcohol doesn't affect me," he explained. "It's a rare disorder, but it comes in handy sometimes."

Before I had a chance to reply, the sound of gunshots rang out from the convenience store across the road. Two thugs wearing balaclavas and brandishing pistols came running out. One of them looked straight at us.

"I gotta go," said Calvin. "I, er, really gotta go."

And with that, he was racing down the alleyway behind me like a frightened little mouse. I stood on the pavement for a second or two not being able to believe either the robbery across the street or that the man I had been drinking with had run off and left me in full view of the bandits.

Another shot rang out, hitting the corner of the pub we had just been in. A chunk of brick went flying over my shoulder, and only then did I drop to the ground.

"That piss-weak bastard is not going to hear the end of this," I muttered to myself as I huddled next to a parked car.

Then I heard a scream. There was another gunshot and another scream. I peered through the glass of the window and saw a man, dressed from head to toe in black Lycra, including a tight-fitting hood that covered the top half of his face to just over the edge of his top lip. Two slits allowed him to see, though his eyes were lost beneath the dense shadows of the costume.

I watched amazed as this masked man snatched the guns from the bandits and crushed them into small balls of metal with his bare hands before throwing them so far up into the sky that I eventually lost sight of them. Next he slammed the two men together, knocking one of them out and giving the other one a pretty nasty headache. He threw one on top of the other and then suddenly a length of barbed wire shot out of one hand. As his hand circled around the two crooks they became more and more ensnared in the razor-sharp wire. Then, even more amazingly, his left hand turned into a large pair of wire cutters that he used to cut himself free of the wire. While the wire cutters morphed back into his left hand, his right hand, the hand that the wire had streamed out of, turned into a pair of oversized pliers, which he used to twist the two ends of the barbed wire together, securing the two bandits.

Blaring sirens ripped through the relative silence. I stood up, as did about a dozen other passersby who had been taking cover.

"Who was that?" they asked each other. "Have you ever seen anything like it?"

I started walking toward the nearest taxi rank. I probably should have stayed, but I figured there would be enough witnesses to tell the police the whole crazy story. I had seen the whole thing with my own two eyes, and I wasn't sure I believed it. I had no idea what the police would make of it.

Back at my apartment, I saw that someone was waiting on the stoop outside. Calvin. I couldn't quite see him, but I knew from the silhouette that it was my new boss.

"Hi there," he said, as though nothing had happened.

"Hi," I replied, rather coldly.

"Oh, you're pissed off with me?" he asked as I turned the key in my front door.

"Nothing much gets by you, does it?" I said. "Thanks for leaving me there. I could have been shot!"

I walked through the door and let Calvin follow me.

"That would never have happened," he reassured me.

"How the hell would you know? You ran off like a little girl."

Calvin went quiet.

I took my coat off and hung it on the back of the front door. I kicked my shoes off and pulled my socks off. I wondered to myself if I was being too hard on the man. He was my boss, after all. And, nothing had happened to me. I guess I was just a bit annoyed at his cowardice. He seemed like such a macho man in every other way.

"I don't know you very well," he began, walking toward me, "but I have a sense that I can trust you."

"I like to think I am trustworthy," I replied.

"Even with big secrets?"

I nodded and continued into the kitchen.

"This is a major big secret and once I tell you I have to know that you will never repeat it."

My mind reeled with all the possible things he could tell me that would warrant such a build-up.

"I swear," I said. "My word of honor."

He stepped closer until he was only a few centimeters away from me. He wrapped his arms around my waist and looked into my eyes.

"You know I think you're a special guy," he said, his voice low and gentle.

I could feel his cock hardening against my growing cock.

"I think you're pretty special, too."

He kissed me, softly and tenderly; his lips lingering on mine for a second before leaving them. He looked at me, and I smiled. He smiled back.

"I didn't run off this evening," he said. "Well, I did, but I came back."

My brow furrowed.

"Let me explain. You see, I was that man in black. I only ran off to change into my costume. I need that costume because it is fire-proof, bullet-proof and it contains other crime fighting elements that I don't know how they work, they just do. I am the one the media dubbed 'The Toolman' because somehow when I put the suit on I can manifest whatever tools I want, and they help me bring down criminals. It does a whole heap of other stuff, too, but I don't need to go into that now."

I backed away from him, breaking the embrace.

"Are you for real?" I asked, smirk firmly in place. "You're telling me that you're some kind of superhero?"

Calvin nodded. "Some kind. Yeah."

I remained silent for a minute, taking it all in, and when I had I realized that the information had made him even more appealing. I smiled, creating in him a similar response.

"Does that mean you're okay with this?" he asked, his eyes daring to hope.

"Of course it is," I said.

"Well that's great news because there is one other tool I have been wanting to show you since I saw you checking it out yesterday."

I stepped into another embrace. Our lips met, but this time they stayed together, our tongues slipping over each other and around each other in a slow, seductive dance. My arms were tight around him, and his were just as tight around me, our hands roaming over each other's backs.

"I have wanted this since the first time I laid eyes on you," he whispered into my ear as his lips sucked on the sensitive skin below it, continuing down my neck, across my throat and up to the other ear.

I moaned, pushing my groin against his; desperate to feel his naked body against mine, to feel his hard cock in my mouth, up my asshole.

His lips found mine again, and while he sucked my top lip, his fingers undid the buttons on my cotton business shirt. He slipped it from my toned torso, letting it drop to the floor below. His hands returned to my chest, running over the twin peaks of my lightly-haired pectoral muscles, sliding down my flat stomach to the top of my trousers. As his hands fumbled with the buckle of my belt, I began to unbutton his shirt, pushing his shirt over his broad shoulders and off his body altogether.

In no time at all, I felt my trousers falling down, exposing my hairy, muscular legs. Still, our lips stayed on each others. I sucked the tip of his tongue as it explored the inside of my mouth, and at the same time I tried to get his belt buckle undone. I felt him push my hands out of the way, and when he pulled his pants and briefs off, I bent down and pulled my briefs off, too.

We were totally naked. Calvin pulled me to him, and I shuddered as our naked flesh touched. I could feel his muscles against mine, his nipples brushing against mine and his thick, engorged cock squashed against mine. But, I wanted to be closer. I wanted to feel him inside my tight hairy fuck-hole.

Suddenly, he broke away from the kiss and spun me around. One powerful hand pushed the top half of my body over the kitchen counter. I felt him kick my legs apart and then his hands were on my muscular butt cheeks. I gasped when they were parted, so forcefully, exposing my puckered, pink love-ring, so this man I had only known for forty-eight hours could examine my most private part. I felt him nuzzle my lightly-haired asshole with his nose; I heard him sniffing at it, breathing in my musky man scent. I pushed my butt out further, wanting him to explore it in any way he saw fit. I felt my cheeks pulled further apart and the firm, wet tip of his tongue push up against my tight pucker.

I brought my hand down and gripped my cock. It was already dribbling like a fire hose. I used the precum to coat the length of my hard eight-incher, smearing it over my veiny cock so that soon my hand was slipping up and down its length with ease.

Calvin's tongue was sending shivers up and down my spine. His tongue darted in and out of my twenty-six-year-old asshole, probing and going deeper with each jab. His mouth kissed my hole, his lips sucking my ass lips; his hot breath making my pucker twitch and pulse. I moaned and began to grind my ass into his face. I could feel the bristles on his chin scrape against the sensitive tissue of my pucker, but rather than hurt, it sent tiny lightning bolts of electricity radiating out across my body.

Without any warming, Calvin stood up. I could feel his cock slide up between my butt cheeks, his arm wrapping itself around my narrow waist.

"I want to fuck you, Jake," he whispered into my ear, nibbling the lobe from behind.

I reached behind me and guided his throbbing meat into my asshole, pushing myself onto it slowly and enjoying every inch that disappeared inside me.

"Feel good?" he asked.

"Yes," I moaned. "It feels so good."

With his cock securely inside me, I reached back again this time cupping my hand over the back of his head, pressing it closer to my neck, and as he began thrusting into me, his thick, moist lips kissed the back of my neck. I felt his tongue flicker on the skin, then his lips, kissing then sucking. Meanwhile my other hand worked on my cock, stroking it slowly to the rhythm of Calvin's thrusts. I was lost in the ecstasy of the moment and almost didn't feel his fingers find my nipple and began to twist and pinch the fleshy nub.

I closed my eyes. I was completely his; his huge, thick shlong deep inside me, his powerful arms around my waist, his strong fingers twisting and turning my nipple, and his firm lips on the back of my neck. I could have shot my load many times, but I wanted to save it. I wanted to try and hold off until Calvin wanted to come, and when he did I wanted to feel his superhuman tool go off inside me, flooding my guts with his super spunk.

We'd been fucking for God knows how long when I felt him guide me out of the kitchen and down the hallway toward my bedroom. With his cock still deep inside me, I led him to my bedroom. I was careful with every step. His cock felt so good inside me that I couldn't bear to feel it slip out, even for a second. I pushed the bedroom door open wider and led Calvin to my bed.

For a minute, or maybe it was five minutes, he pounded my ass so roughly that I had to brace myself on the edge of the bed.

"How does that feel, baby?"

My whole body was rocking. I could hardly speak. "Fucking fantastic," I managed to say. "Fucking wild."

I closed my eyes again. Everything about him felt right. I would have let him do anything to me by that stage.

"Oh baby, fuck my ass. Pound it. I wanna feel that hot cock deep inside."

I didn't usually vocalize much during sex. I thought I always sounded like a bad porno movie, but with Calvin it was different. I actually meant what I said. I did want him deeper inside me. I did want him to ram his rigid rod into me. I wanted to feel him fucking me. Really feel him.

He slammed his cock into me a couple of times so deeply that it bordered on pain. I grimaced. But then, he slid his cock out of me, spun me around and kissed me, his tongue instantly in my mouth, tasting me, caressing my own tongue.

"Oh baby your ass is so tight. I was so close to blowing. But I don't want to. Not yet. I want to enjoy you some more."

His mouth muffled my reply. I could feel his tongue between my teeth, so I dare not try and speak for fear of biting him. His hungry mouth kissed a trail from my mouth, down my chin, my neck and onto my chest. He took first one and then the other nipple into his mouth and sucked on them firmly, paying one attention and then the other.

My head rolled back. A long groan escaped my lips. He took my left nipple between his teeth, biting down on it slightly while the tip of his tongue flicked it from the other side. The sensations were causing me to shudder. My nipples had always been hugely sensitive, but in his more than capable mouth, with his tongue tickling both in turn, I felt as though I were going to explode. I had never felt such an overwhelming sense of pleasure. Even so, I missed his cock inside me.

"Fuck me," I said. "Ride my ass. I want to feel you shoot inside me."

He wrapped his arms around me and kissed me for a moment before laying me down gently on the bed. He grabbed my legs and pulled my ass to the very edge of the mattress and then guided his stiff prick inside. Again, I groaned. I writhed on his cock, bringing my fingers up to continue the work Calvin had started on my nipples.

"Jerk off," said Calvin, almost demanding it.

"I can't. If I touch my cock I'm gonna shoot."

There was no reply. He grabbed my ankles and pushed them wide apart, using them to steady himself as he pounded my puckered asshole. His large ball sac slapped against the hairy skin of my groin. I could hear it slap, slap, slapping and feel it sticking slightly as he thrust out before slapping into me again as his cock plowed into my tight fuck tunnel. Drops of his sweat peppered my pubic hair and my lightly haired abdomen. I could feel it splashing onto my throbbing hard cock, too.

He leaned forward, still fucking me. His lips were slightly puckered. I lifted my head to meet his kiss. Without missing a thrust, he kissed me. I wrapped an arm around his shoulders, holding his lips to mine and steadying myself against his thrusts which were getting more and more powerful. Then he began to moan.

"Oh baby, I'm going to blow. I can't hold back."

I pushed my hand between his stomach and mine and did my best to jerk off. I couldn't grip, it but it didn't matter. There was enough friction between our bodies and my hand to get the job done. Our mouths just rested on each other, our hot breath blowing straight into each other's mouths.

Calvin was grunting and puffing. And, so was I. I was ready to blow, trying to hold off for as long as I could until I heard Calvin come.

"Awwww fuck, I'm gonna cream your asshole baby. Here it comes."

His face contorted. I caught a glimpse of it before I closed my eyes. I wanted to concentrate on the feeling of him going off inside me. And boy, did I feel it. The first gush was a warm splash inside my bowels and enough to set my cock off. As the second jet of cream erupted from Calvin's cock, I felt a spreading warmth coat my hand and stomach. Somehow, I managed to pull my sticky hand free. I leaned forward and cupped both Calvin's muscular butt cheeks, pulling him into me as his cock continued to unload inside me. When finally he had finished, he collapsed on top of me, panting and saturated in sweat.

I held him in my arms and kissed his shoulder and the base of his neck. His cock was still inside me, shrinking but still inside me. For several minutes, we lay in silence, holding each other and getting our breath back.

He was the first to speak.

"How was that? Can I come back?"

I laughed. "That was the fuck of the century," I said. "Of course you can come back."

The following day at work we had to be careful not to be overly affectionate with each other. The firm was okay about gay people just not with intimate inter-office relationships.

It was pay day, a very important day for everyone. I was doing up the wages, double checking my calculations, when I felt Calvin kiss the back of my neck.

I smiled but ignored him. Then I felt him poke me with something. I looked up. He had his cock out.

"Someone wants to say hello," he said, shaking his nine-inch monster cock at me.

"Someone is going to get both our asses fired," I said, looking over my shoulder at the office door.

"No problem," he said as a large metallic claw grew out of his hand, reached across the room and shut the door. The claw immediately changed into a key which locked the door.

"How did you ...?" I babbled. "I thought you needed your suit."

Calvin smiled. "Me, too. I just discovered it. I was told the suit could genetically alter me if I wore it too often. Guess what?" he said, laughing.

"Well just be careful about which parts it alters," I said, grabbing his cock. "I'd hate anything to happen to this."

I took his hard prick into my mouth. I felt his hand on the back of my head. I shuddered. His touch was like an electric charge to me. It got my hormones racing. I swallowed his cock as best I could, opening my mouth wide as it slid down my throat then closing it slightly so that I could feel every vein and the swell of the large mushroom head when I neared the tip. Every now and again, I would lick the piss slit, tasting the salty remnant of his morning piss with the first couple of licks and then nothing, just the soft moist tissue inside.

I gripped his cock with one hand, stroking it while simultaneously sucking it. As I took it down my throat my nose came up against his pubic bush, that fragrant, manly smell of sweat, pheromone and salt soon had my own cock twitching inside my pants. I reached down and freed it, my hand then stroking it as I lovingly sucked Calvin's hot rod.

There was knock on the door.

"Calvin. It's Rachel. Are you in there?"

I looked up, but Calvin shook his head. He mouthed something, but I didn't catch it. I just knew he meant that it would be all right and to continue. My heart was racing now. There was another knock. Calvin started to fuck my face. He seemed to be getting off on nearly being caught. He undid his pants completely and let them drop to the carpet. He was now butt naked, his massive organ down my throat, and I wasn't sure, but it seemed as though he was fingering his asshole.

"Ah that's it baby," he moaned. "You've got a hot little mouth there.'

I could feel his balls tightening. My mouth and hand were working faster on his cock to the point where my own cock jutted into the air unattended, wobbling in time with my sucking and jerking.

I glanced up and saw him playing with his nipple. The other hand was still behind him. I could tell by the way he was sticking his ass out that he had his finger up there. It made me so horny to think of him being so sexual right in the middle of the office building. Finally he began to grunt. I knew what was coming. I sucked harder and worked his cock with my hand.

"Oh yeah, baby. That's it. Don't stop now. Don't stop now."

I flattened my tongue and got it working on his cock, too. My fingers were tight around the base of his prick. My jaw was beginning to ache, but I didn't mind. Calvin was my man. He had hinted as much, and I knew in my mind and heart that I felt the same way. I would do anything for him including tolerating a bit of lockjaw.

His hand left his nipple and rested again on my head. He pulled it onto his cock and a couple of times I nearly gagged. Finally he came – with a loud cry that I hoped no one could hear. His thick man jelly washed over my tongue and ran like a torrent down my throat. I continued sucking and swallowing, not wanting to miss a drop. Even when he had finished ejaculating into me, I kept sucking, making him shudder and laugh.

"Stop it," he laughed. "Stop it."

He pushed my head off his cock. I wiped my lips and stuffed my semi-hard cock back into my pants. I waited for him to get dressed and then went and unlocked the door. Almost immediately there was another knock. I ran back to my desk.

"Come in," I said.

"I just did," said Calvin from the other side of the small office.

"Stop it!" I said.

"Never."

From that first date we spent pretty much all our time together. Of course there were times when he "mysteriously" disappeared, but I knew that whenever that happened there would be some mention of him, or rather Toolman, on the six o'clock news. It was kinda fun being Lois Lane.

MASTER MIND'S DOWNFALL
By Jay Starre

A winter snow storm had blanketed the Pennsylvania landscape in white. Even though it was still afternoon, low clouds cast a grey pall over the countryside. In all that uniformity of grey-white, he almost missed the driveway. Fortunately, his keen senses alerted him just in time to slow down enough to make the turn.

Thick woods on either side of the drive were punctuated by a large mass ahead, more grey that offered little welcome. The granite stone of the mansion implied a stolid sense of permanence. One of the oldest structures in the area, he knew for a fact the home had been built in the early 1700s.

His breath wafted out in front of his face as he rubbed his gloved hands together while mounting the steps. That nervous rubbing of his palms was an indication of his unease.

He was afraid. Not an emotion he enjoyed or often entertained.

Physical danger came along with his work. At times, he felt fear when confronted by obvious threats from burly scoundrels or perilous situations. That kind of fear was not a hindrance. He merely used it to focus and intensify his powers.

This afternoon, the fear was different. It settled down in the pit of his stomach. It refused to be called up and employed productively. That failure only increased his unease.

"Come in out of the cold, Sir. Would you mind waiting in the drawing room? Senator Graham will be with you presently."

The butler waved him in with a military bow. He half-expected the man's shiny black dress shoes to click together and the long arm to snap up in a salute. Hooded amber orbs briefly met his before sliding away.

Unmasked II

    This butler was not as he seemed. Not at all, but he had little time to explore that notion as the man briskly led him across the gleaming hardwood floor into a doorway only a few paces away.

    An ancient oak door was pulled shut, and he was alone. Welcome heat greeted him. The chamber was rather large for a drawing room and dominated by a truly immense fireplace, the likes of which he'd never before seen.

    A semi-oval cavern, at least ten yards wide and ten feet high at the crown, roared with a veritable bonfire in its center. It was almost a room of its own. The heat emanating from it came in intense waves, the light emitted making any lamps unnecessary, even in the gloom of the winter day.

    He removed his overcoat immediately, thinking it odd the butler hadn't offered that service. After being outside, even if it was only briefly, the heat of the room was almost unbearable. Eyes drawn to the mesmerizing flames of the roaring bonfire, he moved closer, even though sweat had already begun to bead his brow and dampen his armpits and torso. He experienced an odd compulsion to strip completely, right then and there. His cock stirred and began to rise up under his sleek leather costume. He was getting a hard-on!

    "Please feel free to make yourself comfortable."

    The disembodied voice hissed with snake-like sibilance above the crackling of the bonfire. He recognized it as the Senator's, even though they'd only spoken briefly over the phone.

    This was very strange. Of course it wouldn't be that unusual for the Senator to have an intercom, but he also felt certain the man was watching him. He tore his eyes from the fireplace and glanced around the room, searching for evidence of that intercom – and a possible hidden camera.

    "Go ahead and remove your clothing, Master Mind. All of it."

    His cock stiffened completely, throbbing nastily. What the fuck was going on? He was accustomed to strange circumstances and odd people. After all, his line of investigative detective work involved both. It was his own unease that was disconcerting. And his raging boner – along with his almost desperate desire to follow that disembodied suggestion to strip!

Self-control was one of his strong suits. Sexually, he had few inhibitions and few urges he couldn't reign in, or use to further his goals. His stiff cock throbbed with undeniable urgency, and sweat ran down into the crack between his compact ass-cheeks to remind him of his own twitching butt-hole.

All right, he thought to himself. There was no profit in fighting it. Follow the blatant trail laid out before him, while employing his keen senses to strip away the obvious outer layers to get to the convoluted meaning beneath.

Against the aged oak-paneling of the wall behind him, a coat tree offered a place for his clothing. With steady hands, but throbbing cock and pulsing asshole, he began to remove his costume.

"Excellent, Master Mind. Our business is best conducted with you in the nude. I look forward to a look at your body, which I've been informed is truly magnificent."

Who would have informed the Senator his body was magnificent? Another oddity!

The disembodied voice had come from the back wall of the drawing room, almost right beside him. He chose not to reply, not yet at least. Let the Senator reveal his intentions before he offered his response.

Of course, he was the one revealing himself at the moment. His emerald leather shirt, supple leather boots, and sleek leather pants came off as he draped each item on a hook of the coat tree with a steady hands. Only his gloves, mask and tight green leather jock strap remained. He hooked his fingers in the straps of his jock and pushed downward, bending over as his hard-on popped out into view. His bare butt and crack were exposed for the no-doubt observing Senator.

He turned to face that roaring bonfire again, naked.

"Yes, magnificent as promised."

Regardless of the heat, Master Mind shivered slightly as he felt the caress of unseen eyes roaming over his nude body. Very tall, with a powerful ass that swelled with muscular firmness below a tight, narrow waist, he reminded one of a cheetah, poised now, but with long lean limbs prepared to erupt in an explosion of blinding speed at any moment.

A lengthy fat pipe of a cock curved out from his crotch, twitching toward his rippling abs. His torso was solid muscle, devoid of hair except for a light auburn tangle at the base of his boner and a sparse trail that led up to his navel.

His dark emerald mask outlined his handsome face, revealing the cloud-grey keenly observant eyes, the mass of auburn hair sprouting above, and the half-smiling bowed lips and strong chin below. His mask and his supple gloves were all that remained of his costume.

"I'd ask you to remove your mask, but I imagine you might refuse. For now, I'd rather ask only those things you might willingly offer."

Willingly? Master Mind caught that key word, and sensed the message beneath, although it was close to impossible to read the speaker's thoughts with only the voice to focus on.

The Senator was counting on that!

He'd received a generous down payment at his St. Louis office before he embarked on the journey east. He'd go along with the Senator's bizarre scenario, at least for now.

Again a shiver ran up his nude body, and this time he noted the chilling draft that seeped in from behind him. The wall, appearing to be made of solid oak paneling, must not be as it seemed.

A moment later, his keen ears caught the sound of rollers sliding just before he turned away from the warmth of the bonfire to the blast of icy air from behind.

"Voila! A present for you, Master Mind! I strongly suspect you'll appreciate the opportunity presented."

The oak paneling separated, and out of the gaping black maw behind it, a rolling apparition of bizarre lewdness emerged. With a jolt, he was struck by a return of the unreasoning fear he'd experienced earlier, raising the hair on the back of his neck and along his forearms.

A man knelt on all fours over a padded, curved column of dark emerald leather. Straps of that same black-green leather encased ankles and wrists as he was effectively bound on hands and knees to the odd bench.

Master Mind stepped aside as the rolling bench slid past him toward the center of the room and closer to the heat of the immense fireplace. The paneling slid shut, and the icy blast was cut off.

He was left gawking at the anonymous stranger. Fear churned around in the pit of his stomach, urging him to reach out toward the man's mind in a swift stab of telepathic probing.

Nothing!

Master Mind's cock, already stiff and twitching, lurched against his belly and emitted a drool of precum. Something was afoot here, totally beyond the mere hiring of his services by the unseen Senator Graham!

Regardless of his suspicious thoughts, his attention was obviously drawn to the sprawled figure in the center of the room. He was oddly dressed, to say the least. Form-fitting leather gleamed along his stocky, muscular body. From head to toe, the leather encased him in shimmering emerald, no coincidence it seemed to Master Mind, that the color of the material mimicked his own dark-green costume.

There were only two areas where the clinging leather did not cover the bound stranger's skin. The leather encasing his head had one large hole where the mouth gaped open, pink and yawning. There were smaller holes at the nostrils and ears, so the man could apparently smell and hear. But the eyes were completely masked behind the gleaming leather.

This encasing of the head, and the eyes in particular, would affect Master Mind's ability to read the man's thoughts. He himself was well-aware of this weakness in his powers, but how could the Senator know about it? Or why would he care?

His eyes were drawn to another area of the crouching man's body. His ass. Big and round and glorious, the fleshy surface was encased in the same leather, but with one exception. The deep divide between those melon-mounds was revealed by a slash in the leather. From waist to leather-encased ball-sack, that slash gaped open to expose the valley between.

The column of leather he was draped over effectively spread apart his powerful thighs. His ass-cheeks opened up in that position, down-coated flesh bared.

Where the man's asshole would have pouted on view, instead, dangled the thick handle of a dildo, the other end, of whatever unknown size, was buried between twitching ass-lips.

He was stuffed full of dildo!

It was all too bizarre. Yet also undeniably intriguing. His sense of curiosity, suspicion, and fear coalesced in an explosion of intense need to ferret out the meaning behind the shenanigans of the mysterious Senator Graham.

And, there was something about this hapless stranger that tore at him. Who was he? Why was he here? Master Mind sensed a familiarity about the body that nagged at his memory. But for some reason, he was dumbfounded by the odd leather costume ... and the absolute silence of the bound victim.

The mouth moved, as if speaking. But, there were no words, no sounds at all. The full lips looked huge as they bulged from the mask's slit, and tantalizingly familiar. He stepped forward, reaching out with a gloved hand, knowing that physical contact would engender at least a limited measure of his telepathic ability.

His reach was stymied, fingers banging up against an invisible barrier. He felt a wall between them! Using both hands, he probed up and down, realizing a flat surface rose from the base of the rolling cart upwards. The victim was encased in a sound-proof cage.

Transparent glass or plastic surrounded the dildo-plugged stranger.

"You will find a sex instrument and a remote control on the stand behind you. I'm sure you know what to do with them. Indulge me, if you will. All will be explained in time."

The Senator's voice trembled slightly. Master Mind could hear the lust in it. Was this merely a sex game for the wealthy politician? No, that was not it, or at least not all of it.

Out of that false wall, a draft and another rolling object materialized. Master Mind faced the approaching cabinet, his back heated from the flames of the fireplace, his front assaulted by the bitter cold that emanated from the other side of that wall.

His cock throbbed against the icy chill, while his tender, sweaty asshole quivered with nervous anticipation as he laid eyes on the dark-green instrument squatting on the cabinet in front of him.

A dildo. A big dildo!

Beside the gross object, a gleaming green rectangular object also awaited. It had to be the remote control the Senator had referred to. Control for what? The dildo's purpose was obvious. He'd make use of it first then see to the remote.

He snatched it up in his gloved hand, the color of both glove and toy almost a perfect match. He turned to face the bound stranger in the middle of the room. Stepping closer until he physically felt the glass barrier against his knees and chest, he peered at the hapless victim within.

The dildo in his hand was slick with lubricant. Thankfully! It was quite lengthy, with a thick handle that matched perfectly the one he could see dangling from the victim's pouting asshole. Emerald green, the other end resembled a rippled cock with a large blunt crown, followed by a series of larger and larger ripples that finally led to the handle.

He reached back and slid the big object up between his compact ass-cheeks. The flared knob found his asshole, and with a deep breath, he began to press inward, one gloved hand gripping the thick handle.

Arching his back and biting his lip, he slowly pushed the big thing beyond his palpitating sphincter. Staring at the bound stranger's large ass, he focused on the deep crack and that dark-green handle dangling between the full, leather-covered cheeks.

As the aching sensations in his asshole grew more intense, the knob slipped inside, his sphincter swallowing it. Then, as he pushed deeper, the thick shank slithered inside, the first ripple and wider girth of the dildo straining to enter his guts, Master Mind stared at the kneeling victim in front of him. A growing sense of comradery grew and swelled within his pounding heart as he continued the steady assault on his own asshole.

The man's head swung from side to side, searching for someone or something. Totally blinded by his mask, contained within the sound-proof chamber, his poor ass stuffed full of huge dildo, he was utterly helpless. Or so it seemed.

Master Mind let out a grunt as the next ripple slid past his stretching ass entrance. He squatted slightly, aware of unseen eyes on him, and pushed deeper. And deeper. The fat thing twisted and turned inside, burrowing its way into the steamy depths of his guts.

He willed the tight orifice of his sphincter to stretch and accept the giant green dildo. Although it was difficult, he focused his sympathies on that bound victim, which somehow made it easier to accomplish than he'd imagined.

Finally, the last ripple pushed inside, his sphincter clamping around it and seizing it. He felt the broad flange of the handle pressing up against his asshole from the outside, and the thick ripple of the dildo pressing outward from inside. It throbbed in his guts, huge and firmly planted.

That larger girth within strained to exit but was prevented from doing so by his own clamped ass-lips, unwilling to open up and release the massive invader.

This was how the bound stranger felt! Stuffed impossibly full.

Master Mind knew whose side he was on. Not the unseen Senator who had engineered this scenario, but this anonymous stranger, dildo-stuffed and bound and blinded. Somehow, he would free him this afternoon!

"The remote, Master Mind. I hope you haven't forgotten it."

The voice still trembled, replete with both anticipation and lust. He didn't feel that boded well! Still, he turned from the caged wretch and stepped over to retrieve the remote, totally aware of the dildo up his ass as he moved, the thick handle swaying down between his thighs, dangling from his asshole just like the one protruding from that poor dupe in his cage.

Master Mind's cock responded to the aching stimulus by jerking and leaking a dribble of precum to splatter the hardwood floor. It reared up from his crotch, thick and pink, as he walked, unashamed and obviously hungry for attention. He couldn't help stroking it briefly with a gloved hand, looking back at the kneeling captive with his big butt stuffed full of fake cock. A fierce desire to ram his very real and very hungry cock up that poor pawn's massive butt took hold of him for one delirious moment before he managed to reassert some measure of control.

What was happening to him? Why was he so flustered and so lacking in self-control?

He looked down at his free hand. The gleaming square object fit in his palm neatly. Sweeping aside his self-doubts and choosing action, he turned back to the victim and aimed the remote. Stepping again to the invisible wall that divided them, lean thighs wide apart to relieve some of the pressure of that big dildo up his butt, he just slightly twisted the knob in its center to test out any response.

"Uhhnnnnnggg!"

Totally caught off guard, he grunted with surprise as a shock wave of vibration pulsed within his bowels. At the same time, the stocky victim's body jerked over the bench, thighs clenching and parting, big butt heaving while the handle of the dildo up his ass pushed outward then sucked inward.

They were both plugged by remote-controlled vibrators!

The dildo up his ass continued to thrum and vibrate, sending waves of pleasure-pain up into his guts and against his tightly clamped ass-lips. He groaned and shivered, half his body bathed in the heat of the bonfire, the other half chilled by the draft still seeping in from the false wall at the opposite end of the chamber.

"Now for a test of your limits, and our victim's. Rest assured the man in the invisible cage deserves whatever he gets. He is my enemy, and you have been hired to punish him."

The unseen Senator's words galvanized Master Mind, but not in the way the politician might have intended.

He did increase the intensity of that vibration, gasping and half-squatting against the jarring eruption of pressure within his own asshole, while staring fixedly at the pawn before him.

Yes, he'd test their limits, but for reasons of his own. Master Mind concentrated on the writhing wretch on the other side of the glass barrier with all the strength of his awesome mental abilities.

Firelight flickered over the crouching form. The husky body squirmed and heaved as the vibration up his ass intensified. Light rippled over the second skin of that emerald leather costume encasing him from head to toe. His biceps strained, the muscles of his broad shoulders bunched, his giant thews clenched and quivered. His mighty ass reared up, the gross handle of the dildo in his ass pushing out, sucking in, as it vibrated wildly with the increasing tension engendered by the remote in Master Mind's hand.

He himself stood with bare feet splayed wide, back arched, half-squatting as the dildo up his own ass thrummed savagely, his solid butt-cheeks jiggling from the intensity of that vibrator humming and pulsating far up his anal channel. His cock grew thicker and stiffer, aching and drooling nonstop.

He felt violated, especially so knowing the Senator was watching it all, spying on the pair of dildo-stuffed victims squirming and heaving around the lubed rubber up their asses.

He also grew more and more certain of what was going on.

Master Mind had looked into minds of utter depravity, entered psyches of men with absolutely no morals, and survived the hellish experience. Now, unable to read anyone's mind but his own, he wasn't shocked by the depraved thoughts he found within his own soul.

No doubt about it, he was enjoying the spectacle of the bound pawn quivering and jerking on his padded leather bench, the dildo up his ass vibrating wildly, his massive body straining helplessly, the masked head craning and weaving in a fruitless search for the source of his torment.

Through that inner understanding, he was allowed a window into the Senator's thoughts and intentions. And, of course, the victim's.

It hit him all at once. Increasing that vibration, he felt his entire body convulse, his naked thighs quaking, his ass-cheeks heaving wildly, his cock spewing a steady stream of precum. And likewise the caged pawn. Shimmering green danced over the trapped man, every muscle of his powerful body jerking. His ass heaved up against the restraints that held it. The big ass-cheeks parted and the dildo's handle vibrated crazily.

Yes! He knew who that poor pawn was!

Even though he could read not a single thought of the writhing man, he recognized the rippling strength, the body tossing and squirming in the throes of sexual stimuli.

Nicolas Cyrnica!

He hadn't seen or heard from the man for over a year, not since that one afternoon in his mansion as they fucked through a thunderstorm and Master Mind had read his mind and found him guilty of the embezzlement he'd been accused of. His accusers had been equally guilty, a circumstance that had mitigated Nicolas's culpability to a degree.

They'd spent another two days together after that, but the intensity of their sexual chemistry and mental sharing had driven Master Mind away. Fear of too much intimacy and fear of too much emotion, that pair of powerful distractions had sent him fleeing the stocky, brooding accountant. He hadn't taken a single call from Nicolas in over a year, effectively denying his existence to himself in an effort to root out the need, and the fear of that need, he felt for him.

The vibration increased as he twisted the control knob up a notch. Now, there was a madness to his method. His thighs and knees jerked and his ass-cheeks quaked. He squatted farther, spreading his ass-crack open, groaning against the powerful vibrations assaulting his innards. The dildo was planted far up his ass channel, a torrent of exquisite pulses tormenting his guts, from where the handle throbbed against his butt-lips to far up near his stomach where the dildo hummed faster and faster.

Nicolas responded as well, heaving upwards, the split in his leather costume wide open, revealing the similar jiggling of his own large ass-cheeks. The sense of shared, and intense sensation, grew to a crescendo.

Between his big butt-cheeks, the outline of Nicolas's cock stretched the leather encasing it. In a bulge pointing downward, pressing against the rounded end of the column of leather he was draped over, that fat rod grew fatter, every vein visible through the skin-tight material. The knob swelled and pulsed.

Master Mind's prostate was on fire, his cock stiffened to the max, his entire body jerked as he squatted even lower, face now pressed against the barrier between himself and Nicolas. It was time!

Gathering his emotional and mental forces, one hand planted on the barrier, forehead flat against it, he sought out Nicolas's mind with a lightning blast of energy.

At the same time, the dildo up his ass shot out, and his cock erupted in a violent, wracking orgasm.

The dildo up Nicolas's ass was ejected at precisely the same moment. Left behind, the stretched asshole pouted and convulsed as he shared that moment of wracking orgasm with Master Mind.

The barrier shattered. The hardwood floor was suddenly littered with sand, the dissolved molecules of the glass that Master Mind's telepathic prowess had uncoupled.

"Master Mind! Watch out for the butler! Ohhhhhh ... God .. I'm shooting!"

The shouted warning had him spinning to face the doorway, just in time. In burst that unlikely butler, a leather mask over his face and goggles covering his eyes. He held an assault rifle in his arms, aimed right at him.

Master Mind experienced several layers of overlapping thoughts and emotions all at once. His orgasm, shared and intensified by Nicolas's equally overwhelming rapture, wracked his lean, nude body. The mystery behind his unreasoning fear, and unbidden lust, also flooded into his consciousness.

And, there was the pressing need to meet the armed butler's threat.

Asshole gaping from the giant dildo expelled, cock spewing, he sprang forward, naked body unwinding and lengthening as it flew through the air and tackled the startled butler. One gloved hand ripped the mask and goggles from the man while the other tore away the assault rifle.

Unmasked II

The man's thoughts were laid wide open as Master Mind stared into his amber orbs and pierced deep into the core of his evil soul. The savage probe totally stunned him, his body flopping on the floor as Master Mind quickly and efficiently bound him with his own belt, wrists and ankles behind him.

Still dripping cum, he moved with lightning speed to release Nicolas. Off came the leather cuffs on ankles and wrists, off came the hood, shreds of leather dangling from the man's bull neck, dark eyes staring into Master Mind's as the pair exchanged a barrage of mental communication.

There was not a moment to waste. The butler knew all, and now so did Master Mind. Totally synchronized, the pair raced out of the room, upstairs to a shocked Senator, who hadn't even had time to dress, stiff cock betraying his lust, and bright blue eyes frantic.

Shortly, the previous scene of debauchery was replayed, this time with roles reversed, pawns now perpetrators, perpetrators now victims.

The Senator sprawled over his own lewd leather bench, hefty white ass on view, ankles and wrists bound. The butler, tall and wild-eyed and moaning, stood in front of the bound politician, thrusting his lengthy cock in and out of a gurgling, protesting mouth.

Both men writhed and jerked as the huge dildos up their asses vibrated with increasing pressure against their hapless butt-lips and prostates.

Master Mind grinned as he stood beside a naked Nicolas. One lean arm draped over the stocky Armenian's shoulder, the other arm down on his lower back, a gloved hand exploring the crack between his hefty ass-cheeks, fingers strumming the well-lubed and well-stretched butthole.

Nicolas twisted the remote's knob viciously, eyes gloating as the pair jerked spasmodically in response. Long, purple cock was driven deep into the Senator's throat. The butler's tight ass clenching and quaking.

There was no need for words. Master Mind finally understood it all. The others had revealed their thoughts in a gusher of revelation. On Nicolas's part, willingly, the others not so willingly.

Since they had last met, Nicolas had turned State's evidence against those who had accused him, and consequently been recruited by the FBI. His task had been to investigate Senator Graham, a suspect in another more massive embezzlement scheme that involved Nicolas's former employers.

Senator Graham had his resources. He'd not only found out about the FBI's plot, and Nicolas's part in it, but also discovered that Nicolas had been under Master Mind's previous investigation. The unsuspecting Nicolas was lured here, seized, and then used as bait.

Graham had hoped to somehow thwart Master Mind's mental abilities, as well as betray him into a debauched sexual compromise, perhaps blackmailing the superhero with the taped evidence of his own actions.

The complicated scheme had now backfired, as evidenced by the squirming, mewling pair of dildo-plugged victims suffering the fate they'd hoped to inflict on their captors. Of course, the politician's own cameras were catching it all on disc.

But, there was more to it. Master Mind was forced to accept that deeper truth as he probed Nicolas's steamy asshole with a pair of gloved fingers and the Armenian twisted the knob of the remote more viciously, while pumping Master Mind's cock with his other hand.

From the moment Master Mind had pulled up to the mansion, Nicolas's thoughts had been intruding on him. That was the reason for his randy hard-on, and for his unease and fear.

Fear of what? The truth, that he had purposely avoided any contact with Nicolas since he'd last seen him. The lightning storm fuck they'd shared had been such a powerful experience, and the bond between them so incredible, it had truly frightened the superhero.

Unmasked II

He'd steeled himself against any emotional entanglement with anyone. This wall against love had been shattered today. Shattered utterly.

The pair shared a grin, and their nasty thoughts, as they again turned their attentions to the squirming, heaving pair in front of them.

How much could they take? How long before they surrendered and shot their loads?

It was certainly enjoyable discovering those limits!

Master Mind moved behind the stocky accountant, replacing his fingers with the slow insertion of his fat, stiff cock. Nicolas sighed and leaned his head back against the superhero's, their minds melding as cock rode deeper and deeper up hungry asshole.

The superhero fucked his new sidekick, lean long arms wrapping around his powerful, naked body, sharing the exciting view of their vanquished opponents heaving and squirming around the vibrators thrumming viciously up their poor assholes.

The bonfire in its giant cavern roared. Their victims squealed delightfully as the vibration in their guts rose and rose. The handles dangling from their heaving asses bobbed and jerked.

The depravity of the scene was very satisfying. Very satisfying. Superhero cock fucked sidekick hole with delicious pleasure intensified by the sharing of those debauched thoughts. Nothing was hidden between them. Nothing apologized for.

It would be a long afternoon. A very long afternoon!

SAVING TERRA
By Armand

As I reached for the phone, Helios headed bare-assed toward the bathroom and called back, "Come help me wash the cum outta my pubes."

"Hello," I almost yelled into the phone while straining to see Helios's round muscular derrière disappear into the shower. My solar-powered boyfriend enjoyed the fucking I'd given him so much that he'd left two hand marks singed into the pine headboard. How the hell would we explain that to friends and family?

"Gravitar, I'm in trouble." Terra usually sounded imperious and snarky, which is one of the things I loved about her, but this time her voice was panic-laden and tremulous.

"What's wrong?"

"I've been kidnapped," she answered. "They want to get rid of us. They say if anyone uses superpowers in Plain City again they'll kill me."

"What! Can't you get to ground?" It was a stupid question. If Terra could touch even a small patch of dirt, she would have used her immense powers to manipulate the earth and escape.

"Listen, Gravitar, do what you have to do. I trust you and Helios."

I heard a smack and jumped as if I'd been electrocuted. "Terra? What was that?"

The male voice was distant but distinct: "Bitch, tell them not to use their powers or you're dead."

"You tell 'em." Her words were sharp and angry.

From the shower, Helios called out, "Baby, I dropped the soap, and I'm about to pick it up."

My head was spinning. "Terra, don't taunt them. Just tell them Helios and I won't use our powers. We'll get you out of this somehow."

"Don't even try it hero," a cocky male voice said. "You come anywhere near us or use your fucking superpowers again and she's toast. I know she's not invulnerable, 'cause I already tested that out."

"You fucking slime ball!"

Click. The line went dead.

Helios stepped out of the shower to show me his staff at full attention. "Baby, I need your help with this." He pointed both hands down at his member.

"We've got a problem. A big one."

By his wry smile, I knew he thought it was a double entendre, so I rushed to the bathroom to tell him about Terra and to take care of my boyfriend's big problem.

# # # # #

It had been six months since Helios and I had made love for the first time after we'd saved eight kids from a group of stupid kidnappers. After confessing he was bi, Helios let me fuck him in true superhero style, and it was mind-blowing. Then he'd asked to know my true identity just before peeling off his black mask. When I looked at his naked face, I realized instantly that I knew him.

Actually, I knew of him. His real name was Bobby Parker, son of our esteemed, yet Republican, mayor. During the campaign, I'd seen the commercials – the ones where everyman candidate Robert Parker was the consummate father to his four children, including Plain City State's star football player, Bobby. I was a senior at PCSU when Bobby was a sophomore, and though team sports make me break out into hives – as a result of traumatic childhood games of Smear the Queer – I had seen Bobby play a few home games. My friends, Bette and Iris, the best hags any gay boy could want, invited me to go with them to salivate over Bobby in his tight white football pants. As he ran up and down the field, I swore he had the best muscle ass I'd ever seen. Every time another player slapped his glorious backside, I burned with jealousy.

Eric Summers

    I had never met him, though I'd almost bid on him when a sorority auctioned off campus hunks to raise money for Malawi. Of course, I would have totally bid on him to help the poor African kids, but I was afraid someone would try to smear the queer, so I let a sorority ho buy him. Alas, I was left to watch Bobby from afar: on campus with his Paris Hilton clone girlfriend (surely a nuclear physics major); in the gym doing his 200th sit-up while I tried gracefully to mount an elliptical machine and look up the leg of his shorts at the same time; on his father's campaign commercial, which I played endlessly for the three seconds of a smiling Bobby throwing football with his pops in the palatial backyard. After graduation, I tucked Bobby, along with Ponch and John from *CHiPs* and Bo and Luke from *Dukes of Hazard*, into the sexually unfulfilled corners of my mind.

    Now four years later, Bobby Parker and I were superhero lovers, and our friend Terra was in trouble. The day after her kidnapping, we still had no leads. We'd met with the Plain City Police, and even spoken with the FBI, but no one had any clues that could help us find Terra. After getting nowhere, I did what I always do to occupy my time – I started organizing. While alphabetizing spices, I decided we needed the latest Ryan Reynolds DVD – mostly because of a brief but oh-so-gratifying nude scene – so we went to Best Buy.

    Standing in front of a TV the size of a New York City apartment, I watched the live newscast about an explosion downtown. "Shouldn't we go help?"

"And get Terra killed? No way."

    The sight of the gaping hole in the side of the apartment building sent chills through my body. People were running amok as firefighters tried to douse the flames.

"But we might save a life." I was the king of pathos when I wanted.

"Look, the goons who kidnapped Terra may have set off the explosion to test us."

    I scoffed, "It was probably a meth lab that exploded."

My boyfriend cocked an eyebrow as he reached down and adjusted his package in his board shorts. For a minute, I thought only of jumping his bones right there in the local Best Buy, but then I regained my senses. "How can we just stop being heroes?"

"Who says we have to stop." There was a glint in his eye as he flashed his best pearly white smile. "Maybe we just have to give up our secret identities."

I looked aghast, like Tippie Hedren seeing birds. I opened my mouth to say 'What!' but no sound came out.

Bobby slipped close and put his arm around the small of my back. A muscleman looking at DVD players scowled at us. Bobby said, "What's up, dude? Isn't my boyfriend hot?" Then he unabashedly grabbed my ass. I jumped as an unmanly giggle escaped my lips. After the muscleman fled – maybe to call security to kick out the homos getting frisky in aisle nine – Bobby explained his plan. "We can help as normal citizens if we blend in, but not as supers."

Looking into his azure eyes, I realized he was good-looking and clever. How did I get so lucky? "No costumes."

He nodded. "We are just Bobby and Tyler, innocent bystanders who might get to help save a life. Maybe a secret burst of sun power or a gravity-defying trick."

"We just can't let anyone see."

"Come on, sweetcheeks." He grabbed my hand and led me toward the exit. We passed the homophobe muscleman in the CDs, and he recoiled as we passed by.

"We've got to go save the world," Bobby announced to him. "And then, we're gonna fuck." Ever the diplomat, my boyfriend was about to get us gay bashed between Alanis Morissette and Morrissey, but we were in his Jeep and on our way to the explosion before anyone could even yell faggots.

#####

Moments later in downtown Plain City, we levitated to the top of a building; then we ran and jumped onto the roof of the burning apartment building. From the roof, I was able, without being detected, to hold the weakened wall in place while the firemen got everyone to safety. Inside the burning building, Bobby, without his Helios costume, opened locked doors and blasted away debris with his sun power. No one figured out a thing, and once we knew everyone was safe, we left the scene undetected.

We were still on an adrenaline high from our first bout of secret heroics when we arrived back at Bobby's place. I couldn't believe we got away with it – helping without being in our superhero disguises.

He tossed his Jeep keys on the credenza and tore off his vintage tee. "That was more exciting than doing it as a super. It was like sex in public."

"I didn't think we'd get away with it, but it totally worked." Giddy does not come easily to me, but there was no other word to describe my emotional state.

"You were awesome, babe." Bobby grabbed me and kissed me deeply.

"Me? What about you! Running through a fiery building saving people, and the firefighters and cops never even caught on." Then I felt the indescribable surge of his power running through me. My boyfriend can control the level of energy he releases through his skin. At the highest levels it could kill, but at the lowest level it titillates, like a vibrator against the taint. My cock grew harder, and my last words were, "So Terra's safe for now."

My mind grew fuzzy in what felt like a drug-induced euphoria. Bobby stopped energizing me at just the right moment and dropped to his knees to suck my rock hard stiffy. I ran my hands through his thick blond mane as he sucked my cock all the way down until his lips touched my neatly trimmed black pubes. "Holy mother of God," I uttered. Only during ecstasy did I show my piousness. "Damn, that feels good."

I pushed him back on the Mondrian-inspired rug and took his thick tool in my mouth for some hot sixty-nine loving. While we sucked dick, we tugged on each other's balls and had some anal finger fun.

Bobby almost threw me off, and as he sat up, and said, "Babe, I want you to fuck me hard today, just like our first time."

I knew what he wanted. Since we'd declared our monogamy and had our HIV and STD tests together, we'd been able to forgo condoms, so I slathered lube on my naked dick and in his sphincter then I entered his ass with one slow thrust. It never ceased to amaze me how tight he was or how turned on he was when I fucked him.

"Fuck me, Tyler. Come on, baby. Give me all you got."

As I started to thrust like a piston, I watched my boyfriend's perfect blue eyes roll up in his head. The rug started sliding with each thrust. That is, until I started levitating us off the ground. I had Bobby's legs over my shoulders and my hands on his hips, so I could pull his body into me. Encouraging me with a nod and a seductive lick of his lips, he reached up and pinched my nipples. The look of libidinal desire on his face was the hottest fucking thing I'd ever seen.

And when his sperm shot from his cock, it flew three feet into the air. Once it left his body, I no longer had gravitational control of it, and it went berserk and landed on his chest and cheek. While his sun power surged through me, my cock erupted inside his ass. Once I had lowered us back to the rug, I licked every drop of cum from his body.

There was nothing like superhero sex.

#

The next day, Bobby and I, as our superhero alter egos Helios and Gravitar, went on the local news channels to announce that we wouldn't use our superpowers until our friend Terra was safe. Of course the truth was that we planned to use our powers in covert ways. We weren't ready to give up our secret identities, even to the police, so we would have to work with them as meddling bystanders rather than superheroes.

The public outrage was instant and extreme. They wanted their superheroes back no matter what it took. Clearly the citizens of Plain City valued us more than we, or the fucking kidnappers, imagined. People organized a citywide hunt for Terra. Local businessmen and women offered a ransom for tips leading to her rescue. Neighborhood patrols were increased to compensate for the lack of superpowers. Helios and I received cards and letters in record numbers. There were editorials and commentaries, prayer meetings for Terra's safe return.

It was delicious. The outpouring of support made me a bit *verklempt*. All my years as an awkward, in-the-closet, Buffy-wannabe teen were now vindicated. Sure it was Gravitar the public loved and not Tyler. I still got attitude from the man at the repair shop, and I still had to wait in line for a five-dollar cup of coffee at Starbucks, and I didn't get a special superhero discount on polo shirts at Abercrombie and Fitch, but I knew that the citizens of Plain City loved me. If they knew that Helios and I fucked like porn stars, they may have felt a wee bit different, but I didn't think about that.

One week after Terra's kidnapping, Bobby and I made our way to a bad pileup on the highway. After parking on a nearby street, we ran across the field to get to the accident. I am not cut out for running through soybean plants and high grass, so I was jonesing for my days in green spandex and black face mask when we could just drive to the scene like the cops. I fell way behind my boyfriend. By the time I caught up, Bobby had zapped a stuck door and rescued a five-year-old boy. Clearly the kid knew Bobby had powers, but Bobby just set him down on the berm, gave him a wink and a high five, and held his fingers over his lips in a "hush" gesture.

It was time for some Gravitar moves. The engine of the Ford Focus had folded toward the body of the car and was pinning the driver inside, so I surreptitiously levitated the behemoth while Bobby tried to block a Good Samaritan's view. After Bobby pulled the unconscious man from the wreckage, the Good Samaritan, who was a doctor, administered medical help while I dropped the engine back into place undetected.

The ambulance arrived, so our welcome was about to expire. We barely escaped the police and the media. It was too close for comfort. We couldn't keep this up for long, and we couldn't do our usual heroics, so I was frustrated.

That night, the police called Helios with a tip from the hotline. They suspected Terra was being held in an old paint factory on the south side of town, so Bobby pulled on his yellow spandex and black mask, and I jumped into my green spandex and black mask, and we launched into action. We hitched a ride on a news channel's helicopter. Once we were over the abandoned building, we stepped out of the chopper, and I used my control of gravity to gingerly lower us onto the rooftop. Floating in an embrace exhilarated me because it reminded me of the first time I had held Helios and levitated.

"I love you, Tyler," he said.

Holy crap! Did he really just say that? Was my smile as big as it felt? "Me too, Bobby."

Once we alighted onto the roof, we peered through the skylight and spotted three men sitting around a table playing poker. No sign of Terra, but these goons looked like trouble, so we were convinced this was the right spot. Helios leaned into my backside, and I thought I might fall forward onto the glass.

"How about I send a light blast and blind them?" His warm breath on the back of my neck sent a shiver right to my groin.

"There may be others," I whispered. "They might hurt Terra if they hear us coming."

"So we gotta slip in and find her." He sounded so confident I started to get a little excited. Then he wiggled his hips.

I pressed my ass into his crotch and said, "You get all three of us outta here alive, and I'll finally let you fuck me."

His eyes grew wide, like a nympho getting a new sex toy. "Oh we'll get out alive all right. Ten minutes or less and you take me out for lobster." I smiled. "In Maine," he added.

"Fuck you."

He grinned. "No, fuck you." Then he jumped up and ran to the roof access door. Placing a hand on the lock, he melted it and eased open the door. When he used his power like that in the daylight, I could swear he started to glow a little, as if sunbeams were bending toward him and infusing him. My boyfriend looked at his watch and said, "Ten minutes."

Silent as Tibetan monks, we traveled along the scaffolding until we could see the poker players below. From our perch, we saw that Terra was locked in the office at the back of the building. Ludicrously, I focused my mind on her to telepathically communicate. Since neither of us was telepathic, I simply looked constipated.

"Fucking hell, Jimmy. How you get so goddamn lucky?" Goon One cried out.

"'Cause he don't get any pussy," Goon Two responded with a laugh and a slap on Jimmy's shoulder. "Everyone knows lucky in cards unlucky in bed."

"Fuck you both," Jimmy responded as he hung his head like a man who knows he is so not the alpha male.

"He has to beat off all alone every night," Goon One razzed.

"Yeah. Thinking about Terra."

"Fuck off." Jimmy blushed and gathered his chips.

"What's wrong? Gotta little crush on our visitor in the office?" Goon Two spoke the last words as if he was speaking to a baby, which was ironic since he was 300 pounds. "She's a hot super, Jimmy. She don't want your little crooked ding dong fumbling to find the hole." I was getting pissed that they were talking about my friend like that. "You're just lucky those other two supers are behaving, or else she'd be dead now, and you'd be fucking a corpse."

"Those two supers are scared bitches," Goon One said. "They didn't show up at that apartment explosion we set, or that robbery on Fifth. They must really like her. Maybe they're banging the bitch, too."

I felt Helios lean over the edge of the scaffolding as if he was going to yell, "Who you calling a bitch, Fat Ass?" Thankfully, he remained still.

"So now we hit the banks like Eddie planned – three at the same time – and we high tail it outta this shit hole of a town with a load of money." He leaned toward Jimmy and said, "Maybe Eddie'll let you fuck your girlfriend Terra before he whacks her."

Jimmy jumped up and walked away.

"Ahh, he's gonna cry," the fat one said.

Helios looked at me and mouthed the words, "I'll handle them. You get Terra."

"We'll handle them," I protested, mouthing exaggeratedly.

"Lower me and close your eyes." He took my hand, and we jumped over the railing together.

As we descended slowly, I closed my eyes and waited for the massive flash of blinding light. There were screams: "What the fuck!" "I think I've been hit!" "Shit, it's Helios!" Furniture and poker chips toppled; then there was gunfire. As I hit the ground, I saw three kidnappers emerge from the back of the factory and run toward us with guns. Where the fuck had they been hiding? Helios blasted one with a beam of energy and then another. Meanwhile, I grabbed a large stainless steel work table and raised it to deflect the bullets. It worked. As I let go of the table, Helios blasted it toward the third gunman, and it slammed into him like a metal wave.

The poker players were bumbling blindly as they drew guns from their holsters. When I grabbed two of them and flew up toward the ceiling, I heard a scream in the office. I knew it wasn't Terra; in fact, it sounded like a man being mauled by a tiger. Helios ran toward the office. The fat goon struggled free from my grip and fell to the concrete below, and I heard the snap of bones. "My fucking legs!" he screamed.

"Well you shouldn't have squirmed free, dumbass." I hooked the other guy's clothes on the edge of the scaffolding and said, "Don't move or you'll end up like your buddy."

Meanwhile, Helios and Terra emerged from the office. When I ran over and embraced her, I saw her bloody knuckles.

"I punched one of 'em," she said matter-of-factly.

"Let's get out of here, and let the cops clean up," Helios said. "We've still got two minutes. Looks like it's time for lobster in Maine and a hot piece of ass."

Terra rolled her eyes in an I-don't-want-to-know way before heading through the exit door. We only made it ten feet before two SUVs charged up and six men with guns jumped out.

"Stop right there, supers, or we'll shoot," the balding, middle-aged one said.

"Eddie." The name seethed through Terra's clinched teeth.

I couldn't levitate shit because I wasn't standing near anything I could touch. Helios could blast two at a time, but the other four would have a chance to shoot. My brain was desperately searching for a way out, and I decided I would jump in front of Helios if the crooks pulled the triggers.

Then I felt my body wobble slightly, as if I'd had a couple stiff margaritas and stood up too quickly. It only took a moment for me to figure out what was happening. I slowly looked down, and bingo: We were standing on good old terra firma and Terra was barefoot. All hell was about to break loose. Without warning a massive wall of dirt shot up between us and the bad guys. I heard gunfire, but no bullets penetrated the swelling mountain. Finally, after reaching thirty or more feet, the huge wave of earth buried Eddie, his posse and the vehicles.

It was fucking awesome. Being a super and having super friends was as gratifying as a Kathy Griffin show.

"Whoa," I uttered.

"He was such a prick," Terra stated as she started to walk away.

I felt a sharp slap on my ass. "Ten minutes, babe." From Helios's grin, I knew we'd be eating lobster in Maine after I got my brains fucked out.

Truthfully, I was looking forward to it.

THE OTTER
By Rob Rosen

The Otter crept along the slate-gray alley wall, slowly and silently, choosing to remain hidden in the shadows until the appropriate moment presented itself. The smell of decay and waste permeated the narrow passageway. Without thought or intention on his part, the dense hairs on his upper lip raised and repeatedly folded, blocking the stench from entering his nasal cavity like a plug in a bottle.

He'd guarded this route numerous times now, had used it himself before the transformation from mild mannered archeologist to queer defender, and knew it was just a matter of time before the inevitable occurred.

Sure enough, the hairs that covered his body, from his well-defined calves, up his sinewy thighs, across his narrow waste, flat ripped belly, and rock-hard, thick-nippled pecs, had begun to stand on end. Like an innate warning signal, they quivered, bristling away from his skin. Danger, it seemed, was fast approaching. It was sadly expected, given the proximity to two gay bars and lack of sufficient lighting down the tight alleyway that led back to the main street.

He inserted the concave metal disc in the half-inch hole that pierced his earlobe. It was more than mere body adornment now; it had become a much-needed sound amplifier. He heard the pair of sneakers in an instant, though they were still many dozens of feet away. He also detected the three pairs of boots just beyond that. His fine body hairs warned him it was more than mere coincidence that four men fast approached. These hairs were quickly joined by an eight-inch, steel-tipped goatee that slithered and sliced through the air like a snake through a grassy plane. His body was preparing for a fight even before his mind registered the need to protect.

"Hey faggot," he heard, echoing down the alleyway.

Unmasked II

The prey moved in double-time. The Otter heard his panting and quickened heartbeat. The predators bounded forward, laughing drunkenly as they kicked over garbage cans and cackled their verbal barbs.

The one in sneakers tripped, skidded across the cement, gasped, and came crashing in a dull thud against the wall. The predators were on him in the blink of an eye.

"Hey, faggot," one of them cooed with a lewd smack of his lips. "Lookin' for some of this?" The Otter heard the sound of a zipper being slid down.

"Please, don't," the one on the ground whimpered. The Otter moved stealthily out of the darkness from behind them.

"You know you want it," the leader of the pack goaded. The Otter heard two more zippers following suit. "Suck 'em, faggot," the leader growled. The three were now surrounding the one.

"He said, don't," The Otter shouted.

The attackers craned their necks to see who had interrupted their sport. Their mouths gaped open. "Beat it," the one holding center court grumbled, with a menacing sneer.

"Or what?" The Otter replied, stepping in closer. "You'll hit me with your little Billy club?"

The man's turgid five inches shriveled at the comment. His friends snickered but otherwise held their ground, not to mention their longer, thicker cocks.

With fists held up high, the leader moved to within punching distance of The Otter. In a lightening flash, the steel-tipped goatee sprang up and straight out, stopping within millimeters of the man's jugular. "I wouldn't if I were you," The Otter warned, with his arms akimbo. "It's got a mind of its own, and right now it's thinking that the three of you should go on your merry way and leave this man alone." The man he was referring to watched in rapt silence from his crouched position.

The offender in the center stopped dead in his tracks, while the other two moved in on either side of the rescuer. One of them stooped down and drew a knife from his sock. He raised it above his head and let it fly. The hairs on The Otter's exposed chest folded flat and locked in place, creating a plate of armor that caused the knife to bounce off and fall harmlessly to the ground.

The sneakered one squealed and clapped in delight.

"Last warning," The Otter cautioned, the briefest of smiles stretching across his handsome face.

It fell on deaf ears. The two moved in to pounce, while the asshole in the center was still being held at bay by the lethal, spiked chin hairs. The Otter lifted his arms, flexing his rock-solid biceps, and, with a mischievous grin, said, "You asked for it."

In an instant, the dense hairs beneath his armpits were set free and sprang to life. They wired and coiled and leapt out in a wide arc, then came boomeranging back as they wrapped repeatedly around the two men's faces, thereby blinding and suffocating them at once.

The two fought to remove their bindings, but it was for naught. In less than a minute, they were both on the ground, out cold from a lack of oxygen. The hairs released their vice-like grip just before imminent death. The man in the center, who had watched the spectacle with bulging eyes, fainted, collapsing in a pile in between his nefarious cohorts.

"They were lucky," The Otter said, the smile now returning in full force. "I could've forgotten to use deodorant today." Quickly, he walked over to the victim and helped him up. "Are you okay?" he asked.

"Better than they are," came the stunned reply.

"Good, then let's get out of here before they awaken."

"Fine by me," the rescued man said. "But, just one more thing."

The Otter watched in amazement as the man walked over to the three downed criminals and, one by one, pulled their jeans and underwear down to their ankles, placing the center man's mouth over the flaccid penis of one of his partners. The third man's face was placed between the leader's ass cheeks. He finished the deed by whipping out his cell phone and snapping a picture of the spectacle, with a rapidly scribbled note added to the pile.

And with that, the two were running down and out of the alleyway. They arrived at the victim's car a minute later.

Laughing, The Otter asked, "What did the note say?"

To which the man replied, "Do this again, and the picture I took of the three of you makes the papers."

"Ooh," The Otter said in appreciation. "I like your style."

The man smiled, and asked, "Can I offer you a ride? It's the least I can do."

The Otter returned the smile and nodded his head yes.

The two drove off into the night and far away from the dreaded alleyway. It was then, in the glow of the overhead freeway lights, that The Otter noticed that the driver was no man. He was just barely out of his teens, and cute as all get out. His sapphire blue eyes sparkled in the moonlight. The Otter was suddenly transfixed.

"Name's Chuck," the driver said by way of introduction.

"Lester," The Otter told him, then quickly amended with, "The Otter."

Chuck paused and massaged his hairless, dimpled chin. "The Otter, huh? Seems appropriate. Do you swim and play with abalone shells, too?"

"It refers to my, um, overall look."

"So if you were older and heavier, you'd be called The Bear?" Chuck laughed. "Okay, seeing as you are what you are, The Otter works fine. By the way, how does all this work?"

"Long story."

"I've got the time. And the place." Chuck turned and smiled at his hirsute passenger, shooting him a sly wink as he did so.

The Otter thought of the implications. The hero never slept with the victim. It was inappropriate to take advantage of the weak. Then again, the weak were rarely this cute, or this willing.

He agreed to the proposal.

Their lips locked as soon as they entered Chuck's small apartment. Their tongues swirled. Their eyes stayed opened. The Otter's hefty cock strained at his nylon pants, while his goatee swished happily back and forth.

"That takes some getting used to," Chuck said, in between eager kisses.

"Tell me about it," The Otter replied.

"No, you tell me, while you're getting out of that outfit." Chuck sat on his couch and motioned for The Otter to get undressed.

It was a simple get-up, actually: a skin-tight, purple, V-necked top, and a matching set of nylon pants and slippers. A lavender "O" covered the center of the upper half. The Otter wisely wore a purple eye mask, as well. A dense matting of chest hair filled in the area between the V-neck. Buried in the hairs was a strange, silver amulet attached to a short, silver necklace.

The slippers came off first, and The Otter started his tale. "I was on a trip to Peru. This was last year. I'd just graduated from college with a degree in archeology. I wandered away from my group and found myself in a small cave hidden in the side of a mountain."

The pants came down next. The Otter had thick, muscular calves and thighs, rife with brown, wiry hairs. Chuck massaged the thickening cock beneath his jeans as he watched and listened.

"Nice purple jock," Chuck said, almost in a moan.

"I like to match," The Otter told him, with a wide grin, as he rubbed his own thick dick through the material. "Anyway," he continued the story, "inside the cave was a lone talisman. It was ancient. Easily the oldest object I'd seen on that expedition. It was beautiful, somehow drawing me to it."

Chuck kicked off his sneakers, and the jeans were quick to follow. He had on a pair of silk, paisley boxers. The tip of his mushroom head poked out from one of the leg openings.

"For me?" The Otter asked.

Chuck nodded and lifted the material up to reveal a curved, seven-inch prick and a meaty pair of balls. It looked gigantic on his small, lean frame.

The Otter grabbed the bottom of his nylon top and lifted it straight up and over his head. His stomach and chest were covered in a thick down, as were his forearms. The only clear patches of skin Chuck could detect were on his rescuer's shoulders and upper arms. The Otter tweaked his nipple with a long, low moan and continued with the story.

"I slid the talisman on my necklace, for safekeeping. It felt like the right thing to do. As if it was predestined, if you believe in that sort of thing; as if the object had been left there, waiting for me over the centuries to find it." The Otter grabbed the silver amulet with one hand as he spoke. His other hand slid inside his jock as began to stroke his cock. "I knew in an instant what powers it held. It seems to turn your weaknesses, what you consider your worst characteristic, into your strongest."

"Body hair, in your case," Chuck interrupted.

The Otter nodded. "I always hated it. I'd been covered in it since I was twelve. All the other kids made fun of me. Even gay guys don't usually dig it."

"Not all gay guys," Chuck told him, removing his boxers. His cock bounced, as did The Otter's goatee. "I guess opposites do attract. I've always hated my own hairless body. It's like a little boy's."

"Not everywhere," The Otter made note, eyeing Chuck's long, hard cock. He then finished his recounting. "The power of the amulet seems to live in my hairs now. As long as I wear it, I'm The Otter." He held it up for Chuck to see and then removed the mask. "The hairs seem to make me invincible."

"And fucking hot," Chuck added. "Now I think you have one more article of your outfit to remove." He stroked his cock and waited. He wasn't disappointed. Not by a long shot.

The Otter grinned and pushed the purple jockstrap down and off. He then stood in the middle of the room – hairy, hard, and fully, totally erect. A massive, thickly veined eight-inches pointed directly at Chuck.

"Maybe you should change your name to The Horse," Chuck quipped as he bounded off the couch and onto his knees. His mouth was around the giant dick in two seconds flat. He downed half of it before gagging, the huge tool sliding in and out of his mouth. Chuck raised his hands up and stroked and caressed The Otters heavy, swinging, hairy balls as he sucked. He then made the near-fatal mistake of pulling down on them, hard.

The Otter winced, more in ecstasy than agony, but still the hairs registered it as a threat; and they reacted, lightening fast. The hairs on The Otter's thighs leapt and clutched at Chuck's hands, while the goatee speared straight down and came to a steely point just above Chuck's bobbing head.

The Otter grabbed for the amulet and quickly removed it from around his neck. The hairs reverted to normal, both men breathing sighs of relief.

"Sorry about that," The Otter apologized.

"You owe me one," Chuck replied, with a wry smile.

"How about eight?" The Otter replied, grabbing at his thick cock and slapping it against Chuck's smooth cheek.

Chuck smiled and opened his mouth good and wide. The Otter face-fucked him slow and rhythmically. In between hungry slurps, Chuck asked, "You saved my ass once tonight, want to do it again?" He didn't wait for an answer. Instead, he turned around and got on all fours, exposing his perfect, hairless rump.

The Otter bent down and spread the cheeks apart, revealing a pink, puckered hole. Eagerly, he lapped at it with his tongue, sliding it around the ring and then deftly inside. He spit into his hand and lubed Chuck's pole up, pulling it in between his legs so that he could alternately suck on it while licking at the tender asshole.

One of The Otter's fingers then gently entered the tight opening, as his mouth engulfed Chuck's hard cock. The finger glided in as the mouth slid down. The Otter continued this motion, like a piston, sucking and finger-fucking Chuck until a second and then a third finger found their way inside. Chuck, after all, would need to be loosened up to take The Otter's enormous prick up to the hilt.

"Ready for it?" The Otter whispered, affectionately nibbling one then the other fleshy cheek.

"Uh huh," Chuck rasped, reaching beneath his couch and magically producing a rubber and a bottle of lube. The Otter slid it on and flipped his host over. Again, their mouths met. Their eyes stayed open – brown on blue, blue on brown. The Otter lubed up his dick and then Chuck's beautiful, tight little hole.

Chuck raised his legs up. The Otter's meaty head pushed against the hairless rim. Slowly, evenly it entered. Chuck sucked in his breath; the Otter momentarily stopped. When he was ready, Chuck reached around and grabbed and pushed at the hairy ass cheeks. The massive, thick cock slid further in, and then back out, and then back in, deeper and deeper with each thrust, until, at last, the entire eight inches had worked their way to Chuck's gripping limits.

Both men moaned and eagerly kissed, swapping some heavy spit, as The Otter rapidly picked up speed. Chuck stroked his cock as The Otter began to pummel his ass, waves of pleasure rolling from his hole up his back and across his tight, hairless stomach; each pump of The Otter's prick eliciting a loud, throaty sigh.

The two men were now soaked in gleaming sweat as The Otter shoved the entire length of his cock in, ramming and pushing at an ever-hardening prostate. Chuck's fist picked up speed around his long, fat cock, until, at last, a thick stream of cum spewed from his dick and across his pale, thin torso. Chuck's asshole tightened around The Otter's cock as he came, causing the hero to fill the rubber with several ounces of his own piping hot cum, with both of them groaning in rapturous pleasure and abandon as their bodies twitched and spasmed.

Spent, The Otter collapsed, his hard cock popping out of the welcoming hole as he tenderly kissed Chuck and teasingly bit down on his bottom lip.

"Mmm," The Otter moaned.

"Mmm," Chuck echoed.

And then, as was his habit, The Otter asked, "Bathroom?"

Chuck pointed down the hall. The Otter jumped up and jogged off, with Chuck intently watching as the avenger's meaty, hairy ass moved away and into the bathroom. He knew what he would do next, feeling it pull at him from the table. He reached for it and slid it around his neck.

The Otter sensed the disruption from twenty feet away. He finished his piss, shook his dangling prick, and ran back into the living room. He was blinded in a red hot instant.

"Oops," Chuck said as he covered himself in a blanket that had been thrown over the couch.

The Otter moved his hands from over his eyes and stared at the man he'd just fucked. The amulet could be seen as a lump beneath the blanket. "It called to you, too, huh?" he asked, with a chuckle.

"Uh huh," Chuck replied, blushing as he hung his head down.

The Otter found a pair of dark sunglasses on the coffee table and put them on. Then he said, "Okay, let's see."

Chuck removed the blanket. His alabaster, hairless skin shined like a beacon in the night. Even with the sunglasses on, he was hard to look directly at. The Otter's eyes watered, but still he laughed. "Your weakness is now a formidable strength," he commented. "What should we call you? The Star?"

Chuck hummed as he thought of a response. "No, too arrogant. How about ... The Twink."

"Cute. I like it." He paused, the smile growing wide. "And, I like you, too." He walked back over and covered The Twink with the blanket before he once again kissed him hard and full on the lips. "Maybe I can work odd days and you can work evens."

"Or we can go back to Peru together and find another talisman." The Twink looked up and smiled eagerly at The Otter.

The Otter laughed. "The hairy and the hairless. Sounds like a plan." Their lips and eyes met once again, their cocks already growing stiff, ready for round two.

And, truly a dynamic duo was born.

UNDOING TANTRAMAN
By Owen Keehnen

"I need to get Tantraman out of the way," seethed Dr. Eel bringing his fist down upon the table. "I'm tired of that meddling do-gooder."

Tantraman had been battling crime in Centerville for years and had put Dr. Eel behind bars on more than one occasion. "That white and silver spandex clad superhero stands for moral fiber and all that rot, everything I despise. He's nothing but a vapid billboard for wholesome living."

It is true. Tantraman is extremely health conscious. The superhero eats right, exercises, meditates, and even believes in great sex – but with one slight difference. Instead of ejaculating, Tantraman redistributes the sexual energy of orgasm throughout his body when he approaches ejaculation. This pooling of erotic energy is the supposed source of his formidable superpowers.

Given the nature of Tantraman's mega-might, Dr. Eel felt certain that the super stud could be rendered powerless if he and his evil gang could cause him to come. "Cracking his nut will be the end of Tantraman!"

However, succeeding is no simple matter. Frau Ruffie tried to get his superjizz while Tantraman was out cold. She's now doing time in villainess prison because she was unaware that the blond superhero needs to be conscious to become aroused. Forcing spooge from the super stud has also been tried. The notorious underground figure, The Dairyman, tried strapping Tantraman to his milking machine. He soon discovered that the dynamic stud also has master control over his muscles with the ability to shut off his body's response to sexual stimulation and arousal all together.

"But I am far smarter than either of those dastardly dolts. My idea takes a different approach." Dr. Eel has reasoned that Tantraman can only be made to come by tricking him into it and sneaking beyond his much heralded self-control. "He must be brought to the edge gradually, pushing him slowly closer over a period of time until he doesn't realize how dangerously near he is to spilling his precious seed. Then by the time Tantraman realizes it, his hips will be bucking and he will be so close to releasing the super surge of jizz from his balls that with one slight stroke of that dynamic tool he'll be over the edge, and his precious pent-up load will be spilled."

To help bring his diabolical plan to fruition, Dr. Eel contracted the services of two of the underworld's most notorious sexual performers – Jack Splat and Nick the Juicer. "They are known far and wide for their prowess and determination, boundless horniness, and their greed. With the two million dollar reward I've promised them upon their success, they will be relentless in their mission to take Tantraman so far that he cannot stop. Once I get his nut, Centerville will finally be mine."

Dr. Eel continued, "Now it's simply a matter of trapping that super stud in a web of his own do-gooder making, and the wheels of that plan are already in motion."

With the development of a phone transformer, Dr. Eel managed to tap into Tantraman's secret hot phone. He also discovered the code to control the top secret crime-fighter caller ID and most importantly, how to replicate the sound of The Commissioner's voice.

"95-96-97 ..." When the special Tantraphone started to pulse, Tantraman took a break from his bicep curls. Lowering the dumbbells, he wiped a white towel across his glistening muscled body before pressing the speaker button.

Dr. Eel (disguised as The Commissioner) told Tantraman that the authorities needed him to go to The Bucking Bronco to obtain information from two of the dancers there – Jack and Nick. "These two party boys are currently lovers with several high ranking members of the underworld including the formidable genius, Dr. Eel." Dr. Eel felt himself smile. "They have information regarding Eel's wicked scheme to crash the Centerville banking system. Tantraman, this mission calls for something extra from you. Jack and Nick are driven by lust, so you'll need to satisfy them sexually to learn their secrets. Tantraman, if I know those two cockhounds, the hotter they get, the more likely they will be to talk. Tantraman, we need you to be at the top of your game to find out as much as you can."

"You can count on me, Commissioner."

"I knew I could, Tantraman." Dr. Eel hung up the phone with a smirk. "The ethical are always so easy to manipulate. Welcome to your downfall, Tantraman! It will be so sweet to finally see you spill your pent-up soy milk and thus be rendered powerless!"

Following the bogus instructions given to him, Tantraman drove to a rundown section of Centerville. Amidst the burned down and boarded up buildings, he saw the flickering neon light announcing The Bucking Bronco. A rolling bank of bulbs formed an arrow to the door.

Dressed in full superhero attire, Tantraman caused Tony the bartender to do a double-take when he entered. Eel told him to expect Tantraman, but Tony still didn't expect him to show up in full costume. After ordering a cranberry juice, Tantraman inquired about Nick and Jack. The bartender said nothing but merely nodded toward the back bar.

"Nothing like a gorgeous stud in spandex," muttered Tony, grinning as he stared at Tantraman's backside. Tony pushed a button to dead bolt the front door. "Dr. Eel wouldn't want any interruptions to the evening's festivities."

Nick and Jack were dancing on the stage. Tantraman took a seat and watched their act for a few moments. As dancers, they were actually quite good. Jack was hairy and slim with the well toned body of a gymnast. Nick had a shaved head and was shorter and stockier with heavily muscled legs.

Tantraman immediately caught their eye. When the song ended, the two dancers hopped off the stage and came directly over to the superhero.

Nick smiled, "We are in luck."

"We sure are! Just think, Centerville's biggest crime fighter at our bar."

"I wonder if he's just as big as his abilities ..."

"What brings you here tonight, Tantraman?"

Tantraman reached down and cupped his basket a bit awkwardly. He felt so strange being lewd, even if it was for the sake of Centerville. "Oh, I'm off duty and just looking for a little relaxation."

"Well, I'm sure we can work out all your superhero kinks," said Jack with a wink. The dancer wordlessly moved forward and brushed his hands back and forth over Tantraman's defined pectoral plates and before running his hand down the muscled stomach.

"Sounds great," nodded Tantraman, "That's just what I was hoping for."

"Well, then let's go." Jack took his hand and led him to a small private room further back in the bar. Inside, there was a table and a bed along with a chair to one side. Along one wall, a TV monitor was playing a gay XXX movie at high volume.

"Can you turn that down?"

"Sorry, the volume knob is screwy. Just tune it out," whispered Jack with a wandering lick about and within the superhero's ear.

Once they entered the room, Tony slipped into the adjoining closet and started the camera. Dr. Eel was adamant about wanting every moment of Tantraman's downfall recorded for his own viewing pleasure. Also, Dr. Eel was sure that seeing the superhero get it on and be gotten off had the potential to be a bestselling adult rental.

The two dancers pushed Tantraman into the straight-backed wooden chair. "Now relax, it's time for you to sit back and enjoy," said Jack, beginning his lap dance by slowly gyrating his pelvis in circles on Tantraman's lap. Pressing and grinding, he gradually built speed before spinning to face Tantraman.

Nick moved behind and began massaging the superhero's shoulders, letting his hands slip down to squeeze and caress the muscled chest, then trailing further to tweak his nipples through the skintight costume.

"Oh, I think I feel something stirring, something that feels real nice," said Jack with a wink.

Nick smiled and gave Tantraman a deep and sudden French kiss.

Tantraman swallowed, "You two are mighty good at this."

"What can we say, we love our work."

Jack rocked his thonged ass harder into Tantraman's lap, making the crime fighter's cock unfurl and grow even harder.

Nick laughed and ruffled the blond stud's hair. "Here, let me snap off this silver codpiece so you can feel a whole lot better." Removing the garment, he lifted it to his nose and sniffed deeply. "It smells like hot superhero crotch sweat. Smell it for me. Yeah, you like the smell of your own crotch don't you? Bet it feels good to have that off and give that swelling monster a little freedom. Now you can really appreciate my buddy's lap dance. Just imagine what it is going to feel like later with your thick slab shoved balls-deep in that tight and talented ass."

Tantraman stumbled over the words to begin his casual questioning. "So you two are the featured dancers here."

"What do you think? We're more than featured dancers! We're the superstars."

"I bet you have lots of fans and admirers."

"Naturally," said Jack, still grinding before looking over to Nick. "I think our super stud here is going to be lots of fun".

"I can see that." Nick reached over to rub the solid lump in Tantraman's tights.

"Shall we get down to business?"

When Tantraman stood, his supercock made a tent in his costume. Slightly blushing, he turned away as he attempted to continue his subtle line of questioning. "Now about the customers here ..."

"Let us get you out of that." The two reached out and slowly peeled the white and silver superhero unitard over his broad shoulders, rolling it down his chest, over his hips, and off his feet before tossing it in a corner. "You won't need that anymore." Tantraman swallowed deeply and fought the urge to run and fold his crime-fighter outfit. Instead, he stood somewhat awkwardly, wearing nothing but his silver facemask.

"Just as we thought, spandex doesn't lie. You're every bit as hot and put together as we thought you would be." The two dancers stepped back and began to circle him, taking in the superhero's full form – wide shoulders drawn back, the powerful V-shaped back and the strong legs below, chiseled and hairless chest capped by small nipples, a big hairy superhero muscle ass, and a rippling six-pack leading down to a slight blond bush. His super tool was roped with veins and hung heavily having now returned to a mostly flaccid state. A full set of low-hanging jism filled bull balls hung below.

"Nice nuts," smiled Nick.

Jack let out a whistle, lifting the pair and bounced them in his hand to feel the heft and gauge the treasure contained inside. "I'll say that's a real pair of beauties."

Despite his physical perfection, Tantraman was slightly uncomfortable under their scrutiny. It was as though the two dancers viewed him as little more than a play thing for their sexual gratification and pleasure. He was hardly comfortable being seen that way. 'The Commissioner did say they were rather one note. Perhaps that is best for obtaining the necessary information to stop Dr. Eel,' reasoned Tantraman.

"Getting naked is a lot easier for us," laughed Jack.

"All we need to do to get comfortable is one little snap," so saying, Nick yanked off his g-string and leaned forward to hold it over Tantraman's nose. "Go on stud, take a whiff of that hot stripper musk. You like the smell of my crotch, too, don't you? I can tell you do. Only one sniff, and your pecker gave a nice little leap."

Unable to hold back any longer Jack dropped to his knees and buried his face in Tantraman's furry muscle ass.

On the other side, Nick took the superhero's pecker into his mouth and began his highly developed throat flutter and tongue massage. After only a moment of his ministrations, Tantraman found himself lightly face fucking the skilled dancer. With every thrust his full pendulous balls swung forward to slap Nick on the chin.

"So you boys must meet a lot of important men here?"

Jack pulled his face out of Tantraman's hairy crack long enough to answer "We do, mostly edgier guys."

"Edgier," said the superhero with a slight panting. The mouth on his dick felt so good, just as good as the tongue working every inch of his ass.

"Well, you know ... underworld guys," Nick added, lifting his mouth from Tantraman's thick cock long enough to jack the saliva slickened rod a couple of times before swallowing the impressive piece to the root yet again.

"Nick knows all right," laughed Jack, "After all, he's dating Dr. Eel."

"It's just casual."

"He is so your boyfriend!"

Tantraman smiled, dangerously unaware of the stripper's larger plan unfolding. Tantraman thought he had the dancers just where he wanted them and was pleased that he was starting to get the information necessary to stop Dr. Eel and put him behind bars where he belongs. "Oh yeah, tell me about him."

"In a minute, Tantraman, do you like it when my tongue circles the mushroom head of your cock?"

Tantraman was unable to suppress a moan.

"I thought you did. How about when I stick the tip of my tongue in your piss slit?"

Jack laughed, "He really looks like he is enjoying that."

"I think he's getting really excited," laughed Nick with a couple of jacks of the superhero's big blue veiner.

When he stopped, Tantraman gradually regained his composure. "Now tell me about Dr. Eel. Does he like your blowjobs?"

"Oh he does, but he's nothing like you, stud. Dr. Eel never gets this hard." said Nick, slapping Tantraman's swollen tube steak on either side of his face. Winking at the hidden video camera, Nick ran his tongue up and down the length of the blond Goliath's shaft. "I want this rod buried to the bush inside me."

"I ... I ..." Soon Tantraman stepped back. Closing his eyes he took a couple deep breaths and found his peaceful place inside.

Jack and Nick looked at each other and smiled. This superhero didn't stand a chance. They were determined to get that load and the two million they'd been promised. They knew it all must be very gradual. They knew they couldn't rush him, not yet anyway. The two dancers gave him a couple minutes.

"That porn movie is so loud it's hard to hear myself think."

"Then don't," smiled Nick. "Just let yourself go. You're here to relax. We'll do all the thinking. You ready for more stud?"

"You know it," said Tantraman with a transparent enthusiasm. At once, the two were upon him. Jack straddled the super stud and was sucking and nibbling on Tantraman's nipples while Tantraman ate the dancer's gorgeous heart-shaped butt. Nick was using his powerful mouth and tongue to probe that beautiful superhero muscle ass, every so often running the bristle of his shaved head over the do-gooders sensitive anus and balls.

"Let me at that cock again," said Jack, hopping off Tantraman's face. While Jack blew the stud, Nick continued his expert work on his ass. Tantraman had never had a rimming that felt quite like this before. The feel of Nick's head was incredible, and his tongue almost seemed to corkscrew through the muscled ring of his butt and explore the musky tunnel beyond.

In a moment, Nick noiselessly opened a drawer at the bedside table and pulled out a special string of beads. With the super stud's butt well loosened from his relentless ass work, Nick was certain the time was right to take their plan to the next level. Keeping his fingers, mouth, head, and tongue in constant teasing motion on and around Tantraman's anus and balls, the super stud was distracted and unaware that Nick had also applied a momentarily desensitizing cream to his anal ring and had then slipped a string of beads inside him one at a time.

Jack looked over and smiled to see the magical stimulation beads being inserted. The beads were another invention of Dr. Eel's, each of the seven warming beads was especially designed to swell and vibrate at a different frequency. The warm throb and slowly expanding nature of the beads could pleasure a man in ways that couldn't be duplicated. The super stud would soon begin to feel the subtle yet mounting waves of pleasure.

The sex criminals knew they needed to keep Tantraman fully engaged. He needed to think he was in control. For their scheme to work, his mind needed to be kept occupied while his body was slowly led astray until mind and body didn't have time to connect before he gave up that load. "Dr. Eel always tells Nick about all his big plans."

"Oh he does not."

"He does so."

"Not everything."

Tantraman tried to sound casual. "I want to hear more."

"Maybe with that gorgeous dick inside me you'll hear every detail," laughed Nick, nuzzling the jizz filled super nuts, which had already drawn up a bit higher in his huge cumsac. Nick could already feel the heat emanating from Tantraman's ass. The beads were beginning to warm and glow. "Jack, get the lube."

Jack took the canister of lube from the drawer. He scooped out a generous amount and stroked it on

Tantraman's supercock; gliding his hand down the thick pulsing flesh pillar and bringing it back up with a firm rotating twist.

Tantraman flinched a bit. It took a moment for him to catch his breath. The sensation was incredible. "What is that?"

"Oh, it's our special blend lube. We save it for special occasions. We gathered it ourselves. It's 98 percent corn-fed college jock jism that's been kept at body temperature."

"Fresh as the day they gave up their spooge."

Jack nodded towards the screen. "Check out the movie."

"It's footage of us having the time of our lives getting every drop of that wholesome college boy jizz. The same stuff we just slathered on your big veined cock."

Tantraman felt an added twinge of excitement knowing that the cum coating his rod had come from the studs he'd been seeing in the movie.

"They were all so happy to give it up."

"So we took every drop," added Nick with a loud lick of his lips.

"That stuff feels fantastic."

"Doesn't it?" Jack wrapped a powerful fist around the base of Tantraman's cock and held it tight before stroking him quickly with the other. "We've got to have you nice and hard if you're going to fuck our tight asses."

Tantraman reached out to still Jack's hand and closed his eyes. Once more he visualized a serene place where he could focus and reclaim that inner calmness.

Once he recovered, Jack and Nick took turns rolling the condom down the impressive length of Tantraman's dick and then layered the outside with another generous supply of the special jock juice lubricant. Nick straddled the superhero and eased the mammoth cock inside his ass before beginning to move his hips. The dancer was an expert at control of his sphincter muscles.

"Oh yeah!" Tantraman felt so good. He heard the moaning from yet another stud giving up his load on the video mixed with some guttural insertion "Ahhhs" coming from Nick. He forced himself to focus. "Now where were we? You were telling me about your boyfriend, Dr. Eel."

Nick was riding him full force. "Was I?"

"Yeah."

"Well, as I said it's more casual than boyfriends."

Tantraman tried not to sound impatient. "You said something about his riverfront meeting next week." The super stud's breathing was slightly labored from the fucking and from a pulsating and expanding warmth that came from somewhere within. The sensation was so gentle and soothing, like a soft lapping wave or several fluttering tongues softly tickling inside him.

"Did I?"

"Yeah."

"Don't you mean, Oh yeah? Hey Jack, how about playing with Tantraman's nips. Those pencil tip beauties look like they're begging for some of your expert manipulation."

Jack reached over and began to tweak and pull on the nubs, lightly twisting and then gripping harder. Jack brought Tantraman to the brink of pain before taking him back to pure pleasure and repeating the cycle. "Here stud, let me move you this way a bit," he said, rearranging Tantraman, so his head was hanging slightly off one edge of the bed and his feet were draped over the other.

"I bet your tits would like some of the stud lube on them," said Jack, putting a little on his hands.

When Tantraman opened his mouth to ask for a little relief from the tit work, Jack grabbed him by the hair and force fed him his thick and sweaty stripper cock. "How do I smell?" he added, draping his low-hanging ball sac on the crime fighter's facemask.

Tantraman got good whiff of them. The scent of a man's nuts always got to him.

"Yeah, suck my cock with your super stud mouth. Man you have a sweet throat," moaned Jack with a rocking of his hips.

Unmasked II

  Tantraman's cock felt so good in Nick's hot hole. The secret stud jizz was making his cock ultra sensitive. Just imagining all those wholesome studs shooting a thick and gooey load kept getting him hotter. And, that strange warmth inside him felt as if it was starting to swell and press in some new and wonderful way. He couldn't recall ever feeling this good. Suddenly panicked, he reached up to still Nick's hips. He closed his eyes and took four deep breaths. He needed to just think serenity and find his happy place, but the guys were coming on the video and shouting so loudly. The air was so stale in the small room that it was difficult to breathe.
  "You okay?"
  "Yeah."
  "Good."
  Tantraman attempted a smile and renewed his thrusts. "Now about that clandestine meeting that The Eel has planned."
  Nick started increasing his speed. "Yeah, keep fucking me faster, and I'll tell you anything."
  Tantraman increased the depth and tempo of his thrusts, moving in and out of Nick's tight hole like a piston. He needed to do this for the information, to save Centerville, and to help protect his community. He needed to keep it up just a little longer. These two go-go boys couldn't hold out much longer. They didn't have his control. Soon he would get these two to give him everything he needed. "Next week you say?"
  "Yeah. Hey Jack, come and get some of this stud's dynamic dong. Man, I can feel every vein in that thing. This super sausage has my ass on fire."
  "Don't worry about me buddy, I'm happy right where I am." Jack began sucking on Tantraman's balls, working his way down to a vigorous rimming of Tantraman's now hot and throbbing hole. The inserted beads had doubled in size and started their subtle vibrations. Jack smiled to see that all was proceeding according to plan. He licked his way back up to give a series of playful bites to the hollow where

Tantraman's leg met his pelvis. A moan rose from the superhero. Jack smiled at the discovery of yet another highly sensitive spot on the stud.

"It's Wednesday," said Nick, feeding the stud the bogus information.

"Huh?"

"The meeting, it's Wednesday."

"Oh, what time?"

"God this feels so good. You like this Tantraman? Is the big super stud forgetting all his troubles yet?" Nick started contracting his sphincter muscles even tighter.

Tantraman swallowed and reached up to adjust his mask. The warmth of the room combined with the heat from the goings on had him sweating. He moaned to feel that vibrating pressure deep inside. It felt so good, like a tickling that's forcing ... Panicked, Tantraman reached out to still Nick's hips.

Jack and Nick exchange looks and a slight nod. Nick bent forward and flicked his tongue across Tantraman's nipple. "Are you okay? You scare me when you do that."

"It's just a matter of control."

"I so admire that."

In a moment, the threesome resumed the action. Nick leaned forward to kiss him and started rocking harder. Jack was lapping at his hole and smearing a handful of the stud jizz all over and around his big swollen superballs. Scooping the engorged nuts into a tight cluster, he then ran his lubricated palm over the surface in fast circles. In a moment, he released the nads and moved to the side of the bed near Tantraman's head.

"Wednesday?" Tantraman was panting. 'God, this pressure. It just feels so ...'

"Huh," said Nick over the slurps of a sloppy blowjob from the video monitor.

"Wednesday." Tantraman reached out again to still Nick's hips. However, this time Nick batted his hands away while simultaneously leaning forward onto Tantraman's chest and wrapping his strong legs tight around his waist as he bucked even harder. Nick squeezed with his sphincter muscles at the bottom of Tantraman's wand, then lifted his pelvis and brought that tight pressure all the way to the swollen crown on each upstroke. Faster and faster he gyrated.

Tantraman's awkward position of hanging off the bed was no mistake. Not only did it put him directly in the camera line, but by elevating his pelvis with no support beneath his feet or head, the superhero had unwittingly been placed in an extremely vulnerable position. It was hard for the stud to take a full breath. When he was finally able to inhale, Jack was ready and quickly shoved a bottle of poppers beneath the super stud's nose, giving him a big whiff of amyl.

Everything exploded in his head. Everything was deep in a cloud. He couldn't think. All he could feel was a throbbing and the pounding, and it all seemed centered in his cock and ass. It felt so good. There was nothing else. In a great show of will, Tantraman managed to return to his senses and push Nick off his chest. When he attempted to take another breath, Jack spread his butt cheeks and sat on the superhero's face, wiggling his anus across Tantraman's gaping mouth.

"Yeah, lick my ass. Come on, eat it," moaned Jack, reaching down to pull and twist on the superhero's sensitized nipples.

Wasting no time, Nick scrambled from the floor and pulled the condom from Tantraman's cock. Grabbing another handful of stud lube he slathered it on the supercock, wrapping a fist around its formidable girth and jacking the stud's steel rod.

"You like all that college boy jizz," he whispered, leaning down to run his bald buzz head all over the struggling superhero's swelling balls.

Tantraman managed to get his mouth out of the furry confines of Jack's ass for a moment, "No wait."

"We've waited long enough. You owe us. You owe us that big fucking load."

Unable to breathe or focus or think of anything beyond the rigid need of his cock and the warmth in his anus Tantraman squirmed, helplessly trying to regain control.

"Shoot it, stud."

"NO!"

Jack leaned down and whispered in his ear. "You know you want to. Do it. Show us how a real man gets his nut."

"Shoot that big superhero load."

Through gritted teeth Tantraman managed to utter, "Never! No, I can't, I ..."

"You can. Let it fly."

"You're there man, just relax and let it go like those studs you've been watching on the TV. Those hot jocks shot it just like you're about to."

"Come on, buddy. You don't have to fight anymore, just let go." Jack whispered. Remembering the stud's hyper-sensitive spot Jack caught Nick's eye and nodded toward the hollow of Tantraman's thigh.

Nick understood at once and promptly spit on the area and with a grin buried his shaved but bristly head in the patch of skin between Tantraman's leg and pelvis while still jacking the supercock.

"Let it go."

"Just think of how good it's going to feel."

"Here you go, stud."

"I can feel it coming up."

"Oh yeah, let it go," said Jack, climbing up to kneel on Tantraman's arms.

"Give it up," coaxed Nick, grabbing the string of warming beads and pulling them one by one from the pulsating superhero's open ass.

Tantraman arched his back and seemed frozen for a moment. A shout from deep in his chest rumbled the room. "No!" His hands clawed the sheets and his teeth ground frantically.

"It's too late to stop it now, your balls are throbbing. That load is already out of the gate. Let it go." Nick fought to keep a stroking grip on the pulsating monster cock.

"Ahhhhh."

With another stroke the first ribbon of superjizz flew to the ceiling.

"No!"

"Oh yeah, let's see it all stud. I want you to let every drop go." With another stroke a river of cum dribbled from the piss slit of his flared mushroom head and onto Nick's pumping fist. In a couple strokes, it was followed by spurts and strings of pent up super sauce. Nick managed to catch some of Tantraman's flying spunk and used it to keep jacking the spasming superhero's sensitive rod. "Give me more."

"No, oh God. No." Tantraman was still attempting to stop the flow from his red twitching rod, but to no avail. The cum continued to fly, so Nick continued to jack him until the spent supercock began to soften.

When it was finally over, ropes of thick spooge covered the TV monitor, the table, and every other surface in the room. The air was suddenly heavy with the scent of sweat and poppers and cum.

The two dancers reached across the super stud's spent body and shook hands.

"Gotcha! Now smile for the camera," laughed Jack turning the superhero's sweat covered face toward the small red record light.

Nick brought a bit of the supercum to his lips before reaching out to smear a little across the defeated superhero's facemask and into his mouth. "See Tantraman, it isn't always so bad when the bad guys win."

#

Could this really be the end of Tantraman?

Will Centerville now be at the mercy of Dr. Eel and his evil cohorts?

Tune in (and turn on) tomorrow.

THE ICE KING COMETH
By Tom Cardamone

The Ice King walked into The Bear Trap off of Twelfth Avenue and stood, allowing the patrons hunkered at the bar to size him up. He liked to be admired. The men mostly looked like him: overly masculine, large and in leather. Several shaved heads wrapped in aviator glasses regarded him, and though no obvious emotion was revealed, The Ice King knew he was lusted after. He always was.

Music pulsed. A few men, pretending to be bored, lifted drinks. Under the red lights the alcohol in the bottom of their glasses shone like diluted, bloody mucus. He stepped up to the bar and placed a boot on the rail. Men in jackets and leather pants turned to exhibit their hard-won physiques. The Ice King's chiseled musculature was strapped by a leather-studded harness that crossed his chest and back, buckling at the waist of his leather chaps. Everyone was dressed like him in his own way, but no one else wore gloves. Cracking his knuckles produced an icy vapor, imperceptible in the darkness of the bar.

When he takes off his gloves, people die at his frozen touch.

The Ice King put a leather finger to his moustache and smoothed his upper lip. He was thirsty, but not for alcohol. Under natural light, it would have been more noticeable that his skin was completely white, but he was not an albino. He was ice. His flesh was steely, like a distant mountain peak; beneath the permanent tundra was cold, lifeless rock. Metallic blue pupils swirled around white irises; his arctic gaze could freeze anyone and anything.

The bartender eyed him wearily, but The Ice King ignored him, absently stroking the long scar that marred his perfect bicep. The memory of that battle, the particular superhero who administered the punishment, bordering on total defeat, filled him with anger. And, anger led to arousal.

Unmasked II

He exhaled frozen breath. The fools probably think I'm smoking. He puckered and blew lazy smoke rings of chilled air toward the ceiling. A fair-haired twink sashayed by, giving him a long look. He had always liked blonds.

The boy cocked his hips as he walked; ridiculously tight vinyl pants shivered low across his shapely ass. He paused at the stairwell to the basement and looked back at The Ice King, his parted lips glossy, feminine. The Ice King followed. The music wasn't as oppressively loud toward the back of the bar. The lights were fewer. No one noticed the icy vapor rising from the snowy footprints he left on the floor. Numerous bars throughout the world are named The Bear Trap. The only thing they have in common is the type of men they attract: ready and willing. Likely, he had been to all of them. He couldn't remember the layout of this one though and relished the anticipation welling up within him; it was rare that any emotion broke through his permafrost of disdain.

He descended the stairs into a labyrinthine bathroom of doorless stalls and leaky urinals. A florescent tube hung askew from the ceiling and flickered weakly. The stale air stank of piss and cheap poppers and cigarette smoke. Now, he remembered there was a backroom. The broom closet concealed a gross curtain that led to an ancient basement, practically a cave, with an earthen floor to soak up the sweat and semen of desperate animal assignations. The Ice King stepped into the antechamber crowded with mops, rancid from the sour scent of bleach. He could hear men panting, sucking and wallowing in the darkness. These men would be his clay, and he would sculpt them.

In bathhouses and backrooms, when the mood struck, he fashioned icy atrocities, orchestras of men frozen in acts of fellatio, masturbating strange flowers of arrested sperm arching in the air, mouths opened in screams of ecstasy or death, stalactites of sweat hanging off their chins. First he would observe the men, pushing away any who approached, so he could better study the action of the room. And, when the men reached a crescendo, he thought aesthetically pleasing, he would take off his gloves and touch the nearest coupling. Walking through the room, he spread winter. All froze, and he would pause by the door and exhale a final, wintry blast of satisfaction. Art wrongly considered a crime when discovered. He knew his vision was unappreciated by the masses, much less the authorities. Still, his only hope was that the police photographers accurately captured his work and preserved it for future generations. Possibly when the sun had dimmed and the world had grown colder, became a bit more like him, only then would his work gain the recognition it deserved.

The twink stepped from the shadows and stood before him. The Ice King had seen enough of the room; he was ready to sculpt. He grabbed the boy roughly by the back of his hair and jerked his mouth open. The boy gasped in surprise but fumbled eagerly for The Ice King's zipper. They kissed, and the temperature in the room suddenly dropped. He savored the swirl of fear and excitement in the boy's eyes and watched closely as they became cloudy with frost. Winter came.

# # # # #

The Ice King slowly rose above the city on a cloud of ice particles. With minimal concentration, he could successively freeze and unfreeze the moisture in the air in such a way as to propel him to serious heights and at great speed. Obscured by clouds, he traveled the world, delivering icy mayhem wherever he pleased. The cold hell he created in the back room at the Bear Trap should have given him immense pleasure, but he was left wanting. The scar on his arm ached as he considered its source: the Canadian hero, Light Stream. The one time they had grappled, The Ice King had felt challenged, alive. Yet, as the embodiment of cold, he was a harbinger of death, so to be thwarted was rare, an odd thrill. And, the earnestness of Light Stream, his sincerity was so touching and, oddly, achingly familiar. The Ice King wanted to return the touch and not to just freeze the blood in those "heroic" veins, at least not at first. The way his long hair had whipped about his face as they fought, hand-to-hand, high in the sky – he had always liked blonds.

It was decided; he turned and flew north over the city. He heard the distant wail of sirens. The Empire State Building stung the low clouds directly below. Appropriately, it was lit white. Snow white.

# # # # #

Mother Bear lived in a simple cabin on an island off the coast of Maine. She owned the island, as well as property in the Rocky Mountains. She often shared the island with the occasional girlfriend, though Mother Bear was short-tempered, and her lovers never lasted long. Mother Bear was one of those mutants the government worried so much about. Worse, she was fully dedicated to realizing their worst fears. As the founder of the Annihilators, she attempted to forge a group to counter the World Guardians; where the Guardians strived to ease the world's ills, the Annihilators worked to both spread and benefit from chaos. Unfortunately, the other Annihilators were jailed or dead. Only Mother Bear had escaped, and though she quietly scoured the world for new villains to reassemble her team, she was battle-weary. She spent more and more time in bear-form, scavenging in the woods, fishing with her paws in streams or napping in dark caves. Of the villains she had originally approached, The Ice King was the only one who had refused to join and survived her formidable anger at being rebuffed. His cold fortitude had earned him her respect and then begrudging friendship.

He landed on her island. Frost from his dispersing cloud mingled with the morning mist and painted a thick mat of pine needles white. The island was covered with tall pines. The rocky ground never really leveled, slowing any approach to the cabin. The cabin was built into a hill, one side on stilts, with firewood stored beneath. He listened carefully as he approached but heard only birdsong. Smoke rose from the chimney; she was home. He formed a snowball in the palm of his hand and lobbed it at a window – a direct hit. He saw movement, and the window swung open. Mother Bear pushed the hair out of her eyes and gave him a casual wave. A rare smile cracked his face.

She was still pulling on a pair of old jeans as he entered the cabin. Her door was always unlocked. This was her island, and anyone who entered uninvited did so at great peril. The cabin was one big room, toasty from the fire in the fireplace. She immediately opened more windows to cool the room on his behalf and then walked over to give him a great big bear hug. The constant cold that radiated from his flesh never bothered her; bears can naturally withstand low temperatures. He relaxed and fell into an old recliner. A four-poster bed under a jumble of flannel sheets consumed one whole corner. The walls were covered with shelves stocked with necessities. The floor was carpeted with deerskin rugs, animals Mother Bear had hunted and killed herself. A giant freezer stretched beside an equally large refrigerator. She offered him coffee, black. He took the mug and blew on it until it was perfectly chilled. He realized that he was jet-lagged and malnourished; he hadn't slept or eaten in days.

"Your handiwork made the news." She blew on her own steaming cup of coffee and nodded toward the television. When she wasn't rambling in the woods for days on end, Mother Bear was glued to the television. She was a news junkie, constantly channel surfing for news of unexplained phenomena that might help her locate new, hopefully malicious mutants. That and true crime novels. He often teased her over her choice of literature, yet he relished the facts she would spout about serial killers and Nazis and the like.

"Yes, it was one of my better sculpture gardens." He yawned.

"You look famished, dear. I'm making stew." The light aroma of which had just reached him.

Unmasked II

Dirty hiking boots much too small for Mother Bear stood idle by the door. A bloody bone protruded from one. He eyed her.

"Oh, you didn't."

"Well she was getting cabin fever, and I was getting hungry." She exaggeratedly licked her lips and smiled.

The Ice King let out a short chortle. "You and your girlfriends. You'll never settle down."

She lifted the spoon to her lips and blew.

"Yes, I'm something of a nomad, but not as much as you. I can tell this is just a stopover; what are you planning?"

His eyelids grew heavy. "Something big, something really, really big," he yawned.

Sleep was an impending avalanche of shadows.

# # # # #

The Ice King awoke in total darkness. It was well past midnight, and the cabin was still. Through the open window, stars were visible in the night sky. He felt rested and ready to leave but knew that would be rude. Not that Mother Bear would mind, but he hadn't come all this way just to power nap. She snored and shifted under a mound of blankets.

He put his hands behind his head. Mother Bear was a large woman, what people would call "big boned." Crooked teeth and a man's chin were softened only by the thick brown hair that curled to her waist. Reading glasses also made her look less dangerous, more librarian than carnivore. Yet besides himself, she was the most treacherous criminal he knew. Likely, they were drawn together because they were equally misunderstood; while often labeled "psychopaths," each had a natural understanding of what other people were to them – just prey.

The room was still lightly scented from the stew. Though he didn't eat as much of it as she did; no one could put away food like Mother Bear. He savored the rawness of the undercooked meat, the naturalness of the sparsely used herbs and spices she had caringly gathered from the woodlands of her island. Both had laughed when she had momentarily gagged and then spat out a human tooth.

When The Ice King reflected on the difference between himself and others among the elite of the super powered, there was one singular factor – determination. Mutants were a genetic crapshoot, some with a less-than-fortunate outcome. None had purposefully sought power as The Ice King had. He had struggled in the industry of cryogenics. His willingness to experiment and take risks was frowned upon by the very management poised to reap profits from the outcome. That was lesson number one: The brightest are always managed by the dim, the weary, the weak. He was once weak. So he trained his body as he had trained his mind, consistently and toward two goals: strength and success.

In his experiments, he asked himself a simple question. If we can preserve a dead body by lowering its temperature, why not find a way to strengthen a living being with the same principles? He thought it was ludicrous and limited that his field was focused solely on conservation and not enhancement. Revolutionary ideas are often dismissed as the ravings of madmen, so he kept quiet. He needed equipment and chemicals and research subjects, not peer approval. He still savored the memory of blowing out the windows of the laboratory. Shocked employees gathered in the parking lot. They thought the clouds, smoke, the initial snow, ash. They were perplexed when they saw their breath. When the first frozen corpse of a security guard was hurled onto the pavement below, shattering like an icicle, they ran for their cars. He laughed as they fled. Testing his new powers, he conjured blasts of icy wind, strong enough to rip through the elevator doors and sever the suspending cables, dropping those trapped within to their doom. Going from office to office, he killed at random. Laughing, he commanded swirls of snow and ice to shoot from his hands and coat every surface. Desks turned into giant ice cubes. And, if a luckless secretary huddled beneath it, so be it. He had made no friends at the company. That thought, in particular, had made him howl in delight. Everyone had called him the "ice queen," and not always behind his back. Now he had showed them he was, indeed, made of ice. He was in control, he was the strong one. A thin layer of ice frost covered his skin and hardened against the words, the snickering – he was finally, truly, impenetrably, cold.

Mother Bear shifted in her bed. The Ice King squinted, trying to discern what shape she had taken. Often she slept in bear form. A most peculiar aspect of her transformation. When she shifted, her animal form was male. Functionally male. Size-wise, impressively male. A massive furry paw kicked the covers away. The Ice King rose from the recliner and thought, 'Isn't it dangerous to disturb a sleeping bear?' He took a running jump and dove into the bed. Mother Bear, annoyed, desolately roared. She swiftly pinned him, bearing her teeth less than an inch from his face. He pulled on her fur. She batted him roughly until he rolled on his stomach. The claw marks that marred his back from their last encounter were permanent. He relished the scars that she could cut through his icy layers. Her rising girth threatened his buttocks; she slashed his leather jockstrap to ribbons and bore down with all her weight. A mighty roar shook the nearby trees, overshadowing his whimpers of delight.

# # # # #

Light Stream flew high over Lake St. Claire. The sight of the desolate, choppy waters below cleared his mind. Though he spent most of his time flying between Vancouver and the newly erected headquarters of the World Guardians in New York, he relished his trips to Toronto. He loved the height of the city, and like the residents there, thought of it as a cleaner, more civilized Manhattan – and the Great North. To be able to dive off the top of CN Tower and rush across the mountains and over untouched forest. It was the only time he felt at peace. Above a large portion of the world without humanity, Light Stream was able to free himself of the confines of the word "hero."

Sometimes, he thought that if he ever wore a cape he would wrap it around his neck and choke himself; of all the members of World Guardians, he was the only one who seemed to live the mission. The others shed all responsibilities when they took off their masks. Well, he didn't wear a mask. He was through with masks. In high school and college, well after he knew he had been blessed with the ability to fly and bend light, he never dared use his powers. He never acted on his desire to soar, to snap his fingers and spurt lightning into the air. No, it took him a long time to know who he was and why he was here. That left no room for masks. Even his costume was designed more for aerodynamics than flash. He had purposefully chosen a dark purple to help pilots see him at a great distance. His hair was long simply because he never thought to get it cut. He didn't think of himself as handsome and was amused by how the press portrayed him as vainglorious. As a flock of geese changed direction to avoid him, he banked low, giving them plenty of room.

Flying close to the water, ocean spray flecked his face. When he was alone and really feeling the pressures of his chosen path, he habitually reviewed those moments in his earlier life when he had failed to grapple with his problems, the opportunities he had let slip away, needs that had gone unexpressed, unfulfilled; often he ended up thinking back to his first roommate. They were both the skinniest boys in the dorm, the bespectacled outcasts. All that they had in common should have bound them together, but they never formed a friendship, rarely spoke beyond the bland pleasantries demanded by their shared space. Yet at night, from the bottom bunk, Light Stream could tell when his roommate was pretending to sleep, that they both were awake, aware of their barely clothed bodies, yearning to be touched. But, they only touched once, the last night of the semester. After summer break, he returned

Unmasked II

to the dorm room, having stored up the courage to confront his roommate about their mutual inclinations, only to find that the other boy had transferred to another college without so much as a goodbye. Though Light Stream was always attracted to the jocks at school, he admired their muscular bodies and the natural ease with which they touched one another, he realized after his roommate left that he didn't desire them, he wanted someone who was like him, someone who wanted him, too.

He rose slightly to avoid a buoy and decided to head back to the city. 'But which one? Wherever I decide to go there will be a problem I need to solve, an emergency to tackle. And wherever I don't visit, a crime will be committed.'

Funny, now that he had finally come to terms with his powers and had dedicated his life to public service, gained the rock hard body such training and discipline demanded, he still found himself attracted to the youngish, thin men who sheepishly asked for his autograph, their intelligence and interest shining through their thick glasses. He knew that his nervousness at their proximity came off as typical superhero aloofness; this in turn fueled their worshipful deference, meaning he slept alone most nights and, when in Manhattan, was forced to dine out with whatever character from the World Guardians happened to be available.

Just as he turned north, he noticed an unusual glimmer from within a dark cloud over Detroit. Even though he had flown all over the continent, he still found it unusual that an oddity of geography placed Detroit north of parts of Canada. The black cloud was stationary over the city. Light seemingly reflected off a new skyscraper from within, impressive at even such a distance. Light Stream decided to investigate.

'I don't remember seeing a new skyscraper the last time I flew over Detroit.' And, Detroit was a shrinking city. It had lost population in the seventies and never recouped.

Its crime rate made him a repeat visitor. New construction of this magnitude and speed was unbelievable.

Instinctively, Light Stream again flew low to camouflage his approach. He slowed his speed to better assess the situation, and as he did so, the hero noticed a considerable dip in the temperature. Large chucks of ice started to crowd the waters below.

'But, it's only September.'

He was close enough to discern that the Marriott, the tallest building in the city, had been engulfed by ice. Frozen towers shot up into the air, so much ice that the massive complex of skyscrapers known as the Renaissance Center that surrounded the hotel was consumed as well. Light Stream hovered and shivered, gripping his thick shoulders he marveled at the giant crystal castle; it was nearly a work of art. But within the frozen turrets, he noticed little black dots. He floated closer. People. A man with a briefcase. A woman still in her robe frozen in mid-leap as she tried to escape the surging cold by jumping out of her hotel room window.

'The Ice King.'

Light Stream's frame glowed with an angry light; his powers roiled, and halos of angry sparks ignited around his wrists. Immediately, he soared upward and sought a defensive position in the clouds. Just as The Ice King had planned. The blow from behind was powerful. The impact knocked the breath out of him. Light Stream exhaled and folded and would have fallen except for the cold arms that embraced him. Consciousness flickered, and for a moment he relaxed into the arms that gripped his chest. The clouds were sheets and pillows, and this was the way he wanted to wake up in the morning, caressed lightly, strong arms around him, protecting him, loving him. But, the embrace was cold. The dull burn of frostbite bit through his costume, and he was revived but at a loss. 'Why hasn't the Ice King tried to kill me?' And with that, he felt a slight nip on his ear, the tickle of a frigid kiss, and he was released.

Unmasked II

Light Stream plummeted. The cold villain floating above shrunk rapidly, mocking waving "bye-bye" as the hero fell. Light Stream struggled to regain flight, but he was falling too fast; the cold of that kiss clung to him like a memory. That last night in the dorms.

It was hot and humid. Both boys slept on top of their sheets, or tried to sleep. The sound of his roommate shifting restlessly above, struggling against the oppressive heat, was just too much. In his mind, he had climbed to the top bunk a thousand times and added his heat to that of his roommate's. His solid cock strained against the stifling, moist confines of his underwear, and in a moment of frustration, he stripped them off and threw them into the middle of the room. Startled by his own rash action, he scrambled to retrieve his underwear but froze when he heard his roommate moving heavily above. The mattress groaned, and he covered himself with his damp sheet as his roommate, too, tossed his underwear onto the floor. Both pairs overlapped – white flags of surrender on the threadbare carpet. Silence. Neither boy moved. And then from the top bunk, his roommate dangled one leg, then the other. An excruciating minute passed. The young Light Stream reached for one fuzzy calf, and then the other, and stroked them. Both boys shivered, and in an instant his roommate had jumped down and turned to face him, proudly displaying his body, his arms above his head gripped the railing of the bunk bed. Shadows leaked from his armpits and painted his ribcage and thin waist in darkness. The silhouette of his long, thin cock bobbed in the weak light coming through from the hallway beneath the crack under the door. His roommate who had always been so cold, never changing clothes when they were in the room together, now allowed his cock to bob seductively, alluringly just inches from his face.

The young Light Stream was breathless, worried that he would accidentally levitate, he grabbed the mattress, and the sheet that covered his nakedness fell away. His roommate examined his body, first with his eyes, then with hesitant fingers. Both boys gasped as each simultaneously gripped the other's heat, sweaty palms demanding that they pull on one another and join, one boy on top the other, lips together, sharing the same hot breath yet never actually kissing, except for a furtive nibble on his ear.

His roommate who had always been so cold.

Falling fast as a bullet, Light Stream blinked. He must have momentarily passed out. With a burst of adrenaline, he summoned all of his power and braked hard. And, The Ice King flew by as Light Stream hovered in midair to gain his bearings. The Ice King banked far below. 'He must have been coming after me, to the rescue?' As he bobbed in the sky, Light Stream was surprised and mildly amused that he had an erection. The memories from college were still fresh in his mind, ignited by The Ice King's kiss.

'Oh my God! He's my old roommate! Impossible, he's so big and so – so cruel. Well of course it could be him; why would I assume he'd still be so skinny. College was almost twenty years ago. Look at how I've changed. I've changed a lot.'

Perplexed, Light Stream levitated and watched as The Ice King approached within a black cloud trailing icy hail. And, he realized that he had changed in all the right ways. No matter his challenges, he had always faced them. His old roommate had run away. And, look at what he had become.

They had battled once before, in the skies above Manhattan. It was a ferocious fight, and Light Stream had struck down The Ice King with a nearly lethal lightning bolt. The World Guardians had joined the Coast Guard in combing the East River, first as a rescue operation, and then to recover the body. Light Stream had continued the search long after the others had called it off, an unnamable pang propelling him forward. And then, The Ice King had resurfaced and committed monstrous atrocities across the globe, against the very community where he could have sought love and acceptance. The community that Light Stream pledged to protect. Yet, when news of his nefarious

Unmasked II

transgressions first reached the hero, his shock and outrage tempered with relief that the criminal had survived.

The hero prepared for the onslaught and turned slightly, so The Ice King would not see the ball of energy forming in Light Stream's hand. But, as he bobbed in the wind, he allowed the powerful globe of light to dissipate. He extended his hands, palms out, and tried another weapon.

The Ice King was upon him; bitter cold lashed his cheeks as the villain raised his fists, now covered with frozen icicles, ready to pummel Light Stream.

"Kevin, is that you?"

The Ice King faltered; the largest icicle protruding from his knuckles cracked and tumbled to the ocean below.

"It's me, Rod, your roommate freshman year."

Different emotions flashed across the tundra of The Ice King's face. Reflexively, he fingered the scar from their last battle. Light Stream floated closer and looked into the eyes of the killer, the madman, the dangerous freak he had known briefly when they were both innocent, when neither knew what it was that they wanted, except that they desired each other. His gaze was met with frosty resistance, mixed with insecurity, and then longing.

They kissed. And Light Stream held The Ice King as the surrounding dark storm cloud dissipated into harmless rain. His hapless former foe fumbled in the air and finally relented and clung to Light Stream, who continued to kiss him deeply, with a kiss of forgiveness, understanding and passion. Their full crotches brushed; each bulge burgeoned with magnetic energy. And, it was too late for the wide-eyed villain to disengage once he realized that it was one of those rare kisses hot enough to melt ice.

SAVING CAPTAIN CUM
By Gerrard Jones

On the corner, a gorgeous young couple shared a lingering goodbye kiss. Their lips brushed softly against each other as the blond flipped the tip of his tongue over his partner's firm upper lip. Their fingertips brushed over pecs and slowly down abs until they circled back to slide playfully into each other's back pockets.

"I'll see you tonight."

One more kiss.

"Love you."

"You, too."

Another kiss, then they went their separate ways.

The dark haired partner passed a middle-aged couple walking down the street holding hands and chatting, laughing, enjoying being with each other. Both of the guys were still in pretty good shape, neither was likely to be an underwear model any time soon, but it clearly didn't matter, they were totally into each other and more than a little in love.

They strolled up the steps to the coffee shop where Derrick nursed his morning frappuccino on the patio. As they passed his table, Derrick noticed matching wedding rings on their fingers.

It was hard not to hate everyone who was in love and getting laid. It looked as if there was someone for everyone – except him.

He tore his eyes away from the happy couple and back out onto the street as he downed the rest of his caffeine. This was his beat. The Confederation of Champions had thought that the village would be the ideal place for a gay superhero to patrol, and they might have been right if Derrick's gift hadn't also cursed him to a life of lonely celibacy.

He'd first known he was different during a circle jerk at his neighbor Steve's house. He'd known he was gay for a few years and been masturbating to exercise magazines and the men's underwear section of the Sears' catalogue in the bathroom, but these were the first cocks he'd seen in the flesh – so to speak. Four hot, naked guys beating their meat in front of him was a fantasy come true.

Then it happened.

He came.

The spunk shot out of his young cock with a force that flattened him against the wall behind him and blew a hole out of wall next to Steven. That wasn't the only thing that happened. Four hard cocks went limp, and four young studs moved away from Derrick. The fear in their eyes spoke for itself. If that spunk had hit any of them, it could have killed them. It was in that moment that Derrick knew he would never have a lover.

Months of experimentation had helped him understand and fine tune his gift. His orgasms would rip through any substance except porcelain. This explained why his parent's bathroom was still intact. He discovered that any orgasm would wreak havoc, but porn increased the intensity and destructive ability of his cum.

Since then Captain Cum had been a regular feature in the gay village. Two years ago he'd been grand marshal of the Pride Parade, he was loved and admired, but he was never laid. No one was willing to take a risk with his cum, and he wasn't going to risk anyone's life for a piece of ass, no matter how tempting some of the asses around here were.

"Can I buy you another?"

The sweet low voice shook him out of his thoughts. "Huh?"

"Can I buy you another?"

Here was another temptation he'd have to say no to. This one was going to be harder than most.

"I'm Peter." Peter held out his hand and grinned. Derrick shook his hand.

There was so much about Peter that Derrick shouldn't be staring at. His face was beautiful, with lips that were desperate to be kissed and dark green eyes. His white T-shirt and jeans did nothing to hide his tightly muscled body. Derrick's eyes lingered a moment too long on his nipples that were clearly outlined through the snug cotton. Nipples were a special weakness, and Peter's were spectacular.

"Is that a frappuccino? Two frappuccinos please." Peter sat down. This was no good.

"Look Peter."

"I'm looking ..." He'd been so busy checking out Peter that he hadn't noticed Peter had been checking him out, too. "... and I really like what I see."

Derrick could feel himself beginning to blush. "Thanks, but I really can't ..."

"You're married?"

"No."

"With someone?"

"No."

"I'm pretty sure you're not straight."

Derrick laughed out loud. Peter flicked his thumb over his nipple and made it stand out even more. "I didn't think so. You've got a nice laugh."

This was going to be harder than he had expected. "I can't. I can't be with anyone."

"Are you sick? If you are, we can work something out. There's more than one way to ..."

"I'm not sick, I just ..."

"You're not into younger guys? I'm not as young as I look. I'll be twenty two next month"

Most guys gave up before this and moved on to some other prospect. There was no shortage of guys for someone who looked like Peter. Derrick wracked his brain trying to find a way out of his situation before he either gave in to Peter's advances and risked the kid's life, or told him the truth and gave away his secret identity. Neither solution was acceptable.

He was so caught up in his own problems that he didn't hear the scream from the bank next door.

He did hear the gunshot.

There was hardly any time to notice that Peter had run off the patio. The other patrons were running for safety as Derrick threw off his street clothes and whipped on a mask.

Seconds later, Captain Cum entered the bank.

All of the customers and most of the employees were out of the bank already. There were three men behind the counter.

A swarthy security guard was nervously dumping tills of cash into a bag as fast as he could.

"Move it or the next shot goes through his head." The man with the mask was no superhero. His left arm was around the neck of a slim, handsome bank teller while his right hand held a gun to the man's temple.

This was going to be pretty easy. Captain Cum whipped the cod piece off his uniform and quickly started stroking his already hard cock. Shit that kid with the grin and the nipples had turned him on. This would be quick.

"What the fuck?" He often got *that* reaction from crooks when he took out his tool.

"Captain Cum!" The beefy security guard and the bank teller chimed in chorus. He often got *that* reaction from hot guys when he took out his tool.

He thought about Peter, imagined him naked, imagined what it would be like to slide his throbbing cock into that muscled little ass. He took careful aim and shot pulse after pulse of vigorous cum across the room where it collided with a security camera that crashed onto the head of the masked criminal. Before anyone could say "I'll get you a towel" it was over, and the crook lay unconscious on the floor.

"That was incredible." The security guard's dark eyes gazed in obvious admiration at Captain Cum's slowly relaxing but still impressive cock. "Of course I've heard about you, but I never imagined I'd ever … I mean it was …"

"Totally awesome. Now do the vault."

Captain Cum stared at the teller. "The vault?"

"Our bank manager's in there. He's the only one who knows the combination, and he's locked in there with explosives strapped to him."

"But I ..."

"He's straight, but he's still a pretty nice guy, and he's got kids. You have to save him."

"But I'm spent."

The two men looked at him in disbelief. If he'd known about the vault, he could have taken out the lock with the second spurt of cum. He looked down at his soft cock hanging heavily between his thighs. He had to do something, and he had to do it before the bank manger was blown up.

"I need some porn. The hotter the better."

"I don't have any."

"Me neither; I'm at work."

"Anything. An underwear ad, an exercise magazine, some Renaissance art."

The two men shook their heads.

"The situation is desperate men. I'm going to need your help."

"I'll do anything I can."

"So will I." Their eagerness was heartwarming, but he was going to need more than their enthusiasm.

"Take each other's clothes off." The words were hardly past his lips when the two had ripped off each other's ties. The security guard moved the faster of the two. He yanked the teller's shirttails out of his pants and over the guy's head exposing the smooth defined chest to Captain Cum's appreciative gaze. His cock started to respond. It swelled and grew further as the security guard's hairy chest and pierced nipples were exposed.

"It's working. Now kiss."

The two came together in a passionate, hungry kiss as they worked at each other's pants.

Two pairs of pants hit the floor at the same time. A pair of snug, white boxer briefs ground into the teller's designer jock. The security guard's rough muscled hands grabbed the smooth, jock-enclosed ass and pulled his cheeks apart.

"I've wanted your ass for months."

"You should have said something. I thought you weren't ..."

"Stop talking and fuck." Captain Cum was hard and throbbing, but this wasn't over yet.

The guys grabbed their underwear and pulled it to their ankles; their hard cock's springing free and glistening with precum. The teller kicked off his shoes and pants while the security guard pulled a condom from his pocket and rolled it over his thick cock. The teller threw his lean, muscled body down on a desk with his legs in the air.

"Fuck me. Please fuck me. Ahhhhh!"

The security guard was home with his cock buried in his co-workers sweet ass. It was all Captain Cum needed. He felt the familiar tightening deep in his guts and his cock exploded violently. Cum rocketed across the room shattering the vault's lock.

The door slowly swung open, but he still had to deal with the explosives. He took a step toward the vault, but his knees buckled from the intensity of two orgasms so close together. He couldn't let his exhaustion stop him any more than he could let himself be distracted by the passionate sex the two bank employees were still having just feet away from him.

He took another step toward the vault when suddenly he saw a streak of vermilion Lycra speed past him and into the vault. Another superhero had come to help.

It was too late.

An explosion rocked the floor of the bank and knocked Captain Cum off his feet. The security guard turned the teller over and started fucking him from behind.

Captain Cum staggered to the door of the vault to view the destruction.

There wasn't any.

A vermilion clad superhero was bent over untying an unconscious bank manager. Even in his exhausted state, the site of the glorious upturned butt got his cock twitching. The young hero turned around, and Captain Cum looked into a pair of familiar dark green eyes and noticed a pair of nipples he would recognize anywhere.

"Peter?"

The young hero grinned. "I don't know any Peter." He held out his hand. "Digesto Boy"

He grasped the outreached hand.

"I heard an explosion. What happened?"

"I swallowed it."

"You what?"

"I have an indestructible digestive system. I can take anything anyone can throw at me." Digesto Boy smiled and flicked his thumb over his nipple.

"Your entire digestive system?"

"From top ..." he pressed his lips to Captain Cum's mouth "... to bottom."

"Bottom?"

"Oh yeah."

For the first time in his life, Captain Cum thought there might be someone for him. He kissed the strong firm lips. "Let's get out of here. I've got a place down the street."

He realized that he was still holding Digesto Boy's hand. Together they walked out of the vault to where the teller was riding the security guard. The two of them still lost in the oblivion of a long anticipated fuck.

"Before we leave ..." The young superhero took Captain Cum's face in both of his hands and kissed him passionately pressing his firm body against Captain Cum's muscled torso before reluctantly pulling back and glancing down with a mischievous grin "... you might want to put your cod piece back on."

When he invited Digesto Boy back to his apartment, he hadn't been thinking. He'd given up on ever being able to invite anyone back to his place, and he'd totally let the

Unmasked II

place go. It was a complete sty. As he unlocked the door and moved into the hallway he started to apologize.

"I'm sorry for the ..."

Digesto Boy's tongue was inside his mouth.

On the way from the bank, they had ducked into an alley to get back into their civilian clothes, and now they desperately fought to get each other out of them. Derrick pulled away from the young stud's lips long enough to get the T-shirt over his head. His breath caught as he saw his naked torso before diving straight at the rigid nipples. Digesto Boy's strong hands pulled his face further into the young man's pecs.

"Don't be so gentle."

Digesto Boy's knees gave way as Derrick took the nipple between his teeth. It broke their connection long enough to get the young man's hands on Captain Cum's pecs. He grasped the fabric and pulled. Button's flew across the room as two strong muscled torsos slammed back together, crotches grinding against each other and tongues meeting.

"Sorry about the shirt."

"Fuck the shirt"

"Fuck me!"

Without breaking their oral connection, Captain Cum whipped the half naked Digesto Boy into his arms and started toward the bedroom.

He should have known better. Half way across the messy apartment, he tripped over a pile of men's fashion magazines. They landed in a heap with Digesto Boy's face pressed into Captain Cum's swelling groin.

"I'm so sorry" He tried to get to his feet, but Digesto Boy grinned and pushed him back to the floor.

"You could have just asked."

Digesto Boy's hands were on his belt on his belt and working his zipper down. His hips rose off the ground, and he felt denim sliding over his tight ass.

"What the fuck are these?"

Captain Cum glanced down his body. It wasn't just his apartment that he'd let go. He was wearing a pair of ancient baggy underwear.

"The next time I see you, you'd better be in some underwear that does justice to your body."

"Next time?"

Their eyes met.

Captain Cum was suddenly very aware of his heart beating in his chest. Was this gorgeous man already asking to come back?

"Is that too presumptuous?"

"No. I'd like that."

"I hope you're going to like this, too. Now get these hideous things off."

He'd never imagined that a pair of lips on his cock could feel this incredible. He started thrusting his hips into the smooth beautiful face of his new lover.

If he hadn't already cum twice in the last hour, he'd have already blown his load; as it was, he started feeling the base of his cock starting to contract.

"I'm ... I'm ..."

The sweet lips were replaced by a firm hand gripping the base of his throbbing cock. "Don't you dare! I'm not finished with you."

The pulsing in his cock subsided – a little.

Digesto Boy was on his feet pushing his shorts down and kicking them off.

"HOLY FUCK!"

The fabric of Digesto Boy's fashion briefs was stretched to the limit by the slim man's inflamed cock. Captain Cum was on his knees kissing the hard cock through the soft fabric. He grasped the muscles of the young man's compact ass drawing him closer before grasping the jock's waistband and pulling them off. The head of the cut cock slapped against his muscled abs and left a smear of precum against the smooth skin.

It was delicious.

Captain Cum wanted more.

He took his first cock into his mouth. It was intoxicating.

His mouth moved naturally up and down the thick shaft feeling the veins stand out hard against his tongue. His hands reached around and started massaging Digesto Boy's strong ass.

Kneading the firm muscles.

Working the cheeks apart.

Tickling his hole with a finger.

"I want you inside me."

The cock slipped out of his mouth as Digesto Boy lowered his body to meet Captain Cum's. Their lips merged again as Captain Cum's aching cock slid along the crack of his partner's incredible ass.

"Are you sure this is safe? I wouldn't hurt you for anything."

"I've had a nuclear bomb go off up there. I can take anything you throw at me."

He lifted himself up until the head of the Captain's cock was pressed against his indestructible ass hole.

He thrust his tongue past the man's lips.

He pinched the Captains nipples.

He pulled his hips down piercing himself on the pulsing virgin cock.

"AHHHH!" The groan came involuntarily from the depth of Captain Cum's belly and forced its way through his body.

"Fuck ... holy fuck" Digesto Boy started rocking his hips, fucking himself on the thick cock buried deeply in his ass.

Captain Cum grabbed the smooth hips and held them still. "Just let me feel you." He pulled the strong ass further down toward his balls and ground himself deeper. Now it was Digesto Boy's turn to groan. His own cock pulsed between their bellies.

"I don't think I can take much more. Please," his breath was coming in short gasps. "Fuck me, Captain Cum."

"Derrick, call me Derrick"
"FUCK ME. PLEASE!"
His new fuck buddy landed on the rug with Derrick's cock still inside him.
His back arched as he pulled himself out and then thrust himself back inside the sweet ass.
Their bodies started moving together, thrusting toward ecstasy.
His instincts took over and Captain Cum started driving wildly into Digesto Boy's eager body. He felt firm hands on his body, grasping at his ass, pulling on his taut nipples, urging him to go even deeper and harder.
He bent over and took a nipple between his teeth.
He reached between their bodies and started stroking Digesto Boy's thick cock.
He pulled his cock out of the boy's ass and then slammed it back with everything he had.
Digesto Boy's cock exploded in his hands.
Cum flew past his head, hit his chin and sprayed between the two lovers. At the same time his ass spasmed wildly.
It was more than Captain Cum could take.
He drove into the smooth muscled ass again and again emptying himself deep inside the young man's body, losing himself completely for the first time in another man.
He collapsed onto the cum strewn sweaty man who lay under him.
There was no sound except the raspy breath of two spent men.
Two pairs of lips found each other again.
Two pairs of eyes met.
Two sets of fingers intertwined.
"That was ..."
"Incredible."
"Fucking incredible."
Digesto Boy reached up and stroked Captain Cum's cheek.
"So, would you consider taking on a sidekick?"

"No. I wouldn't."

"What?" The hurt in the young man's face was unmistakable.

"I'd consider a partner."

Digesto Boy wrapped his legs around Captain Cum's ass and pulled him closer. "Put 'er there partner."

They sealed the deal with a kiss. Actually, there were a lot of kisses!

KOSHER MAN GETS PORKED
By Milton Stern

For those of you just joining us ...

Mordecai was tall, over six-foot-four, with very broad shoulders, large, naturally hairless pecs, six-pack abs, bulging biceps, and powerful muscular legs, all covered in dark olive skin. He was also known for his rather round and huge muscular *tuchus*. His feet, at size fifteen, were not only quite large, but also magnificently beautiful. But, it was Mordecai's face that drew people to him. He had black, curly hair, and at over forty, his temples were graying, making him look all the more distinguished. Mordecai also had thick, black eyebrows, hovering over bright green eyes framed in double rows of lashes that gave the impression he was wearing make-up, and his prominent Semitic nose led one's eyes to his full lips and gleaming white teeth. Mordecai's innocent smile could melt the coldest of hearts and made all the *yentas* and *bubbies* want to pinch his cheeks.

By day, he was a cataloguer at the Jewish History Museum in Greenberg, a popular metropolis on the East Coast that drew the cosmopolitan as well as the seedy. But, cities have a tendency to do that, and Mordecai didn't mind. However, when the sun set, Mordecai emerged from the basement at the Jewish History Museum and headed home, and at the first sign of trouble, he donned a white mask and dark blue tights with a large white circled "K" emblazoned on his chest, along with white boots and a flowing white cape to become "Kosher Man."

Mordecai wanted to forgo the cape as it always got in the way, but his mother insisted, and a good Jewish boy always does what his mother says. He also wore a dark blue *yarmulke* on his head with a white circled "K" as well (it was actually the flip side of his everyday *yarmulke*, which had a Star of David). His best kept secret was how he never lost the *yarmulke* while fighting evil even though one never saw a *yarmulke* fly off an Orthodox Jew's head during a wind storm either.

But, the cape was his biggest nemesis. Often when flying, it would flap in his face, making it difficult to navigate, or he would go to punch a crook and end up tangled up in the cape instead. Whenever Mordecai experienced these mishaps, he thought of the joke:

"What do you call a Jewish ballerina?"

"A klutz."

He thought the same applied to Jewish superheroes as well.

Mordecai could have lived a normal, quiet life, but he displayed special abilities from a young age. While still a toddler, he showed great feats of strength, lifting furniture and other heavy objects around the house.

As he entered puberty, his body transformed without ever having lifted a weight or participated in sports. His mother insisted he read as one could get an eye poked out playing sports. In high school, coaches wanted him to play football, but participation in various geeky academic clubs precluded his lettering in any sport. Mordecai was relieved because he was aware that he sometimes did not know his own strength, and he was afraid he would more than poke someone's eye out if things got out of hand.

One day, when he was in college, he was late for class, and as he started to run across campus, he suddenly found himself airborne and gaining altitude. Startled at first, he held onto his books while extending one arm in front of himself to guide his journey, and within days, he mastered his newfound talent.

Mordecai then flew home to show his mother, and she did not act surprised, for she had expected this day to come.

"When I turned forty, I knew I did not have much time left to become a mother," she told her son, after he landed in their front yard and sat beside her on the porch. "I prayed, and an angel appeared before me and told me I would have a son and this son would be very special. He would be one of the chosen ones. He would have abilities not seen for thousands of years. He would have the strength of twelve men, the wisdom of twelve rabbis, and he would soar like an eagle, yet have the heart of a dove."

Mordecai listened intently as his mother continued.

"But, the angel made me promise that no forbidden food would ever touch his lips. He would learn the Torah and honor his parents," she said. "I was told he would have one weakness and that he also would never father children of his own."

"Why would I never father children?" Mordecai asked.

"I asked the same thing," his mother answered. "The angel told me that if I wanted a child, there were sacrifices I would have to make, and mine was to never be a grandmother. I asked if you would be sterile, and the angel said it was more complicated than that. So, I never pursued it any further. He then made me promise again that no forbidden food would ever pass through your lips."

"And, I have kept kosher for you, Mother," Mordecai said as he kissed her on the cheek.

Only a few months later, his mother presented him with his first getup as Mordecai referred to his tights.

And, for the last twenty-four years, he has been Kosher Man in Greenberg, where his mother owned Mother Rose's Kosher Restaurant.

#####

Unmasked II

Mordecai arrived home, flying in through the window (how no one ever saw him arrive home that way every night was mystery) after a long night, mainly dealing with gang-related violence. Somehow, the AN66 gang found its way to Greenberg, and they were wreaking havoc on the citizens of this fine metropolis. Our hero was both exhausted and exhilarated as his moonlighting activities usually had that effect on him.

He stripped off his tights and walked into the bathroom. As he turned on the shower and tested the water temperature, he looked down just as his kosher cock started to rise. He stepped into the shower, and no sooner had he reached for the soap when his member was at its full twelve-by-seven attention. Mordecai wrapped a soapy hand around the huge appendage and with just a few strokes shot a load that reached up to his chin. The shower rinsed it away before he could scoop it up for a taste. As usual, it had been months since he had sex, and with each passing day, it took less and less time to come as he was hornier than a Bonobo monkey.

Mordecai climbed into bed and looked at the clock – 3:00 am – meaning he would barely get four hours sleep before heading to work at the museum. He dozed quickly.

"Help!" someone screamed from a good distance away. "Help!" he screamed again.

Mordecai sat up.

"Help!" the man screamed again.

He strained to determine the direction of the scream. When he did, he jumped out of bed and, in a flash, transformed into Kosher Man. He jumped through the window, and the sound of breaking glass reminded him that once again he forgot to open it.

"Now, I know somebody had to have heard that," he said out loud as he flew in the direction of the man's screams. "And, my landlord must be suspicious about all the broken windows."

He located the man in distress; he was standing in the middle of a dark alley.

"Why are they always standing in a dark alley? Wouldn't it be smarter to go out to the street and call the police, so I can get some sleep?"

Mordecai landed in a flourish, and his cape temporarily covered his head before he grabbed it and straightened it out.

"Are you OK?"

"I am now that you are here, Kosher Man."

Our hero stepped forward to help, but he noticed something that made him suspicious. The man's hair looked like a wig. He reached up to the man and grabbed the wig, and just as he thought, there was a swastika tattooed to his skull.

"You are an AN66 member!" Kosher Man yelled, but before he could grab the hoodlum, a vat above his head flipped over, and before he knew it, he was covered in a hot, white creamy liquid that had lumps and smelled like soup.

Almost immediately, Kosher Man slumped to the ground, for it wasn't the heat that affected him, but the soup's main ingredient – clams, which had grazed his lips as the soup cascaded down. He had been doused with New England clam chowder. *TREYF!* (For those of the Gentile persuasion, *treyf* is non-kosher food.)

As he lay there writhing in pain, more AN66 members, all with shaved heads, swastika skull tattoos and dressed identically in jack boots, tan pants and leather jackets appeared.

"Grab the kike," one who appeared to be the leader yelled, and several of them picked up Kosher Man, straining to lift him up over their heads and carry him away.

Kosher Man awoke several hours later and found himself in a sling, his hands tied above his head with pork sausage, and his legs tied separately with the same vile ingredient. He was stripped naked, except for his mask, as even villains never remove a superhero's mask when they capture him, which remains one of life's great mysteries.

Whereas under normal circumstances and tied in the same fashion without the use of pork sausage, he would have been turned on and probably sporting a massive hard-on, his dick hung limply, and he was in excruciating pain.

He also knew that if he remained like this for too long he would die, for pork was his Kryptonite.

The AN66 leader walked over to him and looked down at the dying hero with a smile that more resembled a grimace.

"Before long, you Jew bastard, we will be rid of you, and we'll rule this town." He then tried to laugh maniacally, but he was not that good of an actor, which Kosher Man mentally noted as he was unable to speak.

"Get the tenderloin," the wannabe supervillain barked at his charges.

Three of the AN66s brought a large slab of meat over to where our hunky hero was slung up and held it up to his exposed anus.

'If that is a pork tenderloin, I am a dead man,' he thought as he braced himself for the assault.

"I figured pork would be your downfall, Jewboy," the not even B-movie worthy actor/leader said to Kosher Man as he signaled for his flunkies to shove the pork tenderloin up his ass.

They aimed, and just as they got about eight inches of it up his hole, a loud commotion was heard outside the dungeon. There were loud crashes and bangs, cracking and yelling, slumping and dragging, kapowing and moaning. Then, the door burst open, and a tall, muscular man in beige tights with little black dots all over them and a matching mask and cape leapt into the room, followed by a smaller, but no less muscular man, wearing beige tights that were not adorned with the black dots but appeared light and fluffy nonetheless.

"Who the fuck are you?" the AN66 leader yelled.

"I am Matzo Man, and this is my sidekick, Matzo Ball," he answered as they proceeded to kick ass all over the dungeon, eventually tying up the leader and the three men who were porking Kosher Man.

The two newly arrived superheroes then raced over to the sling and quickly untied the pork sausage restraints. They both looked down and saw the remainder of the pork tenderloin hanging out our hero's *tuchus*, and they pulled it out so quickly, that his sphincter popped.

"Aunt Rose, get in here," Matzo Man yelled to the outer hallway.

Kosher Man's mother then entered the room and immediately opened her purse and pulled out a syringe. "What did they do to him?"

"They rammed a pork tenderloin up his *tuchus*," Matzo Ball said.

"MB, she's a lady," Matzo Man said to his sidekick.

"That's quite all right," Rose said as she prepared the antidote and filled the syringe. She plunged the needle into her son's chest, and he coughed before opening his eyes.

He then closed his eyes, for he thought he was hallucinating. He opened them again, looked at the two beige rescuers and asked, "Who are you?"

"Mordecai, you don't remember your Hebrew school friend, Bernie? And, this is his partner, Morty," Rose said.

Unmasked II

"I knew you were in trouble, so I called them on the *Yenta Line*."

"Bernie and Morty?" he asked.

"Bernie is Harvey and Sheila's son. He is also Matzo Man, and Morty is Matzo Ball," she said as if anyone knew that, while she placed the syringe and other items back into her purse.

"We better get him out of here before the police arrive," Bernie, aka Matzo Man, said as he and Morty, aka Matzo Ball, lifted Mordecai, aka Kosher Man, out of the sling. "Where are his tights?"

"Never mind his tights. Get him home and give him three enemas and a hot *Silkwood* shower. The Manischewitz Blackberry won't take full effect until all traces of pork are out of his system," Rose ordered as she left the dungeon.

"Manischewitz Blackberry?" Matzo Ball asked.

"The woman is amazing. She knows just the right wine to serve with *treyf*," Matzo Man said with a wink.

Once back in his apartment, Mordecai was treated to three extreme enemas by his superhero comrades, and he was starting to feel better.

"Now for your hot shower," Bernie, who had stripped down to his briefs, announced as he grabbed one arm and draped it over his shoulder. Morty, who had also stripped out of his costume, grabbed the other arm.

They propped Mordecai up in the tub and turned on the water. As Bernie grabbed the handheld shower and rinsed the hunky hero from head to toe, Morty grabbed a bar of kosher soap.

"You should take off your underwear and get in there with him. It will be easier that way," Bernie said.

Morty, always the loyal partner and sidekick, did as ordered. He was slightly shorter than Bernie's five-ten, but with a thickly muscled, hairy body and a nice thick eight-inch dick with a mushroom head, he was just as sexy. He stepped into the tub and soaped up Mordecai. "He has an incredible body," he swooned as he worked both his patient and himself into a lather, sporting a hard-on in seconds.

"He also has a huge dick," Bernie said as he pointed the shower head at the now rising cock. Bernie then stripped off his briefs revealing his nine inches of thick kosher meat. All the penises were beautiful as a *moyel* does a much better job circumcising than a doctor – even a nice Jewish one.

Although Mordecai had not said much since they arrived home and he endured the invasive enemas, he had a smile across his face as his comrades in tights both cleaned and scrubbed his body of any remnants of the pork that almost killed him.

Morty then eased Mordecai over so that his butt was totally exposed, and he grabbed the showerhead from Bernie, so he could rinse the soap from the big muscular *tuchus*.

"Sweet," Morty said as he looked at the luscious mounds. He just couldn't help himself as he pressed his raging hard cock against the opening that had been through so much abuse only hours earlier. "I want to plow that so badly."

"Don't do it badly, do it right," Mordecai said, finally uttering a complete sentence for the first time since being doused with New England clam chowder. Mordecai, who was a bit of a neat freak – and anal retentive, usually wouldn't dream of being topped, but the hunky side-kick with the big Hebrew National and his freshly cleaned colon made for a perfect opportunity. And, Mordecai was not one to pass up a good opportunity.

"And, you," Mordecai said to Bernie, "feed me that cock of yours," for this was the rarest of good opportunities.

It didn't take long for Mordecai to be getting it from both ends like a nice brisket on a rotisserie. With the hot water cascading down on them, they fucked and sucked until the walls shook. Morty rarely topped and this was a treat worth more than anything he would get during the eight nights of Hanukah. For Mordecai, who rarely got laid, this was heaven on earth. And, he struggled to remember the prayer thanking God for good sex.

His own cock was hard and throbbing although he had not touched it as his hands were all over Bernie's *tuchus* while he swallowed every inch of his kosher meat. The copious precum made it all the more pleasurable, and Mordecai didn't fear any remnants or *treyf* coming from this treat.

There were moans and groans, cries of "Oh God," and lots of heavy breathing.

Bernie came first, filling Mordecai's mouth with a kosher protein shake, which he swallowed like a superhero. Bernie immediately dove between Mordecai's legs and stretched his mouth over the foot-long bull cock that was leaking buckets of precum just in time to taste and swallow Mordecai's load, which shot without so much as any handy work, for Morty was fucking him in the most glorious manner, both strong and gentle at the same time, massaging his prostate perfectly. The spasms from his anus drained a load from Morty, who filled Mordecai's guts with his own kosher protein shake as he yelled, "Hallelujah!"

After cleaning each other off, Bernie and Morty stayed the night with Mordecai, sleeping on either side of him – an additional treat for our lonely superhero, who always slept alone.

The next morning, after bagels and lox, they returned to their own metropolis, Mogen David City. But before they left, they promised to come and visit Mordecai at least once a month, and he promised he would do the same and smiled as he waved goodbye, and they drove off in their brown 1976 Eldorado.

"All we need is a female superhero, and we can form the Jewish Justice League of America," Mordecai said to himself as he walked back upstairs to his apartment.

When he entered, his phone rang.

"Hello?"

"So, *nu*?" his mother asked.

HUMMINGBIRD II
(GETTING BEHIND ON THE JOB)
By Sedonia Guillone

In spite of the constant tension between Liam and me over the issue of my keeping our memoirs, I continue on despite our first really serious lover's quarrel and my really creative, hot, erotic way of getting us to make up. This is just too delicious not to keep a record of, even if I'm the only one who will ever read it. Here goes:

Just because Hummingbird saved my ass from murderous thugs back in Hong Kong, had hot passionate sex with me and then got me into the Agency, so I could become a master in fifteen forms of martial arts and work as his sidekick, known to the world as Black Ninja, doesn't mean he had the right to do what he did to my memoirs. I didn't know at first what Liam's problem was, but whatever was going on in Liam Connor's gorgeous Irish head led him to the act that caused our first real fight.

We were taking some R&R after a particularly harrowing job in the Middle East. I had wanted to go to Thailand and bum around the beaches of Phuket (nothing is hotter than Liam in a Speedo). But, Liam insisted on India. I could only guess that something about our last assignment had thrown him into a spiritual crisis, and maybe he figured that going to India would help him find the answer to what was troubling him. I tried to discuss it with him numerous times, but each time I broached the subject, he'd stare at me, his blue eyes taking on a strange, faraway look and mutter, "You just wouldn't understand, Kit," in that sexy lilting brogue of his.

Liam's answer alone was enough to throw me off balance and make me worry that maybe it was I. Maybe I'd done something wrong. Did he not want me as his sidekick anymore? Or worse, no longer as his lover? I couldn't begin to imagine going back to work in my parents' rebuilt little grocery in Hong Kong, hauling crates of vegetables and cooking oil all day from trucks after having been years with the love of my life, living one crime-fighting adventure after another.

And then, during one particularly sweltering day of trudging around in Calcutta, we stopped into a public toilet where Liam and I shared one of the holes in the ground to relieve ourselves. For whatever reason, Liam's eye fell on the small notebook tucked into my shirt pocket. I jotted down notes here and there of things I was worried about forgetting when I wrote our memoirs.

"Kit Chang," he growled, "what the hell are you doing carrying that thing around with you?"

"What thing?" I knew perfectly well what he was talking about, but I didn't like the sharpness in his voice. Usually, he teased me good-naturedly about not wanting me to write our memoirs, threatening to spank me if I persisted. He's made good on that threat several times, which has only served to spur me on with my writing, hoping to exact another punishment.

"You know damn well what thing. That bloody notebook. Think I don't know what you're doing, sneaking around when my back is turned?"

I stared at Liam. His chiseled face was growing red, having remained relatively pale until this moment, even in the Indian heat. He hadn't shaved in two days, and the dark stubble over his chin and jaw only emphasized his rugged Irish looks.

"Come on, Liam," I said, "relax. I just can't let anyone find these. They're precious. Until I'm finished, I …"

Liam surged forward, grabbed my shirt by the collar and yanked the notebook out.

"Hey!" I yelled and lunged for it but not before he dropped it into the hole in the ground where we'd just pissed. I knelt down but could only watch, helplessly, as my notebook splashed into the shitty, murky depths of that cesspool. It wasn't actually too deep, probably shallow enough to find the book, but even a superhero doesn't go fishing in a public toilet in Calcutta.

Several moments of utter shock kept my gaze rooted into the black hole before I could even speak. Liam had never shown such temper before, especially not over something so trivial as a notebook full of harmless anecdotes. When I finally could move, I stood up, my hands in fists and glared at him. "What the hell is wrong with you?" I shot out, even though in the midst of my anger, a tiny voice in the back of my head told me that Liam had been pretty distressed to do such a thing.

He narrowed his eyes. "Nothing is wrong with me, Kit. You're the one who insists on writing this nonsense about two insignificant piss-ants who are going to pass away into nothingness in a few years. Who the hell is going to care about us anyway? What are we?"

I put my hands on my hips. Liam's existential ranting was having many emotional effects on me all at once, a sort of terrifying melt that made it hard to think. All I could do was shoot back with arguments I knew could not possibly quell him. "That's bullshit," I said. "What about Superman and those guys in the comics? They're beloved decade after decade, and they're only characters on paper! We're the real deal!"

Liam poked at my chest with one large finger and continued his rant. "That's because people love to watch us fly about in our skintight outfits, muscles bulging, beating up the evil blokes of the world. How far off our pedestals would we fall if they saw us now, two lovers arguing over a few papers in a public shithole? And that, after we'd just had our cocks out, pissing together. How heroic is that?" He poked me again, his face darker than I'd ever seen it. "Cut out your sentimental crap, Kit. It all means nothing in the end. Nothing."

That last word raked over my insides as if it had been made of spikes. I stared at him. "You're the Hummingbird," I insisted. "Nothing can change the fact that you've saved countless lives, mine included, not to mention the whole world a few times from megalomaniacal nut jobs who wanted to blow it up."

Liam waved me off. "Yeah, and each time, we get a silver plaque, a round of applause, and then it's what have you done for me lately?"

He had a point about that. The Agency dicks were more difficult to deal with than a spoiled teenager in the throes of adolescence. We superheroes and sidekicks could never do enough for them, and then, when a guy hit forty-two ...

Oh, shit! Liam was nearly forty-two! How could I have been so selfish I'd forgotten? He was mere months away from forced retirement. No wonder he was acting this way.

I sighed. The shit-soaked papers suddenly meant nothing in the face of Liam's angst. Besides, I'd already managed to enter most of it into my computer. But, Liam didn't need to know that. "Your retirement," I said gently, "that's what this is about, isn't it?"

Liam just looked at me. "Whatever."

Again, the way he said that word threw me into my life-without-Liam fears. "Not whatever, Liam. We'll still be together. That's what's the matter isn't it?" I said, hoping that my presence in his life would be enough to take the sting out of losing his beloved career. Being the Hummingbird, a man who could fly at top speeds, hover and move up and down, pulling villains right out of airplanes was not an easy gig to give up. Not to mention that his superhero status was what had really brought us together. He'd have never been in Hong Kong otherwise, swooping from the sky to pull the Triad thugs off me before they beat me to death. Liam was probably terrified of being reduced to civilian status. After all, what did a guy do after saving the world? Drive a bus?

In spite of this understanding, I still wasn't prepared for Liam's response.

"Fuck you," was all he said.

That was it! Reaching out, I went to grab his sleeves and shake him when his Agency beeper went off – the signal of an emergency job.

He looked at it then at me. "Shite," he muttered. "Change now. They'll be here in minutes."

There was no time to continue our talk, as much as I ached to. Liam was pushing me away with both hands and feet, and I could do nothing about it.

Already in a somewhat private spot, we pulled our uniforms from our knapsacks, got them on and went out, just as an Agency helicopter approached the airspace above us. In the next second, Liam put a beefy arm around me, and we were gliding up toward the hovering copter, drifting above the cries and pointing fingers of shocked civilians.

Liam deposited me inside and climbed in. We rode silently all the way to a series of large rock outcroppings that hid caves, somewhere near the Pakistan border, a hotspot where it was left to me and Liam to take out the terrorist holding and defuse the weapon they'd stolen.

My role was to sneak in, disguised as I always was by my skintight black outfit and soundless shoes. I kept easily to the shadows of the front cave in which they were hiding out and rendered several terrorist in paramilitary dress unconscious using pressure points on their necks before they even knew I was there. Liam was at work in another part of the caves. I knew when he'd made his presence known by the shouts, yells and sound of bullets in the distance, muffled by the thick rock walls.

My heart lurched, but I had to concentrate completely on my task, working my way to the inner depths where the weapon was, hidden in a room full of grain sacks. I managed to take all the enemies out by pressure point except for three whom I had to fight hand to hand.

Minutes later, panting and a bit scraped, I had the way clear. During the helicopter ride, I'd memorized the instructions for dismantling the weapon, and in several more nail-biting minutes, had the weapon defused and ready to be repossessed by its proper government, which was done in the minutes that followed. By the time it all was over, the caves were empty of guerilla fighters and of weapons.

There was only one thing missing.

Liam. Where had Hummingbird gotten to? My blood ran cold.

Left alone to wait for the Agency to retrieve us, I searched the caves for Liam, calling out his name as loudly as my lungs and vocal chords could muster. Finally, I heard him yelling my name in response and followed the growing sounds to the very rear of the caves. One more yell, and I heard his voice emanating from behind a heavy door. I dragged the door back and froze. "Liam? What the hell?"

Liam glared at me from where he stood, balls ass naked, shackled in the center of the room, his wrists and ankles in heavy cuffs, connecting him to a thick chain bolted into the rock ceiling. I followed the line of the chain from his wrists up to the gigantic bolt. Titanium. The one substance that sapped Liam's strength. Much like Superman's Kryptonite. No ordinary criminal had been behind this job. There was only one who'd go to the trouble to make titanium chains. Had to be …

"What the frig are you waiting for, Kit? Get me the hell down."

Something held me in place, kept my boots rooted the spot where I stood and stopped me from pointing my wrist lasers at the chain to free him. Maybe it was Liam's growled demand, an echo of the withdrawn, brooding, crusty asshole he'd been these past weeks, pulling away from me, keeping me off balance, closing me out every time I tried to get him to open up.

"Kit!"

I looked into his eyes, their blue glaring. Sweat gleamed on his forehead and cheeks. I followed the trails of the droplets and found myself perusing his naked body in all its broad, chiseled perfection. More sweat gleamed off his dark chest hairs, which drew my eye to the pattern in which they funneled into a thin trail down the center of his cut abs. "Are you in pain?" I asked.

"Kit, dammit!" He tugged, uselessly against the chains.

No. Apparently not in pain. I resumed my ogling until I reached his eyes again. A knowing look came into them.

"I get it," he said. "You're leaving me hanging here like a side of beef to punish me. Well that is just rotten."

"Come, Liam. You like chains. You know, prisoner ditch digger and warden?" I reminded him. It was a little game we played together sometimes in private.

He glared some more. "You know who did this to me, don't you?"

Of course I knew. Hummingbird's nemesis, Kendo Ishihara, a multi-billionaire from Japan. However, Ishihara wasn't here. He had his own devious expensive methods of getting around the world, unseen. My scanners did not detect any other human presence. This little chain thing was, I knew, a mere gesture, Ishihara's way of letting Liam know he was still in our lives and getting ready to do something else dastardly. Which is why I'm extra pissed that the Agency would force Liam to retire. Hummingbird is the only one who can keep Ishihara at all in check.

So now, it was just Liam and I, alone in this cave, Liam naked and chained, and our relationship desperately in need of some drastic measures.

Aware of my sudden power, I folded my arms and leaned against the doorway. In doing so, my eyes shot down, catching sight of his cock. I stared, and watched it twitch to attention under my gaze. My body tightened. No matter how hurt or pissed I felt, I could never be anywhere near Liam and not get hot. Not only was he so close by, but he was naked, sweaty and chained up. I could do whatever I wanted to him, and he was helpless to stop me. "Sort of," I said finally.

"All right already. You want me to apologize for throwing your book into the shithole? All right, I apologize. There. Are you happy? Now get me the hell free."

Feeling suddenly evil, and a bit more randy now, I grinned and took a few steps toward him. "Or what, Hummingbird? You'll spank me?" I laughed and closed the distance between us, stopping a mere foot away.

In spite of Liam's anger, I didn't miss the change in his blue eyes, the way they darkened slightly under heavy lids. I struck a pose, knowing the effect my Bruce Lee shaggy black hair and sleekly muscled physique under the skintight uniform was having on him. After all, it was my looks that had drawn Liam from the Hong Kong sky to check me out the day before the thugs attacked me.

Liam remained silent, but I saw the heavy rise and fall of his broad chest. I glanced down. Liam Junior had also risen to attention and stood hard and full, already leaking a shiny trail of juice over the plump head. "Kit," Liam said. The anger had drained from his voice and sounded husky now. After all our years together, I knew exactly what it meant.

I reached out and trailed my fingertips through his soft mat of black chest hair. In teasing swirls, I caressed him, brushing over his cinnamon-colored nipples. Each one hardened into a tiny disk at my touch.

He groaned.

"I don't so much want an apology, Liam," I said, reveling in the power.

"Then, what do you want?" he rasped.

I slid my fingertips down, following the pattern of hair where it funneled into that delicious trail. Right down the center furrow of muscles to his belly button I glided and pushed the tip of my index finger in. Liam groaned again. His navel is one of his major pleasure zones, and I used it to my greatest advantage, rubbing and playing around the small indentation. His huge cock bumped my wrist, as if to remind me of more important parts needing attention. No worry, I'd get there soon enough.

Then I thought of something else. Ishihara probably had hidden cameras all over these caves. If so, he'd be getting quite a show on his closed circuit. Screw him. I wanted to save my relationship with Liam more than I cared about some nemesis voyeur.

I went up on my toes, and leaned into his ear. Our chests pressed together. Raw heat emanated from Liam's body, so hot it practically burned through my skintight suit. "I want you to be open with me," I said close to his ear. His musky scent invaded me. My body was weakening. It wouldn't be much longer before I got to the point of cutting the chains and bending over for him. "I want you to cut out this shutting down crap and talk to me." I followed with a lick over his tiny earlobe. Mmmm, he tasted so good and the moan that vibrated from him urged me on.

Liam panted. "Open about what?" His cock pushed like a hot brand into my stomach and rubbed against mine. My mouth began to water in the need to fill it with that meaty rod.

I pulled from his ear and nibbled along his jaw. Meanwhile, one hand cupped his heavy balls and kneaded them teasingly as I licked a trail down his neck and chest. I'd answer him when I was good and ready. Heading for one nipple, I closed my mouth over it and sucked greedily, pulling one low growl after the next from Liam. The hard tip tasted so good I was more than ready to continue devouring him.

When I finally lifted my head up and looked at Liam, his eyes were practically closed, pale face flushed, lips open to let out his groans and pants. Oh yeah. A little while more of this, and he'd tell me whatever I wanted him to.

"Kiss me," he said in a tight whisper.

Even though I was the one in power, the order sent a jolt of heat right to the tip of my cock. Liam's lips are so perfect, gracefully shaped and dusky pink. The contrast of their softness to his rough black stubble turned my insides to mush. I obeyed.

Our kiss was hot, moist and hungry. I slid my tongue against his as if to devour him. I'd heard once in a poem somewhere that a kiss was the way to taste a lover's soul. That's what happened now in the chafe of our lips and the rub of his stubble against my smooth chin. No matter how much Liam tried to stay mad, I could feel what was really going on inside him. His anger was melting, giving way to the one searing reality that glued our souls together:

I was his man, and he was mine.

Finally, I pulled away, panting. My body was on fire. We stared at each other for several hot seconds. Liam's eyelids were heavy, his face completely flushed, chest heaving, his ruddy cock straining to get at me.

It was time for more.

"Kit," Liam panted. "Cut me down. I want you."

I grinned, knowing how wicked I looked. "Not just yet, baby."

He tried to look pissed, but I'd gotten him too worked up. He was my slave ... for now. Our play always reached the point where the prisoner turned on his warden, tossed him down and had his way with him.

Slowly, teasingly, I stripped off the top of my uniform. Liam loves my smooth golden skin and dark nipples. I flexed my muscles for him, turning this way and that, then arching my back, face tilted upward and raked both hands through my thick hair. He groaned each time. Finally, I stepped back up to him and closed my arms around his broad torso. His back muscles bulged under my hands. I squeezed then slid my palms down, following the wide V of his lats, down the sides of his tight waist as I dropped to my knees, and cupped his hard, pale ass cheeks. "Hello," I whispered hungrily when his leaking cock bumped my lips.

The straining member bobbed against them, as if begging admission. I caught the shaft with one hand and licked teasingly across the head. Mmmm. *Hao sik* (that's Cantonese for delicious). Liam's salty-sweet flavor hit my tongue like the sweetest nectar. I held his cock long enough to guide it between my lips and then went back to his ass, squeezing with both hands as I took him in deep.

"Ohhhh, Kit."

Good thing the chains were holding Liam up. He pushed his hips forward, making me gobble him up to the base. I closed my eyes as my mouth filled with heaven. Liam's cock, silky skin, hard muscles, veins and all. His musk filled the air around me, and I sucked, with just the amount of pressure he loved. He pumped his hips against my mouth, and the air of the cave filled with both our moans. One of my hands crept into his crevice and played around the tight bud of his hole.

"Oh, Kit! Aye!" Liam's voice slid back down to a growl, and he let loose with the now-familiar string of Gaelic curses, which, I'd learned over the years included things about fucking my pretty ass raw until I couldn't breathe. The litany of smutty phrases rang in my ears as Liam's thick cock slid against my tongue, back and forth, making my whole body feel completely melted.

It was time.

Forcing myself to pull away, I took a deep breath and aimed my wrist lasers at the shackles. Even the titanium couldn't resist the sharp heat of the lasers made by the Agency's weapons developers. James Bond's Q has nothing on those guys.

One by one, the shackles fell open, and Liam lunged for me. Beefy arms closed around my waist, and the walls of the cave appeared to tilt and sway as he lifted me up and carried me. Next thing I knew, I was face down over a pile of grain sacks and Liam's large hands were yanking at the bottom half of my uniform. The heat shimmering off his muscled body invaded my bare skin, and his broad, sweaty muscles closed over my back.

"You're mine now, Kit," he growled by my ear.

I moaned and turned my head. "Always, Hummingbird," I panted while one of his thick fingers pushed into my ass, invading with a hungry thrust, stretching me open.

This was the moment I always loved. Better than any crime-fighting, a higher high than flying, Liam's body on top of mine was the height of my human existence. I'd always been that kind of romantic, and the moment Liam took me over and filled my ass with his cock made my life as complete as it possibly could be on Earth.

From the corner of my eye, I saw Liam wet up his *lok chat* with his own leaking juices. In the next second, the plump head pushed into my aching hole. His large hands closed over my shoulders, and his breath pulsed hot against the back of my neck. I closed my eyes and smiled, my cheek pressed into the grain sack beneath me. This was heaven. "Do it, Liam," I breathed, not so much an order as a plea.

It always makes Liam hot when I beg him for it, and it had the same effect now. Liam groaned and thrust, one satisfying slide that sheathed his cock deep inside me. I let out a sharp breath and clutched the grain sacks to brace myself against the sheer power of his body slapping against mine.

"Kit," he ground out then pulled back and thrust again.

His meaty thickness rubbed that magic spot inside me, and I nearly howled. I pushed back against him, my ass up and rocked back and forth. My vision darkened and tiny lights sparkled, as if I were floating right out of my body. I couldn't help smiling, my chest sagging into the sacks of grain serving as our bed while I dug my fingers into the burlap and pushed in a delicious rhythm against Liam. Slap, slap, slap. The sound of our sweaty bodies meeting filled the air of the cave, along with our musky scent. I squeezed and Liam groaned, the long, low sound that went with the gush of his life force into my ass. Sometimes, I swear it's been Liam's yang mixing with mine that gave me the strength and will to learn what I had to in order to become his sidekick. We believe that kind of thing where I come from.

In my erotic haze, I felt Liam's large hand close around my cock and stroke it.

"Come for me, Kit," he breathed into my ear. His body sank onto mine, and he leaned back, with me against his front, rubbing my cock in the kind of light quick strokes that always get me off. He closed his lips on the side of my neck and nibbled. The other thing he knows I love. I smiled again, eyes closed. That's my Liam. I had him back. My seduction had worked.

I hoped ...

He closed his lips more firmly against my skin and rubbed faster. That did it. I shot everywhere, as much a release of ecstasy as from the tension of everything that had been happening.

Spent, I collapsed back against him, listening to our heavy breaths rising and falling.

Liam slid his large hand up my stomach to my chest. "I don't mean to shut you out, Kit. I can't help it," he said finally. "It's just, I know I'm going to lose you after I retire."

I turned over and stared at him. "That's the most ridiculous thing I've ever heard."

He frowned. "Kit, you're barely thirty. You've got so many good years left in you to work for the agency. They'll find you someone else to side for. Or they'll step you up."

"I don't give a shit. I'm not working without you and that's that." I can't help it. I was born in the Year of the Cock. We cocks are fiercely loyal.

"Don't be daft. You're the best."

I gripped his arm. "If they force you to retire," I said, "They lose me, too. Besides, they're complete assholes if they do that. If they think someone else will be able to deal with Ishihara, they're really wrong."

Liam's eyes got this misty look in them. "Thanks, Kit."

"Now, will you stop pushing me away?"

"I'll do my best."

I sighed, partly in relief, partly in chagrin. At least we'd made up.

"And, I really am sorry I threw your papers in the loo."

I grinned. "It's all right. I have most of that stuff saved on disk anyway."

"What? You!" His eyes flashed. "I ought to spank the crap out of you right now."

I laughed. "I'm taking you up on that." I started to get back up on my hands and knees when Liam's Agency beeper went off again from somewhere in a corner where his clothes had been thrown when the terrorists stripped him.

"Oh, shite. Always at the worst moments." He followed the sound to the corner and picked up the mechanism, which miraculously, had been spared. Then he looked up. "They'll be here any minute. We gotta go. Ishihara's on the move."

Damn. Oh well, the spanking would have to wait.

And so would the Agency, on the matter of Liam's retirement. They just didn't understand what Ishihara is capable of. A nemesis needs his superhero and vice versa. And now, Ishihara probably had videos of me and Liam, sweaty and naked, doing ... well ... you know what. The Agency would go ape shit when they found out. But, it wouldn't do any good. They need Liam. The world needs Liam and will for some time to come.

I grinned at him as we finished dressing and headed for the door. Yep, the worst that would come of a possible video was that Ishihara might try to use it and blackmail us. That would only irritate Liam who'd turn to me and threaten a spanking.

He grinned back at me. "Let's go."

I followed him out, taking one look back at the chains in a useless heap on the floor. I'd used the chains to my advantage as much as the villain had. But with much better results.

Hey. Whatever it takes.

ANTIMATTER MATT
By Derrick Della Giorgia

Matt wasn't a physicist, but he knew the thing he emanated from the tiny red bump on his right arm was antimatter. Ignoring all the theories and lab experiments the concept involves, antimatter is, like its name states, the opposite of matter. Just as banal as black is the opposite of white, night is the opposite of day, full is the opposite of empty, antimatter functions as the complementary side of matter.

Matt was born with the "secret button" – as his father used to call the round fibroma an inch below his right deltoid – and never really paid much attention to it unless somebody questioned what the pea-sized foreign body on his smooth skin was. Usually, people preferred to describe and praise his emerald green eyes, which were the exact copy of his mother's, or make fun of his orange freckles on his nose and cheek bones. All in all, nothing worth considering his life any different than any other adolescent's in Maglie, southern Italy.

It was with the pleasurable experience of the rise of his sexual hormones that diversity came up. He grew taller, his childish body bloomed into a lithe and well proportioned shape and he discovered something stupefying about himself. His secret button, the odd imperfection on his white skin, became Matt's power button. Whenever Matt pressed it or simply rubbed it for enough time with his fingers, an imperceptible ooze of antimatter spilled out from it producing an immense amount of energy.

Everything in the known universe is made of matter. The stars above, streets, tables, cars, houses, our own flesh, the air around us, the clouds and water ... nothing but pure matter, which obeys, like the rest of us, to the law of the opposites. Opposites attract. Positive and negative, dark and light, cold and hot; they are drawn to each other, but put them together, and one will cancel the other.

Unmasked II

Opposites attract and annihilate each other. When antimatter reacts with matter, they both disappear, being converted into a flux of immense energy – photons, the scientific term. With a simple touch, Matt could cause antimatter to come out of his slender but well defined arm and create an incommensurable quantity of energy when the thing hit the matter outside.

Antimatter power was the second gift adolescence gently awarded Matt. The first being the ability of enjoying orgasms. Both types of entertainment proceeded arm in arm in Matt's life and as naturally as he shared his body for the first time at the age of fifteen with his next door neighbor Marcus, at the same age he learned how to share his antimatter with the rest of the world. Once, he powered the light clock of the main square in Maglie for two months, simply by rubbing his secret button against it, and he made public his special ability. The whole town celebrated him in awe, and an unstoppable avalanche of SOS calls of the most unthinkable genres commenced to mark his existence.

When he wasn't helping some machinery stay alive or studying astronomy, Matt worked in the bookstore on via Galileo and dated Mediterranean guys that were taller than he. However, at the age of nineteen, he didn't have the luckiest stories to tell when it came to his love life. He had avoided a couple of black outs, alimented the environmental experiments on the coast by the port of Otranto, promoted art events, even enhanced the fun in a couple of night clubs after a drink too many, but none of those deeds helped the initial semi-disasters in bed. Not that he wasn't sexy or intriguing – some guys had even nominated him the hottest catch in the area, but the extracurricular happenings when engaged in physical exchange of love were of the oddest. The first time, he had inadvertently prodded his bump when hugging Marcus's beefy body atop his, and every light in the apartment by the train station where he lived with his family had turned on, followed by the kitchen and bathroom appliances. "What the hell are you trying to do, Matt?" His parents had banged on his bedroom door at two in the morning and, with that, had vanished the chance of having his first orgasm. It took him two more months to convince Marcus to try again, when nobody was home. This time he wore a band-aid on his bump and made Marcus's eyes roll in the back of his head, while he exploded with pleasure for the new energy flowing through his body, something totally different than the power provided by the antimatter.

Another time, Matt was enjoying the results of his efforts to hook up with Elijah, the son of the owner of the record store a couple of blocks down the street where he worked, and the antimatter interfered again with his sexual performance. They were by the sea, on the deserted beach of Laghi Alimini, right before dawn toward the end of August. Elijah had finally melted to Matt's asphyxiating courting him, and after pizza, he had accepted to take a drive to the beach "to look at the sky. Tonight there are so many stars ... I can tell you about them ..." Matt wasn't completely sure whether it was his astronomy knowledge talking or his heart-arresting sexual attraction for Elijah, but he didn't stop. Taller than he, of course, Elijah was twenty-four and a soccer player. Sturdy body, black short hair, amber smooth skin, he had never showed particular interest in Matt, and that turned Matt on in an unthinkable way. Everything was perfect, and despite the fact that the star talking hadn't added anything at all to the romance of the night due to Elijah's almost null curiosity about astronomy, the sand smeared clothes went off, leaving their naked bodies tightly laced under the moon light. One of the most satisfying orgasms of Matt's life crowned the exhausting twenty minutes of rough riding with the soccer player, except that an hour of hard work awaited them immediately afterward because of the unwanted antimatter that had activated the white Fiat Punto and driven it off the road into the sand.

"I really don't know how you deal with that!" was Elijah's only comment.

Unmasked II

It was during his solar system class that Matt received a disquieting call from the director of the Zoo Gargano della Regione Puglia, the biggest zoo south of Rome. Matt knew it inch by inch, having spent most of his pre-adolescent weekends running from exhibit to exhibit, away from his parents' incessant recommendations. The zoo was a five-hour drive away from Maglie, but Matt always managed to convince the whole family, on Thursday night, to go back and check on the Africa Savanna animals. "They didn't look very happy last week. We must go and check on them."

"Honey, they weren't very active because it is very hot, and they try not to waste energy and liquids." His mum used to explain, even though she knew that the trip was unavoidable.

"Yes, this is him, sir," Matt whispered while exiting the classroom.

"We need your help. We are experiencing an unsolvable electrical problem, and the Northern Trail sector is in danger. The temperature is rising, and we don't know how to protect the animals." The old man sounded sweet and sincerely worried that something bad could happen to the animals. Northern Trail hosted the wolves, the brown bears, the arctic foxes, the polar bears, the elks and a couple of more species that Matt couldn't remember on the top of his mind, despite his numerous visits to the zoo. They were all animals that needed low temperatures to survive and the lowest temperature in Puglia in mid-July was 30 degrees Celsius.

"I perfectly understand. I will leave right now. I should be there in less than five hours."

"Thank you so much. We will be waiting for you. The whole community is very thankful."

Matt catapulted himself into his car and got on the driveway, the radio blasting "Incredible" by Madonna. His air conditioning system was useless, and the temperature started rising under the roof of his Fiat Punto. He opened both the windows, took his shirt off and poured the entire bottle of water over his head. Puglia didn't look very different than Africa during the summer. The asphalt in front of him divided the dry golden country exactly in half and far away liquefied into a white substance that absorbed all the colors into a wet silver glare. Everything was incandescent.

Olive trees, burned bushes, sparse cacti, abandoned houses and on the far right the blue of the sea that was only slimly darker than the resplendent sky. All immobile against him, despite the high speed.

The water on his chest dried in a blink of an eye, and his white skin went back to sizzling. The hot air on his neck and chest numbed him. It was a sensation he knew very well. That sense of communion with nature, with his land. Matt wondered what the meaning of all that beauty was. The meaning of his existence, why he had been picked to be different. Where the red bump on his arm came from and how he was supposed to use it. He looked at it for a moment in the mirror, right under the tense deltoid engaged in controlling the wheel as the roar of the road and the wind dove into the car deafening him. He had just passed Bari.

When he got to the Zoo Gargano della Regione Puglia, Matt was completely drenched in sweat. His jeans were glued to his legs, and he had to dry off with tissues the rivulets populating his slender torso. Then he put his shirt back on and rang the number from which he had been called earlier by the director.

Antonio Rizzello was waiting for him by the main entrance, right past the ticket booth where his family had gathered so many times to make sure everybody had their food and drinks ready before buying the entrance.

"I am so glad you came Matt." The man was overweight but agile and fast. His short sleeves collar shirt had sweat spots where the fabric adhered to the opulent body, which he tried to cool down swinging the zoo brochure as a fan. He rapidly started moving after a brief but strong hand shake.

Unmasked II

"No problem. How can I help you?" Matt started trotting after him, abandoning the idea of refreshing. They were directed to the African Savanna sector. A few parents were sitting on the benches as their kids admired the giraffes, the only animals in the mood for a walk at that hour. The thick silence made you forget you were in a zoo, the pungent smell wafting toward you when you walked closer to the animals being the only remainder of its inhabitants.

"We had an electrical problem. We don't seem to be able to get power past the Australasia and the Tropical Asia sectors, exactly where we need it the most. Technicians are already at work, but the temperature in the Northern Trail is rising so fast that I'm scared I will have to move the animals somewhere else. The closest zoo, as you know is in Rome! It would be a disaster ..." Rizzello never stopped his curious galloping during his talk, and by the time he was done, they were in front of the endangered species.

"Do you think I can power the machines with the antimatter?"

As Rizzello worked the key inside the door of the power generators, Matt eyed his favorite polar bear. Ghiacciolino was sprawled on the melting ice looking tired and sad, not lazy and contemplative as when he slowly paced up and down his iceberg looking for fish.

"You are our last hope before preparing for the transfer." They walked through the tall towers of buttons and little green and red lights, toward the back of the room. The machine they stopped in front of read "Northern Trail Generator" in blocky black letters on a fluorescent yellow sticker.

"Is it this one?" Matt bent on the knot of cables behind the generator and commenced his ritual after Rizzello nodded speechless to his question. He circled his coral red fibroma with his left index finger and gently conveyed the flux of antimatter into the grey rubber tube. Nothing happened. None of the indicating lights in the front turned on. The director's desperation invaded the room while the tall black obelisk in front of Matt suffocated him, stealing his air as the mechanical heat cooked his brain. Matt took off his shirt, passed it over his forehead and tried again. Nothing.

"This is bad." Rizzello moaned, nervously shifting his weight on his feet.

"Let me get more in there." Matt pushed his tight body in the dark slit between the generator and the wall and spilled the antimatter directly into the machine. An iron burp preceded Rizzello's scream of two seconds.

"You got it! It's on! The generator is on again!" Matt exhaled, careful not to hurt himself more than he already had. Then he made sure to drop enough power for a couple of weeks and squirmed out of his hole. His torso was tattooed with wide stripes of grease, and even in the torrid weather, he could feel the burning of a couple of scratches on his back.

"Thank you, son! You saved us!" Rizzello was so genuinely happy that he threw his heavy arms around Matt and ingested him into his embrace. The animals were safe!

"I am very happy, too, sir."

After his success, Matt had no choice but to accept Rizzello's invitation to lunch at his house. He would eat and take a shower before heading back south to Maglie.

The drive in the director's car was pleasant, short and air-conditioned. His white and pastel pink villa arose by the sea, a beautiful mansion outside of Peschici, twelve miles of Adriatic Sea away from the paradise of the Tremiti Islands. But San Domino, San Nicola and Capraia were not the only gems Rizzello treasured.

Connor, the only child of the family, erupted into his room the exact moment Matt lay his hands on the button of his jeans.

"You must be Matt! I'm Connor. Lunch is almost ready!" The tall, tanned, energetic Adonis jumped out of his navy blue Adidas shorts before Matt could say anything, and stood naked in his sneakers as he took his sun glasses off his hair. He looked like the perfect ad for a porn Web site. Beautiful, hot and sincerely comfortable being nude in front of a public. In no rush of covering his most intimate secrets, Connor's smooth and turgid body dropped into the armchair by his queen size bed and engaged into some mind-blowing positions to take his shoes off.

"Nice to meet you ..." A burst of embarrassment took possession of Matt's body and an inexplicable wave of shivers destabilized his posture. He awkwardly turned around giving his back to Connor in an attempt at removing the source of his unease, and his eyes ended up in the mirror of the closet in front of him, where flaming Connor triumphed. More spasms ran down Matt's back, and he did it again. The antimatter freed into the room only increased the tension. George Michael's "I Want Your Sex" loudly emerged from the hi-fi system hanging on the wall, filling up the air that separated them and Matt became flushed, liquefying the green of his eyes on his reddened cheek bones.

"Was that you?" Connor seemed to know more than Matt imagined. He rarely stopped to think that people talked about his life and his exceptional power. To him it wasn't anything life altering, but more than a few couldn't hide their morbid curiosity. "Are you taking a shower?" He asked next, staring at the zebra stripes of grease on Matt's extended back.

"Right now!" Matt mumbled and hid into the bathroom, impatient to peel his jeans off and lock himself into the shower cabin. Away from the guy that seemed to obstruct his will and movements. Unfortunately, his stratagem didn't provide him more than two minutes of protection.

Connor burst into the bathroom as antimatter boy was still underwater. He announced his presence with a simple "Brushing my teeth! Gotta show up at the table in five ..." and started maneuvering the faucet singing, "I want your sex."

Matt rinsed off desperately trying to come up with something to talk about, but the only thoughts that crowded his mind were sexual fantasies of the naked guy bent over the sink. He swallowed his excitement and came out as natural as he could.

Connor turned to him and smiled as soon as the glass door swung open. Then came a laugh.

"You're still covered in grease, Matt!" He stepped forward and grabbed him from behind to point at the grease still smeared on his left trapezius. "Come on, I'll help you." Devoid of any saliva for his state of alert, Matt found himself trapped between the column of water spilling from the white tiles and a wall of toned warm flesh behind him. Two curious hands landed on his hips, and he felt his surrendered body being lifted, to the point where Connor's lips whispered into his ear commands he wasn't able to comprehend.

Less inhibited now, Matt faced Connor and pressed his white skin against the guy's tanned abs. He felt his chest burning again, nothing that the cold water falling on them could counteract. They intertwined and kissed without catching their breath until Connor helped Matt climb onto his body to obtain what they both couldn't wait for any longer.

With the exception of the contortionist skills required to make love in a shower box, it was definitely Matt's most exciting and trouble-free orgasm so far ... until Connor frowned and wondered: "What's that noise ... It sounds like my dad's helicopter!"

THE LEGACY OF CALIBAN
By Kale Naylor

It was nearly 3:00 am when Zane reached his mattress. The night's patrol proved to be a bust for the hunter. For nearly two years, he had been tracking the lord of the international underworld; the mysterious demon known as Caliban. Though Zane had been successful in dismantling a number of his operations, the young man had yet to come face to face with his sworn enemy. Running a hand through his shaggy blond hair, Zane released a heavy sigh before drifting off to sleep.

He awoke with a start. His finely honed senses alerted him to another presence in the apartment. Clad in only a T-shirt, boxer briefs and a crucifix necklace, he didn't have time to don his body armor. He reached underneath his bed and grabbed a glock and a sheathed katana. Zane placed the strap of the sword over his broad chest and nimbly ventured into the pitch-black hallway.

Arriving in the living room, it occurred to Zane that luring him into the open may have actually been the intruder's intent. A masked figure leapt from behind and swiftly kicked Zane's gun from his hand. Zane smashed his fist into the assailant's jaw and leveled him with a spin kick. He slammed the attacker face first through the coffee table before he was tackled from behind by additional intruders. Zane struggled to break free, but he was immobilized.

A figure emerged from the shadows, and the hunter's eyes widened. Though he had never seen him prior to this moment, Zane immediately recognized him as Caliban. While he expected the immortal demon to possess a human guise, he hadn't anticipated Caliban being so visually striking. Appearing to be in his fifties, the man's chiseled face was clean-shaven. The dark attire he wore did little to conceal his powerful build. His silver hair was closely cropped, and his gray eyes emitted a faint glow. As Caliban drew closer, Zane noted a strong sweet odor permeating the room. It was intoxicating, and his body buzzed as a result. He shook his head to remain coherent.

"Caliban," Zane hissed.

"The infamous Zane," he replied. "It's a pleasure to finally meet. Though I have to say I wasn't expecting you to be this young." He rubbed a hand across Zane's cherubic face. "Or this cute."

"Sorry, but I don't swing that way," Zane replied.

"Hehehehe," Caliban chuckled. "Not yet."

Zane's body continued to buzz. His terror grew as the realization hit him. The sweet musky odor was emanating from Caliban. In addition to the slight inebriation, Zane felt his cock swelling in his boxer briefs.

"Why so shocked?" Caliban asked. "Oh. Someone didn't do his homework. You knew that I was a demon, but you didn't know exactly what type. Let me spell it out for you. I'm an incubus. That sweet scent that's getting you nice and primed is my pheromones."

Zane shuddered when Caliban squeezed his swollen cock.

"Nice," Caliban said. "I'll be enjoying that soon enough."

"Get your fucking hands off me," Zane protested.

He strained futilely against his captors.

"That recent stunt with my drug factory cost me millions," Caliban said.

"You're going to pay a hell of a lot more," Zane warned. "You can trust me on that."

"You know, your problem, Zane, is that you're too uptight," Caliban said. "You need to loosen up. Learn to enjoy yourself. Let's see if we can help you along."

Caliban gave his men a slight nod, and the men straightened Zane's right arm.

"Let me go you fucking bastards!" Zane cried.

Caliban removed a syringe from his trench coat and plunged it into Zane's forearm.

"Ah!" the demon hunter grunted.

Caliban squeezed the liquid contents into Zane's vein. The soldiers released Zane. Warm torrents of ecstasy permeated throughout his entire body. His breathing labored, Zane had never experienced anything so intense or so pleasurable. He shook his head and tried to resist the effects, but his body became warmer and hornier.

"Feels good doesn't?" Caliban asked. "It's called Bliss. A little cocktail I've been brewing for quite some time. It was supposed to hit the streets last month until a nosy blond demon hunter went and blew up my factory."

Zane lunged at Caliban who simply side-stepped him. The boy crashed on the couch. The demon ripped Zane's crucifix from his neck and tossed it away like litter. Caliban tugged off the boy's boxer briefs before running a tongue over the pale well-muscled glutes.

"Delicious," Caliban said. "Buttery even." He whispered into Zane's ear, "I'm going to enjoy pounding it several times a day. And, I'm going to enjoy making you beg for it."

The demon's eyes emitted a crimson glow. Zane writhed until everything faded to black.

#####

He wasn't certain how long he had been unconscious, but when Zane finally came to, he found his arms shackled to a dungeon ceiling. Completely nude, Zane continued to experience the influence of the drug and found himself fully erect. He pulled against his restraints.

"It's no use," said a familiar voice.

Caliban was clad in a thin silk robe, which only accentuated his broad chiseled body. The incubus ran a hand over Zane's muscular smooth chest.

"Those chains are designed to hold men twice as strong as you," Caliban said. "But, feel free to keep struggling. I do love seeing you flex this body of yours."

With his jaws clenched, Zane remained poised, staring past Caliban at the stairs, which led to the door.

"Oh I get it," Caliban said. "Bracing for the worst like a soldier that's going to be tortured. You needn't worry. I have no intention of inflicting pain on you. You can just stand there and listen." He caressed the side of Zane's face. "I did some research on you. Tragic business with your parents. You were practically an infant when they were murdered. No doubt that inspired you to go on your one-man crusade to annihilate all demons. You've had to raise yourself. No parental figure to guide or mold you. Out in alleys fighting nasty creatures, you should be in college. Attending classes and parties. Fucking a few cheerleaders or maybe a few frat boys."

"What do you want?"

"Bliss is not your run of the mill narcotic," Caliban continued. "It's also a mystical aphrodisiac. The euphoric high can last for days, and the users will be fucking their brains out the entire time."

"You plan to feed off of the sexual energy."

"Absorbing such an enormous amount will make me unstoppable."

"So why haven't you killed me yet?"

"It's true you've been the one loose end that could have ruined everything. And then, it occurred to me. In order to annihilate you completely, what better way than to make an ally out of an enemy? You're an exceptional young man Zane. I have big plans in store for you."

"You've been using too much of your own product if you think I would join you."

Caliban whispered into Zane's ear, "You put on a brave front, but I can read your thoughts. A lonely boy striving so hard to be strong."

The demon gripped Zane's chin and ran his tongue across his cheek.

"But the truth is you yearn for freedom," Caliban said. "Freedom from the burden of this futile crusade. Freedom from self-denial. You yearn to yield control, to be dominated by someone powerful. I can sense it. You're trying to resist, but deep down, you want to give in. You know what? I think you need another taste of Bliss."

He removed a syringe from his robe and plunged it into the side of Zane's neck. The prisoner twisted and pulled against the chains as he attempted to resist the euphoric waves. Caliban removed his robe and revealed his chiseled body. Zane's eyes trailed the demon's broad hardened chest, which led to his taut abs to the monstrous bulge that was barely contained in his bikini briefs. The incubus grinned and gave the bulge a squeeze.

"Don't worry," Caliban said. "You're going to enjoy it. Soon enough you're going to be begging for it."

Zane's heart pounded rigorously and his erect cock became harder. He tugged against the chains. His lust raged, his body continued to betray him.

"You like what you see?" Caliban asked as he massaged the back of Zane's neck. "Your lust is giving me quite a buzz. Poor boy, all those years of repression. I bet you don't even allow yourself to jerk off."

"Caliban," Zane gasped, "I promise I'm going to end you."

"Take your best shot."

Caliban waved a hand, and Zane's shackles clinked. Rubbing his wrists, the hunter contemplated his next move only to discover that thinking coherently was becoming more difficult. He lunged at Caliban, hurling a flurry of punches and kicks. The incubus simply guffawed. He gripped Zane's wrist and twisted his arm behind his back. Caliban pressed his younger prey against the cold stone wall, grinding his crotch against him.

"Oh Zane," Caliban said. "Do you honestly think you're the first? I've had centuries to perfect my technique on knights, soldiers and emperors. By the time I was done, they were more than willing to forfeit their kingdoms and souls just for a taste of my cock."

"The drugs," Zane gasped. "Your powers."

"Truth is I didn't need them. All of that repression made you primed. I might be supplying the nudge, but you were already at the ledge. Truth is I love your resistance. It'll make your surrender all the sweeter."

Caliban slipped two fingers between Zane's cheeks.

"Oh God!" the boy cried.

"Those muted human senses cannot prepare you for what it feels like to be an incubus. Just give in Zane. No more fighting, no more struggling. There's no shame in letting go. Let me show you what real power feels like."

The demon's finger tips massaged his prey's prostate.

"FUCK!" Zane gasped.

With that, his final thread of resistance was severed. Zane thrust to meet the incubus's skilled ministrations. Caliban grinned and savored his triumph. He dropped to his knees and parted Zane's cheeks. His tongue relentlessly penetrated the blond's hole.

"Feels good," Zane gasped.

"I'm just getting started."

Caliban placed his prey on top of the bed in the corner and removed his only article of clothing. Zane's gaze was transfixed on the incubus's long swollen organ.

"Holy fuck," Zane moaned.

Caliban parted the boy's legs and impaled him. Despite its size, Caliban's cock slid in and out of Zane like butter.

"So tight," Caliban moaned.

Like a well oiled piston, Caliban drove his rod into his prisoner. His vacant eyes glazed over, Zane occasionally muttered, "More ... more ..." while drifting in and out of consciousness. He was hooked. As an incubus, Caliban's cock was far more potent than any narcotic. The musky pheromones emanating from his sweat-drenched body further intoxicated Zane.

With a yelp, the incubus discharged onto Zane's prostate. The hunter spastically arched his back and released a guttural cry.

"Time for you to cross over," Caliban said.

A stinger emerged from Caliban's tongue. Zane gasped before he lost consciousness.

#####

That evening, Caliban returned to the mansion. Expecting to find a sleeping Zane in his room, he instead found an empty bed save for broken manacles.

"Mystical shackles my ass."

With a sniff, the demon smirked, for his charge was still in the mansion. The musk of sex was both pungent and fresh. Caliban's trek led him to a string of his soldiers strewn across the floor, unconscious with satisfied grins. While most of his men were nude, a few of them had their pants and underwear pulled around their ankles.

Caliban's search inevitably led him to the pool room where his charge was in the shallow end, mercilessly slamming his cock into the ass of a nude redheaded guard. Caliban removed his clothes and lounged in the steaming Jacuzzi, enjoying the show. Eventually, it concluded with a cry from Zane. The guard crawled out of the pool seconds before passing out.

"I don't understand," Zane said. "I've come over a dozen times, and I'm still horny."

"The hunger is overpowering for the newly turned," Caliban said. "In time, you'll learn to control it. In fact, it's usually around the time you'll develop your own stinger. In the meantime, there is only one thing that can satiate it. That's the semen of other incubi."

"I need it."

"Not so fast. I'm not sure if I'm ready to give you a taste. You've been a naughty boy. Fucking all my guards without my permission. Besides, I like you in heat like this."

Zane pinned Caliban against the wall of the Jacuzzi with the side of his forearm.

"Don't screw around," Zane warned.

Caliban chuckled. He swiftly grabbed Zane's wrist and twisted his arm behind his back.

He whispered into Zane's ear, "I think someone needs to be reminded of his place around here."

Zane pressed his ass against Caliban's erect cock.

"Ah I get it," Caliban said. "You want me to remind you of your place. A naughty boy wanting to be punished by his master?"

"Yeah."

Caliban chuckled, "Someone's learning quickly. God you're turning me on."

He placed his hands behind his head and savored the sensation from the blond's eager mouth.

Gazing out at the city, the two demons toasted their champagne glasses. It had been a year since Zane was turned, and with no one left to oppose Caliban, his reign as kingpin of the underworld was absolute.

"And our London contacts?" Caliban asked.

"It's a go. I checked out the warehouses when I flew over there last month. Bliss will be ready for distribution throughout Europe in a few weeks."

Caliban downed his champagne. "Perfect. We should take a trip to England next month and …"

A wave of vertigo struck him.

"You okay?" Zane asked. "Must've been something you drank."

His vision blurred, Caliban staggered for a few more moments before he finally collapsed.

#####

Caliban's eyes fluttered open. Peering about, he found himself in a very familiar dungeon. What's more, his wrists and ankles were shackled to the floor. The nude incubus tugged at the chains, but in spite of his superhuman strength, his restraints would not yield. It was then he realized that a silver collar rested around his neck. He tugged at the collar, but like the chains, it wouldn't break.

"It's a little trinket I picked up while I was in Europe," Zane said.

Caliban's protégé stood before him in a thin silk robe.

"I managed to persuade a few warlocks to create that collar for you, after I made it worth their while," Zane said with a smirk. "Completely indestructible, it can't be removed, and it neutralizes most of your powers except for your hunger of course."

Zane waved a hand, and Caliban involuntarily dropped to his knees.

"Gotta love those warlocks," Zane said. "With Bliss being sold and taken like candy and all of the sexual energy to feast on, I'm going to be essentially a god."

"What is this?"

"Isn't it obvious? I've decided to take over. And, don't worry about your men. Let's just say they're all too happy to serve under me, in more ways than one. Don't look so shocked, Cal. I told you I was going to end you. In effect, I have."

"After all I've done for you."

"You think this is a betrayal?" Zane asked. "I'm giving you exactly what you wanted."

Caliban stared at his charge with a bewildered expression.

"You forget I can read thoughts now, too. All of the people you could've turned, you picked the one person who was your biggest threat. Deep down you weren't looking for a charge. You were looking for a successor. You yearn to yield control, to be dominated by someone powerful."

Caliban's averted gaze confirmed the truth in Zane's words. "So what happens now?"

"You're going to retire."

"You're leaving me down here to rot?"

Zane laughed and caressed his prisoner. "Of course not. You're going to spend the rest of your days doing the one job you do best."

Zane opened his robe. His cock was at full mast.

Caliban grinned, "As you wish ... master."

RAZED
By Evan Gilbert

I've got this thing for Raze.

We met professionally, so to speak, shortly before midnight on a warm, cloudy, dying Tuesday in March, outside a bank in the rolling little city of Vicksburg, Mississippi. The funds in my offshore accounts had gotten uncomfortably low, and for the past week, I'd been taking steps to replenish the old coffers. Robbing banks isn't as much fun as some of my subtler methods, but it's quick, and I was in a hurry to move on to other things. This was my fourth hit in as many nights on a Vicksburg bank. As my little spree had made the local news, I decided to move on after this. Turns out I'd pushed my luck just a bit too far.

In the last fifty years, the world has become absolutely lousy with meta-humans of every stripe. Metropolis has the heavy-hitting Superman. The American deserts are the preferred grounds of a half-ton monster called the Hulk. Russia is home to a twenty-member team of telekinetics known as the Red Brigade. Japan has people who can fly and toss fire bolts from their hands. The oceans are lorded over by Sub-Mariner, Aquaman and Triton. And, it would take an encyclopedia to list all the super folk living in New York.

The Mid-South has Raze. Think of a cross between Spiderman and a Ninja. He's tall, slender but well built, has the strength of fifty men and flings razor-sharp discs with deadly accuracy. Like Batman, he does most of his work at night, putting down the petty thugs who prey on the law-abiding. Technically, he's a fugitive himself. His discs have maimed many a ne'er-do-well. Good Southern folk, however, think those wounded criminals got what they deserved. While there are warrants for Raze's arrest floating around in Tennessee, Arkansas and Mississippi, the police aren't exactly working overtime to bring him in.

Unmasked II

I'm a meta-human, too, a mutant born with some rather unique abilities of my own. Primary among those is the power to alter my body. I can change my height, shape, skin color, hair, even my hormones. (And yes, I have done some very freaky things on the side.) I can look like a teenaged jock, your elderly next-door neighbor – or a bank manager.

The security guards patrolling Vicksburg Savings and Loan were a bit surprised to see the pale, skinny, balding Mason Wentworth walk up to the main entrance that Tuesday night. They unlocked the doors and let him in, of course. "Sorry, boys," he told them, "I just realized there's some work I need to finish up in my office. Here, I brought you some coffee and donuts."

While the guards took a break, Mr. Wentworth went to his office, switching off the bank's security cameras along the way. The vault was locked and on a timer that would not allow it to open again until 8:00 am the next day. Mr. Wentworth was a technical genius that night, using his office computer to access and override the timer. The door to the vault hissed open. Mr. Wentworth slipped inside and quickly stuffed more than three hundred thousand dollars into a backpack that still smelled of glazed pastry. Then he returned to his office, reset the timer, listened as the vault's door hissed shut and logged off the computer. He switched the cameras back on, said goodnight and made sure the guards locked the main entrance when he left. Switching off the cameras, along with the late-night computer activity, would be damning, but those were issues the real Mr. Wentworth would have to face, not the one with the load of cash strapped to his back.

I'd barely made it around the corner when the air in front of me suddenly sang three brief, successive notes, ending in a rather solid thunk. I stopped, startled by the sight of three thin half-moons of shiny gray metal protruding from the brick wall just inches from my head. In that same moment, I became aware of a presence, above and off to my left. I looked up.

Raze was dangling by one hand from the sill of a third-story window in the building across the street. Bracing his feet against the wall, he launched himself into the air, did a somersault, and landed nimbly on the sidewalk in front of me. He wore a black, loose-fitting outfit, and a black hood that left only his eyes exposed. There was a thick red sash around his waist, a kind of utility belt that held his fearsome throwing discs. His eyes had a slightly Asian cast to them, with long, thick lashes, and the surrounding skin had a bronze hue. My first thought was that there could be someone very cute under all that black cloth.

"That backpack has put on some weight since you went into the bank," Raze said. "What've you been feeding it?"

I responded by slipping the backpack off my shoulder and whipping it around at Raze's head. Raze leaned back, just enough to let the bag swing past his face without touching him. That was sufficient diversion for me to increase the mass in my thigh muscles, slightly lengthen my legs, and dart off at far more speed than a human could muster.

"Well, that wasn't nice," Raze called after me. He must have pulled some of that Ninja shit, bouncing off walls and car hoods, because the next thing I knew, he dropped out of the sky in front of me. I stopped.

"Come on, dude," he said, holding out his hand for the backpack. "Give it up."

He was, I realized, much younger than he appeared, twenty or twenty-one at most. Just a kid. His cocky self-assurance was sexy and irritating at the same time. The idea of taking him down was tempting, but I couldn't afford to spare the time. While downtown Vicksburg was all but dead at that hour, there were still cops on patrol, not to mention the fact that the bank guards might become just a wee bit suspicious if they spotted Mr. Wentworth going toe-to-toe with a superhero.

Unmasked II

    Time for a Ninja move of my own. I crouched down and jumped, vaulting over Raze's head.
    "You're not as old as you look," Raze said coolly.
    I was off and running again, racing across the street. There was an alley between the two buildings ahead. I made it to the entrance and then Raze was on me, which actually wasn't a bad thing. He took me from behind, one arm going around my neck as he used his momentum and prodigious strength to force me to the ground. I could feel his muscular body through the baggy material of his outfit, thick pectorals crushing into my back while the warm, rubbery mass of his dick and balls pressed against my left thigh.
    He wasn't such a little boy after all. And, he obviously wasn't into underwear. Or deodorant. The ripe smell wafting from his underarms hit me like the pheromone it was. I started to get a hard-on.
    "This is cozy," I murmured.
    "Oh, you can speak," he said with mock surprise. "Good. Now, can you say, 'I give'?"
    "Sure." I could have increased the muscle tissue all over my body to match his strength and then thrown him off. But, there was an easier and much more enjoyable way to get myself free. I reached down between his legs, grabbed a handful of his substantial equipment and started stroking. "How's that?"
    Raze leapt three stories straight up, a shuddering, disgusted gasp exploding from his throat. "Fucking faggot!" he screeched down at me.
    Another talent of mine is mind reading. It requires proximity to my target. Physical contact gives me even better reception. Touching Raze told me everything there was to know about him, including a weakness that I intended to exploit. I got to my feet as he landed some distance away from me.
    "What's the matter, hero?" I said, smiling. "I thought you were having fun."

"Shut the hell up!" Raze snapped. His eyes were tight with fury. "Touch me like that again, and I'll kill your nasty homo ass. Now take that goddamn money back to the bank!"

"I don't mean to be rude, but go fuck yourself."

Raze flinched at that, as I'd expected. I used his moment of discomfort to send my right arm stretching four stories up. Snagging the edge of the roof above with my hand, I snatched myself atop the building that bordered the eastern side of the alley.

Thoroughly pissed now, Raze came bounding after me, using windowsills and fire escape landings to mount the building. I was halfway across the rooftop, running hard, when he shot over the edge. There was a single tingling note, and the backpack suddenly dropped to the turf behind me. The punk had used one of his discs to cut the straps that held the pack to my shoulders. It was no accident that the blade also left a ten-inch slash across my back.

I slid to a halt and sent both hands stretching toward the backpack.

Raze landed in a crouch, three discs gleaming between the fingers of his right fist. "Touch that bag, and I'll take off your fucking hand!"

In the blink of an eye, my right arm slid between Raze's splayed legs and up to his butt. I grabbed his firm, round buns, my fingers stabbing deep into the valley between. As he screamed in rage and leapt away, I grabbed the backpack with my left hand. Before Raze even touched back down on the roof, I had the pack clutched to my chest and was on the run yet again.

There was a snarled, unintelligible curse behind me. It masked the sound of the discs as they sang through the air. The impact pitched me forward to my knees. Raze had thrown the damned things with such force they sliced through both my body and the backpack before burying themselves in the wall of a taller building two blocks down.

Unmasked II

    The split pack slid from my arms, spilling gray-green bills that wafted across the roof on the night breeze. I stayed on my knees as Raze walked around and grabbed the pack. Then he stood there, glaring down at me, waiting for me to keel over and die.
    I winked at him.
    His eyes widened. He watched as the wounds in my chest knit themselves shut. "What the fuck are you?" he hissed, stepping back.
    Another benefit of being able to manipulate your body parts is that you can heal yourself. There was still some internal damage to take care of, however, and I didn't want to fight Raze while doing so. "You win this one, kid," I said with a wink. Then I shot out a fist that swelled to the size of a refrigerator as it slammed into Raze. Still clutching the pack, he went airborne and came down on his back, sliding across the roof. I hurtled away, over the edge. By the time he peered over to look for me, I'd managed to hide myself in a trashcan below.
    I watched. Raze came down from the roof with the backpack and headed for the bank. Two police cars were flashing out front. The guards must have discovered that the bank's security system had been breached and called the cops. Seeing the cars, Raze faded back into the shadows. He was too far away for me to pick up his thoughts, but I was pretty sure of what he would do next. Namely, take the cash home with him, then go to the police tomorrow in his civilian mode and turn the money in as a lost-and-found.
    I didn't bother to follow him. I knew where he lived.
    Jackson, the Mississippi capital, is a thirty-minute drive east of Vicksburg. The suburbs are pretty ritzy, sprouting malls and housing developments as upper middle-income people of all colors vacate the city proper.
    Diego Lopez was one of those stuck in the inner city. It was 2:30 am, Wednesday, when he finally entered the two-story apartment building on the city's south side where he made his home. Head down, he walked somewhat

wearily along the upper corridor, a bulging, black plastic garbage bag slung over his left shoulder.

He didn't notice me until I slumped against the door of the unit at the end of the hall, sighing impatiently.

"Oh," he said, looking up, his voice boyish. "Hi."

"Hi," I greeted testily. His gaze sharpened, and suddenly he didn't seem quite so tired. His eyes roamed up and down my body with such blatant hunger that I couldn't help smiling.

"Sorry," he said, embarrassed. "I didn't mean to, like, stare."

"That's okay." I liked what I was seeing, too. Diego was about six foot three. He was good-looking, with curly black hair atop his head, thick eyebrows, slanted dark brown eyes, a long, narrow nose, plump lips and a close-cropped, triangular goatee on his chin. His skin was reddish-brown. His broad shoulders and chest angled down to a narrow waist and long legs. He wore an oversized brown T-shirt, baggy black jeans and white sneakers that were as big as shoeboxes. The overlarge clothing could not hide the fluid motion of his muscular body as he walked closer.

He stopped outside his apartment, eyes still on me. "Something wrong?"

"I'm just waiting for my friend, Ella," I replied, pouting. "She said she'd meet me here at her place after she left work. I just got in town. She's going to let me crash with her for a couple of days."

Diego frowned. "I hate to tell you this, but you must've gotten your signals crossed. Ella doesn't get off work until seven."

"What? That bitch!" I became the very picture of distress. "I told her what time that damn bus would put me in town, and she swore she'd be here to meet me. Now I have to sit in this godforsaken hall for four fucking hours. That bitch!" I slapped the door with both hands in frustration.

Unmasked II

"You could wait for Ella here," Diego said, nodding toward his apartment door. "With me."

"Oh. Thanks, but that's okay. I'll be fine right here."

"You can't just sit in the hall ..."

"Yes, I can." I rolled my eyes in a do-I-look-like-a-fool motion. "Hey, I appreciate the offer, but I don't know you. And, how can you be sure it's okay to trust me? For all you know, I could be a bank robber. Or a contract killer."

"You're too pretty to be any of that stuff." He actually blushed when he said it. "And, I promise you have nothing to worry about in me. If it'll make you feel safer, I'll leave my door open and put a chair right there so you'll see Ella the minute she walks down this hall."

I hesitated just long enough to make it look good. "All right," I said skeptically, picking up a pink overnight bag from the floor.

Diego grinned, unlocking his door as I approached. "What's your name?"

"Iona Dick."

"Iona. That's a pretty name."

"Thanks. And you are ...?"

"Diego."

"Diego, you're cute." Dense, but cute.

He blushed again.

As promised, the door to his apartment stayed open. Diego took a chair from his dinette set and placed it practically on the threshold for me. There were only four rooms to his apartment, and from where I sat, I could look into every one of them except the bathroom. The furnishings were modest, scrounged from various family members when he moved out of his mom's house. The place was just what you'd expect from a college student working a part-time mechanic's job in his uncle's auto repair shop. I watched as Diego walked through the kitchen into his bedroom, where he dumped the bulging garbage bag behind his bed.

I was everything Diego liked in a woman: tall, buxom and long-legged, the perfect 36-24-36 package with silky auburn hair flowing down to my shoulders. The tight blue jeans and tucked black blouse I wore emphasized my assets. Diego was attracted to women of every race, but I happened to be black. He lost his virginity at seventeen to a black woman. A towering, leather clad, whip-cracking black woman with a PhD in anal torture. She left a lasting impression. And not just on his tender little pucker.

Diego returned to the living room and sat on his sofa, so we could talk. He wanted me desperately but, sweet kid that he was, thought that he would take me out on a proper date before he tried to get into my panties. Alas, I didn't have that kind of time. So, as the chitchat flew between us, I flirted with ever-increasing gusto. Diego flirted back. Ere long, the door was closed, the chair was back at the dining table, and we were in Diego's bedroom with my pink overnight bag at my side.

I immediately took control. Seated on the bed – shoulders back, breasts bulging, legs crossed sultrily – I gave him an imperious stare and barked, "Strip!"

Standing in front of the bed, Diego flinched. "Wh ... what?"

"Don't talk! Strip!"

Diego grabbed the hem of his T-shirt and lifted his arms, raising the curtain on what promised to be one hell of a show. First up was a set of tight, brown, rippling abs. Next came a furry, chiseled chest with tiny nipples begging to be bitten, followed by hairy, wonderfully sweaty pits that immediately filled the air with a pungent, enticing aroma.

As he dropped the shirt to the floor, Diego got a whiff of himself. "Wow. Sorry," he said. "I had a rough day and didn't get a shower ..."

In one swift motion, I sprang to my feet and slapped him a stinging blow across his luscious nipples. "Did I say you could talk?"

"N ... no, ma'am," Diego stammered. "Sorry, ma'am."

"Shut the hell up and get those jeans off."

Hooking a thumb into the waistband, Diego undid the button on his jeans, then unzipped quickly, revealing the dark mass of his pubic foliage. The pants dropped and his cock bobbed up at me, thick and wickedly curved, above a furry, low-hanging ball sac. He had a nice set of male plumbing, but that didn't interest me at the moment.

"Turn around," I commanded.

He dropped his chin humbly and obeyed. The ass was every bit as beautiful as I'd imagined, smooth, round and compact. I slapped that rump hard enough to draw an ecstatic gasp from Diego, but his buns were so tight with muscle they didn't even quiver.

"Okay, punk, get down on your knees like a dog," I snapped.

He dropped immediately to his hands and knees. Still wearing his sneakers and with his jeans bunched around his ankles, he made for a very tempting sight. I pulled a two-foot long wooden paddle from my overnight bag. Then I stepped in front of him, took him by the chin, and forced him to look up at me. As he stared, I shucked my blouse and jeans. My big, naked breasts defied gravity, and my hairless kitty cat was perfect down to the last detail. (I'd had to do a long, close examination of a real live vagina in order to morph my manly parts appropriately. Not the most fun thing I've ever done, let me tell you.) The display was like Pavlov's bell to Diego. His mouth dropped open as his eyes went to my manufactured pussy. He leaned forward, sticking out his tongue. I waited until he was just shy of licking me, and then brought the paddle down on his butt with a resounding whack!

"Did I say you could touch me, bitch?"

He flinched away from me. "No ma'am."

Another whack. "Did I say you could talk?"

Diego shook his head.

"I see you need some stronger discipline." I strutted around him, heading for my overnight bag. "Is that it? You need stronger discipline?"

He looked over his shoulder, nodding at me.

I dropped the paddle, grabbed the bag, and produced a butt plug. It was rather modest in size, a mere six inches long and four inches around at its widest, and it was bright blue (Diego's favorite color). His eyes widened at the sight of it.

"Do I have to use this on you?" I wagged the plug at him.

The boy's head bobbed enthusiastically.

"Stick that ass out!"

Trembling with excitement, Diego arched his back, poking out his butt. Those gloriously meaty globes parted slightly, and his cute little pucker winked at me. Now it was my turn to salivate. I wanted to dive in and take some laps, but I settled for slathering his valley with KY.

Without further preamble, I put the butt plug at Diego's back door and slowly began drilling it in. Diego groaned, grimaced and gasped as the plug disappeared into him inch by inch. Once the base of the plug hit home, I gave his buns another swat with my hand and stood up.

"There," I said with all the primness of a Catholic grade school principal. "Are you going to be a good little boy from now on?"

"Yes, ma'am."

Whap! I smacked his plugged booty yet again. "Damn it, you just can't keep that fucking mouth closed, can you?" I shoved my hand in the overnight bag again and came up with a twelve-inch dildo as thick as my dainty forearm. I waved the monstrous piece in Diego's face. "Am I gonna have to use this on your ass?"

"YES MA'AM!"

"Get that ass up higher!"

Diego put his chest on the floor, pushing his butt up until his buns splayed apart. When his eyes squeezed shut in anticipation, I slipped the dildo back into the bag as the innie between my legs morphed into an outtie. My dick is normally seven inches when it's at attention. For Diego, I supersized it, sprouting an appendage that a mare would love. I yanked out the butt plug and rammed my humongous cock up to the root in Diego's juicy little opening.

Unmasked II

He screamed, a long, bellowing yell born partly from pain, mostly from delight. His hole was hot, deep and wet, clutching at me in oh-so-delicious spasms. I pounded away, plumbing depths the buff, brown boy didn't even know he had. He yelped with each thrust, and I began slapping his ass, snapping, "Yeah, pig! Take it, pig! Squeal, pig!"

He bucked.
I bounced.
He shook.
I spanked.
He cried.
I cursed.

And for fifteen long incredibly hot minutes, I rode Diego around his tiny bedroom. In the seconds before my blast-off, I did him the courtesy of reaching around to grab his drooling, rock-hard cock. Two strokes were enough to set him off, and he grunted loudly as he sprayed the dirty carpet beneath us. His orgasm caused his hyper-stretched hole to grip my dick like a fist. I drove in deep, smashing Diego to the floor, and exploded.

When we were both done, Diego lay there, completely spent, muttering, "Oh, God ... oh, God ..." Seconds later, he began to drift away with my mega-cock still inside him. It was the best piece of ass I'd had in a long time, and I could feel myself getting hard once more, ready for round two. But, I didn't want to push my luck again, so I slowly withdrew from Diego's plundered bubble butt.

I turned my outtie into an innie again (no easy task when you've popped a woody) and quickly got dressed. I reached over the bed and retrieved the garbage bag Diego had deposited there. Inside was the cash from Vicksburg Savings and Loan, along with Raze's hooded superhero outfit. Money and a memento. What more could I want?

I slung the bag over my shoulder and tippy-toed my way to the front door. The last thing I heard on my way out was a soft, satisfied moan from the slumbering Diego.

RIGHT HAND MAN
By Erastes

No. The mask stays on. There's no way you can know who I am, not with what I'm going to tell you. Ironic, isn't it, that I'm the one wearing the mask now?

I know, I know. But I'm jumpy and I'm having to watch my words even now. No, I won't have another. Gotta keep sharp. One slip, and I'm out of a job, out on the streets, and probably a dead man.

So how does this work? Do you ask questions – or do you just want me to talk? Fine. I can do that.

I got the job six years ago. I was fresh out of the best butler school in England, and my first job was as prestigious as I could have wanted. I was working at ... hah. Nearly named names. Let's call him Lord B. He paid well, and the perks were great, good apartment, great car. Time off for a little cruising around town if you know what I mean – British guys are cute, and I love the way they talk, especially when it's dirty. As long as I was discreet, Lord B didn't mind even if I brought them home. I didn't, though. Never met anyone who mattered that much.

Anyway. About six months after I started working for him, Lord B tells me that he's got some political party needs arranging, bigwigs from the shadow cabinet and heads of huge corporations. I gave the invitation list a once over with the impassive face I learned at school and said, "Very good, sir," although I have to admit that I was impressed, even though I was trained not to be. I worked hard at the arrangements and the night went without a hitch; the food was perfect, the quartet unobtrusive and the warm "thank you" from Lord B was more rewarding than the bonus he later slipped into my pay-packet.

What? No, not in that way. Lord B was a decent employer (for a British aristocrat), but he had a face like a codfish, no chin and no hair. I never thought of him in that way. Plus the fact he wasn't into men, was famous for it. As

Unmasked II

the tabloids have often gloated about, and to the eternal shame of Lady B, he liked his girls young, blonde and slutty. That's why she lived in the country. Of course, he went too far, went too young, and that was his downfall.

Anyway. I was serving drinks at the party when the bell rings, and I was surprised because everyone who had RSVP'd was accounted for, so I excused myself with a murmur and went to answer the door. There was this guy on the doorstep, in the required tux, and a white scarf and he was ... beautiful. I had to fight my face for control because perfect butlers' jaws do not drop open when encountering one's boss's guests.

But hell, yeah. You've seen his face, or at least most of it. You know he's gorgeous. You wouldn't be asking for an interview to your magazine if he wasn't hot as hell and you wanted to know what it was like under the Lycra. It amazes me that a scrap of green fabric hides who he is so effectively. But that little mask can't hide the way his cheekbones stand out, like he's had surgery (he hasn't), the way his hair sweeps back from that wide forehead, the way the light hits those golden curls. The way his eyes shine, even in the dark. The suit now, that hides nothing, but the first time I saw him he was in normal evening clothes, and although I remember thinking back then that his body was made for a tux, when I finally saw him in the Lycra, I cursed the fact that he couldn't wear it all the time.

So, I asked him to wait, civilly, took his name, and quietly told Lord B that he had an extra guest. It was clear that Lord B had been expecting him, and I was a mite put out that I had not been kept informed. I made my way back to the unexpected guest and announced him, rather stiffly, but he turned to me with those emerald eyes and thanked me so beautifully that my annoyance melted away.

He was a frequent guest after that; he always came unannounced and at odd times of the day. I found myself warming when the doorbell would ring late at night, and I took a lot of pleasure taking his coat from him, still warm from his skin and musky with his scent.

Eric Summers

    I don't know to this day what business he had with Lord B, but I can guess, as what happened to Lord B could only have been done by someone who was able to get into a locked safe without keys and then to – pretty effortlessly – reach the top of Tower Bridge carrying two people without being seen. On the day before Lord B was found naked with an underage prostitute on top of the biggest stage in England, the unexpected guest – let's call him ... Mr. Alan ... said to me, as he took his coat from me, "If you need a job soon, come and see me, all right?"

    I thanked him politely in my perfect butler manner but said I was perfectly suited. He shook my hand, and my body reacted as violently as it ever had to anyone. Nothing showed in my face, I'm sure, but had he been watching below my waist, he would have seen just how much my skin liked the touch of his, and had I listened to my cock's demands, I would have said: "I'll come with you now, sir." but my training held sway. Well-trained butlers do not take jobs for sentiment. Perfect butlers do not take jobs with men because they want to see them naked. Or, because they want to explore their skins with their tongues.

    But, I remember wishing that they did.

    Of course, the scandal hit the papers the next day, and the day after that and the day after that, so I left. I had no choice; it would have been suicide for my CV to stay and support a man like that, who'd fooled the country so. I checked in with the school, mulled over the offers that were available – all tempting – and found myself turning Mr. Alan's card over in my hand. There was no reason for me to consider his offer – I didn't even know if he could afford me, but all of the other jobs were abroad, and I was growing to love England, warm beer and bad traffic aside. So I phoned him, was unsurprised when he answered the phone himself, after all he was butler-less, and was invited for an interview that afternoon.

    Long story short, I got the job, obviously. I had no idea what he was hinting at when, at one point in the interview he said: "What is your stand on client confidentiality?"

"It is the butler's creed, sir," I said, honestly. "Butlers from my academy are employed by some of the most important men in the world, and we would not hold the reputation, or have the gall to ask the salaries we ask were we to run to the tabloids after we left one position for another."

"Or other governments," he said. He was observing me closely.

"Just so, sir."

"And you are gay."

I was startled and for the first time in my trained life I showed it. "I trust that that would not be any obstacle in my performing my duties, sir."

I must have sounded as nettled as I felt, for he said. "It's not obvious, believe me. It's just a ... talent I have. And no, it doesn't matter in the slightest. I'm ..." he paused. "Not entirely straight, myself."

I wondered then, why he had mentioned it, but soon forgot the matter as we talked about the work involved, although "not entirely straight" gave me a delicious hard-on in seconds. He offered me the job on the spot, and I had the dignity to tell him that I would think it over – never let an employer know you are too keen – and would let him know. That seemed to amuse him, and he treated me to one of his rare laughs as he saw me out.

I moved into the country house the week after.

How did I find out who he was? I didn't. He told me. He was so circumspect, I don't think I ever would have found out by myself.

I'd been there a month or more and I liked it. A butler is happiest in a house where there is a strict routine, and Mr. Alan certainly kept to that. He slept until noon, and I was not permitted in his rooms until the stable clock struck midday. A light breakfast, then he'd take the car out – always drove himself – and he'd be back for a light dinner around eight, after which he would go out again, and I would not see him until after noon. I was, of course, enjoying working with him because that all-over body warmth I'd got from him the first time we'd touched hadn't gone away.

Over his breakfast one afternoon, he simply said, "I'd like you to accompany me today."

"May one enquire to where, sir?"

"Does it matter?"

"It might, one should like to know what clothes to lay out for sir, and what sir would like me to wear myself."

He looked thoughtful for a moment. "I suppose you are right. Nothing special for me, but you might want to change into something a little less formal. Bring the car around at half one."

I was standing by the car at the appointed time, dressed in a pair of smart trousers and a windcheater. He jumped in the driving seat, and I slid into the Morgan beside him. We drove out of the main gate and left toward the Chichester Road, and then as we passed the south lodge, he turned back into the estate and stopped the car at the back of the lodge itself. Puzzled, I followed him as he led the way inside the lodge, which seemed unpopulated although I had seen lights on and off at regular times across the park at night.

He turned to me and gave me that look he'd given me the first time he'd mentioned my sexual orientation and said. "I've done some research on you, and it seems you weren't lying. You've never said a word about your employers to anyone – not even the last man you were with."

I inclined my head, and he continued. "I'm going to trust you with this, God alone knows I've been wanting to tell someone for years," and he opened the door to what I had presumed was the bedroom, or kitchen. Instead it was a stainless steel lift, with a glass panel on a wall at head height, and small holes in the ceiling. "Come on."

I stepped in beside him, holding my excitement and nervousness in check. He leaned his head toward the glass panel and spoke. "Mr. Alan," he said, then he turned to me and gave me that libido inducing smile. "Iris scanner, voice activation. If I'm not me, then whoever who was pretending to be me would be gassed in ten seconds. Nonlethal, of course. At first," he added, with a leer. "No questions? That's the sangfroid I know and love!" The lift hadn't appeared to be moving at all, but the doors opened, and we were in a large – no, huge – space; so large that I couldn't see the darkened end of it. As we stepped forward, lights – presumably activated by movement or body heat – flicked on, and finally, I caught my breath, completely unable to maintain my impassive exterior any longer. Under a glass dome in the center of the room was a bright blue Lycra suit on a shop dummy – figure hugging with a matching mask across the dummy's sightless eyes. I turned to him with amazement and said. "You – you are Priapus?"

"That's me," he said with a wink. "Never think it to look at me would you? A bit of hair gel to darken the hair a little, a mask and a revealing costume and suddenly people see someone else."

We've got used to him now, but this was back when he was a breath of fresh air in the city. Priapus the Pruner appeared from nowhere, dressed in Viagra blue, and from the first night, he was a sexual savior, rescuing two young women from rapists, a young man from a homophobic attack and a boy of eight from his step-father's "little game." In the morning, four men were found on the city hall steps, bound, gagged and so efficiently gelded by his "shears of light" you'd never know that they'd ever had sexual organs at all. He'd turned the predators into Ken dolls, and we loved him for it.

We soon learned, from what little PR he did, that he could sense what he called "Sexual Peril" within a four mile radius, and whilst he couldn't fly he could jump – his body treated our gravity as ours treats the moon's – and he would use the high rise buildings to get around.

Yeah yeah, you know all that, of course. What you don't know about is the night he lost his power.

The shears of light were the key behind it all; people who had been rescued said that once he'd taken the predators out he'd lay them flat, with their legs apart, hold his hands out towards them and – well then the stories vary. Some say laser beams shot from his fingers, others say his palms, some say that actual shears are created from a life force that his body makes. The light is so bright when he gelds them that no one can see for sure. And it's clean, and it's painless. And it's better than the filth deserve, in my opinion.

One thing he's never told me is how he got his powers, and I've never asked of course. From that first day, I just became his butler – with a few additional tasks – and it was no big shift in routine. I had a few extra clothes to look after, a blue motorcycle to service along with the Morgan and the Rolls. What he did at night only affected me when his costumes were ripped or occasionally bloodied. I never asked him about them. I read the newspaper reports and the court convictions – and I cheered along with the rest of the city.

I was in the hideout at seven in the morning when he came back that day, and I'll never forget it. I'd got into the habit of sleeping there, for I was never sure when he'd return, and there were always things needing doing, that he had been doing for himself for too long. Those moments when he returned, tired and dirty, sometimes hurt, were the best times of all, for I undressed him, bathed him and helped him to bed.

When the bike roared down the hidden ramp into the bunker that morning I didn't know how badly things had gone for him until he fell from the bike's saddle the moment he'd propped it up on its stand.

I dropped the tray I was holding and ran to him, picked him up and carried him to the bed, he didn't look injured, but his face was unnaturally pale, his lips bluish. Frantically, I stripped his suit from him, checking for puncture wounds or signs of internal bleeding, but there was nothing. If it had been poison, I would have lost him that morning, and I made a vow right then and there that I would need to have poison kits and antidotes within reach, and know how to use them.

To my great relief, his eyes fluttered open. "I'm all right," he said weakly.

"What is it? What happened?" I felt helpless.

His face twisted as if making a decision. "I guess you know everything else, one more thing – isn't going to hurt."

"You can trust me, sir."

He gave me a strange look then spoke. "Someone said that before. Someone I loved."

My throat was dry. I had to fight my emotion down. I knew that I loved him, had done for many weeks but had not allowed myself to admit it. "Sir?" was all I could manage.

"The last valet I had," he said quietly, "I told him everything."

My heart lurched. He was gay then. I'd hoped, but never dared to think it might be true. "And he let you down." He wasn't a member of my school; that was unheard of.

"More than that. He's Pederast."

I was shocked, then at the mention of the notorious villain. "He knows everything?" I looked anxiously toward the entrance as if expecting him to come barging in with his hordes of black clad supporters behind him.

"He's dead. It's all right," he said "but I've lost my powers, and I can't get them back."

"How?"

"I killed him. Pederast knew it would happen, and he laughed that while I stopped him, I wouldn't be able to stop anyone else. It's a natural law from where we're from. If we kill – anyone. We're from the same ... place, you see."

"Same planet, you mean?"

"There isn't a word for it. Place is easiest." He winced as he tried to sit up, and I helped him, propping pillows behind his back. "We were both cast out at the same time. Me for loving men, and him ..." he made a face.

"... For doing what he does." The thought of the man made me feel ill. Him. And the "elite club" he had formed, "the adoration of the young," he called it. The boys went willingly, ensnared and seduced by the power of Pederast's mind, but it was filthy, no matter how he tried to wrap it up in Greek ideals. He had Websites that moved servers when they were shut down, there were actual meeting places where the members indulged in their "adoration." Priapus had made a crusade of it, focusing his energies on closing it all down, but hydra-like it always seemed to spring back. Close down one den in Bangkok and another two would open in other countries.

I attempted to reassure him, but he was adamant. "I know how this works," he said. "So did Pederast. He chose to die rather than kill me – give up his powers of persuasion and mind control. I chose to give up my powers rather than let him stay here another moment. To let him touch one more child."

"There's nothing you can do?" It seemed magical to me – that powers could be given in the first place, that powers could be lost under certain rules. Surely then, powers could be regained? "Nothing to get them back?"

He was quiet for a long long time, and I knew that there was, even before he spoke, but that it was a price he didn't want to name.

"Tell me," I said. "Please."

"No," he said, finally. "There's such a thing as being too loyal."

"If there's something I can do," I said, a hope rising within me, "then you have to let me do it. You have to."

He shook his head.

"Just tell me, then." The conversation took a long time, and eventually, as the color returned to his face a little, he told me.

"And it has to be a willing sacrifice," he said. "Whatever punishment I chose to exact on the guilty, when I came here from that place, that's what I have to do, to a willing victim. Or my powers are lost forever." He looked so unbearably tragic that my heart burned with love for him. "Don't ask me to do that, not to anyone. And if anyone ... not to you." He looked up at me then, and I knew what he meant.

"You don't have to ask," I said, and I leaned down and kissed him. If I had to do without in the future, then I vowed I'd make use of what I had, before it was taken away.

His skin felt hot under my eager hands, hotter than skin had a right to be; I stretched my fingers wide and seeped the warmth in through my palms, running them up and down his chest, over the hard peaks of his nipples, and down, letting my thumbs trace his hard, sculptured stomach. He tipped his head back, his mouth twitching each time I touched his nipples so I started there, tasting his skin for the first time, as I'd wanted to do for so long, flicking my tongue teasingly over one hard little point, then the other. Then I claimed his mouth, just briefly before learning the remainder of his body with my tongue. That he cried out surprised me, that I, his butler could make him do so startled me. That he rolled over and pushed his ass up in blatant invitation drove me mad with want.

All my reserve, all my repression fell away from me in that moment and fumbling like a schoolboy I grabbed the lube from his nightstand and slicked his beautiful, wanting hole with it, then pushed my cock against him. I wanted to speak, then, but there was nothing I could have said that would express my longing – and yes, just a little fear.

Taking a deep breath, I pushed against him, breaching his hole, and the head of my cock disappeared inside. I tried to hold myself back while I let my body, my mind, relish the sensation. He was mine now – and if it only could be once, then it was enough. I grasped those beautiful narrow hips and clung to him while he looked back at me, his eyes wicked and full of want. I felt a restless desire, knowing that, if I didn't have to pay the price I was going to pay, I'd never be satisfied with normal sex again. Hey, now I'm getting prosaic. He pushed back against me and I'm ashamed to say that I fucked him hard then, unable to hold back, unable to do all the teasing and wonderful things I wanted to do – all I could do was to fuck and fuck until, breathless and empty as a drifting paper bag, I fell against his sweating back and kissed the back of his neck.

I didn't need to pull out – there was nothing of me left to pull out. I'd paid the price, but as he took me in his arms and swore he'd never let me go, I knew I'd serve him, in any way he wanted, for all my days.

#

You don't believe me, do you? Well, has Priapus got his powers back or has he not? Exactly. Still skeptical? Right then, feel, right here. See? As flat as a showroom dummy. Yes, it takes people like that. Do I care? Not really. The plumbing works with care, and for one night I loved a god. Fucked a god. I paid the price for that, and it was one worth paying, and hey – it's not like my sex-life is completely over, after all – it's better to receive than to give, right?

FORGET-ME-NOT
By Logan Zachary

"I don't love you anymore," Tony said.

How my partner's words hit me. The man I loved couldn't have said it.

My cell phone rang.

Tony glared at the offending piece of equipment and nodded at it. "Go ahead, answer it." He dared me. "Like you could ever ignore it. Me, yes, work, no."

I flipped open the phone and said, "Yeah."

"Detective Vance, the First National Bank has been robbed." I recognized the voice of Sam, the dispatch officer.

"I'll be gone by the time you get back." Tony turned his broad back to me and walked out.

My heart ached.

"I'm on my way." I snapped my phone shut as I closed the door to my home and to my heart.

#####

"Detective Vance, I'm Officer Ramsey. We have the guard who was on duty during the crime." The officer at the bank held the door open for me as I entered.

"Where is he?"

"He's back here." Our footsteps echoed across the marble floor as we walked to a room off the bank's main entrance.

As we entered the room, the security guard finished buttoning his uniform shirt.

"A strip search?" I turned to Ramsey, "Already?"

The guard's face flushed red as he straightened his uniform pants.

"Not exactly," the Officer Ramsey said. "Mr. Newman was found naked in the empty bank vault."

I took a deep breath and held it before saying anything. "Where are the surveillance tapes?"

"We're collecting them right now."

"Newman, were you drugged? Were you drinking on duty? What happened?" I asked the guard.
Russell Newman rubbed his head. "I'm not sure, sir. I don't know what happened."
"What do you mean?"
"I was checking the doors with my partner last night, and then the next thing I knew Officer Ramsey was waking me up in the vault."
"Naked," Ramsey added.
I looked at Newman and wished I had arrived sooner. He was tall and muscular. A thick patch of hair disappeared as he buttoned his last shirt button.
"Sir, I don't know what happened last night." Russell pulled his long hair away from his face and stood stock still as he waited for his next order.
"Did anyone run a drug screen? Collect a sample of blood or urine?" I asked.
"Sir, I don't do drugs," Russell started, but stopped.
"Someone could have slipped you something. Where is your partner?"
"My partner?" Confusion played over his face.
Was he still dazed? I turned to Ramsey. "Where can we watch the surveillance tapes?"
Ramsey motioned for Russell to sit, and led me out of the room. "Did you want Russell present for the viewing of the tape or ...?" his voice trailed off.
"I guess we should see them first and then question him. Maybe he'll sweat out a few answers or remember something if we're absent for a while."
"Good idea. I'll bring the tapes into the room at the end of the hall." Ramsey motioned, and I followed.
The boardroom housed a huge table and a wall mounted video screen, which covered most of the wall. It must make for an impressive presentation. I settled dead center of the screen and wished I had a cup of coffee.
As if on cue, the door opened and a tray with muffins, cookies, coffee and orange juice was placed next to me. The bank secretary nodded at it. "The meetings been

canceled since the robbery, so no use letting the food go to waste." She left before I could thank her.

Ramsey returned a few minutes later, two videotapes in his hand. He walked to the video player and slipped one in. He picked up the remote and rewound.

I sipped the steaming coffee and savored the warmth in my hands. A lemon poppy seed muffin sat on a napkin in front of me.

"Where did you get the food?"

"The secretary brought it in."

The tape clicked to a stop, and Ramsey pushed play. Four images appeared in each corner of the screen, covering areas of the bank. One showed the vault, closed and locked, one of the front door, the parking lot, and the lobby.

In one corner, Russell walked down the hall and through the lobby. He checked the front door and looked out into the parking lot. He turned his head and spoke.

Another guard approached him and rubbed his shoulder. Russell pulled away and spoke harshly to him.

"Who's that?" I asked.

Ramsey flipped through a clipboard. "It says that Dominic Stone was on duty with Russell last night."

"But, Russell doesn't remember that?"

"No sir." Ramsey lifted the remote and pushed fast forward. The images sped up; white lines ran through the pictures and little changed in the quadrants without anyone.

Dominic and Russell spoke for a while and walked around on their rounds. After twenty minutes, the corner with the vault camera changed. Ramsey slowed the tape to a normal speed. The huge door slowly opened, and Dominic stood in the entrance. He smiled as he rubbed his hands together. He entered and went about opening drawers and dumping money into a garbage bag.

"Where's Russell?" I asked.

Unmasked II

A shadow filled the door, and he appeared, his gun was drawn and aimed at Dominic. They spoke for a few seconds, and Russell's gun arm lowered.

Dominic walked to him with a wad of money in his hand and kissed him. Russell responded and embraced him. Then Russell pushed him away and started to raise his gun.

"Can we get this for the whole screen?" I asked.

Ramsey used the remote and the four quadrants vanished and turned into one big picture.

As the tape continued, another muscular man entered the vault and filled the doorway. He wore a skin tight blue outfit, covering his six foot frame. A mask covered his face; yellow flower petals surrounded the eye holes. The quality of the picture wasn't perfect, but the details emerged easily. A narrow waist held up broad shoulders. His powerful legs and arms would make any bodybuilder proud.

"What the heck?" Ramsey said.

On the screen, Russell stiffened up and stood frozen as Dominic and the Spandex-wearing-guy emptied the bank vault.

Dominic dragged the bags of money out and didn't return.

The man in the Spandex plucked a small bunch of flowers off of his head and let it fall to the floor. He stepped in front of Russell and gently blew something into his face.

Russell breathed in deeply and smiled as he looked into the man's eyes. He caressed his face and drew it closer to him. His lips puckered as he pulled the masked man's mouth to his. A passionate kiss filled the screen. Russell slowly unbuttoned his uniform shirt, exposing his muscular hairy chest.

The SpandexMan helped open his shirt and gently tossed it to the floor.

Russell loosened his belt and let it and the holster fall to the ground. His fingers worked his zipper down and then unhooked his waistband.

His pants pooled around his feet and his boxers tented in front. The fly opened and revealed a dark thatch of hair. A thick veined cock strained against the cotton as two heavy balls hung down a loose leg opening.

The man in spandex reached between his legs and freed his own bulge. A long thick penis snaked out from his outfit and wrapped around Russell's hairy leg. His hands pushed the boxers down and the waistband followed the furry torso, along the treasure trail and stopped at his thick dark bush. His erection prevented the elastic from slipping down any further.

SpandexMan's mouth moved, saying something to Russell. It looked as if he repeated it over and over again.

Russell smiled as the words washed over him. His boxers fell the rest of the way to the floor, and he stepped out of them. He raised one hairy leg and wrapped it around the man in blue. He rubbed his body up and down.

I saw the static electricity build up between the two men. I felt it run across my body and surge between my legs as my erection pulsated with every heartbeat.

What looked like "Forget-me-not," played over SpandexMan's lips.

We watched as the huge penis slid between Russell's legs.

Russell stood still and then an expression of pure joy took over.

SpandexMan stroked Russell's hard cock as he rocked his hips, driving his penis in and out. He continued to repeat his mantra as he rode deep into his perfect furry bubble butt.

I had to wipe the side of my mouth to prevent drool from running down my face as the screen filled with raw sex.

Russell's eyes rolled back into his head as his body rocked.

SpandexMan increased his speed on Russell's dick and humped his rump, faster and harder. He continued to whisper in his ear.

Unmasked II

Russell's cock exploded and wave after wave of cum shot onto their chests. As his balls emptied, his legs slowly gave way, and he slipped to the floor.

SpandexMan carefully slipped his penis back into his suit and readjusted himself.

Russell smiled as he fell asleep.

The tape continued to play, recording him sleeping.

My cock oozed in my underwear. The wet cotton clung to the tip. I pulled on my groin under the table, pulling the fabric away from my skin.

"What do you think that man did to him?" Ramsey asked.

"A fuck to forget," slipped out of my mouth before I could stop it.

#

I reached into my pocket and pulled out my cell phone. I couldn't wait to tell ... wait ... no.

Tony was gone. He had left me. I had abandoned him many years ago, and now I was alone.

Blindly, I drove home and sat in the driveway, dreading that empty house. No warm light burned inside welcoming me home, no more hearts and flowers.

Flowers ... flowers ... forget-me-nots. The flowers found at the bank and the words the man in Spandex spoke.

The Arboretum.

I backed out of the driveway and headed toward the University. Parking outside the greenhouse, my mind whirled over the events of the day: Tony, Russell, SpandexMan, the surveillance tapes, and forget-me-nots.

A knock on the roof of my car startled me. "May I help you?" a male voice asked before I could open my door.

I turned to see a man in bib overalls, no shirt and one strap undone. The denim hugged his body like a second skin. The blue denim had faded to white in the high stress areas.

Instinctively, my eyes darted down to his inseam and an impressive outline rose from the cotton, rubbed white from time. I looked into his eyes and my heart stopped. The bluest eyes looked back at me. His crystal clear sapphires held me in place. "I'm ... ah, I'm Detective Vance from the Minneapolis Police Department."

The man stepped back as I opened my car door and offered his hand. "I'm Carl. I work here." He motioned over to the greenhouse. "Is there something I can help you with?"

I reached into my pocket and pulled out a small plastic evidence envelope with a blue flower inside. "Do you know what this is?"

Carl took the envelope and looked at it. "That's easy, it's a forget-me-not. They grow all over the place, mostly in the shade."

My heart fell.

Carl must have seen the disappointment in my face. "It looks like you were expecting more information. Come on." He guided me to the greenhouse and held the glass door open.

We walked down rows and rows of flowers and plants, weaving in and out of a maze of tables and benches. Humidity hung in the air as did the rich earthly scent of black dirt and plant life.

"We try to use only natural fertilizers here."

"Are you a student here at University?"

"The biology department has a few labs down here to work on genetics and hybrids."

"Are you a professor here?"

"I teach a few classes, but my main job is research. I'm studying the medicinal properties of plants." He stopped in front of a table covered with forget-me-nots. He held the bag close to several plants and shook his head. "See how your flower is finer, more delicate than these prairie strains."

I leaned forward and saw the difference.

He moved down the line and held it up to a few more plants. "Wrong shade. Wrong arrangement." He stepped back and looked at the flower. "How important is this?"

"A bank was robbed, and that was the only clue left at the scene."

"Follow me," he said as he walked down the row to the back room. He twisted the handle that looked as if it should be on a submarine. Slowly, the bolts retracted. "This is my research lab." He pulled the hatch door open and stepped back.

I hesitated as I entered. What kind of plants needed to be locked up? What was he going to do? Feed me to the plants?

Growth lights illuminated the lab. He guided me to a workbench covered with plants. He placed the envelope next to them, and they were a perfect match.

"There are many legends about the forget-me-nots, from God naming all plants and almost forgetting this one, to the flowers calling out to Adam and Eve as they left the Garden of Eden. Even the Christ child, in the hope that the world would remember Mary's eyes, waved his hand over the flowers and they turned blue. The most romantic comes from medieval lore. A knight was walking with his lover by the river before battle and slipped into the water. As his armor pulled him down, he threw the flowers he carried to her and yelled, "Forget-me-not," before he drowned."

Carl turned to face me and caressed the side of my face. His other hand rose and slipped the strap off his shoulder. "My research is on memories, how we can use these flowers to get rid of bad memories."

His bibs slipped down his torso and rested on his hips. "Your guard last night was betrayed by his lover when he robbed the bank. He took off and abandoned him ..."

A jolt of lightning shot through me. This was the man from the bank's videotape. SpandexMan.

"... just as your lover left you sad and empty." He unbuttoned my shirt, reached in, and caressed my hairy chest. "But I helped him forget his lover's betrayal, and I can help you." His hand slid down my abs and combed along my treasure trail to my jeans. His fingers probed the waistband. He unzipped my fly and worked the button.

My erection swelled and burst forth as the pressure of my jeans released.

His mouth sought mine and our lips touched. A soft gentle kiss played between us as his hand found my underwear's waistband.

I took a deep breath in as his tongue and hand entered at the same time. His wet tongue tasted mine, fresh mint exploded in my mouth, as his fingers trailed along my sensitive tip. He grasped my shaft and stroked me down to the root and cupped my dangling balls. As his fingers worked up my length, he milked my sap out. Precum oozed out, and he spread it over my mushroom head.

My hands caressed down his torso and pushed his bibs lower, below his waist. His beautiful body was chiseled and perfect. He wore a pair of bright yellow bikini briefs. He slipped off his shoes and kicked the bibs away as he pulled me closer.

My body wrapped around his in a tight embrace.

Tony.

Carl felt the change in my body. His foot pulled down my pants. We stood underwear to underwear. His eyes scanned my body and his mouth worked down my neck, along my furry pec and devoured my nipple.

I'm all alone.

He stood up. My pelvis plowed into his body, erection to erection, hard-on to hard-on. I grabbed onto his tight ass and ground against him.

He buried his face into my neck again as he nibbled my ear.

"Forget-me-not," he said.

I threw my head back and savored his touch. Turning my head to the side, I found his lips and kissed him. Our tongues hedged against each other and passion bloomed. Desire flowed from me to him and back into me.

I was cheating on Tony.

No, he abandoned me. I abandoned him.

His hands dug into my briefs and pushed them off my butt. His fingers kneaded my gluts as his pinkies started to push down the front of my underwear.

My pubic hair crackled with static electricity as the elastic pulled down over my bush. My penis sprang free and my balls swung back and forth. The cotton fell to the floor, and I stepped out of them.

He pushed me back against the workbench and helped my ass onto the top. He kissed down my chest and trailed his tongue lower. He circled my navel as his stubbly chin brushed my tender tip. He gave me a whisker rub, sending painful pleasure through my very root.

His mouth worked lower. His tongue explored the slit at the end.

Precum flowed out of me and onto his tongue. His tongue collected the ooze and spread it along my hard shaft as he swallowed me whole. His five o'clock shadow bristled over my balls.

I ground my cock deep into his throat.

Drool and precum flowed down my shaft and cascaded over my balls. A small pool formed on the workbench. My ass slipped closer to the edge.

Carl's mouth released my dick, and he spread my legs wider. His tongue tickled my balls, sucking one at a time into his mouth. He rolled them gently between his teeth and tried to swallow them.

My hands combed through his curly hair as I guided his head.

He pulled my ass closer to the edge and spread my cheeks. His hot tongue touched my opening and dug in. Saliva lubed me up as he sought entry. I relaxed my sphincter. His tongue plowed into me. His hot, wet tongue filled my tight hole. I threw my head back and enjoyed the ride.

"Forget-me-not."

I rode his tongue, willing it in further, deeper. My balls drew up alongside my dick. Tingles and waves pulsated along my cock. Carl's hand stroked me as he continued to work my ass. My balls threatened to unload.

Carl sensed my approaching climax and slowly pulled out of me and stood. He helped me to my feet. He stood in front of me, legs wide apart, and underwear straining to their limit.

I looked at his erection and rubbed it through the shear cotton. A wet spot spread over the cloth, making it see-through. His huge cock sprang out as I pushed his underwear down. His dick stood straight out in front of him. Facing him, my hand grasped his shaft and massaged it. It seemed to swell and lengthen in my hand. He rocked his hips, and his hard-on slipped between my legs. It rubbed against my balls and snaked between my cheeks. Its thick tip dove deeper and tickled my tender opening.

My body pressed against his, demanding more. My hole wanted him inside me. I kissed him deeper and wrapped my arms around him, holding him closer, trying to become one.

Carl's body reminded my heart that it ached from losing Tony, and then he entered me with a swift thrust. The precum and saliva made for easy access and my desire sucked him in. His cock gently explored as his tongue had, but his dick slipped in deeper and thicker.

My ass milked his cock and demanded more. "Harder," I whispered.

Images of Tony's naked body flashed into sharp focus in my mind. His huge cock, his washboard abs, his furry bubble butt. "I don't love you anymore." The vivid memories burned on my retinas, and then, the details faded, the color bleached out into black and white, and disappeared, forever.

Carl plowed into me again. His thick cock burrowed deep, stretching and filling me.

"Faster," I demanded as I pressed down onto him. My cock grated against his abs. My dick combed through his hair.

Unmasked II

    Tears slipped down my face as memories of Tony flooded my mind. His body, his kisses, his laugh ...
    Carl's handsome smile, sexy body, full dick, and twinkle in his eye, burned in my memory.
    My balls exploded. Cum spurted out over Carl's muscular chest and my ass clamped down on his cock.
    Carl's dick exploded inside me, filling me with him, filling the empty Tony place forever.
    My whole body felt invaded. His white hot load tingled deep inside. It seemed to have fingers that stretched out and radiated through all my senses. The tendrils wove their way into my mind, curling around Tony and all my images and memories of him. They wrapped around them and held him tight.
    Carl moved away, withdrawing his still hard cock. It sprang free and slapped against his torso.
    I reeled in the afterglow.
    He knelt down and brought his mouth to my tender opening. He slipped his tongue in with easy access. His mouth formed a seal around my hole as his tongue burrowed in. He sucked on me, as his tongue held me open. The tendrils of cum still held tight to the memories of Tony in my mind. He drew down harder, and I felt them slowly start down my spine and from every nerve fiber in my body. Carl continued to drink, pulling all of what he put into me, out.
    Images faded from my mind. I couldn't remember what Tony looked like.
    I couldn't remember ... something important.
    Flashes of my life flew by, faster, faster.
    I ... Tony ... Bank robbery ... Blue Spandex ...
    The sensory overload racked my body, and the world went black.

#####

    The phone's ringing woke me up, and I struggled to remember what had happened last night.
    "Hello," my voice croaked.

"Ramsey here. The tape from yesterday is blank."

"What?" My mind tried to focus. Bank robbery, naked guard, and ...

"I'm not sure what they did downtown, but the tape is blank. Did you find out anything at the Arboretum last night?"

I swung my legs out and over the side of the bed. Naked. I never slept naked. I pulled the sheet over my lap and felt my body flush talking to Ramsey as if he could see me through the phone.

"Sir, you sound happy this morning."

I thought for a moment. I did feel great. I knew I was missing something as I scanned the other side of the bed, a glimmer of someone flickered in my mind, and then it was gone. "Just had a great night's sleep."

"No need to hurry in today; we have nothing to work on." And Ramsey signed off.

I padded to the bathroom and looked out into the backyard as I stood at the toilet.

A man was planting flowers outside. He looked up as he caught my glance.

I grabbed my robe and went into the backyard. "Morning," I called.

"Morning Vance, I'm glad you're up." He gently planted a bunch of small blue flowers into the dirt. He wiped his hands on his pants and stood. He stepped over to me and touched my robe.

My body responded immediately.

He smiled, "Well, I'm done. The flowers are planted."

"Want to come inside for a cup of coffee?" I asked.

He bent over and pinched off a small sprig and handed it to me. "Forget-me-not?"

CAPTAIN VELVET DOWN UNDER
By Ryan Field

Ross was a man who had always been highly underestimated, is how he would have described himself. After college he went straight to New York. First he got a job in advertising, then he was discovered by a producer of adult films: all male videos that brought him extra money and more orgasms than he'd ever expected.

His stage name was Captain Velvet, a superhero with exceptional anal powers that could bring all men to their knees. He wore a mask and kept his anonymity. He missed sleep to balance his advertising career with his film career. Some nights, he didn't sleep at all. He didn't mind the dark circles under his eyes or the accidental yawns at three in the afternoon. When word got around that his ass was a tight, steel trap lined with velvet, men from all over the world fantasized about tagging his hole. And for five years, he worked hard to please them all.

Then life changed. He went back to his dreary hometown to open a small advertising firm of his own, so he could take care of his aging mother. He moved to Martha Falls, MD, a small, square hamlet about fifty miles outside of Baltimore, and a million miles away from any hint of the lifestyle he'd known in New York. He put his film career behind him and settled into the banal, uninspired existence of caregiver, and didn't bother to leave again until a week after her funeral.

He was in his thirties by then, but looked more like twenty-five; an only child who had been left with the responsibility of dealing with Alzheimer's. He could have put her in a nursing home. But he didn't.

Though many of his nights were spent rubbing the clenched fists of his mother's boney hands, and softly explaining to her there was no need to rant about being lost and afraid, there had also been plenty of free time to work out with weights in the basement and run endless miles on

Unmasked II

the treadmill in his childhood bedroom. While saving his sanity with exercise, Ross developed strong, solid legs that led upward to a lean, tight waist. His hard chest muscles popped out after bench presses; when he squeezed his arms across his chest, a thin line of muscle cleavage made his dick grow long and hard. It wasn't unusual for him to masturbate in front of the faded workout mirror against the dusty cinderblock wall and fantasize about his former life in New York.

Two or three times a year, he'd make sure his mother was slightly over medicated and sleeping soundly, and then he'd sneak off to a highway rest stop for a little safe action. The married men on the down low liked to tug his soft reddish-brown hair when he kneeled on the pavement and blew them in pubic; the way the closeted young guys in college were always in such a hurry to pull his pants down and bend him over the hood of a car made him smile when he was alone in bed at night. He liked spreading his legs and submitting to them; the exhibitionist in him couldn't resist their hungry stares and heavy breathing. After they fucked him and discovered his velvet hole, many asked if he was a professional male stripper. In the summer months, he sometimes undressed, got out of his car and walked slowly into the woods, knowing all too well the guys who had been sitting alone in parked cars couldn't resist following him.

A week after his mother died, he phoned his old producer and mentioned that he'd be interested in making films again. He missed the attention and the action; he craved his old Captain Velvet costume. The sheer, see-through, black cape and the black velvet hood that completely covered his face made his lips quiver. And, the outrageous black leather boots made his heart beat fast. They were black Hyde and mid-calf, with hard chrome trim and six-inch Cuban style heels. The chrome-tipped toes pointed like arrows. And, when he pointed his toes in the air while a group of hot guys fucked him in those boots, he saw streaks of lightening.

Eric Summers

The producer said they were shooting a film in Australia in a month; he could make a guest appearance as Captain Velvet. But, he had to pay all his own expenses because it was such short notice. It was a very small part, but it could lead to bigger things. When he agreed to go, he hung up the phone and took a long, deep breath. He hadn't had a vacation in a long time; he hadn't been out of Martha Falls in years, and he'd never been out of the country.

This film was being shot in the most exotic place he could find on the map: Cairns, in the heart of Tropical North Queensland, which is Australia's primary gateway to the Great Barrier Reef Islands. There were tropical dreamlands there, with names like Lizard Island and Green Island. He was so tired of jerking off in the mirror; he was bored with the frustrating routine at the rest stop (on a good night two or three guys would nail him; but most of the time he sat there alone in the darkness waiting for dick that never came). Cairns looked like the kind of vibrant, eclectic city he needed to visit in order to stay sane. Oh, he'd been dreaming about a trip like this for some time. His heart raced at the thought of walking the reef island beaches at twilight in nothing but a skimpy Speedo while other men stared at his smooth legs and round ass; his cock pitched a tent when he imagined all those hot, hairy-legged Australian men in rowing shorts. The thought of traveling to such a far off paradise to bring back his role of Captain Velvet not only stimulated his intellect, but also stirred his starved libido.

The day he arrived in Cairn the sun was bright and a balmy breeze blew the lush, green palms toward the bluest sky he'd ever seen. But, more than that, the young man who escorted him up to his room was dark and beefy and hairy. He wore white short pants and you could see the outline of his dick; a thick portion of meat pressed to the right. Just the sort of guy he preferred; a complete opposite to his smooth body. "Are you a native?" Ross asked.

"Oh yes, I am that," said the young man. "An authentic island boy, I am." His accent was unmistakably

Aboriginal English. It was very similar to Australian English but distinct in certain ways. No mention of the "h" sound, and when the young man said "that" it sounded more like "dot."

Ross smiled. He didn't care how the little island cutie sounded. "Can you recommend some of the local attractions?" The guy was so hot Ross had to bite his bottom lip and turn toward the window.

"Oh, yes sir. You must sign up for a four-wheel-drive day trip to the Daintree Forest. It is magical." He became animated, his voice rose with a lilt. "The temperature there is always around 85 degrees, and it's never too hot because all the greens create a canopy of shade."

Ross smiled again. "How do I do that?"

"Ah well, this is your lucky day, man," he said. His dark brown eyes were wide; he began to wave his hand in the air and a bicep jumped from his upper arm. "Two of my friends and me, we just started our own very nice tour of the forest. You can be one of the first good customers."

Ross laughed. The cute little guy couldn't have been more than twenty-five years old, but he had all the moxy of a fifty-year-old. "How much does this cost?"

"Very cheap. Two hundred American dollars," he said. "And, my friends and me, we know how to take real good care of good looking American men."

Ross' eyes bugged, and he smiled so wide you could see his upper gums. The young man had just paid him a rather blunt compliment. He liked that. "I see. I have something important to do tomorrow, but the next day I'm free," he said. He was due on the film set, but his appearance was so small it was only one day, and he was free to do what he wanted after that.

"Nine o'clock the day after tomorrow," he said, "We will be waiting in front of the hotel for you."

#####

He was glad he'd made plans to do other things, because the film turned out to be a huge disappointment. It was a cliché Australian outback rip-off, and a couple of the actors were so young and nervous they couldn't even get hard. This film didn't have a storyline, and they worked Captain Velvet in at the very end as a set up for future films. It was campy at best. The producer said that if he was serious about coming out of retirement for at least two years, he'd do a series of new films in the future that were all based on Captain Velvet. He smiled and did his best that day; he'd been out of the business for a long time, and he didn't want to piss anyone off. He wanted to make more films, and if this was what he had to do to get there, he was willing and able.

And, it turned out that his small part was the best scene in the film. When he crossed onto the set in his Captain Velvet costume and the other guys saw him, their dicks grew, they licked their lips and went right to work. When one of the younger, nervous actors saw his ass, his cock grew four times its size. They took turns fucking him over a broken fence. When they lifted his cape in the air and mounted his ass, their eyes rolled and their tongues fell out. His hole was still that same tight, velvet trap; it could still suck big juicy cocks to wild climaxes. They couldn't get enough, and he couldn't spread his legs wide enough for them.

Later that night while resting in bed, Ross remembered his plans for Daintree Forrest. But, he had second thoughts about all this four-wheel-drive business now. He'd said yes so impulsively just because he liked the way the dark little guy looked in short pants. What if these guys took him out to some remote rainforest, robbed him and left him there to die? What if they stole his wallet and wristwatch and stabbed him to death? What if he disappeared, and no one heard from him again? But, he eventually fell into a deep, heavy sleep, and when he woke the next morning, he decided he'd worried enough in the past few years.

So, he put on a skimpy black, mesh tank top to show off his chest, a tight pair of white shorts to show off his ass, and heavy black boots just in case there was any walking to do. Then he pulled six bottles of cold water from the hotel mini bar and dropped them into his nap sack; he snapped a baseball cap to the shoulder strap. The only money he brought was the fee for the tour; everything else of value he shoved into the hotel safe.

As promised, the little guy was leaning against an ancient four wheel drive outside the hotel entrance with his arms folded and his legs crossed. He wanted to get down on his knees there in the driveway and start licking his ankles. A tall dark man sat behind the steering wheel on the right side of the front seat, and someone Ross couldn't see because the rear windows were tinted was sitting in the back seat. When the little guy saw Ross, he jumped forward and opened the back door immediately.

Ross lowered his eyebrows and stared at the boxy SUV. There were dents in the fenders, the off-white paint was faded and chipped, and the right side of the rear end sloped downward. The tires were massive; you had to jump up on the running board and climb inside. "Are you sure this thing is safe?" he asked.

"This is so safe; drives like a dream, man," he said. He motioned for him to get into the car, and said, "My name is Abim; it means ghost. You have the two hundred bucks, yes?"

Ross struggled to reach into his tight shorts to pull out the money. He noticed Abim staring at his hairless legs; the young guy's eyes were wide, and he puckered his lips as though he were about to whistle. "My name is Ross," he said, and then handed Abim the cash.

"Nice short pants, Ross," he said. "Most Americans don't look so good in them."

He laughed. "Oh really." He was glad he'd shaved his entire body that morning. He'd shaved it the day before for the film, but he liked being smooth all over just in case.

"We better get going," Abim said, "Get ready for the tour of your lifetime, Ross."

He climbed into the back seat, and Abim closed the door. While Abim walked around the back of the truck to get into the passenger seat up front, the driver started the engine, and a tall young man in the back seat whipped out a huge dick and said, "You like banana?"

His eyes widened. "Ah well …" His brown dick was long; the head was covered with foreskin.

Abim was in the car by then and shouted, "Put that thing away. You'll scare him!" Then he shook his head and looked back at Ross; when he said "thing" it sounded like "ding." "I'm so sorry, man. He's new with this tour. He means no harm. His name is Bambra, which means mushroom."

Ross wanted to say, "That's okay, I like banana a lot," but he simply smiled and nodded at Bambra. His name suited him well; when he pulled the foreskin back, the head of his cock reminded him of a nice fresh mushroom top.

Abrim sighed and then motioned the driver to get moving. "And this is Keli, which means dog. He will be our driver today. He's very strong and very good; he knows the tropical rainforest with his eyes closed."

Ross looked at the driver. He certainly was a large man; his head nearly hit the ceiling of the SUV. And his skin was ebony and smooth. "It's nice to meet you, Keli."

Keli nodded. He clearly wasn't much of a talker.

But then, no one really had much of an opportunity to speak with Abim in the car. He spoke endlessly, explaining the town of Cairn, how to get to the Great Barrier Reef and how to avoid being eaten by a "croc." His voice went high, with run-on sentences, and the more he spoke, the more he left behind the aboriginal English accent. Ross wondered how anyone could speak so much without taking a breath. But while Abim rambled on about how the Rainforest was over one hundred and thirty-five million years old, and 430 species of birds lived among the trees, Bambra whipped out his dick again and started to jerk it with slow, steady motions. Ross's eyes bugged out, and he pretended to stare out the window, as though he hadn't noticed anything unusual, but it was awfully difficult to keep his eyes off the nine-inch cock of a good looking young guy who was just waving it in his face.

A few minutes later, Abim said, "I think Bambra likes you, Ross. I think he wants to play."

Bambra smiled. "You like Banana, Ross?" He spread his dark hairy legs wider and leaned back in the seat; his dick stuck out of his shorts like a flagstaff.

Keli, the driver, covered his mouth and laughed.

Ross hesitated. But Abim said, "Go ahead."

That's when Ross leaned to his left, rested his body against the wide backseat and said, "Oh yeah, I like banana."

And as they entered the Daintree Rainforest, he began to suck the sweet brown banana. Bambra hadn't showered that morning, and his cock tasted a bit cheesy, but that didn't stop Ross from slurping the entire shaft all the way down his throat. His lips rubbed against the young man's wiry pubic hair; he could smell the watered down vinegar aroma of his balls. When they passed another group of tourists taking photos of a magnificent waterfall that was set back in an alcove of lush green palms, the only thing Ross saw was the head of Bambra's dick oozing with precum. When he licked a drop with the tip of his tongue, it occurred to him that he probably wouldn't see much of the Daintree Forest at all that day.

Abim leaned over the front seat to watch Ross sucking off Bambra. Then he poked Keli and said, "I think our friend Ross might like some more banana."

Keli laughed while Abim threw his legs over the front seat and climbed into the back and kneeled down on the floor. Without looking up from sucking Bambra's dick, Ross reached around and grabbed Abim's crotch. Abim smiled and unzipped his shorts; he spread his hairy legs and put his hands on his hips while Ross reached into the young man's pants and wrapped his hand around a thick, chunky erection. It wasn't as long as Bambra's dick, but it was also uncut and thick. It reminded him of the last time he drank beer from a can. These guys were hot; it's too bad they hadn't been on the film set with him. They would have loved Captain Velvet.

The driver made a quick left turn and drove down a dark, unpaved one-lane road. He drove well, avoiding bumps and holes. Ross looked up from sucking Bambra and asked, "Where are we going?" His lips were puffy now; his chin was wet with his own saliva.

"I have a friend who has a small villa here in the rainforest," Abim said. "We can park there, and no one will bother us." Then he reached forward, grabbed Ross by the back of the head, and pushed his puffy lips to his cock. "See if you like my banana, too."

Ross had to open his mouth as wide as it would go in order to take Abim's cock through his lips and down his throat. He closed his eyes and started to moan when Abim's shaft rested on his tongue; his cheekbones indented and his lips went soft and spongy. While he sucked, he grabbed Bambra's cock with his left hand and started to jerk it off; he placed his right palm on Abim's hairy thigh for support.

When the truck came to a stop, Abim grabbed the back of Ross' head. Ross looked up with innocent blue eyes. "Let me help you take off your clothes, Ross," Abim said.

Ross sat up and looked around to see where they were parked. His hair was sticking up in the back and there were beads of sweat dripping down from his temples. The truck faced a magnificent wall of exotic green shrubs: bushes with spiked palms, tall trees with wide symmetrical leaves, and prickly round ground cover layered the edges of the driveway. Every so often a hint of red or yellow or purple popped from the green. When he looked out the back window of the truck, set up higher on several layers of carefully placed rocks, he saw a small wooden villa that reminded him of a tree house. A natural waterfall, with perfectly placed rocks, ran downhill along the left side of the villa; Abim rolled down his window, and Ross could hear the water rush down the slope.

"Don't worry; no one is here," Abim said. "This place is totally private."

Ross raised his eyebrows and smiled. Abim laughed while he pulled off his black mesh shirt and slid the short pants down his legs; he wasn't wearing underwear. Then Ross pulled off his heavy black boots and white socks. Keli, who was watching the strip show from the front seat, rubbed his hands together and licked his lips. When he was completely naked, Bambra ran his wide palm across Ross' smooth thigh. Bambra's brown eyes were now as wide; he was fascinated by all that smooth, fair skin. Abim slipped his hand up Ross' other thigh and rested it on the small of his back. It occurred to Ross that neither of the young men was reaching for his dick, and that he was surrounded by dominant types who were only interested in his ass. He knew they were in for a nice, unexpected surprise.

So he spread his pretty legs for the guys, arched his back so his ass would be in the air, and leaned over the front seat. Keli's uncut dick was hanging out of his jeans by then. Ross bent all the way over the seat and slipped it down his throat. It was as long as Bambra's, and about as wide as Abim's, with a slight curve. It tasted salty, as though he'd wrapped a slice of bacon around the shaft. When he started to suck off Keli, both Abim and Bambra leaned forward and began to play with the backs of his legs and his ass. Bambra licked and nibbled; Abim turned his large hand sideways, pressed his fingers together and shoved the pinky side of his hand up the crack Ross' ass lengthwise. Ross spread his legs wider; his toes curled against the back seat. He continued to gulp and suck, while Keli held the back of his head and Abim's hand pressed against his ass crack.

When Abim removed his hand, both he and Bambra began to spread Ross' ass cheeks wider. Bambra licked the pink hole first; Ross moaned when the young man's rough stubble brushed against his tender skin. Then Abim took his turn. He buried his face between his ass cheeks and shoved the tip of his tongue into the pinkness. A moment later, Bambra placed both palms on his ass, spread his cheeks as wide as they would go, and Abim shoved his middle finger all the way up his wet ass.

Ross stopped sucking and gripped the steering wheel. His eyes began to roll and his mouth fell open. When Abim saw how well he was reacting to the finger fuck, he looked at Bambra, shrugged his shoulders, and stuck two more fingers up his sweet ass.

"Ah yes, deeper guys," Ross whispered.

"You like?" Abim asked. He was biting his bottom lip and watching his own fingers probe Ross' hole.

"Can we go outside, guys?" Ross asked. He wanted them to take turns on him against the rocks in the stream; he wanted to get nailed hard and fast in this special tropical paradise.

"Ah well, but not too far," Abim said. "We can go out, but not too far from the truck. You never know if the tourists will be walking around. This is private property, but they don't always care."

Ross nodded yes, and then he climbed into the back seat while Abim opened the rear door.

Abim got out first. "Here, let me help you." Though he was short, his strength was amazing. He reached up into the truck, grabbed Ross by the waist and lifted him down gently on the dirt driveway. Ross held his wide shoulders for support; his legs were a bit wobbly from being spread wishbone style for so long. "There you go, babycakes. You're never going to forget this tour."

Ross smiled. He knew they weren't going to forget his velvet hole either.

Bambra and Keli got out of the truck and stood on either side of Abim. Ross was the only one completely naked; the others were still fully clothed, but their dicks were still sticking out of their pants. These guys were ready to pounce: their dark pupils were dilated, their legs were spread wide, and they bounced on the balls of their feet.

Unmasked II

"We don't get too many good looking American guys like you," Abim said, "I think Bambra and Keli want to have a go at you first."

Ross smiled; he knew what these boys needed. "Just let me get some condoms from my bag in the truck."

He bent over slowly, so they could stare at his ass, pulled three condoms from his back pack, and then handed one to each young man. While they opened the small packets, Ross slowly walked to a grassy area about thirty feet from the truck and stretched his arms all the way in the air. Keli walked up from behind, grabbed him by the waist and pulled him down slowly. When Ross was on his hands and knees, he spread his legs and arched his back again. Keli spit down on his dick and pressed the tip to Ross' hole. Keli was awkward and his dick was large. As he shoved it into Ross' ass, there was a moment of shooting pain – but only a moment. Ross took a deep breath, sighed and then started to back into Keli's dark cock. He squeezed his anal lips; Keli's eyes bugged and his head rolled in circles. He kept moaning, "Ah, Ah, yes, yes ..."

Abim and Bambra stood beside them and watched. When they saw the expression of pure delight on their friend's face, they looked at each other and raised their eyebrows. They held their condom covered erections while Keli started to buck and pound Ross into the grass; it didn't take long before Ross was flat on his stomach. Keli was a strong boy; he nailed him to the green damp carpet. He fucked hard and fast, and he blew a full load of seed into the tip of the condom quickly.

Ross clutched a rock with his right hand and spread his legs wider when Keli pulled out. Keli's legs were trembling and his face was red. Of course Ross was paying for the tour, but he knew these guys were having a good time, too. When Keli pulled the condom off, he stared at the other two and said in English, "This is good."

Bambra was next; he didn't need any lube to get inside. Ross' hole was already open and ready for action. He fucked with a distinct rhythm, as though he were pounding away to the minute waltz. One, two, three ... bam, was how it went. Ross opened his mouth and bent his legs at the knees. His toes curled and his eyes rolled. Bambra's hard fucking caused his dick to rub against the grass. Keli had been so silent. When he came, he simply grunted and bucked faster. But when Bambra reached orgasm, he started to shout, "Ah ... Ah ... yes ... here goes. Fucking unreal ... it's so soft and tight." Ross felt the cotton fabric of Bambra's short pants rub against the backs of his thighs. Bambra went deep and shouted: "Fuuuuck!"

He didn't pull out right away; he wanted to linger inside the velvet trap as long as he could. He fell on top of Ross' naked body and whispered, "Ah, that's nice, man. You're so soft inside I could stay forever." And then he slowly began to buck, so he could squeeze out the last few drops of cum.

But Abim kicked Bambra in the leg. "Get off now; it's my turn, man. You've been in there long enough."

Bambra pulled out and Ross smiled. What more could a nice looking guy from Martha Falls want? He had two hot young boys with aboriginal accents fighting for a turn to fuck him.

Abim shoved Bambra out of the way and gave him a nasty look. Then he went down on the grass, ran his hand across Ross' ass and guided his cock to the opening. By then his velvet hole was like a vacuum ready to suck up anything long and hard. But when Abim's extra thick dick entered the pink tunnel, Ross thought he saw a white light. Though the other two men had been good fucks, Abim clearly had the advantage with his girth. It literally filled him to the point of losing consciousness; the sensation of fullness began at the lips of his hole and spread all the way up his ass to that special spot where his orgasms usually began.

"Ah, Abim," Ross said, "Go deeper man, please."

Abim smiled. "This is the sweetest, softest hole I've ever fucked. It reminds me of these videos I once saw about this Captain Velvet."

Unmasked II

Ross clamped down on his cock as hard as he could, then he made the lips of his hole suck the shaft as if he were jerking him off with his ass. He didn't want to let down a fan of Captain Velvet. He had no idea anyone even knew about Captain Velvet in Australia.

Abim's breathing grew heavy and drops of sweat fell from his forehead. He fucked him slowly and sporadically at first. He'd pull all the way out, shove it in deeply, and then repeat that two or three times. And just when Ross was ready for another plunge, Abim would bury his cock all the way in and hammer his pelvis against his ass cheeks.

But Abim was so overcome by the powers of his hole, he was just like the other guys. He wanted to come fast. And when he started to really pummel away, it wasn't like Bambra's waltz-fuck. His fucking rhythm was more like the beat of a disco drum, and it looked as though he were doing pushups in fast forward motion. The harder he fucked the closer Ross came to blowing his own load. Abim's hands were on either side of his head by then. Ross leaned to the left and began to suck one of Abim's thick fingers while the young guy continued to smash him into the grass.

"Ah, Abim," Ross said, "I'm so close. Harder, yes!"

The other two guys were still watching, but they'd already shoved their dicks back into their pants. Keli was tapping his foot and looking at his watch.

Abim didn't say a word. He started to grunt; another drop of sweat fell from his temple onto Ross' back. The ass thumping grew more intense.

"Ah, yes," Ross shouted. His head was bouncing and he expanded his arms as far as they would go. This was good dick; better than he'd had in a long time.

Abim gave one hard stab and they both came together. Ross could actually feel Abim's chunky dick head swell and blow through the latex condom; he knew Abim felt his hole constrict and twitch when his ass exploded into an orgasm.

A moment later, the young man rested his body against Ross' back and sighed. His dirty black boot brushed against Ross' leg and he whispered, "I never felt ass like that."

Ross clamped down on his dick and held it tightly. He could make the muscles inside his hole feel just like a hand. "Can I make you my official tropical tour-guide for as long as I'm here?"

"We'll take you anywhere you want to go, mate," Abim said. Then he laughed. "With a hot fucking pussy hole like that, we'll fuck you for free."

Though he was still nailed to the grass, and a big dick was still buried up his ass, Ross distinctly noticed that Abim's accent had all but disappeared. He sounded Australian, but not at all aboriginal. "Hey Abim," Ross whispered, "What happened to your island boy accent?"

Abim smiled, and then reached around and grabbed a handful of Ross' chest muscle. "That's for the tourists. My real name is Bobby, and I was born in Sydney. And Bambra is Mike, and Keli is really Tommy. The Americans and English love it, all the stereotypes. And, they really don't know whether the accent is Jamaican or Aborigine. Sometimes I'm not sure myself. I hope you're not disappointed."

Ross smiled. "Not at all, Bobby. I've got a little secret of my own to tell you." He couldn't wait to see the expression on his handsome young face when he told him he was really the authentic Captain Velvet.

LOVING CALVIN PANARO
By Jamie Freeman

I step up to the podium and I am instantly blinded by the barrage of lights, popping, flashing, and pulsing in front of me. This was a bad idea, I think, shuffling the papers in front of me and looking up into the lights.

"Good evening, ladies and gentlemen. I have a short prepared statement then I will take your questions." I feel my eyes watering, and I'm thankful that I have rehearsed the statement so thoroughly because I can no longer see the paper between my shaking fingers. As my eyes adjust, I look around and can see four, no five members of the Council security team, three in costume and two holding cameras at either side of the stage. I look out and my eyes meet Stefan's. He is in costume, The White Eagle, standing quietly near the rear door, arms bulging beneath sleek white Kevlar. His expression is stony, but I hear his voice in my head, 'It's OK, Mark,' he assures me, 'you're doing fine.' A fitting tribute to a fallen comrade.

I finish my prepared statement and look up at the crowd. Eyes clear, breath even, hands lightly touching the sides of the podium.

There are a few questions about how Eveningstar died, the wounds, the sequence of events, the current whereabouts of the Jackal and Pandora, the health status of the Secretary General and President Obama. Then one of the FOX reporters asks whether Eveningstar prayed before he went into battle.

"I'm afraid only he could have told us that," I say curtly.

"Steve," I acknowledge the CNN reporter with a nod. He's covered the Council for a decade. I'm hoping he'll go easy on this solemn occasion.

"Yes, Mark, would you please comment on the rumors that Nicholas Eveningstar was romantically involved with Athena the Huntress."

"Sorry, Steve, that one is just a rumor. He was close friends with Athena for years, and, as you know, co-chaired the organization with her for five years after September 11th, but the relationship was purely platonic."

"Don," I point to the reporter from *Entertainment Tonight*.

"Is it true that Rupert Everett is being considered for the role of Eveningstar in the DreamWorks bio-pic?"

"Yes, I understand Mr. Spielberg is interested in Rupert for the role. Nothing definite yet though."

"Margaret," I point to blonde from the local CBS affiliate.

"Would you care to comment on the more widespread rumors that Nicholas Eveningstar was, in fact, gay?"

I am prepared for this question, of course, but as I look into Margaret's dark brown eyes, I hesitate.

# # # # #

I first formally met Calvin in 1987, but I'd seen him around the city on and off for several months without ever realizing he was the masked figure whose heroics we all followed in the papers and on TV.

I was fresh out of college, my expensive journalism degree stuffed in a box of clippings, short stories, and poetry I'd shoved in a corner of the tiny closet of my efficiency apartment. My dreams barely sustained me through an underpaid internship at the *Metro Voice* and two separate bartending gigs. I was running around with a couple of junior reporters from CNN and my roommate Glen, a friend from college who had landed a gig in the press office at the Council of Superheroes. We spent late nights dancing and early mornings making excuses for being late to work. When I had an hour between jobs or when I could sneak away from my internship for a while, I'd haunt the Kent Baths down on 3rd Avenue. Glen's boyfriend Davey worked the door and would let me in for free if the place wasn't too crowded and if his boss wasn't around.

Eric Summers

The first time I saw Calvin at the Kent, he was coming out of the showers, his body glistening with water, dark fur slick against the muscles, rock hard nipples peeking out from his pecs. He was sweeping a towel around his body, but in the moment I saw him, time became distorted and slowed to a crawl. The towel swung in a slow arc around his side, long muscular legs stepping solidly through the doorway. His enormous cock lay nestled in a dark tangle, pendulous balls sliding along his thigh as his legs moved. By the time the towel finally wrapped around him, concealing his perfection from my astonished eyes, he was looking directly at me. His dark eyes glinted with an electric power I took for angelic annoyance. I jumped back against the wall, letting him pass, large perfectly formed feet and legs propelling him down the hallway, the wet towel molded tightly to his perfect ass, water droplets dappling his broad back.

And then, as quickly as he had appeared, he was gone.

I stood still for a long time, staring down the hallway in his wake. He had never looked back, though later, when Calvin had cause to tell the story to friends, he claimed to remember the moment and to have glanced pointedly back at the astonished boy in the bathhouse corridor. He was kind that way, claiming to remember moments that were cherished by the people around him, though I am doubtful that he ever really remembered that particular moment. I, on the other hand, was dumbstruck by his very presence. For me, it was one of those moments that you never lose track of. Even twenty years later, I can close my eyes and relive the moment, smelling the chlorine and the sweat and the hot air that followed him through the doorway in a burst.

When I finally recovered my senses, I hurried down the corridor after the dark Adonis, but he was gone. I asked Davey about him, but Davey just said there were a lot of hot guys at the Kent, and I needed to be more specific.

Unmasked II

  I watched for him at the baths, but weeks went by without a sighting. I talked to Davey, but he was useless, so overdosed on naked bodybuilders, models, and pot that he could barely tell one man from another anymore.
  A month passed without another sighting. My desire had slowly diminished as the weeks passed, nights no longer relentlessly haunted by jarring sexual dreams of my dark god. My hormones had nearly returned to normal when I saw him again, this time at the Metropolitan Museum of Art in the Greek Salon, standing with the most beautiful woman I had ever seen.
  I was standing next to a statue of Athena, beautiful marble curves in bold opposition to the statue of her brother, Apollo, whose likeness dominated the wall to my left. I had been contemplating the two statues for quite some time, pacing back and forth between them. In truth, I had been composing a sonnet, working the rhyme and rhythm of the beautiful pair into the compact structure of my notebook, jotting notes, changing words, adjusting phrases to heighten the flow of my aesthetic passion. I was making the security guard uneasy, pacing, talking, writing; my Doc Martins and ripped jeans to his outer-borough eyes a symptom of inner-borough insanity or worse. He watched me carefully, as I ran my hands through my hair, whispered, and wrote.
  I turned on my heel, charmed by a particularly good rhyme and ran into a brick wall that had not been there before. I looked up. My heart exploded in my chest as I realized I had literally run into my dark Adonis from the Kent. Our eyes locked and I felt something snap between us, like the feel of unlived days standing at attention before us. I stumbled back from him.
  We both stood stock still for a long moment, our eyes locked together in silence.
  "Oh," I mumbled, "I'm sorry. I didn't realize you were there."

The beautiful brunette woman at his side, reached out a perfectly manicured hand to touch his arm, plum nails and diamond rings flashing along his tanned skin.

"He didn't mean anything, sweetheart," she said.

The guard stepped forward. My cheeks flushed.

"I'm sorry," I whispered.

The dark giant looked down at me, eyes focused so intensely on me that I felt my body urging me to flee through the galleries and out into the street, my genetic legacy recognizing the superiority of this alpha male.

I stepped back.

But then, he smiled, lush lips drawing back to reveal a row of movie-star perfect teeth. "You like the statues?" he asked.

"They're magnificent," I said, pointing at Apollo and Athena with my notebook, flustered, overcome by his presence. He stepped closer, as if to view the statues from my own vantage point. I felt his scent curling into my nostrils, a heady mix of sweat and expensive cologne that made me more lightheaded.

He smiled. "Yes, they are magnificent," he said.

The woman smiled, tugged on his arm and laughed. "Let's go Cal; I think you've had enough beautiful things for today."

I stepped back from the two of them, feeling shabby, wondering if my hair needed combing, if he could smell my cheap cologne or the smoke from my clove cigarettes.

The man of my dreams and the most beautiful woman in the world walked past me through the doorway. Cal, she had called him. I watched them walk arm in arm through the next gallery. As they passed through another doorway, Cal looked back, flashed me another smile and waved, fingers moving back and forth. The gesture was too feminine for such a hulking masculine man. I laughed out loud and waved back.

The guard frowned at me, but I sat in front of the statues for another hour until I had finished my sonnet.

Unmasked II

A week later, I crawled home from a late-night bartending gig as the sun crept up over the river. The morning air was cool and the soft semi-darkness of the far side of night was somehow comforting. When I arrived at the apartment, Glen and Davey were asleep, naked and snoring in a pile on Glen's bed. I stumbled around them and collapsed on my own bed. When my head hit the pillow, I felt paper crinkling against my cheek. I pulled the torn scrap of notebook paper out from under me and leaned toward the window. Glen's serial-killer scrawl and sparse staccato phrases were unmistakable: *Interview Thursday morning. 10am. Council HQ. Press Assoc. Dress nice. Resume.*

I looked at my watch. I had about five hours to sleep, shower, shave, dress, print my resume, and get across town to the CHQ. Perfect, I thought, setting the alarm and collapsing into sleep.

I was four minutes early for my interview. I looked presentable in khakis, white shirt, tie and blue blazer. I had my resume in a folder I'd bought on the way and a pen in case I needed to complete an application. Glen, who had already left for work when I woke up, met me at the door, grabbed my resume, and pulled me through a doorway into a giant room packed with office cubicles. We hurried down a long hallway, then another, then took an elevator down ten floors and hurried to the end of another hallway, this one paneled in shining steel with dark grey industrial carpet.

When we reached an oversized doorway with the silver shooting star insignia of Nicholas Eveningstar emblazoned across it, Glen finally stopped. He reached over to smooth my forelock, looked at me closely and said, "Press Associate for Eveningstar. You can do this." Then Glen, who was about as sportual as anyone you will ever meet, attempted to give me a high five. He fumbled, tried again, then gave up and kissed me quickly on the cheek. He knocked three times on the door and beat a hasty retreat down the hall and out of sight.

I stood in astonished silence in front of the closed door. Press Associate for Nicholas Fucking Eveningstar?!? Holy shit! He had saved the planet about a dozen times, including repelling the Kr'aLor invasion in 1985 and ending Alexei Sargasso's nuclear showdown last summer. Holy shit! My hands were shaking, and a cold sweat was sweeping up from my cramping stomach to my chattering teeth.

The door slid open.

"Mark Belmont?" a deep voice called.

"Yes, sir," I said, stepping through the door into my destiny.

#####

Now as I stand at the podium nearly twenty years later, I hear myself say, "Nicholas's love life is something he always kept private while he lived, can we not allow him the honor of maintaining that privacy in death?"

There was a long, puzzled silence in the room, then a flashing cacophony of light and sound, shouted questions overlapping. "Are you saying he's gay?" "Was he involved with the Hammer?" "Is it true he dated Sir Ian McKellan?" "Was he scheduled to be on the next season of *Dancing with the Stars*?" "Is it true that he and the Scarlet Skull were married in Rhode Island?" The tide washes over me, and I can feel a reluctant smile spreading across my face. The time honored game is afoot.

"Ladies and gentlemen," I say when I am finally able to speak over the shouting, "I can only answer one question at a time. We do this in an orderly manner, or we don't do this at all."

#####

I worked for Nicholas Eveningstar for nearly three years before I pieced it all together. The Council required all active duty, full members to maintain mask status while on the property or while on assignment, so I never saw him without the mask. True, he was huge and imposing and clad in tight black leather or synthetic Kevlar blends all the time. True, he had a smoking hot body. True, he had the most piercing dark eyes I'd ever seen. True, he wore the same expensive cologne I'd smelled on Cal. But I never pieced it together. Perhaps his super powers extended to some kind of glamour, holding my comprehension at bay. Perhaps it was the mundane glamour of masks and costumes and the bureaucracy of superherodom. Whatever the reasons, I failed to realize that the man for whom I now worked was in fact, the man I had secretly fallen in love with in the Greek Salon at the Met. I accepted the position working for Nicholas Eveningstar and continued to look for Cal, haunting the Kent baths and the lonely galleries of the Met whenever my new position afforded me a few spare hours. Since my down-time usually coincided with Eveningstar's teleportation to another dimension, or a Council mission to fight some super villain or another, I didn't see Cal again for a very long time.

When I did see him next, it changed everything.

#####

During the First Gulf War, the Council met with representatives of the European League, the Arab Convocation and about a dozen other major hero groups and hammered out a non-intervention agreement. I went with Eveningstar, Athena, and the White Eagle to the conference, one of a group of about ten support personnel who coordinated the press appearances that surrounded such an unusual gathering. I was busy for the first three days, primarily working as a press escort keeping reporters from the American print media informed of the details of the meetings and the evolving accord. When the signatures were committed to paper, there was a long press conference and a precipitous dénouement that left me in London with a week of vacation and a generous expense account. I museum hopped, drank, and bought too many books.

One afternoon, I was wandering in the streets near the hotel and found a small movie theater that was showing the new movie *Longtime Companion*. I bought a ticket for the matinee, wandered into the nearly empty theater, and pulled out a paperback copy of *Jane Eyre*.

"Is this seat taken?" The voice startled me off the moor. I glanced up into Cal's dark eyes.

"You're here?" I said, looking at the gentle curve of his chest, the tuft of hair curling over the collar of his shirt, tracing the set of his jaw with hungry eyes. I could smell him, the cool cologne that he and Eveningstar shared.

Then something registered suddenly; he saw it clearly in my face.

"You knew all along," he whispered, and I wanted to believe him, but I hadn't known until that very moment. The clues had been there, but I had never pieced them together in the right order, never fit the pieces this snugly together.

"Of course," I said, shrugging, dropping my feet off the seat in front of me, sitting up straighter. "Join me, Cal," I said smiling broadly. "Or should I call you Nicholas Eveningstar?"

"Cal from now on," he said, sitting beside me with a cryptic smile.

We watched a movie together, and he dropped his warm hand over mine when I sniffled back tears. After the movie, we walked out into the early December twilight, bundled against the cold and walking shoulder to shoulder through the streets of the West End, talking. We bought carryout curry and took it back to the hotel, riding the elevator in silence to my small third-floor room.

He flipped on the television, dropped his scarf and jacket on a chair, sat on the bed, and began taking off his shoes. He pulled off his socks slowly, eyes locked on mine. I stood in front of him holding the bags of carryout, my hands fiddling with the tassels of my scarf.

He grinned and stood in front of me, barefoot in jeans and a tight black T-shirt. I had seen him every day for almost three years, but he looked so different now. The man behind the mask was alive and beautiful in a way the professional hero was not.

"What?" he asked, his soft baritone rumbling through me like a passing train.

"You're so different today."

"So are you," he said, taking the bag of curry and setting it down on the table. He reached inside my jacket, hands sliding against my sides as he pulled my jacket off and tossed it on the chair behind me. He stepped close to me, and I marveled again at how huge he was. He towered over me, his shoulders twice as broad as mine. I felt like a child in the embrace of a giant. His hand touched the small of my back; we moved together, our legs touching, warmth transferred through the dark denim. Then he leaned down and kissed me, gently at first, as if he was afraid of breaking me, but as my own passion took over, I pulled him roughly toward me, and he unleashed a little more of the beast. His tongue brushed roughly along the inside of my mouth, eager lips sucking on mine.

The kiss lasted longer than I expected, as if neither of us was sure what to do next, so I stepped back, pulling away from him.

"You ok?" he asked.

In answer, I reached up and pulled his shirt up over his head, peeling him like an orange, then licking his exposed flesh from the center of his breastbone down to his navel, the hair coarse and salty beneath my tongue. A shudder rippled up his body as I reached for his belt buckle.

I parted the two halves of the enormous buckle, pulling the long black belt out through the ring of loops with a flourish that cracked the belt behind me. He laughed at this and reached down for me. I pushed his hands away, intent on undressing him myself, intent on removing all the layers to see the naked man beneath everything, as if removing the clothes would remove the myths that surrounded him, that set him apart from me and from the rest of humanity.

I unbuttoned his jeans, unzipped him and slowly eased them down his powerful legs, revealing the tanned muscles and dark hair of his highs, then his long legs. He stepped out of the jeans, standing before me now in a pair of black briefs, like the heroes of the 1940s wore, but with a bulge that was bigger than anything I remembered from the old news reels or the costumes in the Smithsonian.

I stood in front of him, my eyes running across the broad expanses of furry muscle, taking in every detail: the jagged scar across his right pectoral muscle, the round plugs of scar tissue that marked entry wounds on his left arm and his right shoulder. The strong smell of sweat emanating from his feet and from the hot skin beneath his mantle of fur. He wrinkled his nose, but I shook my head in answer. No, he's perfect, I thought to myself because he's not perfect. The flaws somehow made me hungry for him, his humanity finally indisputable, hot and acrid and scarred in front of me.

I reached out and ran my hand lightly along the length of his rearing erection, barely contained by the dark cloth. A wet spot marked the spot where the tip of his hulking cock rubbed against the fabric.

He reached out to grab my arm, but I pulled back, catching his arm in mine, my fingers barely touching around the thickness of his muscled wrist.

I shook my head, and he hung his head slightly, eyes playful, silent.

I stepped close to him and ran my fingers up his sides, feeling the spray of goose pimples my caress elicited. I leaned close, feeling the pressure of his cock hard against my stomach, my chest. Precum soaked through his shorts, hot against my skin as I moved gently against him.

I pulled him down roughly to kiss me again, our faces grinding so hard against each other I could taste the salt of blood. I pulled back, but he kissed me again, harder, sucking the blood from my lip, holding me tight against his chest. I could feel his hands trembling, his breath heavy as a bull. I pulled back again, this time forcing him back, toppling him onto his back on the broad bed, all in one wily movement. I dropped my jeans and underwear to the floor, my own erect cock popping playfully out in front of me. I flipped my shirt over my head and tossed it behind me. I took one long look at his chiseled body, then let myself fall naked on top of him, his body hot and rock solid beneath me.

  I slid up to kiss him again, straddling his stomach, rubbing my cock against the center of his chest. His hands grabbed my buttocks, pulling me close to him, grinding me into him in rhythm with his deep breaths. I rode his chest for several moments then pulled back from the kiss. I moved down until my erection was grinding against his, our cocks separated only by the black cloth of his underwear, now almost completely soaked through with precum.

  I reached down to strip the briefs off him, moving back momentarily to pull them over his granite thighs, down the furred calves and muscular ankles, finally disentangling them and releasing his enormous feet. I dropped the briefs on the carpet and knelt to run my tongue across the sole of his foot from heel to toe. The tang of his foot sent shivers down my spine and elicited from him a soft contended growl. I licked around to top of his foot, sliding my tongue along gentle plain, inserting my tongue between his perfectly formed toes, letting my mouth cover one then the next until they are slick with my saliva and he was squirming on the bed above me. I stood up, sliding his big toe between my lips, bending his leg up and back and catching a glimpse of the hairy dampness of his anus. I sucked his toe gently, sliding it in and out of my mouth and watching his eyelids flutter in cringing abandon.

  I worked my way up his legs slowly, my tongue caressing each crease, wetting each hair as I made my way toward my ultimate prize. As my tongue glided down his inner thigh, Cal lifted his legs up, grabbing them behind the knees, folding himself in half with extraordinary agility, and exposing the tight bud of his ass to me. I breathed deeply, his musk was strong and damp, intoxicating and primal. I climbed onto the bed, kneeling over his ass and letting my face plunge into the jungle of fur and sweat. When my tongue touched the rim of his ass, I felt his whole body shudder, like boulders rolling down a mountain. I licked gently around the edge of him, teasing him before I plunged into the sweet winking opening. I tongued him, my hands sliding beneath the giant muscles of his ass to position him beneath me. He groaned and writhed, his voice quavering between a deep rumble and a surprisingly high-pitched breathy sound.

"Oh yeah, baby," he gasped as my tongue slid up along the ridge connecting his anus and his avocado-sized balls. "I want you to fuck me," he said then, surprising me.

I looked up at him hungrily. Our eyes locked and he winked. He rolled over to reach the nightstand, his body a tight broad arc of muscles, as if Hercules had posed for Myron's *Discobolus*. I felt my cock twitch in angry anticipation, a glob of precum sliding down the tip, unbidden.

I rolled the condom on, stretched and lubed him gently with my fingers and plunge into him as quickly as I could, my own excitement building too quickly toward the point of no return. My heart was hammering its way through my ribcage and my cheeks were on fire.

As my cock pushed into him at last, a cold wave flashed across my face and chest, the hairs standing on end. 'I am fucking Nicholas Eveningstar,' I thought, then, in immediate rebuke, 'don't be a starfucker, Mark!' My momentary hesitation registered with Cal, who leaned forward, pulled his legs back and whispered, "Come on babe, fuck me hard."

The grin on his face and the deep throb of his voice was enough to pull me back into the moment. I thrust slowly the first time, then, when I was rewarded with another long, trembling baritone groan, I started to fuck him harder. I braced my hands against the hairy back of his thighs, pushing them into his broad chest as my cock slid in and out of him.

Cal's hand was sliding up and down his astounding length, the fingers of his large hands unable to close around his girth.

I looked down and watched myself pistoning in and out of him, the pressure behind my balls building slowly. Heat radiated up from his huge body, our sweat and funk mixing into a vaporous cloud that intoxicated and enflamed me.

When the first orgasmic tremor rippled through his body, I could feel it beneath his skin like a wave, the great muscles shifting beneath my hands. I sped my thrusting and felt my cock nudging his prostate. He began to groan wordlessly in rhythm with my thrusting; my breath grew ragged and the blood drained from my face. I heard myself cry out, but I could not focus on anything but my cock thrusting in and out of him. Cal quaked and suddenly he began to come, a milky gusher that spewed over both of us from his uncontrolled cock. This tipped me over the edge, and I came into him, thrusting feebly until the strength was tapped from me. My arms grew shaky until I finally collapsed onto Cal, our bodies meeting in a lake of sticky whiteness. I fell onto him, his legs and arms pulling me in tight, the rocketing sound of his heart pounding in his chest the last thing I remember hearing before sleep overtook me.

#####

"I'll take one more question," I say, pointing to an unfamiliar Asian woman.

"Yes, with Eveningstar's offices closing down, what's next for you, Mr. Belmont? Will you remain with the Council in another capacity?"

I smile involuntarily. She has surprised me.

"I plan to take an indefinite leave of absence from the Council. I've had some book offers, as you can imagine, and it's been a grueling couple of months, so ... um, that's all I have to say." I look up, placing a thoughtful expression on my face for the final eruption of flashes, photos and shouted questions. "Thank you very much, ladies and gentlemen; it's been a pleasure working with you all."

I step down from the podium, surrounded immediately by my security contingent and escorted through a side door.

Once in the back hallway, I dismiss my protectors and walk through the CHQ hallways to the main bank of elevators. I wait and ride in silence down to the office suite I have shared with my lover for nearly twenty years.

The reception desk and lobby are silent, recessed lighting and glowing computer monitors casting dim illumination across the empty desks and grouping of chairs and sofas. I walk through the silence, my shoes clicking on the cold, hard floor. I push through a glass door and enter the private row of administrative offices, passing the chief of staff's office, the library, the conference room, and a small medical suite, all dark and silent.

At the end of the hall, I stand for a moment, looking at the broad double doors with the silver shooting star insignia emblazoned across them. I open the door and step inside, perhaps for the last time.

"How did it go?" I hear the clink of ice cubes in crystal beneath the deep thunder of his voice.

"As well as can be expected," I say, reaching out to take the glass from his giant hand.

He steps close to me, lowers his unmasked face to mine and kisses me gently on the lips.

"So nobody suspected anything hinky?" he says when he pulls back.

"Not a thing, darling, you are officially and permanently retired."

"So where next, Mark?"

"Somewhere warm and sandy and sunny, Cal," I whisper, leaning my head against his chest and letting the familiar scent of his body surround me.

THE CAPTURE OF CLOUD RUNNER
By Jay Starre

Cloud Runner's strengths were obvious. Just as obvious, at least to me, was his main weakness. I hoped it wasn't so apparent to his numerous enemies.

Appearing out of nowhere to swoop down out of the sky and apprehend a fleeing criminal, he seemed almighty and unassailable. His power of flight, a power he shared with the creatures that inhabited the clouds and stars and the sun and moon, lent him an ethereal omniscience. That appearance of armored strength served well in intimidating the scoundrels he and I worked to bring to justice.

I didn't press him about his weakness, even though I mentioned it now and then. I had to respect his boundaries. He revealed as much as he dared to me, and I felt privileged to have his trust. But, there were limits. Wasn't that true of everyone, friends or lovers – or even enemies?

Cloud plucked me up from a green space in the center of the city, River Park's lonely hillock in a landscape of glass and steel that radiated in all directions. Burly arms wrapped around my back, slate-silver wings flapped wide, and we soared. It was the deepest night, a fat full moon visible as it rose between the tall spires of Midwestern Metro's gleaming skyscrapers.

"What's your pleasure tonight, Dag?"

The orange mask was a vivid slash across the upper portion of my hero's handsome face. Full red lips above a dimpled chin grinned at me. I grinned back.

"We haven't had a proper sixty-nine yet, a flying cock-sucking fest. How about it?"

Cloud's answering chuckle sent a little shiver through me. He was always so damn chipper, the opposite of my own more pessimistic, and I believe realistic, attitude. I loved him for it and always felt uplifted in his company.

Especially now that he was actually lifting me – through the air!

Unmasked II

It was late, past midnight, and although the city still glittered, traffic was winding down, and offices in the downtown towers were empty. Even though we soared right through the center of a metropolis of millions, I felt alone with my masked lover.

Capable hands on my lower back immediately began to spin me, while those broad wings curled down to embrace me in a silver cocoon. I found myself turning in the air, spinning head to toe so that my face was buried in Cloud's crotch, his head in mine.

"Oh yeah! Gimme some of that cock of yours," I shouted out against the rush of wind in my ears.

"Go ahead! It's all yours," he shouted back.

My hands slid around his solid waist. I pulled my body closer, feeling his lengthy form press back. I opened my mouth and gobbled at his crotch, feeling the fat tube of his cock lengthen beneath his silken black costume. The material was unusual, thin as a second skin, and totally aerodynamic, but practically bullet-proof, as he'd revealed to me recently.

The second skin heated up instantly as my warm mouth explored the bulge beneath. Satisfyingly, that bulge grew into a stiff column, throbbing against my lips and tongue. I could actually feel every pulsing vein along the thick shaft, and when I stroked up toward the crown, feel the outline of the flared knob and even the deep crevice of the piss slit right on the head. The material of his costume was practically nonexistent! Practically, but not quite.

A hand dipped between my face and his crotch, releasing a nearly invisible seam. Cloud's cock fell out of the slender opening, slapping my face as it dangled down stiff and pulsing. His big nads escaped the confines of his suit, nestling on my chin as I groped with open mouth for the plump knob of his meat in my greed for cock.

Air whooshed past as he unfurled his wings, and we terminated our spiral downwards. Now, we rose in a dizzying arc between the downtown spires, the wind rushing past my flopping ankles as one of my hero's hands seized my ass from beneath and tore open my fly from above.

Just as I gobbled up the oozing head of Cloud's bobbing boner, his wet mouth burrowed under the waistband of my underwear and captured my own stiff tool.

We sucked each other. Feet first, head down in Cloud's crotch, I licked and chewed, inhaling that substantial tube of hero-pole with snorting gurgles. He fed it to me, humping upwards, while I did the same, thrusting down between his sweet lips, shaking all over as tongue twirled over my sensitive glans and full lips smacked around my pulsing shank.

Craning my head backwards, I caught glimpses between Cloud's legs of glass towers as we wove in and out of the downtown landscape, and heard the sound of the traffic below ebb and wane as we rose and fell. One moment we strained skyward, my head almost upside down between Cloud's thighs, cock plunging far up my throat, the next moment we dove, and I was upright, my cock driving down into my hero's gulping gullet.

Who might have seen us? A late night office worker stunned as a silver-winged, superhero sped past his window, a pedestrian making his way home after a night at the bar, chancing to glance up just as a pair of soaring cock-suckers whizzed overhead, perhaps a fellow cop on his beat always on the lookout for the unusual, and getting an eyeful!

It didn't seem to matter to Cloud, who was usually the most secretive of superheroes. That night, he dared to soar through the glass canyons, cock in mouth, slurping, smacking, snorting. I gasped for breath as I mouthed his tasty meat, swallowing it to the root as I buried my own boner deep in his throat.

The harsh glare of moonlight struck me in the face now and then as Cloud careened in all directions, managing to keep his keen eyes alert even while he sucked me off and I, him.

Unmasked II

I admit I had room for fear only once, and that was at the point of our mutual orgasm. The constant suck and lap bombarding my aching rod had my balls churning before too long, while the taste of sweet precum oozing from Cloud's burrowing knob heated me from head to toe.

I slammed my cock to the root as I felt the jizz boiling up. At the same time, the cock in my own throat pulsed and expanded. Cum shot out as I swallowed, my body convulsing in Cloud's arms, air whistling past as we spiraled downwards and I emptied my load into his gullet.

How did he maintain his sense of space and equilibrium while orgasm gripped us both? I have no idea. We were falling, dropping like a stone as I pumped my steamy juice into his throat and he did the same to me.

Glass whirled past on my right. Would we hit the pavement in seconds? I was breathless, limp and draining, swallowing all of that warm nut-juice with fearful gulps, when all at once we twisted, reversed direction and I was head-down, cum filling my throat and facing the moon between Cloud's wide-open thighs.

It was a memorable suck-job. Very memorable.

The memory was still fresh in my mind the following day as I entered Chief Mason's office at the Midtown Cop Shop where we both worked. He sat at his immaculate desk, oval glasses perched on his broad nose, soft blue orbs direct but quiet.

"I want you to establish contact with this new superhero, Acrobat. He's been working solo, as you know, and although capturing a number of wanted criminals, working outside the law to do it. See if you can get him to work with us, like that other superhero, Cloud Runner."

"You've been told about my association with Cloud Runner, I suppose," I answered slowly. A brutally direct response wouldn't have been good. This was the Chief, after all, even though he was young as hell and had a reputation as the most easy-going boss in existence.

"Yep. What do you say? I'd like to see Acrobat become as much a law enforcement asset as Cloud Runner."

"Not in a million years," I blurted out, before taking a quick breath and rushing on. "I don't trust this Acrobat dude. He's not made of the same stuff as Cloud Runner."

"Hmmm. So far, we've only seen good things from Acrobat. Time will tell, I imagine. In the meantime, see what you can do, Officer Smith. I have confidence in your persuasive abilities."

I held my tongue, staring at the Chief helplessly with my hands clutched in front of a raging boner tenting my slacks. His thick blond hair was plastered down with pomade, his muscular body disguised under a somewhat oversized uniform, but I recognized the dimpled chin, the full lips, the pale blue eyes I adored.

I'd realized Chief Bradley Mason was Cloud Runner the first time I met with him after Cloud and I experienced that amazing flying fuck a few months earlier. I was disgusted with myself for not realizing it sooner.

But I hadn't let on, not to anyone, including Cloud.

I nodded curtly and fled, even though I wanted more than anything to leap over that tidy desk and tear off the Chief's uniform and tongue every inch of his glorious body – from taut nipples down to deep navel, fat cock and plump balls, and up between the ass-cheeks then way up into the palpitating asshole ...

Instead, I did exactly as he'd ordered. It was easier than I'd thought possible, which alarmed me. As if I needed alarming. I was in a constant state of alarm, recognizing our bustling Midwestern metropolis was awash with vicious criminals preying on the law-abiding innocents relying on myself to protect them.

He answered the phone. I was speechless for about two seconds. "This is Detective Dag Smith. Is this Acrobat I'm speaking to?"

I'd leaned on a friend in the press, a dude who worked for one of those tattle-tale rags, and he'd provided the cell number. It was registered to John Smith. No relative of mine, I felt sure.

"Yes, Detective Dag. You are speaking with Acrobat himself. I won't be so crude as to inquire how you discovered my number. Would you like to meet? I'm free this afternoon."

The voice was pure prairie drawl, a local I assumed. There was more than a hint of amusement in the tone, too. Was this dude amused by the police checking up on him? I was irritated, but held my tongue as I jumped on the chance to come face-to-face with the new hero in town.

"One thing. Please come alone."

I wasn't surprised. Nor was I foolish. I arranged no back-up, but I did place a call in to Cloud, leaving him a message about the meeting, and the time and place.

I found myself in the seediest part of town down by the river. I entered an empty warehouse, discovering a scrap of paper left behind that gave me directions to another run-down building, empty as well, but offering a trail of small crimson arrows pointing the way to a rickety elevator, across a filthy rooftop, down a dark stairway, into another abandoned apartment, clambering out an open window then across another roof and finally into a strange-looking egg-shaped tower nestled between other grimy towers.

"Welcome, Detective Dag. I see you managed to sniff your way along my trail of clues."

The drawl was still amused and condescending, too.

The dude himself was quite a sight.

Acrobat greeted me inside that egg-tower in an oval hallway, behind him the glow of a much larger chamber illuminating his form with garish clarity.

I was not impressed, although he was without question a fine specimen of athletic manliness. That much was obvious – his costume left little to the imagination. Blood-red boots hugged his lower calves, a skimpy pair of emerald trunks outlined cock and balls with total clarity, a tight-fitting hood of that same blood-red encased his finely-shaped skull. His hands, snugly gloved in green, perched at his slim waist. Red on top and bottom and green in the middle – he looked like a fucking Christmas ornament!

The sight of sculpted muscles from neck to ankle, tanned, smooth and hairless, would have left most breathless. I thought him merely vulgar. As a wide gash of mouth smiled out of that red mask, and dark eyes roamed up and down my more bulky body, that bulge in his trunks lengthened and stiffened right in front of my eyes.

Vulgar, yes, and dangerous!

"Come into my lair. I promise to be nice!"

He turned, and treading with a light bounce, displayed the rolling globes of his taut butt encased in emerald. That ass did impress me, although I still disliked him.

That ass proved my downfall. My eyes should have been darting all around in search of pitfalls, rather than glued to the sight of pumping cheeks and an inviting crack. Just as I entered the larger chamber beyond the hallway, a net shot up from beneath my feet and surrounded me. In a moment, I was trussed and struggling, dangling several feet off the floor.

"Don't resist and I'll keep my promise to be nice." The drawling voice oozed like liquid lava. The wide grin surrounded by crimson gaped as tongue came out and wagged at me with vulgar wetness.

I was furious. With him, and with myself. In fact I was so angry, I almost succeeded in tearing off the net that held me. Too late and too little, though, as Acrobat acted swiftly to stem my resistance. Leaping around my dangling form in an impressive display of acrobatic skill, he snatched an ankle at a time. He then bound it to one of my corresponding wrists with silken rope he produced out of a cupboard that rose out of the floor like magic.

My ankles in the air, my thighs wide apart, my ass was totally vulnerable as he reached deftly between strands of silken net and sliced open my slacks with nothing more than a small pocket knife. My shorts were next, and I was left with ass-crack gaping, trussed and helpless.

"We'll have to stuff that tender hole of yours after I get a good taste of it."

The irritating drawl grated on my ears as I stared through my raised thighs at his nasty grin and that wagging tongue. I have to admit, my asshole did twitch at the thought of that lengthy tongue tickling it, but I was pissed off, to say the least and determined not to enjoy the rim-job apparently coming up.

I struggled some more, but there was little I could do as that masked face jammed up into my parted crack, pocket knife slashing open the netting to allow lips and mouth to clamp right over my exposed butt-hole.

Sucking and smacking ensued. I gasped and bit my lip as my anal defenses resisted bombardment by that wet suction. Regardless of my state of mind, those defenses were quickly annihilated by the biggest, longest tongue to ever fuck me as it slithered deep inside my churning gut.

Tongue drilled way up in me as I thrashed around in that damn net, but that wasn't all. I realized we were rising and falling in the air, as Acrobat bounded up and down, carrying my slung form with him. How was that possible?

Through the fog of an impossibly exquisite rimming, I realized the floor beneath us was actually a strange type of trampoline. He bounced up off it, taking me with him, while jamming that maddening tongue far, far up my asshole with each leap.

Even though I gave in to the slithering snake up my ass, my pouting ass-lips wet and throbbing, I kept my head, somewhat. What was this perp's motive? Did he merely enjoy bondage sex with cops? Was he after more?

I suspected he was after Cloud Runner. But how would he know we were buddies?

Acrobat's gloved fingers slid between the strands of the severed net and attacked the rim of my hole, pulling it apart as that tongue wriggled deeper, twirling and stabbing relentlessly. I squirmed and gasped, angry and hot all over from my exertions, my emotions and the slobbering wetness invading and transforming my tender asshole.

His tongue slithered from my hole, leaving behind a spit-soaked orifice that gaped open between my bound thighs like a pink gash. A red-head, my ivory white skin flushed easily, and now I felt it glow crimson as the nasty superhero produced a gross object in one of his gloved hands and laughed as he did.

"One plug for one end, Detective Dag! Another for the other end to come shortly."

His mouth was coated in drool. His eyes shone with dark greed. I offered no reply, but couldn't hold back a grunt as he rammed the tip of a bright red butt plug into the center of my eaten-out asshole.

He laughed brutally as we rose and fell in an odd cadence, his booted feet bounding off the spring-board floor, each rise that plug sliding deeper, and deeper yet with each fall. I was experienced enough to will my poor asshole open as the girth of the plug increased, and increased. And increased!

With a vicious chuckle, he forced it all the way in. My asshole strained and expanded and finally gulped the plug in with a final contraction around the smaller base as the rubber toy was planted home.

The square base, bright red, now quivered in my crack as I allowed my uneasy sphincter to relax around it. The fatter bulge of the plug pressed against it from the inside, which was admittedly pleasurable, but I was far too angry to really enjoy the sensation.

"Sweet! That nice pink ass looks good all plugged up. Now for the other end."

I had no time to contemplate what he meant to do, swift action following his threat. Gloved green hands snatched up another nasty implement, pocket knife quickly slashing an opening in the net near my face. I caught a brief glimpse of a red leather strap, with a fat red rubber cock attached before the thing was shoved into my mouth.

Unmasked II

The strap was snapped in place behind my neck, the dildo trapped in my mouth, effectively silencing me. I was plugged at both ends!

"Now to phone your friend. I suspect he'll rush to your side!"

The gloved hands slid over my trussed body until they found my cell phone, then deftly sliced through net and coat to pluck it out. I gurgled around the dildo in my mouth and squirmed ineffectively as he grinned in my face and punched in the last number I'd called.

"This is Dag. I need you to meet me now."

To my astonishment, the drawl transformed into a perfect mimic of my own huskier voice. Would it fool Cloud? With cock-gag stuffing my mouth, and butt-plug filling my asshole, I stared into the dark pools of Acrobat's masked eyes.

As he spoke with my voice and gave directions to Cloud's voice mail, I experienced a revelation. This was no stranger facing me! Those same eyes had met mine more than once.

Stanley Matthews!

The Chief's private secretary! No wonder the scoundrel knew about Cloud and me! And, he'd been watching me as I phoned Cloud just before I left the station for my rendezvous with Acrobat. And, he'd been on the phone at his desk when I called Acrobat. Talking to me right there – just across the room!

Jealousy, that might be this fool's motive, then. I'd sensed it before, a secretary who maintained a vigilant watch over his boss, using his position to prevent others from gaining access.

And, this was Cloud's weakness, unable to see the deviousness in even his closest associates!

Even as these revelations struck me, I was hoisted up into the air, noticing now how large the chamber was surrounding us. The egg-shaped structure was immense and open, with netting attached to all the surfaces from floor to rounded ceiling. With that trampoline floor, I suspected it was some kind of practice room for the bounding villain.

Dangling helplessly high above the floor, I prayed Cloud would ignore that message, or at least come forewarned. My anxious wait was short. Cloud Runner always answered my calls, and I never called for his help unless it was important.

A surge of dismay and hope coursed through me as I saw my hero enter, silver wings furled around his powerful body. Acrobat stood in the center of the room, red-booted feet planted wide and ready for action as he welcomed Cloud.

"Detective Dag asked me to entertain you while we await his arrival."

The drawl dripped honey as the masked face smiled pleasantly. Was Cloud fooled? Regardless, I knew something about him Acrobat might not. With dildo gagging my mouth, I couldn't cry out, but even trussed up with my ankles in the air, I could affect some movement. I arched my back and reared, feeling that immense plug up my ass as I did, but managing to rock and sway the netting surrounding me.

High above, Acrobat assumed I would be out of Cloud's range of vision. Not so. Eyes that missed nothing, my superhero was instantly attracted to movement. He glanced up and saw me.

Almost too late!

The same trap laid for me erupted from the floor, but Cloud's furled wings spread in a silver blur and up he soared, just out of reach of that dangerous netting. My heart leaped as I saw him approaching, then sank when a red-and-crimson form smashed into him from below.

The trampoline floor served Acrobat well as he bounded upwards and seized Cloud with emerald-gloved fingers. The pair whirled and plummeted in a blur of silver, black, green and red. I snorted air in through my nose, slobbering over that cock-gag as I watched the action from above.

Unmasked II

What a battle! At first, it seemed to go all Acrobat's way, after all this was his home base and his game. He bounded up off the floor and whirled in a blur of spinning arms and legs. He caught himself on the netting, dangled upside-down, and then shot out like a red and green bullet as Cloud raced skyward toward me.

It was like a sparrow attacking a hawk, pestering the larger creature from above and below, clinging to the flying back with sinuous arms and legs, dropping off just before he was smashed against either wall, ceiling or floor by the amazing gyrations of my agile hero.

Silver wings beat and furled and snapped. The black shape of Cloud's powerful body spun and rose and dove. Several times, he approached me, his soft blue orbs meeting mine, and once he managed to reach out and grasp me, before that tenacious villain again latched onto him from behind.

They were right there next to me, hovering in the air, the wind from Cloud's broad wingspan beating in my face, Acrobat's slimmer body clinging to my hero's back when Cloud did something even I had no idea he was capable of.

A shrugging of his broad shoulders rippled his mighty body, and like a snake shedding its skin, the black body-suit he wore opened up and peeled away. Acrobat fell with it, clinging to the sheer material as he dropped like a stone.

I was treated to the almost totally naked sight of my amazing hero hovering in the air beside me. His wings remained, strapped to his body across his chest and back by criss-crossing leather that outlined and emphasized the swell of his powerful chest.

His thick body was packed with muscle, his thighs huge, his waist narrow and his thick cock dangling down half-hard through his exertions. Blond fur surrounded the base, big balls dangling below that.

Still, Acrobat was far from vanquished. He managed to spin and land on his feet, only to bound skywards again while Cloud was focused on me and my predicament.

"Looo ... oott" I gurgled as the villain appeared behind Cloud.

He spun and dove, reaching out to snatch at Acrobat's waist. Material ripped, and as the villain careened off sideways, he was stripped of his flimsy suit, and I was now treated to the sight of two bare-assed superheroes battling in the air below me.

I ogled those bare asses and rearing cocks as I squirmed around the plug up my own tender asshole and slobbered around the crimson dildo between my lips. Dangling there, I had the perfect view of the furious action.

Cloud's huge thighs splayed, offering me a view of his pale ass-cheeks, deep ass-crack and even a glimpse of his snug hole. The same with Acrobat. The slender, tanned body whirled and leaped and careened, arms and legs a blur, plump little can heaving with exertion, crack opening wide as he spun upside down and his hole was right on view.

Again, he managed to attach himself to Cloud's naked back, and this time he did more.

Limber brown thighs snaked around to clasp Cloud's waist and powerful ankles crossed. The pair executed a mid-air turn as they almost careened into my trussed form, and there they were upside-down and asses in my face. I couldn't believe it!

Acrobat's cock was planted up Cloud's butt! He was fucking my superhero up the ass!

My cock reared up against my fly, my butt-hole palpitated around the plug stuffing it, and I drooled around the cock-gag in my mouth. What a sight! As Cloud whirled and dove and twisted in an attempt to dislodge the tenacious villain attached to his back, Acrobat hammer-humped into the rounded white ass-cheeks he clung to.

Acrobat knew what he was doing. His arms pinned Cloud's in a hammer-lock under pits while wrists locked behind his powerful neck. Cloud's hefty biceps tensed and strained in an effort to break that hold, but though Acrobat was lean, he was made up of hard-packed muscle, and insane with lust.

They rose to my level a number of times, and I caught a glimpse of Cloud's eyes. I was buoyed by the steady glint of blue, fearless and determined. Even though Acrobat seemed to have the upper-hand, his lengthy cock up Cloud's battered butt-hole while I was trussed and helpless, that look gave me confidence in the outcome of the ferocious battle.

Cloud slammed his back into the netting on the walls, but Acrobat maintained his hold, his tanned butt pumping furiously as he got the one thing he seemed determined to attain, a deep fuck of my hero's white ass!

Cloud's wings spread wide as the pair fell away from me, his white body nude, those silver leather straps that held his wings in place crisscrossing a smooth and hairless torso, his own cock fat and raging, his giant thighs splayed, the tanned legs of the evil Acrobat entwined around his waist, cock driving up between the flying superhero's ass-cheeks. I watched Cloud's face and expression as they dropped toward the floor, intent and loving as he looked back at me.

It was about to be all over.

They slammed into the floor, Acrobat pinned under Cloud's weight. Immediately they rebounded, as the trampoline structure pitched them skyward again, but that only meant they dropped another time, just as heavily as Cloud flapped his wide-spread wings to add velocity to the downward direction.

I stared down at them, Cloud's awesome body spread wide, cock rearing pink against his ivory flesh, Acrobat's tanned limbs all at once going limp and falling away. My hero wasted no time in whirling in mid-air as they rebounded, this time scooping up the winded, half-conscious villain, arcing sideways and slamming into the curved surface of the wall.

In seconds, Acrobat's hands and ankles were enmeshed and confined in his own netting. Now he was the one trussed up!

Cloud soared skyward as I flushed with exhilaration. He'd won! It took only moments for him to release me from my humiliating trap and wrap me in his tender, naked arms as we descended in a floating embrace to the floor.

"What should we do with him?" Cloud asked with a wicked grin.

Acrobat was barely coming to when he discovered himself on his knees, wrists cuffed behind his back, crimson boots splayed wide apart, and my cock ramming up his snug brown asshole.

From in front, Cloud fed the dazed super-villain his own fat meat. The wide mouth opened even wider as the stunned Acrobat realized he was getting what he wanted after all, his own hero's big meat in his gullet.

Cloud gazed into my eyes as he plunged past gurgling tonsils with vigorous enthusiasm. "I think he might be reformed by the time we finish up with his mouth and ass."

I rolled my eyes and groaned. Not only because I was balls-deep in a snug asshole that clamped and pulsed delightfully, but also because I could see my hero hadn't learned a thing! His weakness, a pie-in-the-sky belief in the goodness of man, was still deluding him!

I had stripped down quickly, but hadn't bothered removing the crimson plug planted deep in my own ass, nor the red cock-gag in my mouth, so I couldn't reply, at least not yet. There would be plenty of time to chastise my blond superhero later.

For now, I rammed my cock deep into the churning bowels of the vanquished supervillain as my super-buddy's cock slithered in and out of the gaping slit in that crimson mask, drool glistening along the pink shank and down over his big nads as they bounced on Acrobat's chin.

Unmasked II

The slut-villain moaned loudly, rolling his tanned butt in circles as he gulped up my drilling bone with rising enthusiasm. Maybe he was reformed.

Anyway, we loaded him up with steamy jizz, right there in his own lair.

SUPER SLIDER AND THE WARDEN OF BATON ROUGE
By Jay Starre

Super Slider liked to go barefoot whenever he could. His feet were not only toughened from years of unshod trekking, but also he was naturally gifted with skin that resisted abrasions, cuts, and similar wounds.

That gift seemed a contradiction compared to his more astonishing powers. He could walk through walls. Tough skin notwithstanding, he was able to metamorphose himself into a shimmering wraith, and like a sea breeze through a mosquito net, he could literally slide right through solid objects.

Right now, he wouldn't have minded one of those metaphorical mosquito nets.

The Louisiana bayou was infested with the critters. Even though their sting could not penetrate his tough flesh, their swirling buzz was annoying enough. Still, much nastier beasts inhabited the dank woods.

The nastiest beasts of all were not bayou-born, but strangers all to that steamy wetland. These vile creatures were concentrated in one locale ahead, behind the brooding walls of a massive structure known simply as Baton Rouge.

Baton Rouge. Not the city itself, but a secret federal prison hidden away in the Louisiana wetlands where only the most heinous of criminals were ensconced, no visitors allowed, no contact with the outside world.

Slider sniffed the air with his wide-spaced nostrils. The stink of the wetlands was not what he found offensive; it was the wafting reek of that prison, and the prisoners within. The stink of cruelty and fear.

Keen senses guided him through a shadowy world of cloud-obscured moonlight. Toes and heels found squishy purchase on vine-and-root-covered ground. Nimble fingers found grips among tangled branches.

He spotted the dark edifice ahead not long after he smelled it. Then he heard it. His amazing ears, large and hound-like, had no trouble hearing through walls, or across distance.

Among the chatter of cursing shouts and murmuring whispers, he picked out the pertinent voices and the details he required to further his intended goal.

The bold superhero was going to free one of those prisoners.

Slider's cock, encased in a zig-zag-striped multi-colored leather pouch, swelled and stiffened, oozing out a dollop of precum. Just the thought of that particular prisoner affected him so strongly his cock grew hard and his asshole palpitated.

Bartolomeo.

He whispered it aloud. Even the sound of the name sent shivers up and down his spine – and into his swelling cock and quivering asshole. The rolling consonants and full vowels rumbled in his chest and outward, eliciting a tingling heat in his pierced nipples.

The superhero was generally cavalier about his sexual conquests, but this Cuban-American stud had stamped his mark all over Slider's psyche.

Love, perhaps not, but the emotions he felt were definitely more than mere lust.

He would rescue his one-time lover, however improbable it seemed at the moment.

The watchtowers high above the sheer stone walls were occupied by sleepy guards who randomly played their spotlights over the dense woodlands below. Slider's keen hearing picked up their bored voices as they chatted amongst themselves about nonsense before he made his dash for the fortress across a patch of open ground.

Safely at the looming wall, he immediately took a deep breath and made his plunge through two feet of solid concrete.

It was a blurring of his sensations, his hands first meeting the firm concrete, then shimmering and disappearing. The remainder of his body quickly followed. He tingled from head to toe, his gut churning, his cock throbbing, his asshole twitching, his vision blurred by chaotic images of swirling molecules.

It was over in a second, and he was inside, appearing in an empty storage closet among buckets and brooms. He grinned and shook off the electric tingle, focusing on the task ahead.

Easy enough to look through the locked door and out into a dimly lit corridor. No one was immediately evident outside, so he once more melted through an obstruction effortlessly. The metal doorway was a snap to negotiate, and he found himself in the glaring light of a prison corridor.

Footsteps approached from around a corner!

Rather than sliding through another wall, he chose a different tactic. His power of disguise was as unique as his power of sliding. Practically melting against the wall in front of him, he spread himself flat, arms wide, thighs fanned out, face turned so one cheek pressed against the concrete.

A pair of guards rounded the corner and approached, chatting quietly. They came, and then passed, eyes ahead, never noticing the blur of flesh splayed out against the wall beside them.

The appearance of Slider's body, mostly naked, was a confusion of stripes and patterns that simply failed to register in the onlookers' brains. Tattoos, colorful images of dueling dragons and angels, or symmetrical bands of Greek and Arabic script, splashed across his shoulders, arms, upper back, thighs and calves. His rounded ass was free of them, though, smooth and pale. His platinum blond hair was buzzed short in a zigzag pattern. His costume was all leather, and striped with zigzags of alternating platinum and plum.

A band of thick leather encased his muscular neck, a strap running down the middle of his thickly muscled back and right down into the deep valley between his jutting butt-cheeks. A jock-strap encased his cock and balls. A harness framed his full chest. A dozen rings of mixed silver

Unmasked II

and copper and of various sizes glinted in each ear. A pair of copper hoops dangled from each pointed nipple. A thick silver ring hung from his wide-spaced nostrils. A silver and opal stud was planted in his navel.

And, under that jockstrap, a huge silver ring pierced his swollen cock-head.

The overall effect was so disconcerting, most people struggled to take it in. And when he chose, as now, to melt against any given background, they simply saw only that background.

Slider's eyes were the only give-away. No one could even glance at him without being arrested by those fascinating orbs. Under platinum, wide-spaced brows, a pair of honey-hazel spheres shimmered in a mixture of gold and emerald and azure. If he chose to look directly into your eyes, you simply could not look away.

That's why he closed his eyes now, as the guards meandered past. They didn't see him and were quickly gone beyond another turn in the corridor.

Slider turned his concentration onto his daunting task. The first step was merely to find Bartolomeo in that pile of cement, steel and vile humanity.

Focusing his keen perceptions, almost at once he sensed Bartolomeo nearby, quivering nostrils searching for the distinctive aroma of pits, crotch, breath, ass – and cock, beloved cock – that belonged to no one else. There! First that warm, heady scent, then the sound of his one-time lover's breathing. Slider's big, keen ears zeroed in on the Cuban's sighing moan, so familiar, as if it was right there next to him.

A moan of pleasure. A moan of lust.

His expressive hazel eyes swiveled, focused, sought and found. Through one wall, another, another, a hallway, bars ... there.

No!

Bartolomeo, sprawled out in his narrow bunk, chocolate-brown thighs spread wide, a man between them, naked and crouching, wet mouth slurping as it rode up and down the thick length of the Cuban's stiff prick. The image was right before the stunned superhero's eyes. Cock, rampant, with that distinctively wicked curve, blunt mushroom crown and deep piss slit, veins slobbered on and pulsing, impossibly thick shaft – now appearing and disappearing between the gobbling lips of a stranger, gurgling and slurping.

Those slurps, and Bartolomeo's corresponding sighs, reverberated in Slider's head, hammer blows to his pounding heart.

That was his downfall. Just as it had been once before, in the recent past when he'd stormed out on the Cuban after a jealous argument. That had been the last time he'd seen Bartolomeo.

"What have we here? An intruder, as expected!"

The grating voice was right behind him. Slider whirled, instinct galvanizing him into a defensive crouch, hands out and prepared to attack.

He faced a trio of burly guards, and the flame-haired sneering owner of that growling voice. In the instant, he had to assess his options, he decided flight would be the simplest. He prepared to back away, toward the wall behind him and a swift exit.

But, it was not to be.

One of the massively built guards flung something at him. A length of glittering chain flew through the air and whipped around his neck.

Slider gasped, hands flinging up in a futile effort to tear away the offending tether. But his entire body was all at once trembling with a staggering weakness.

Gold! The chain was made of gold!

No one knew of his weakness for the metal. No one except his ex-lover and intimate friend, Bartolomeo!

"Ah-hah! Perfect! Now these gold hand-cuffs and we'll have our little superhero nicely under our control. Take him, men!"

Unmasked II

"Yes Warden," the three brutes chimed in together as they leaped on Slider just as his knees gave way, and he was about to collapse to the floor.

The Warden of Baton Rouge!

The red-head's brutal reputation was a matter of record. Slider had hoped to avoid any contact with the man, and since it was almost midnight, he'd believed his chances were good.

But gold! Gold was his downfall, which was why all his piercings were of silver or copper.

Although extremely athletic and well-muscled, the superhero was not a big man. At only five-eight, he was dwarfed by the behemoth guards and the Warden himself, who was several inches over six feet and boasting an ex-football player's broad physique.

They dragged the feebly resisting superhero down the hallway and through a pair of barred and locked metal doorways. His body was useless and limp, but his mind raced. How had this come about? What did the Warden want with him? Why had the Warden claimed Slider was "expected"?

The grunting guards revealed nothing while the leering Warden merely directed his minions to keep pace with him. A final door swung open to outside air.

A bare yard, concrete walls and floor, open night sky high overhead. And one square, padded stool firmly planted in the middle of the area.

It only took a moment for the brutes to dump their victim onto that low stool and shackle him in place. Thick gold fetters clamped over his wrists, which were then pulled back and behind him. Kneeling over the stool, his ankles were pulled apart and another pair of gold fetters clamped over them. Then, each of his wrists were attached by gold chain to each of his ankles.

Slider quivered all over with a languid heat, his usually taut muscles limp, his big lips gaping open as he sucked in deep breaths of fetid bayou air. The moon was high above the prison yard, illuminating his kneeling form in shimmering luminescence.

The gold shackles that attached his wrists to his ankles were icy cold, yet heat throbbed out from them, into his veins and then pumping through his entire body. His knees slid apart, his ass-crack opened wide.

The stool itself reeked. Of sex – men's juices and men's fears. It seemed as if the echoes of their outcries still reverberated in the confines of that cement yard.

The Warden's evil cackle was joined by the others' harsh laughter. Their victim was immobilized and helpless, and they were about to abuse him to slake their own perverted lusts. A sharp command from the hovering Warden had the largest of the guards, a huge black stud by the name of Tiger moving in for first dibs on the creamy white ass glowing in the moonlight.

"Open him up for us, Tiger! That prick of yours is bigger than a fucking mule's! He's going to feel it."

The Warden moved around to straddle Slider's lolling head. Big, cruel hands gripped the sides of his face. "I'll feed his face-hole some white cock at the same time."

It happened. He felt the thick, firm poker of black flesh lunge into his spread ass-crack. The hot pole was slippery with some kind of lubricant, thankfully. He heard the spurt of more lube as he felt it splash over his plump ass and quaking thighs.

The striped leather strap of his costume that ran down from his neck and back and divided his creamy butt was snug against his asshole, a final defense against the intended invasion. But, that was easily remedied. The behemoth Tiger laughed as he rubbed his massive prick all over Slider's round ass and unsnapped the strap from the superhero's collar.

It slithered down and out of his ass-crack, leaving the deep divide bare and vulnerable. With his knees wide apart, that crack gaped open. His pink asshole twitched then convulsed as the massive shank of hot cock began to rub against it.

Unmasked II

Framed by the platinum and plum striped jockstrap, that hefty white ass heaved, away from and toward that thick meat as Slider's body betrayed him. It felt good!

The massive crown settled on the pulsing hole. Beefy black paws seized his pale butt-cheeks and pulled them even wider apart. His back arched just as that knob pierced his quivering sphincter. He gasped, only to be gagged by the sudden intrusion of another cock. The Warden was fucking his face!

Two cocks forced their way into him, one at either end while he writhed helplessly between them, sprawled over a stool and shackled in gold fetters. The other two guards snickered from the sidelines, shedding their uniforms as they began to jerk off over the bound superhero.

The huge black poker up his ass stretched and massaged his poor ass-lips and anal ring as it slithered deep into his guts. His mouth gaped open in a muffled groan as all that enormous flesh burrowed relentlessly – a seething, black python exploring his innards.

The Warden's hands clamped the sides of his face as he pumped his big white cock in and out, rubbing against Slider's fat lips and silver-ringed nostrils. He snorted in the reeking bayou air as cock impaled him from both ends.

While he was helplessly getting fucked up the ass and in the mouth, his nimble mind at first refused to submit. It darted and careened down twisting alleys of self-examination and searing memory in an effort to understand his current predicament. At only twenty-one, he was young enough to be both somewhat naïve, and a lot of bold, bordering on arrogant. He understood that about himself, which was a sign of his burgeoning maturity. But, he was still a victim to those traits.

The only person that knew of his weakness against gold was Bartolomeo. How and why had the evil Warden pried that secret from his ex-lover's lips? Bartolomeo was not easily intimidated. Nor was he greedy. Neither physical threats nor offers of money would have moved the tall Cuban. Something else. What?

Was Bartolomeo angry with Slider? Duh! Of course he'd be. The superhero had outright accused him of being a whore in his jealous rage at discovering the dusky-skinned stud in the arms of another man. That man had been the Chief of Police Gordon Reynold himself, older, wiser, handsome, powerful. Slider's boss and Bartolomeo's.

Cock thrust deep into his guts, massaging his innards relentlessly. Very big cock. Big, black cock. The hammer-head knob at the crown banged deep inside Slider, then pulled all the way out with a sloppy squish. That blunt knob immediately slammed against his tenderized ass-lips, stretching and spreading them as it burrowed right back inside the superhero's warm insides, driving home till those hefty black balls slapped against his spread, pale ass-crack.

He was fucked! So fucked. And not just by that black python-prick, but by the one he cared about the most in life! Bartolomeo! Why had he betrayed Slider?

Self recrimination and self-pity nearly overwhelmed him, until two things happened simultaneously to wrench him out of his miasma of inaction.

"Fuck him good, Boys. The little slut is going to be our butt-whore for many days to come. Until we've trained him well enough to turn over to the prisoners!"

That cloying voice was so annoying in its arrogance, Slider found himself growing suddenly angry. Very angry.

At the same time, his keen ears quivered and caught wind of a familiar, much more welcome voice. Bartolomeo.

Walls, corridors, bars separated them. Other voices, murmuring, crying out, angry, fearful, all chattered and clambered to confuse him. But, that one voice carried above them all, soft-spoken yet firm and unyielding.

"It's no use. I won't blow my load. No matter how goddamn good you are at sucking dick, I've got one man on my mind. And he sucks dick like on one else. In fact, he's like no one else. He's the one. The one for me."

Unmasked II

Heat suffused Slider's limp body, a heat more intense than the steamy bayou's stifling pall, more intense than the burning friction of cock thrusting in and out of his battered butt-hole.

Bartolomeo hadn't betrayed him, not with the Police Chief, and not with the Warden by offering him Slider's secret weakness. He suddenly believed that. Or, more importantly, even if the Cuban had committed either or both of those offenses, Slider didn't care. He forgave him.

Just as a renewed sense of power began to infuse his quivering muscles, cum began to spurt all over his muscular back. The pair of guards who stood on either side of him shot their loads.

"Welcome Chief. Look what we have here, just like you ordered."

Slider's hazel eyes swiveled. He gasped and gurgled just as the Warden's fat cock yanked out of his mouth to leave a trail of spittle down his dimpled chin.

The New Orleans Police Chief, come back from the dead!

Bartolomeo was incarcerated in this very prison because he'd been convicted of murder. The man he'd supposedly killed was right here! Chief Gordon Reynold, tall blond and handsome. The man in whose arms Slider had caught Bartolomeo, then, who a few days later had disappeared, leaving behind a trail of blood but no body found.

Alive!

"Sweet ass. I've been dying for a crack at it ever since the super-punk started working for us! Now I'll get my wish. All because of that fool Bartolomeo!"

The suave voice and easy smile no longer fooled Slider. The cop was a slime-ball! No doubt as corrupt as the nasty Warden of Baton Rouge.

Bombarded by the stink of cum as it dribbled down the deep V of his muscled back, the reek of the Warden's red-furred balls in his face, and the swirling realizations that flooded his head and heart with conflicting emotions,

Slider arched his back and allowed the massive black meat pummeling him to drive all the way home. He was stuffed with cock!

And, he was about to get even more stuffed.

The handsome blond Chief tore off his uniform in a rush, greedy blue eyes roaming all over the superhero's helpless form, in gold fetters and oh-so-butt-fucked. In an instant he was straddling their kneeling victim, his lean body just in front of the brutish Tiger.

"How's this feel, Slider? Another cock up the ass? Can you take two at once?"

He felt it pressing against his battered ass entrance. As Tiger continued to slam into him, the blond Chief aimed his cock downward and began to force it in, too.

Slider grunted against the sudden ache of an additional cock pressing beyond his straining ass-lips. The thrust of black cock actually pulled that white bone along with it, and suddenly a second rod was inside him.

"Fuck yeah! We got him double-drilled! And cum-coated, too!"

The Chief's usually smooth voice cracked as he drove downward with his cock into Slider. The tightly clamping orifice must have felt amazing, along with the slide of heated, thick black cock pressing against his own.

At the same time, the nasty Warden of Baton Rouge rubbed his furry nut-sack all over Slider's face, against his lolling lips, pressed up against his flared, ringed nostrils, over his eyes and forehead, cackling like the crazed brute he was.

Behind him, a pair of degenerates butt-fucked him. The huge black body of the guard pressed against the lean white body of the Police Chief. Sandwiched together, they forced one midnight-black prick, and one pink pole into Slider's stretched slot. The contrast of black and white was lewd and exciting.

Slider's keen mind, now galvanized into action, realized any resistance was futile. There must be some other way to turn the tables on his captors. He began by sticking out his fat tongue and swabbing at the plump nuts in his face, then opening wide and sucking in both at once with his big lips.

"The little superhero enjoys it! He's sucking on my big nuts! He's a fucking slut!"

At the same time, he reared back against the pair of pricks goring his helpless hole. He willed the sphincter and the fuck tunnel beyond to open, and then to push outwards. He swallowed the pounding black and white shanks whole.

"Fuck ... ohhhh ... his asshole is a sump pump ... uhhhh ... what a little whore," the blond Chief muttered between gasps.

The powerful stuffing and stretching brought back a sudden and sharp memory of his ex-lover, and the lengthy fat prick he owned. How he'd so expertly used it on the superhero!

They'd first met in New Orleans during a sting operation, ordered by none other than Chief Reynold himself. Bartolomeo, an undercover officer, and Slider the secret tool the Chief employed to slide his way into the den of a group of drug lords.

The tall Cuban-American, with his soft, dark eyes and gentle smile, had instantly mesmerized the superhero. The band of crooks was arrested and carted away, and in the aftermath they were left alone.

Eyes locked, hearts pounding, without a word spoken, the pair found themselves in a heated embrace. The Cuban's wide mouth opened to suck Slider's fat tongue, the big bone in his jeans rearing and pressing into the hero's bare belly.

That amazing brown cock had sunk deep into Slider's gullet, and up his warm, willing asshole, then down his throat again, and up his ass again, pumping and massaging as steady hands spun him and rolled him and controlled him.

From the time of that first amazing cock-drilling, they'd become inseparable. Sex had rapidly grown into an obsession for both of them. Slider had worshiped the Cuban's foot-long dong, and Bartolomeo had made sure to use it on the superhero in every way possible until the day Slider had arrived unannounced at the undercover cop's apartment in the French Quarter to find the Chief there. The two had been locked in a lusty embrace, arms around each other, tongues buried in each other's mouths.

Slider had felt like he was about to die. Jealousy raged inside him. He shouted words he would later regret and stormed out without waiting for an explanation. Two days later, the blond Chief disappeared, his blood-spattered bedroom the supposed scene of his murder, and Bartolomeo's finger prints discovered all over the bloodied knife left behind.

It had taken no time at all for the trial and sentencing, an unheard of two weeks. Slider was tormented during that time, unwilling to speak to his ex-lover, boiling with jealousy and disappointment.

But by the time Bartolomeo had been sent to Baton Rouge, Slider had experienced a change of heart. He just couldn't believe the soft-spoken, gentle Cuban had committed murder. He still lusted after that huge brown cock, of course, but there was more. He still cared for him.

Now the platinum-blond superhero found himself captured, chained, and very, very fucked. But not entirely helpless. He renewed his sluttish writhing and sucking.

"The whore is on fire ... uhhhnn ... let's turn him over onto his back ... yeah ... and fuck his hot holes good. Unshackle him!"

The Warden's orders were swiftly obeyed by the others, to a man enthralled by the squirming and moaning of their victim, now apparently enjoying his own violation.

To their downfall, they unlocked the chains binding his wrists to his ankles, then allowed him to roll over and face them.

Honey-hazel eyes, large and compelling gazed up at the five. For a frozen moment, they were immobilized, gawking down at that butt-fucked body, tattoos writhing in colorful cacophony, smooth flesh awash in sweat, silver and copper piercings glinting in the moonlight. Leather harness and jockstrap glowed in confusing stripes of bright platinum and plum.

They were amazed and enthralled, all with cocks stiff and drooling, all with bated breath, all hot to use those stiff cocks on their lolling victim in as many nasty ways as possible.

"Remove the fetters. I'll make it worth your while. My holes are so wet and juicy and willing. I'll swallow all your cocks to the balls."

Slider's suggestive voice urged. His huge eyes grew even larger, more compelling. He stuck out his tongue and licked his plump lips, he rolled his hips and raised his thighs to pull them back toward his chest and expose the drooling hole between his round white butt-cheeks. That hole pouted and pulsed. Every man there groaned, their cocks throbbing with the need to impale that juicy well-used asshole.

At the same time, Slider's tattoos seemed to writhe with a life of their own. It was the Chief himself who moved forward, stiff, pink cock rearing in front of him, to release the shackles. Gold cuffs and chain clattered to the cement floor.

The superhero disappeared, right before their eyes.

He grinned to himself as he stared up at his astounded captors. They couldn't see him, even though he was right there! He moved swiftly, now that gold no longer bound him. Rolling over, he fell to the floor and slid right through it, hands first, sweaty, butt-fucked body following.

He ended up in a basement chamber, dropping to the floor beneath him on all fours like a cat. Now, it was time to act, and quickly!

He slid through more walls, shimmering like a ghost. In moments, he was in Bartolomeo's cell. The Cuban was on his feet, pacing. The rejected, naked cell mate sat on his bunk, nursing a boner.

"Let's go. Wrap your arms around me."

Bartolomeo's brown eyes were full of tears as he obeyed. "Do you forgive me?"

"Of course. You can explain it all later. We have to get out of here!"

There was one more trick up the superhero's sleeve. Once he had his lover's body wrapped tightly around his own, it was possible to slide through the prison walls together, as one.

Bartolomeo moaned aloud as the disconcerting physical disruption occurred, first once, then in a rapid succession of blurring, melding and reappearing. Their bodies tightly clasped, their cocks swelled and thrust against each other. Their assholes pulsed in matching rhythm, Slider's oozing, gang-banged hole aching for his lover's deep attention.

They coalesced outside the prison walls together, stinking bayou before them. Hand in hand they raced away, leaving behind a prison in turmoil as their thwarted enemies searched high and low for them.

"Thanks, Slider. I knew you'd come for me. I was about to turn in the Chief for all the corrupt shit he was up to, when all this came down on me. I was framed."

Slider glanced over at his lover as they raced through the wetlands toward freedom. He'd guessed as much once he saw the Chief alive and well, but knew there was more Bartolmeo would have to explain.

More importantly, Slider had figured something else out. He'd learned something vitally important that night. About himself, and about his friend.

Trust.

It was not always easy, but it was worth it, "I'll always be there for you," he answered.

They couldn't wait. Time enough later to find answers to all the questions that night had brought up.

A copse of weeping willows offered a dark retreat. Slider bent over for his Cuban lover, his plump, creamy ass gleaming in the faint light. His pink pucker pouted and swallowed. Brown cock slid deep. They were one again.

Unmasked II

LEATHER MAN
By Wayne Mansfield

There were UFO sightings. There was thunder and lightning, and torrential rain. There were blackouts across the city. Eighteen-year-old Jake Jamieson had been bumping and grinding away in a cage at the GRUNT Club. Surrounding him in the crowded and dimly lit club were men dressed in leather, men that were naked and men that were getting fucked on the dance floor in front of him. The place stank of sweat, piss and cum.

Then the lights went out, and the music stopped. A collective murmur rose up from the crowd. Suddenly, the room was filled with a brilliant light as a bolt of lightning pierced the tin roof of the club. Unfortunately, Jake had been about to push the door to his cage open. The electricity traveled through the metal bars to his body, making him glow blue in the darkness. Strangely, the electricity didn't exit his body but seemed to be absorbed into it. Some say they even saw something moving down through the electricity, feeding into the young boy's body.

Then the lights came on again.

The last thing Jake saw before his eyes rolled back into his head was a sea of naked assholes, some gaping and glistening with cum and some red and swollen from being recently fucked. Then everything went black.

#####

From the downtown apartment he shared with his lover, Marcus, Jake Jamieson was able to hear the blaring police sirens and the ringing of an alarm bell at the Metropole Bank. Since that night long ago at the GRUNT Club, he had been able to hear a pin drop in a neighboring apartment. He had been able to hear people's conversations on the sidewalk fifteen stores below. Sometimes, he thought it would drive him crazy, but it was an extraordinary ability that had come in handy on more than one occasion.

"That sounds like trouble," said Jake.

Martin rolled his eyes. "Here we go," he muttered to himself.

Jake leapt out of bed. Already a chemical reaction had started deep within him. His body was beginning to bulk up. His chest was sprouting hair that was soon so thick that it was almost impossible to see any flesh. A thick, handle-bar moustache had appeared above his top lip.

The transformation never ceased to amaze Marcus, who watched with wide-eyed amazement.

After his body had finished expanding, Jake pulled on his leather pants and stuffed his now massive cock into the small confines of the skin tight garment. He pulled on his motorbike boots and strapped himself into his harness. Two leather cuffs that extended up his forearm almost to the elbow protected his otherwise bare arms. The entire outfit was bulletproof, fireproof and self-mending. Not one penny had been scrimped on when designing and manufacturing it. A studded leather mask that came down over his eyes, nose and cheeks completed the outfit and kept his identity a secret.

"How do I look?" he said turning.

"Stunning," Marcus replied. "My very own super-queero."

"Well I'm off. People need saving and criminals need catching."

"Be careful!" Marcus called as his lover leapt through the window. "And, would it kill you to use the damn door?!?"

Jake landed on the concrete pavement fifteen stories down with a thud that sent jagged cracks spearing out through the cement.

"Shit!" he exclaimed. The city council were getting mighty sick of having to redo the same patch of sidewalk every week or so. 'Have to start using the door,' he thought to himself before speeding to the scene of the crime.

To onlookers he appeared as a blur. The lightning hit had given him more than one power. Super-human speed was another talent he'd discovered he had.

"Leather Man! I thought I'd see you," said Sergeant Collins, his blue eyes sparkling beneath black eyebrows. "Not much escapes you, but I think we've got this one under control."

Leather Man adjusted his substantial package and smiled as the Sergeant Collins glanced down. He did it deliberately to tease the upstanding heterosexual sergeant, whom he suspected also harbored a secret desire to feel it sliding down his throat.

"What have we got?" asked Leather Man.

"A small gang of about four men. All of them are armed, and they have taken the bank staff hostage. Our men have surrounded the building. We have snipers up there, over there and on that building over there."

Leather Man's dynamic vision made it easy for him to spot the capped heads and rifle barrels of the specially trained tactical response group. He nodded.

"Any of your men inside?" he asked.

The sergeant shook his head and glanced at Leather Man's bulging crotch a second time.

"Not yet. Can't get in. It's too dangerous. I don't want any of my men risking their lives or those of any of the hostages."

"You mind if I check it out?"

Leather Man flexed his muscles, making the hair on his chest ripple like heads of wheat in the afternoon breeze. The leather of his pants squeaked as it rubbed together between his legs and a button popped open on his crotch flap.

The sergeant could hardly speak. "S-s-s-sure go ahead," he babbled before coming to his senses. "I mean, no, you can't. This is police … Come back!"

But, Leather Man had already disappeared behind the large pillars at the top of the steps.

Unmasked II

As he approached the double wooden doors, Leather Man used his incredible powers of hearing to locate the bank robbers. He could hear one of them breathing, so he deduced that the criminal must be near the door; a look out. Two others were stomping around further inside, but the fourth one was undetectable. He paused for a moment and thought, but he was not a man big on thinking.

He burst through the door like a hurricane, knocking the sentry unconscious. Immediately, the other two men opened fire. Several of the women screamed and scrambled for safety underneath the counters. Everyone else flattened themselves against the polished floor and covered their heads with their hands as if that was going to help protect them from the bullets.

Leather Man walked confidently toward the two men as their bullets bounced off his leather cuffs. With almost no effort at all, he deftly deflected the bullets away from the unprotected parts of his chest and belly.

"Let's get out of here," one of the men shouted.

"Where's Larry?" said the other one as they both started backing up.

"Still in the vault."

"No he's not," said a third man appearing through a great hole in the wall of the security-heavy vault. "How could he not resist a good shoot out? And with Leather Man no less."

"Larry the Lizard!" said Leather Man taking his belt off. "We meet again."

Leather Man swung the belt above his head, the motion of which lengthened it, turning it into a kind of whip that he cracked over the heads of Larry the Lizard's two henchmen.

"Let's get out of here," one of them said. "Rather be alive to enjoy the money we got than rolling in it and dead!"

Larry was inclined to agree. The last time he'd encountered Leather Man he'd ended up doing eight years in prison.

Eric Summers

Leather Man marched forward, cracking his belt whip until the end of it caught one of the men on the back of the head. He retracted it and swung it again, flicking the man's gun out of his hand while he was rubbing the swelling bump on the back of his head.

The other two took the opportunity to flee, as did the few dozen hostages, though in opposite directions.

"Show him your ass," Larry called back over his shoulder.

His fallen comrade scrambled up onto one elbow. His brow wrinkled. "What?"

"Show him ya fuckin' ass. Just do it!"

Larry and the other man disappeared around a corner into a back corridor leaving their colleague to wonder why the hell he should take his pants down. Yet when he looked up and saw Leather Man hurtling towards him across the vast polished floor of the bank reasons didn't seem so important any more. His hands went to work on his belt buckle and then on the button to his jeans. The Leather Man's belt cracked overhead, threatening to inflict more damage at any moment. It seemed like an eternity before he could get his jeans and underwear down, but he managed the task just in time. As Leather Man arrived, he flipped over and stuck his ass in the air.

"Well, hello Christmas," said Leather Man with a grin.

The gangster's sweaty pink hole glistened invitingly. Nestled in a thatch of dark blonde hair it called to Leather Man, puckering and relaxing in a mesmerizing rhythm.

Leather Man's throbbing twelve-inch cock strained beneath the leather of his pants. Even through the futuristic fabric, a small spot of precum had appeared and was growing rapidly. Leather Man could not resist. It was his one weakness. Larry the Lizard knew it, and that's why he had shouted back the strange directive.

As though he had no will of his own, Leather Man dropped to his knees. The musty aroma of the gangster's man hole lured him closer and closer until his nose was brushing against the tangle of ass hair. Leather Man breathed in the heady scent while his hands unfastened the buttons of his pants. It didn't matter that Larry the Lizard and his cohort were escaping with a large amount of money, Leather Man was powerless to do his duty when there was a naked ass to be had.

While the man in front of him quivered with fright and expectation, Leather Man slipped his tongue into the sweaty groove and licked. So sensitive was his tongue that he could feel each and every pucker of the man's asshole. Each ridge seemed to get his huge cock to grow even more than it already had. He breathed in the heady aroma of man-crack and rubbed his stubbly chin gently over it, covering it in the man's stink.

At the same time, he managed to release his monstrous cock, which sprang forth flicking a small ribbon of precum across the immaculate floor of the bank.

"Get in there," he said in his deep, commanding voice.

The gangster looked toward the office where Leather Man was pointing and then crawled the short distance on his hands and knees.

"Kick your pants off."

The gangster opened his mouth to protest.

"Do it!"

Leather Man stood behind the quaking man, basting his engorged man meat with his own lubricant. Soon the whole swollen member was glistening in the electric light, every vein accentuated and the huge purple head looking smooth and polished.

"What's your name?"

"Sid," the gangster replied with a slight waver in his voice.

"Well Sid, this is gonna hurt," said Leather Man lowering himself to his knees. "But just take it like a man. If I hear you scream, I'm gonna bitch slap you, alright!"

When the tip of Leather Man's cock kissed the gangster's asshole, it puckered, tightening and then relaxing again.

"Are you ready?" asked Leather Man before a great glob of spit spilled over the top of his bottom lip and landed squarely on the head of his cock.

Sid didn't get the chance to reply. Leather Man grabbed the trembling man by the hips and pushed his cock head past the sphincter and into the warm cavern beyond, causing the thirty-something man to cry out.

Leather Man smacked one fleshy cheek, leaving a red hand-shaped mark.

"What did I tell you?" he said sternly before softening his tone. "Aahhhh mate, that's one tight asshole you've got there. Gonna be loose by the time I'm finished with it, though."

Leather Man thrust forward, plunging his rock hard rod deep inside Sid, stretching the gangster's man cunt till the skin around it was taut. After he was all the way in, buried to the bush inside the moaning man, he stopped for a moment until he felt Sid's ass muscles relax.

"That's better," he said.

But time was short. The police would be swarming all over the bank in a matter of minutes, if they weren't already. The thought of being caught fucking sent a wave of adrenalin through his body. His cock twitched inside Sid.

"Here we go," he said.

He began to gently fuck the man's ass, sliding his spit-lubed prong in and out at a steadily increasing rate. His grip tightened on Sid's slim hips as he began to pound the young man's hole. Soon Sid's whole body was rocking as Leather Man, desperate to shoot his load, drove his tool home, deep into Sid's smooth, warm bowels.

He didn't know if it was Leather Man's thick cock rubbing against his prostate or the whether he was just enjoying being ridden like a fairground pony, but Sid soon realized that he was as hard as a rock himself. So leaving himself balancing on one arm, he reached back and began stroking his engorged pole, fast. It seemed to lessen the discomfort. Only it wasn't long before he could feel himself building up to an almighty orgasm.

"I'm about ready to feed your ass," panted Leather Man. "You wanted it and here it comes!"

Leather Man pulled the young man deep onto his cock, impaling him so that when he blew it was deep inside Sid's guts.

"Awww fuck mate! Feels fan-fuckin'-tastic!"

That was all Sid needed to hear. The thought of Leather Man seeding his tight, virgin manhole aroused him to a degree that he would have previously thought impossible. But, the sensation of Leather Man's large veiny tool rubbing against the sensitive tissue of his asshole and knowing his guts were swimming in the superhero's thick, creamy man paste caused him to spray a decent load of warm man jizz all over the carpet.

Just as Sid was shaking the last drops of pearly-white ball cream from his deflating cock, the door opened. It was Sergeant Collins.

"Leather Man what are you doing?" he asked, as if it wasn't obvious.

"Couldn't help it," he said, "he showed me his asshole, and you know what that means. I had to fill it. It's a weakness, but it's one I have to bear."

"Yeah, it must be a real burden," said the Sergeant sarcastically.

"Well it looks as though you like what you see," said Leather Man noticing the tent growing in the front of the sergeant's navy trousers. "But shouldn't you be out catching Larry the Lizard and his off-sider?"

"My men nabbed both of them as they were running down the utility hall. Don't worry about them. It's gonna be a long time before either of them sees the light of day again."

"You'd better get over here then. I got something you might want to work on."

Leather Man pulled his still hard cock out of Sid's asshole. It was glistening with anal juice and cum.

The sergeant's cock was now so rigid it threatened to tear right through the fabric that was restraining it. He locked the door to the office and watched as a small drop of milky white semen dribbled out of Leather Man's piss slit. He undid his belt and dropped his pants, stepping out of them as he hurried to Leather Man's waiting cock.

The sergeant's cock wobbled in front of him; a flagpole without a flag. Eight and half inches of thick, uncut cop meat that stuck out from a thick black bush of tightly curled pubic hair.

"Come on man. Get on the end of it," Leather Man said gripping his cock with one powerful hand. "I know you want it. You've been aching for it for years. Now's your chance."

The sergeant dropped to his knees and took the pulsing prick into his gob. His eyes closed for a moment as he swallowed the super-cock down his throat. He'd waited to feel Leather Man's cock inside him one way or another for so many years he had long ago given up ever imagining that it would happen.

"If your wife could see you now," snarled Sid, curling his top lip as he watched the sergeant gobble down Leather Man's cock.

Leather Man silenced him with a blow to the back of the head.

"You shut up! Start sucking his cock!"

Sid went to protest, but Leather Man raised his fist, and soon the gangster was sucking Sergeant Collins' cock like a babe on the teat. He was a bit rough at first, his teeth were getting in the way, but the Sergeant hardly noticed. He was too busy sucking Leather Man's massive cock and savoring every mouthful.

"That's it, mate. Suck that fucking monster."

The sergeant did his best to accommodate the hefty tube of man steak sliding down the back of throat and back again. While Leather Man pumped his mouth, he made sure his flat, wet tongue cushioned the thick shaft as it went back and forth down his throat. He could feel each and every vein in the thick cock and taste the juice that dribbled out of the swollen cock head. He felt as though he were in a dream. He became light-headed. It was hard to breathe; to get enough oxygen into his system when something so large was blocking his windpipe was difficult at best. But the dizziness only added to the sensation.

He could even smell Leather Man's crotch. A heady mixture of sweat, piss and cum. He sucked in the aroma through his nostrils as the superhero continued to fuck his mouth. The scent made Leather Man even more appealing and the sergeant felt that he could explode into the gangster's mouth at any minute.

When it got too much he pushed Sid away from his cock and then took his own mouth off Leather Man's cock.

"I want you to fuck me," the sergeant said.

Leather Man's brow came down. "Are you sure?" he asked. "Can you handle ... well, can you handle this!"

His cock was wet with saliva and glistened in the electric office light. The mushroom-shaped cockhead seemed to throb, to beckon. Then a small amount of clear precum beaded at the piss-slit, swelled until it had doubled in size and then fell to the floor as an almost invisible string.

The Sergeant's tongue was hanging out of his mouth. He nodded. "Oh fuck yeah," he babbled. "I gotta have that thing inside me."

He turned around and pulled his meaty white ass-cheeks apart. The purplish-pink skin of his sphincter was already twitching in anticipation.

Leather Man knelt down. He closed his eyes and breathed in the Sergeant's musty man stink. He sighed.

"That smells unbelievable!"

He brushed the sensitive skin with his nose, nuzzling it as tenderly as any lover before giving it a gentle lick.

The sergeant groaned and pulled his cheeks further apart.

Leather Man ran his tongue up and down the quivering mass of wrinkled ass tissue, stabbing at it with a firm, wet tongue and then flicking at it. But only for a minute or so. All of a sudden he grabbed the sergeant's hips and pulled backwards as hard as he could, burying his face in the smooth aromatic ass crack. His tongue punctured through the muscular sphincter, and soon he could feel the wet, smooth inner lining of the sergeant's man-cunt with the tip of his tongue.

The sergeant arched his back, pushing back and wanting more of Leather Man inside him.

"Fuck me," he begged. "You gotta fuck me."

Leather Man let his tongue linger inside the sergeant's fuck-hole for a few moments longer, savoring the smells and the sensations while he could. Then he withdrew his tongue, kissing and sucking on each ass lip one more time before he grabbed his dripping cock and guided it slowly into the police officer's tight, unfucked manhole.

"This is what you want?" asked Leather Man.

Sergeant Collins closed his eyes and remained silent. His breathing was heavy and his own cock was dribbling all over the carpet, creating a growing stain, which bled into the carpet beneath him. He pushed back, forcing the head of Leather Man's cock into his ass. A wave of sharp pain shot through his body. The nerves inside his ass were spasming.

"You want me to take it out?" Leather Man asked, hoping the answer would be no.

There was no reply. A pause. It seemed that no one knew quite what to do and then the sergeant slowly slid himself onto Leather Man's cock, somehow managing to take the whole length. Leather Man looked down and saw that the skin around the Sergeant's hole was stretched to tearing point. It was so tight that the pink skin looked white.

"Are you sure?" he asked again. "Because I want to pound your cop ass. I've wanted you as much as you've wanted me."

The sergeant nodded. "Just start slowly."

Leather Man did the best he could. Slowly wasn't a word in his vocabulary. He began thrusting, his hands grabbing the man's hips and using them as handles to pull him deeper onto his cock.

"Hey you," he grunted to the gangster who was sitting in the corner stroking his cock.

Sid looked startled. He thought he had been forgotten.

"Get over here and get your tongue on my balls," Leather Man snarled.

The gangster was too frightened not to. His ass was still throbbing from the plowing it had received earlier. If lubricating Leather Man's cock was all he had to do he considered himself to be quite lucky.

"On ya back and slide under," Leather Man said with a scowl. "And give my balls one fuck of a good licking."

The gangster scuttled headfirst on his back between Leather Man's thick, muscular thighs. When he had settled into position, he lifted his head slightly and wrapped his tongue around the big, bouncy hairy ball-sack.

"That's it," said Leather Man. "Lick those salty nuts."

Dribbles of sweat ran down from Leather Man's pubic hair and dripped onto the gangster's face, but he persevered. When he was able to, he took one of the oversized testicles into his mouth and sucked, gently rolling it around his mouth like a boiled lolly before slipping it out again and sucking on the other nut.

The sergeant had begun to stroke his cock. The prostate massage he was getting from the thick piece of meat invading his ass was almost too much for him to bear. It was addictive. The more cock he got, the more he wanted. Soon he was riding Leather Man's meat like a seasoned slut, grinding his ass backwards against Leather Man's hips, meeting each powerful thrust then pushing back harder, so he got every last millimeter of cock inside that he could.

The sergeant's enthusiasm was contagious. Not only had Sid begun to stroke his seven-incher while tongue-tickling the biggest set of balls he'd ever seen, but Leather Man had begun to pick up the pace, too. He was slamming into the sergeant, sending strings of ass juice and sweat all over Sid's face. He could feel his nuts beginning to tighten, and he knew that it wouldn't be long before he was shooting a thick wad of sticky man goo up inside the sergeant's well-fucked asshole.

Sid blew first, ejaculating a stream of thick, white jizz into the air and hitting the small of Leather Man's back. As Leather Man pounded the sergeant's hole, he could feel the slimy man-cream running down through the hair on his back and into the even hairier crack of his ass.

Then the sergeant shot his load; an orgasm that made his whole body shudder. Each time Leather Man drove his cock deep into the sergeant's fuck-hole, it seemed to produce another jet of cock-cream. He came and came until his nuts began to hurt.

The contraction of the sergeant's pelvic muscles was the final straw for Leather Man. He had Sid licking his balls, Sid's jism trickling down his hairy ass-crack, the sergeant's moans and groans filling his ears and the sergeant's ass muscles spasming around his cock. It was all too much. With a grunt that the officers outside in the main bank building could have heard, he filled the sergeant's bowels full of superhero spunk. Even as his cock slipped out amidst the continuing assault on the police sergeant's asshole, the spunk kept coming; splashing onto Sid's face as he hurriedly pushed his cock back into the gaping, dripping cop cunt that had been so desperate for his load.

When he had finished, Leather Man collapsed onto the sergeant; poor Sid only just managed to scramble out in time. He lay on top of Sergeant Collins for a few moments, puffing and panting and trying to catch his breath.

"That was fantastic," Sergeant Collins said.

"Tell me about it,' said Leather Man. "For an ass virgin, you sure were a good fuck. You and Marcus are the only two people who can willingly take my super-thick man-cock. "

Sergeant Collins smiled.

Leather Man rolled off the sergeant and leapt to his feet. He pulled his pants on, stuffed his shrinking though still impressive cock back in and did his pants up.

"Would love to stay and chat," he said, "but time is short."

Already he could feel the cells in his body beginning to change. He was shrinking slowly but surely back to his original size. Even the belt on his leather pants had to be tightened a few seconds after he'd buckled it the first time.

"Leather Man, I'd, er, appreciate it if you, ah, my wife and ..."

Leather Man grinned. His teeth sparkling white against the dark stubble of his jaw. "Yeah, I know the drill. This never happened. Only it was the best thing that has never happened to me."

Sergeant Collins sighed, visibly relieved.

"And if you know what's good for you, you'll keep your mouth shut, too," he said directing the warning to the gangster who was getting dressed in the corner. "Take him away Sergeant Collins. He looks like he's missing his friends."

And, as the door to the office was forced open by a couple of police officers, Leather Man bounded out of the room and sped through the main hall of the Metropole Bank. Taking one look back he leapt onto the roof of the nearest building and disappeared into the sea of skyscrapers.

Exhausted and with his leathers almost hanging off him, he landed on the balcony of his own building. Then he remembered Marcus. He was probably still at home and would not be happy to see him walk in via the bedroom balcony. He jumped off the balcony and landed on the freshly cemented sidewalk, sending drying concrete flying in all directions.

"Aww that's just fuckin' great, mate!" shouted one of the council workmen who was tidying away his equipment. "I've just done that!"

Leather Man felt his cheeks start burning.

"Sorry, mate. I'll remember for next time. Would love to stay and chat, but ..."

And with that he disappeared into the building.

HERO WORSHIP
By Stephen Osborne

  Rob's hands shook as he picked up the package. Somehow he'd imagined the box would have been bigger, but never mind. This is what he'd been waiting for all those agonizing weeks. Yep, there was the sender's name, Costumes and More, Galore! Hurriedly, he ripped into the package and pulled out his new superhero costume.
  Oh, yes. The black leggings. The dark gray tunic with the black V coming down to the navel area. Long black gloves. And best of all, the mask. It was the same dark gray as the tunic and covered everything except the lower face, so he'd be able to talk and breathe easily. Rob wondered if he should have chosen the mask that had ear holes instead. Would his hearing be impaired? It didn't matter. The costume was wonderful. He had to get it on immediately.
  Even though he lived alone, Rob closed his bedroom door carefully before he began to don his new outfit. It was probably a silly precaution, but suppose one of the maintenance men from the apartment complex came by unexpectedly to change an air filter or something like that. How would Rob explain that he was stuffing himself into tights? It's okay. I've got a Superhero fetish. Lots of guys do. Don't let it bother you.
  Rob's apartment was filled with shelf after shelf containing superhero comic books. He had posters of Omega Squad Three, The Blue Avenger, and Quantum Man adorning his walls. The few boyfriends Rob had dated were amused at first over Rob's obsession but generally balked when he admitted to them that he often masturbated over the battles between superheroes and supervillains. They suddenly acted as if they had an attack of heterosexuality and had to extricate themselves from Rob's clutches as soon as possible.

Unmasked II

  The real life superheroes also fascinated Rob. Ever since the costumed vigilantes had started cropping up several years ago, Rob never went out at night without his camera. You never knew when you might catch sight of Hawkboy gliding through the sky or see Xeon swinging between buildings downtown. In fact, Rob had a photo he'd taken of Hawkboy, having caught sight of the superhero last October. Granted, Rob had fumbled getting the camera ready, so it was hard to tell it was actually Hawkboy and not just a blur of red and gold, but Rob knew who it was. Sometimes Rob drove around the downtown area at night just in hopes of seeing one of the city's several costumed avengers in action.

  With the sudden influx of superheroes, Rob figured he wasn't the only person with a hero fetish. A quick search of the Internet showed several groups and chat rooms dedicated to the love of superheroes.

  It was in one of these chat rooms that Rob discovered a guy who went by Xeonguy1. The two quickly bonded and it was a rare day that Rob didn't have a long chat with Xeonguy1. As Rob struggled to get into his outfit, he found himself hoping that Xeonguy1 would be on line. Xeonguy1 had, apparently, a perfect replica of Xeon's costume and often wore it while chatting. What a conversation they could have with Rob in his new outfit and Xeonguy1 dressed in his!

  Just the feel of the tight material was driving Rob crazy. By the time he was putting on his black boots, Rob was feeling light headed and ready to burst. He bounded over to his computer desk in his best superhero style and signed into his usual chat room, praying that he'd find Xeonguy1's name on the list of chatters.

  Sure enough, there he was. Rob's fingers (encased in his new and very hot gloves) raced over the keys, typing out a private message for Xeonguy1.

    Herolvr: I got it! I got my new costume!
    Xeonguy1: Fantastic! Do you have it on?

Herolvr: Sure do. It fits like a glove. I've decided my supervillain name should be The Eliminator!
Xeonguy1: Bet you look hot in it.

Rob hesitated before typing out his next message. After all, he and Xeonguy1 had been chatting for ages now and hadn't actually met in person. Xeonguy1 had emailed Rob some pictures of himself in costume, but even though they lived in the same city, no mention had ever been made of a face-to-face encounter. Rob had always assumed it was because he didn't have a costume of his own, but there was always the possibility that Xeonguy1 was an online-only guy. Still, he had to try.

Herolvr: Want to see me in it?
There was a pause before Xeonguy1 replied with: You've got some pics?
Herolvr: I sort of meant in person.

The pause was even longer before Xeonguy1 answered. And let you find out my secret identity? LOL
Rob smiled as he typed. I can leave my apartment door unlocked. I'll be in the bedroom, ready for you. You can come in and dress in the living room, then meet me in the bedroom for a battle royale!
After hitting the enter key, sending the message, Rob held his breath.
Xeonguy1: Sounds hot. Loser gets vanquished in more ways than one?
Herolvr: Of course! See you soon?
Xeonguy1: I can be there in about fifteen minutes. Be ready to feel the might of Xeon!

Rob's heart raced. Finally, he was going to meet Xeonguy1! The two had cyber-wrestled often and Rob knew that they would have an even hotter time in the flesh. He searched through his pictures folder to find the ones Xeonguy1 had sent him. The guy looked enough like the real Xeon that he could easily pass as the superhero. The Xeon mask covered most of the face, but by the exposed chin Rob could see that Xeonguy1 was a handsome black man. It was a great costume with the white mask, gloves and boots and the blue tights with the white starburst over the chest. If it wasn't for the fact that Rob could see a kitchen with dirty dishes in the background, it might have been assumed to be a photo of the real Xeon!

Rob used a search engine to find an article about Xeon. The excerpt from a newspaper story was fairly recent, recounting how Xeon had foiled a bank robbery. An accompanying photograph, taken by one of the witnesses, showed the superhero smacking the armed robber right in the chops. The picture was grainy, but Rob could still see how nicely the blue tights showed off the black man's muscles. Looking at his computer screen, Rob began to feel his cock harden. It was amazing how good his engorged dick felt against the material of the tights.

Rob was so engrossed in his thoughts that he hadn't realized how much time had passed. Xeonguy1 would surely arrive soon, and he hadn't even unlocked the front door! Rushing to the living room, Rob unlocked the door just as footsteps sounded coming down his hall. For a moment, Rob thought about staying in the living room to greet his friend. After all, Xeonguy1 really didn't have a secret identity. He was just a regular guy who, like Rob, liked to fantasize about superheroes and even had purchased a costume, so he could dress up like one! Still, Rob had promised to remain in the bedroom.

Once back sitting at his computer desk, Rob listened with growing excitement as he heard his front door open. There was some shuffling sounds, and then Rob heard what sounded like a duffel bag being unzipped. He could imagine his chat friend taking off his street clothes and donning the tights that would transform him into Xeon. It seemed to take forever, but Rob's erection remained rock hard in anticipation.

Finally, Rob heard footsteps approaching the bedroom door. With a loud bang, the door opened, and a blue clad figure entered. In a deep voice, Xeonguy1 said, "I've finally tracked you down to your lair, Eliminator! Prepare to meet the might of Xeon!"

Rob rose so quickly that his chair crashed to the floor behind him. Assuming character, he clenched his fists and faced 'Xeon.' "I've been waiting for you, Xeon. Luckily, you're as predictable as always!" Rob picked up a hunk of quartz off his desk and held it towards Xeonguy1. Rob never knew why quartz was supposed to zap Xeon of his super-strength and ability to fly, but that was the apparent effect the mineral had on the superhero.

Xeonguy1 reacted immediately, doubling over as if in pain. "You fiend!" he muttered. "You'll pay for this!"

Rob kicked out, his boot connecting with the other man's midsection. He made sure to pull back and barely make contact, of course. After all, this was just for fun. When Xeonguy1 collapsed convincingly to the floor, Rob leaped onto him, tossing the quartz onto the bed.

The two men wrestled on the floor, grunting and groaning with each blow. Rob (or, rather, The Eliminator) clearly had the upper hand with Xeon weakened from the quartz. Rob pummeled the other man with blows that looked convincing, although they wouldn't in reality even raise a slight bruise. Rob was glad to see the bulge in his friend's tights as they tussled. It was an impressive bulge.

Xeonguy1 used Rob's momentary distraction to pull at the bed covers. The sheets fell off the bed, covering the lump of quartz under a pile of blankets and pillows. Immediately, Xeonguy1 shoved Rob off him. The blue clad hero got Rob into a headlock, shouting, "Now that I've got my strength back you will soon be vanquished, villain!"

Rob doubted that the real Xeon spoke with such flowery language, but he went along with the scenario. "I'm not beaten yet, Xeon!"

Xeonguy1 wrapped his legs around Rob's midsection and squeezed, forcing the air out of his body. "Give up, Eliminator! You're no match for the might of Xeon!"

Rob found himself trapped and unable to move. Remaining in character, he whined, "I give up, you blue freak!"

Releasing the hold, Xeonguy1 crowed, "Xeon is once again victorious! Now I will take my prize!"

While Rob was eagerly anticipating seeing Xeonguy1's package unwrapped, he wished that the guy would drop the superhero rhetoric. It was fun for the foreplay, but was Xeonguy1 going to stay in character during the sex as well? Rob wished that he knew the guy's real name. Somehow he couldn't envision shouting out in the middle of the act, "Fuck me harder, Xeon!"

The man in the white mask leaned close to Rob and whispered in his ear. "Do you have some condoms?" he asked. "One should always play safely."

Rob pointed. "On the nightstand. There's some lube as well." His voice came out a little shaky, and Rob realized he was nervous over the prospect of having sex with a guy whose face he still hadn't seen.

He expected Xeonguy1 to start pulling off his outfit, or at least to remove the mask, but the man merely pulled down his tights enough to release his cock. Any hesitation Rob had felt left immediately. The black man's dick was huge and stiff and Rob yearned to know how it would feel to be fucked by such a monster. What did a guy's face matter when he had a dick like that?

Rob watched in fascination as the other man sheathed his cock and applied the lube. He was so entranced, staring at Xeonguy1's dick that he forgot that he was supposed to join in. When Xeonguy1 gave him a questioning look, Rob got to his feet and began to yank down his tights.

"Bend yourself over the end of the bed," the man in the white mask said in a low growl. "I want you to feel the power of Xeon's mighty prick!"

Rob wanted to feel it as well, but as soon as his friend got into position behind him doubts began to form. In spite of the copious amounts of lube the man had applied, Rob hoped Xeonguy1 would take it slow to begin with. After all, Rob hadn't had a dick that large up his ass since ... well, never!

Rob willed his muscles to relax as he felt Xeonguy1 press the head of his huge cock against Rob's ass. All the relaxing in the world, however, couldn't have prepared him for the jolt that went through his system as the head of the man's monster cock entered his hole. Rob's head involuntarily jerked back as he let out a loud gasp.

"Relax, you're going to love this," the masked man said.

Rob frowned. Relax? What did the guy think he was trying to do, clench up? Rob took a deep breath as Xeonguy1 pushed forward, shoving more of his cock into Rob's ass. Amazingly, the deeper it went the more the pain subsided. It was almost as if Xeonguy1's dick had super powers of its own, erasing the pain of entry. Rob's groan quickly turned to a moan of pleasure as Xeonguy1 began to slowly fuck Rob's ass.

"How does that feel?" the masked man asked.

Rob nearly couldn't answer. When words finally came to him, all he could say was, "Faster! Faster!"

Xeonguy1 obliged.

The bed slammed against the wall with each thrust of Xeonguy1's hips. Rob found it hard to breath. All he could think about was the enormous cock sliding in and out of his butt. The masked man was holding on to Rob's hips tightly, and Rob could hear Xeonguy1 starting to pant from the exertion. The trusts came fast and hard and Rob knew that Xeonguy1 was ready to explode. He reached down to his own aching cock and began to pump furiously.

"Yeah!" the black man shouted, "I'm coming! Fuck, yeah!"

Rob's own cock exploded just as Xeonguy1 slid his cock out of Rob's ass. The man quickly removed the condom and shot a large load onto Rob's back. Rob wondered if cum stains came out of spandex.

The two men stood, shaking and panting, for several minutes before Rob said, breathlessly, "Let me get a towel or two."

The masked man grinned widely. "Good idea."

As they cleaned up, Rob, trying to sound casual, said, "You know, I don't even know your name. All I know you by is Xeonguy1."

Tossing his towel onto the bed, Xeonguy1 replied, "It's probably better that way."

With a shrug, Rob began to pick the bedclothes back up but was stopped my Xeonguy1 putting a restraining hand on his wrist. "Don't do that," he man said, seemingly serious. "You'll expose the quartz."

Rob had thought that once the fantasy session was over they would forgo the pretense of being superhero and supervillain, but apparently Xeonguy1 liked to stay in character. That was okay with Rob. He would give quite a lot of leeway to a guy with a cock like that. "I had fun," he said. "I hope you enjoyed yourself."

The man in the white mask nodded, smiling warmly. "I had a great time. I hope we can meet up again sometime. For right now, though, I've got to run. I hope you understand."

Rob laughed. "Of course. There are villains out there to thwart! Xeon has to make sure the city stays safe!"

Xeonguy1 nodded. "I'm glad you understand. Look for me again online soon. I'd like to do this again." With that, the man turned and headed for the door. He moved so swiftly that Rob was taken aback. Surely, he wasn't just going to walk out without changing back into his street clothes? When Rob followed the guy into the living room, though, he saw that Xeonguy1 had picked up the bag that must have his change of clothes inside and head for the door.

"You're not going out like that, are you?" Rob asked, rushing to keep up with the man.

Having opened the door, Xeonguy1 paused. "I've got to run, but we'll do this again sometime soon." He leaned in to give Rob a brief but tender kiss on the lips. "Be safe," he said before turning to rush down the hall to the apartment building entrance.

Rob followed, frowning. "But ... the neighbors! They might see you!" It suddenly donned on Rob as he spoke that he himself was now outside his apartment dressed in gray and black spandex.

Xeonguy1 either didn't hear him or chose not to answer. He burst through the door and out into the night. Rob rushed forward, catching the door before it closed all the way. "Wait," he said. "At least tell me your first name!"

The masked man was standing on the sidewalk, his bag in hand. Luckily, Rob thought, no neighbors seemed to be out and about to see the two men in tights. Xeonguy1 nodded at Rob. "My name," he said, "is Xeon."

And then, the blue clad figure raised a fist into the air and impossibly left the ground. Rob's mouth fell open as the man flew off into the night.

ABOUT THE AUTHORS

ARMAND published nearly a dozen stories – ranging from sports erotica to superhero stories – in a variety of anthologies. Writing adult stories comes easily to him because he has so many sexy fantasies to put down on paper. He's hoping some day one of them will come true.

DERRICK DELLA GIORGIA was born in Italy and currently lives in Manhattan and Rome. His short stories have recently been published in several anthologies: "Courtesy of the Hotel" in *Island Boys* (Alyson Books), "Couch with a View" in *Cruising for Bad Boys* (STARbooks Press), "A Secret Worth Keeping" in *Pretty Boys and Roughnecks* (STARbooks Press), "Pyramids in Rome" in *Best Gay Love Stories 2010* (Alyson Books). Visit him at www.derrickdellagiorgia.com.

ERASTES short stories have appeared in many anthologies such as *Love in a Lock-Up* (STARbooks Press), and *Ultimate Gay Erotica*. She lives in Norfolk, UK.

EVAN GILBERT, a lifelong Memphian, writes professionally for an international corporation. In his free time, he writes gay fiction. Evan desperately needs a life.

GERRARD JONES is a writer, college professor and active member of the Toronto gay community. He lives with his partner, their two adopted children, their two cats and a philodendron.

JAMIE FREEMAN resides far from Metropolis or Gotham, but has been addicted to superhero hunks since he first basked in the television glow of the incomparable George Reeves. More of his erotic fiction can be found in *Flesh to Flesh*, *Best Gay Erotica 2009*, *Daddies*, and *Cruising for the Bad Boys* (STARbooks Press). He has also previously published a children's book and has a completed novel manuscript waiting patiently on the edge of his desk. He can be reached by email at JamieFreeman2@gmail.com.

Published in dozens of gay erotic anthologies, **JAY STARRE** pumps out fiction from his home in Vancouver, Canada. He has written regularly for such hot magazines as

Torso, Mandate and *Men*. His work can be found in titles like *Love in a Lock-Up, Don't Ask, Don't Tie Me Up,* and *Unmasked: Erotic Tales of Gay Superheroes*. His steamy gay novel, *Erotic Tales of the Knights Templar*, was released in late 2007. Look forward to his upcoming erotic book *Lusty Adventures of the Knossos Prince* in the spring of 2009 from STARbooks Press.

KALE NAYLOR is an Atlanta native who has been a freelance writer/artist for a number of years. An All-American frat boy, many of Naylor's stories are based on his real life misadventures. That is, the stories that won't get him in trouble with the law are the only ones he's fessing up to.

LOGAN ZACHARY is a mystery author living in Minneapolis, where he is an avid reader and book collector. He enjoys movies, concerts, plays, and all the other cultural events that the Twin Cities have to offer. His stories can be found in *Hard Hats, Taken by Force, Boys Caught in the Act, Ride Me Cowboy, Best Gay Erotica 2009, Ultimate Gay Erotica 2009, Surfer Boys,* and *Rough Trade*. He can be reached at LoganZachary2002@yahoo.com.

With almost a quarter-century experience in the publishing industry, **MILTON STERN** has written several short stories for the Eric Summers anthologies, including, *Unmasked: Erotic Tales of Gay Superheroes, Don't Ask, Don't Tie Me Up, Ride Me Cowboy, Service with a Smile, Unwrapped – Erotic Holiday Tales,* and the upcoming *Teammates*. He is also the author of several books, including *Harriet Lane, America's First Lady, On Tuesdays, They Played Mah Jongg* and *Michael's Secrets*. Residing in Washington, D.C., with his toy parti-poodle, Serena Rose Elizabeth Montgomery, Stern is also an active volunteer in his community, where he serves as a neighborhood representative for the Leukemia and Lymphoma Society, club liaison to the Washington Animal Rescue League, and the president of the Straight Eights, a gay antique car club. He is presently researching his next book about a boxer in

New York in the 1880s. You can learn more about Milton Stern at www.miltonstern.com.

OWEN KEEHNEN's fiction, interviews, essays, and poetry have appeared in dozens of periodicals and anthologies nationwide. He is the author of the *STARZ* series of interview books with gay male porn stars. He currently lives in Chicago with his partner Carl and their two dogs Flannery and Fitz.

ROB ROSEN, author of the novels *Sparkle: The Queerest Book You'll Ever Love* and *Divas Las Vegas*, has been published, to date, in more than fifty-five anthologies, most notably in the STARbooks Press collections: *Ride Me Cowboy – Erotic Tales of the West, Service with a Smile, Cruising for Bad Boys, SexTime: Erotic Stories of Time Travel, Pretty Boys and Roughnecks, Unwrapped – Erotic Holiday Tales*, and the upcoming *Boys Getting Ahead* and *Teammates*. His erotic fiction can frequently be found in the pages of *Men* and *Freshmen*. Please visit him at www.therobrosen.com.

RYAN FIELD is a freelance writer who lives and works in New Hope, PA. His work has appeared in many collections and anthologies. He is currently working on a novel. He's written several stories for STARbooks Press anthologies, which can be found here with links: www.ryan-field.blogspot.com.

Multi-published, award-nominated author **SEDONIA GUILLONE** lives on the water in Florida with a Renaissance man who paints, writes poetry and tells her she's the sweetest nymph he's ever met. When she's not writing erotic romance, she loves watching spaghetti westerns, Jet Li and samurai flicks, cuddling, and eating chocolate. She offers more delicious m/m erotica at her Website: www.sedoniaguillone.com/gayrotica.

STEPHEN OSBORNE has been published in quite a few anthologies, including *Unmasked, Ride Me Cowboy, Frat Sex 2, Ultimate Gay Erotica 2008, Hard Hats,* and *Best Gay Love Stories: Summer Flings*. He is also the author of

South Bend Ghosts and Other Northern Indiana Haunts. He lives in Indianapolis with a neurotic cat and a spastic dog.

TOM CARDAMONE is the author of the erotic fantasy novel, *The Werewolves of Central Park*. He has published numerous short stories, some of which can be read on his Website: www.pumpkinteeth.net.

TROY STORM has had hundreds of super hot stories published in dozens of super hot mags that have mostly burnt themselves out, but, yeah! the anthologies – like *Unmasked* – burn on. He now writes in many genres, straight, bent and decidedly crooked. "Junior OHO ... Sort Of" is a sequel to "Superheroes in Waiting," which first appeared in *Unmasked*.

WAYNE MANSFIELD lives in Mount Lawley, Western Australia. He is currently employed as an English language teacher and counselor. He has had stories published in STARbooks Press anthologies such as *Boys Will Be Boys, Ride Me Cowboy, Boys Caught in the Act, Service with a Smile* and *Pretty Boys and Roughnecks*. Find out more at: www.myspace.com/darknessgathers.

ABOUT THE EDITOR

ERIC SUMMERS resides in West Palm Beach, Fla. This is his seventh anthology for STARbooks Press. He has had superhero fantasies for years, and in them, he is usually the superhero. He has actually seen one of the authors in this anthology wearing tights, but he'll never tell who it was!

LOOKING FOR **MORE HOT STORIES?**

WOULD **YOU** LIKE TO **CONTRIBUTE** TO AN **UPCOMING ANTHOLOGY?**

VISIT

http://www.STARbooksPress.com

Hot Deals!

Subscribe to Our FREE E-mail Newsletter!

Submission Guidelines for Authors!

Buy Books and E-books Online!

VISIT

http://www.STARbooksPress.com

TODAY!